THE LAST SANCTUARY

WILLIAM R. LOWRY

First Edition

PAGE PUBLISHING
Conneaut Lake, PA

First originally published by Page Publishing 2022

ISBN 978-1-6624-8630-2 (pbk)
ISBN 978-1-6624-8631-9 (digital)

Printed in the United States of America

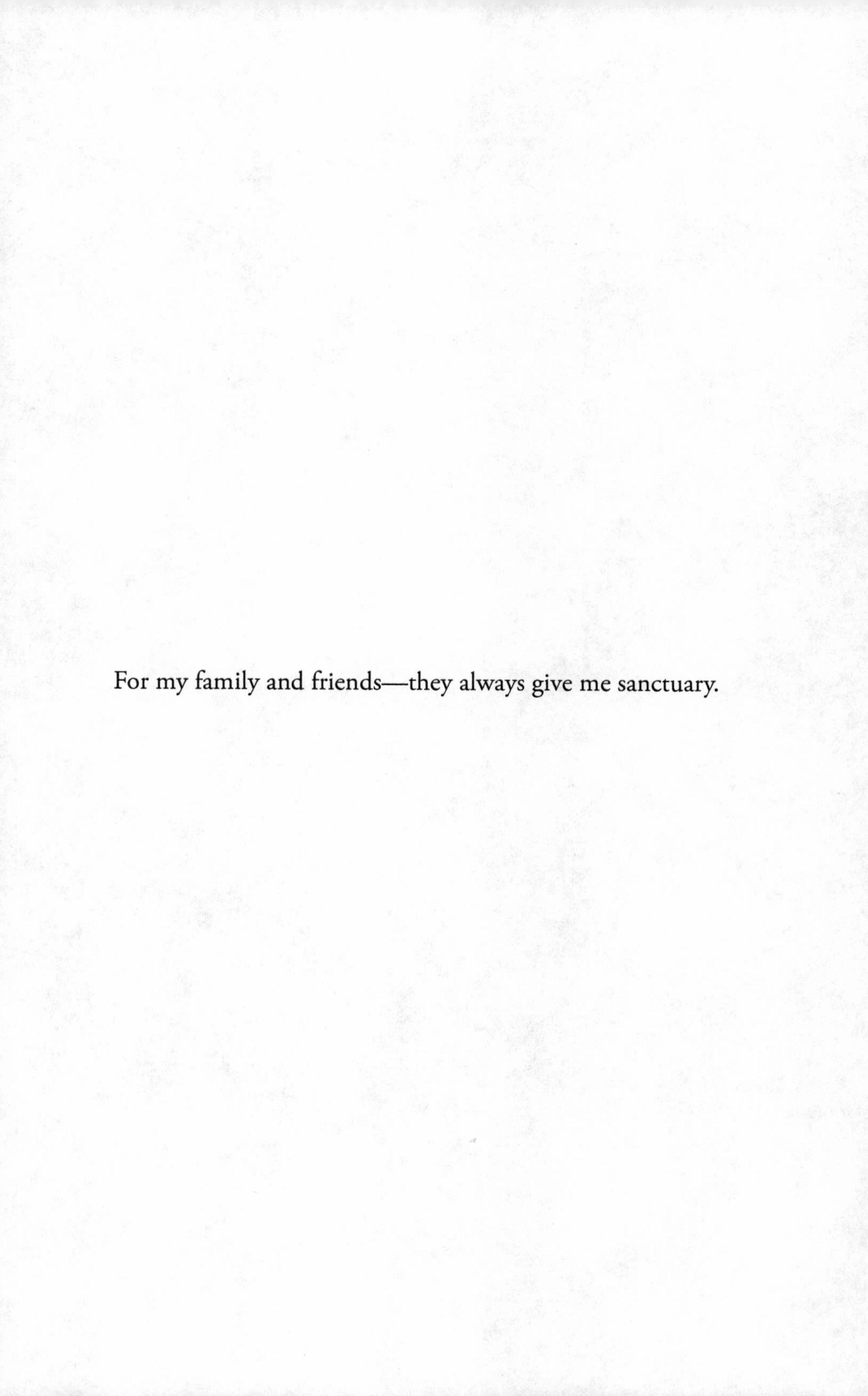

For my family and friends—they always give me sanctuary.

CONTENTS

List of Characters

Hill Family on the Ark
Oliver Hill
Owen Hill
Sarah Everly-Hill
Annie Hill
Roscoe
Beth Hill
Billy Hill

Ark Deckhands
John Hunter
Frank Sanders
Tomas Rodriguez
Jessie Rivera
Glen Miller
Tyrone Green
Hiluka

Brooks Family
James Brooks
Janice Brooks
Jamal Brooks
Jonah Brooks

Ark Personnel
Joseph Mitchell, captain
Hannigan, first mate

Willis, second mate
Rebecca Steinberg, head of lab
Mi-Sung Lee, lab tech
Maria Rivera, head cook
Irene Doyle, cook
Susan Harris, computer specialist
Naomi Harris
Harrison Smith-Garvey, doctor
Jordan Smith-Garvey, cook
Joseph Grimaldi, radio
Eric Griffiths, supply
Carter, boiler tech
Hari and Dee, family of Hiluka
Lee Myerson, computer tech
Bao Ling, civil engineer
Ashram Sirpathia, food production
Mairu Sirpathia, food production
Naveena Sirpathia, food production

White Diamond *Personnel*
Henry Hill
Helen Jefferson Hill
Richard Hill
Charles Perreau, helmsman
Mike Reese, machinist
Linda Reichardt, deckhand
Syszmanski, deckhand
Wilkes, deckhand

Adamstown Residents
Helen Turner, governor
Archie McLeish
Rita McLeish
Ronald Kitchener
Keith Allison
Deborah Allison

Reed, bass player
Lisa, piano and accordion
James, drummer

Darwin *Personnel*
Decker, captain
Gibbons, executive officer
Evans, navigator
Reggie McLeish, sailor
Lyle, baritone
O'Rourke, clarinetist
Fitch, sailor

Others
Joe Washington, friend
Roy, traveler
RC, traveler

PROLOGUE

January 2027

Thou know'st 'tis common—all that lives must die. Passing through nature to eternity.

—William Shakespeare, *Hamlet*
act 1, scene 2, line 72

From the hilltop, they could look in all directions at the ocean surrounding the island. During the night, not much was visible other than the natural lights from the full moon that drifted through the sky and the thousands of stars that seemed to follow in its wake. But they were happy with that. They did not want to see any unnatural lights.

Billy lifted the binoculars again and scanned the ocean. Still nothing. But wait. There, in the eastern sky, he could finally see some light below the horizon, as if someone were opening a chest with a candle in it and the light was starting to seep out. Sunrise was coming. He wasn't sure whether to wake Jessie or let her sleep, but when he glanced at her, she had taken care of the decision. She was watching him from her spot under the blanket, the light from the dying fire revealing a gentle smile on her face. Billy smiled back. She stood, the blanket still wrapped around her shoulders, moved over to him, and took the binoculars so she, too, could look.

Dawn arrived with more lights in the eastern sky, a mix of pink, orange, and blue rays peeking out over the horizon on the far side of the world. A breeze blew down from the mountain off to the west, so the hilltop was cool. But that was only one of the reasons they had wrapped themselves in the blanket. They were enjoying being so close while watching the morning come. And they knew that down in the settlement below the hill, their friends and families were sleeping, and the precious sanctuary that they had built was well protected. So much had happened to them and the world over the last five months, but they were still here and still very much alive. The new day promised new possibilities for a new world.

"Billy," Jessie said softly.

Billy looked where she was looking, off to the north, and then he saw it too. There was light out there, and it was not natural.

He asked quietly, "How many?"

She focused the binoculars and then answered, "Two ships."

Billy unclipped the walkie-talkie from his belt and punched the button. "Hunter," he called and then released the button.

The voice on the other end came back quickly, impressively, given that he had surely just been awakened. "Yeah."

Billy said simply, "They're coming."

Yes, it was a new day with new possibilities, but the new world was like the old one in at least one unfortunate way. They still had to fight for what they held so dear, or it was destined to disappear for eternity.

PART 1

The Ark
September 2026

But you tell me, over and over again, my friend,
Ah, you don't believe we're on the eve of destruction.

—P. F. Sloan, 1964, "The Eve of Destruction," recorded by Barry McGuire

CHAPTER 1

New Orleans

As Hurricane Oscar bore down on New Orleans, Billy Hill and James Brooks were nailing up plywood boards on the windows of Charity Hospital. The hope, however ephemeral, was that such preparations would prevent the kind of disaster that had devastated city hospitals during hurricanes like Katrina in 2005. Then again, so-called hundred-year events like Katrina and Oscar were hitting American coastal cities annually now, as if mocking those who tried to resist nature's power.

"Where do they get these names, anyway?" Brooks yelled. He was only ten feet away from Hill, but they could barely hear each other's voices over the wind. Brooks was a middle-aged Black man, stout but not overweight, with a weather-beaten face and a graying beard that made him look a bit older than he was.

Hill, the other man, was White, in his midthirties, medium height and weight, with sandy-brown hair and a stubble of brown beard on a wide face. He glanced at Brooks as he shouted the answer back.

"It's alphabetical, man."

"I know that, but why *Oscar*?"

Hill paused for just a moment. "Well, how many first names can you come up with that start with *O*?"

After a second, Brooks started, "Oliver…Orville…Omar…"

Hill grinned, a toothy smile that seemed to come easily. Brooks was good company, even when things were rough, as they had been lately. He and his family's apartment in the lower Ninth Ward had been flooded and a tree blew down on their car, destroying the vehicle. Hill, doing disaster preparedness for the Red Cross, had been staying in the apartment, so they had all loaded up a few things into his car and moved into the hospital shelter.

A sixty-mile-per-hour wind gust roared down the street, carrying all kinds of debris with it. Hill started to cite the Bob Dylan line that the wind was "howling like a hammer," but before he could say anything, a cardboard box hit Brooks in the back.

"Ouch!" Brooks exclaimed.

Hill yelled back over the wind, "Good call! That's an *O* too."

Brooks snarled, "You're a smart-ass, Billy."

It was gallows humor. They all knew the Katrina stories, and residents like Brooks still remembered bridges being closed to those trying to evacuate by going across the Pontchartrain. The two men finished up and went back inside the hospital lobby, where hundreds of others had also come to seek shelter. The place was chaotic, with children crying, parents pacing nervously, pets trying to find a corner in which to hide. A radio played at full volume, spewing ominous warnings.

Brooks went to check on his family as Hill sat down next to a broken ATM in a corner of the lobby to rest. He reached into a jacket pocket and pulled out a couple of letters that looked like they had been read at least a few times. He read them again and then dozed off, thinking about California.

The crowd stirring woke Hill up. He wasn't sure how long he had been asleep, but the radio blared with the announcement that all nonessential people should evacuate the city. The announcement was not unexpected, but now that it was here, many had no immediately apparent way to follow the order.

Brooks came walking across the lobby with his wife, Janice, and the two boys, Jamal and Jonah, just steps behind. He liked to joke that all their initials were *J* and *B* so they could use monogrammed towels, as if they had any of those.

When they got within ten feet of him, Hill tossed Brooks some car keys. Brooks caught them and stared back. "What the…?"

Hill stood and said, "It's old and rusty, but it should get you out of the city." When Brooks didn't say anything right away, Hill added, "Hell, it might get you all the way to California." Hill knew that Brooks had read the letters that had motivated his dreaming and was interested in the opportunity. He was a good carpenter, and it sounded like work was available.

"I can't take this," Brooks said.

"Sure you can. It's not a big deal."

"Why don't you just take it and leave?"

Hill had expected an argument and was ready. "I don't have a family, JB, and we can't all fit in that car. Besides, I'm not going anywhere for a while."

Brooks glanced at the stairs as he asked, "Washington?"

When Hill just nodded, Brooks asked, "Why don't you get him and get out of here?"

Hill shook his head. "Washington isn't going anywhere." He looked intently at Brooks. "And nobody should die alone. That happened too much during that damn pandemic. And Wash might last days and then the city will be so flooded that I wouldn't be able to get the car out of here anyway."

They both stood, staring at each other. The announcement to evacuate came over the radio again, as if emphasizing the need to move.

Brooks looked at his family and then back at Hill.

"I owe you, Billy." He stuck out his hand.

Hill grasped it. Brooks's grip was like a vise, not surprising for a carpenter. Hill smiled. "Call it payback for me staying in your apartment the past week."

As the Brooks family started to move away, Janice came back and gave Billy a hug. The two boys stared at him, not sure what to do. Then they were gone.

Hill turned and headed toward the stairs, fighting the crowds of people who were on the way down. When he got to the seventh floor, it was eerily quiet. The sounds of his work boots on the linoleum floor echoed down the hallway. Some patients were still in the rooms, but few nurses or doctors were evident. The halls were littered with empty potato chip bags, candy bar wrappers, and discarded medical gloves. The televisions in the rooms were on, but only irregularly, as the pictures often deteriorated into static. And although it was only late afternoon, the darkness outside seeped through the windows and into the rooms like death come calling.

Hill found Washington sitting upright, tubes still attached to his nose and arm, playing solitaire with a faded deck of cards on his empty dinner tray.

"Hey, Wash." Hill tried to sound upbeat. "Deal me in."

Washington shook his head slightly, as if disappointed to see his visitor. The hair on top of his head looked grayer, and the wrinkles on the brow of his dark face seemed deeper than just days before. He looked thin and vulnerable under the sheets, a far cry from the strong man Hill had first met nearly a dozen years before. They had worked barges on the Mississippi River together, along with Brooks, on and off for several years after Hill had been discharged from the Navy. Washington had shown Hill the ropes on the towboats, literally and figuratively. But even the heartiest boatman can't defy the damages from chain-smoking forever. He was dying, and they both knew it.

"What are you doing here, White boy? You a doctor?" Washington's voice was raspy and thin.

"Nope."

"A nurse?"

"Nope."

"Good. Nurses got to be prettier than you."

Hill smiled.

Washington went on, "You ain't a priest, are you, Billy?"

Billy's smile widened. "Hell no. I'm just waiting out the storm here with my buddy."

"Shit," Washington muttered. "You crazy to stay here."

"Maybe," Billy answered.

Washington frowned. "I mean it. What the hell are you doing?"

Billy just looked back at him and then fell back on his favorite explanation for his own behavior. "Hey, Wash, you know what I always say: eternity is just over the horizon."

Washington was unimpressed. "Don't hand me that, boy. You keep looking for it, but you got to get a home, start a family…"

Hill cut him off, having heard it before, from Washington as well as others. "The American dream, you mean?" His tone sounded more cynical than intended.

"Call it what you want, son, but you got to commit to something."

Billy answered the way he had in similar conversations before, with a deflection. "Right now, I'm committed to this."

Then Washington surprised him. He reached up and grabbed Billy by the front of the shirt and pulled the younger man's face down near his. Billy didn't know he had that much strength left in his grip. Washington looked intently into his eyes.

"You're trying to help, Billy, and that's good. But you only got so much time. You think by moving around and doing different things, you can delay it, but you can't. You got to find something. I don't know if it's that thing in California or what. But you find something and then you dig in and you hold on to it as long as you can."

Billy didn't even try to make a joke. He knew that his friend was serious. And he knew he didn't have much time. Washington released his grip and sank back into the bed.

Billy fought off the lump in his throat and finally asked, "We gonna play these cards or what?"

CHAPTER 2

Yellowstone

At some point during the night, Washington fell asleep, the cards in his hands dropping softly onto the bedsheet. Hill sat quietly, watching the television. An anchorwoman on CNN said they were going to take a break from covering Hurricane Oscar to show footage from another disaster taking place in a different part of the country. The report started with a view of a reporter, a young guy wearing a field jacket, standing in front of the Mammoth Hotel in Yellowstone National Park. Behind him and the hotel, smoke covered much of the hillside.

"Good evening. I'm Jason Warner, live from Yellowstone National Park, where today the Mammoth fire entered its second week. This was a tough day out here as the fire took a tragic turn, killing one firefighter and injuring another. We're talking with Beth Hill, the foreman of the crew who lost the man."

Billy sat up straight and turned up the volume. The camera shifted to show a solidly built woman of average height with light-brown hair, wearing a yellow Forest Service firefighting shirt. Behind her were seven other firefighters standing loosely together. A diverse group, the common feature between them the grime and ash on their dirty yellow shirts. They looked like they had been in a war zone and not at all interested in being on television. As the camera rolled, a thin Hispanic man poured water over his head, letting it run down through his brown face and black goatee. He glared at the camera.

Warner: "Foreman Hill, we appreciate you talking to us today."

Hill: "Okay."

Warner: "I see that your ten-person crew is down to eight. I can only imagine how you must feel."

Hill: "You're right."

Warner: "Losing Ms. Sheffer is incredibly tragic. How is Mr. Miller?"

Hill: "He's in the hospital. He'll make it."

Warner: "Can you tell us briefly what happened?"

Hill: "Okay. We were on the south side of the Yellowstone [River] when the wind shifted to come out of the north. Fire jumped the river and caught us. That's a big river, but these fires are big and there's so much fuel…shit happens."

Warner: "It seems to happen more often lately. This is the fourth fatality for firefighters in the Rockies this summer. After eight deaths last year and seven the year before, is this a trend?"

Beth Hill paused and looked around. The camera followed her gaze to show the hills in the background behind her. Smoke was heavy.

Hill: "What do you think? Winters are shorter every year. Summers are hotter. And all those dead trees from the pine beetles, they're just kindling."

Warner: "The president has referred to these fatalities as a tragic anomaly."

Hill: "A tragic what?"

The camera came back to focus on Hill. Her face looked tired, but the light-green eyes were intense. Behind her, a large Black man with an earring in his right ear and a tear in his yellow shirt just above the name *Sanders* moved to her shoulder.

Warner: "Anomaly. In other words, this is a bad season, but not part of any larger phenomenon."

Hill stared at the reporter for just a moment and then snarled as she answered.

Hill: "Like hell. It's not just a bad season. It's a bad situation, and it's gonna get worse every year. And we're gonna keep losing people if we don't do something about it."

Behind her, the Black man put his hand on her shoulder and said in a deep voice, "Come on, boss, let's get outta here." But Hill stared at the reporter, as if daring him to ask another question. The reporter, sensing blood in the water, was happy to oblige.

Warner: "By saying 'Do something about it,' I assume you mean climate change. Some say these fire seasons are getting worse because the climate is changing. But the president says he doesn't believe in it. Do you?"

Hill paused again before answering, almost long enough to think she wouldn't say more. But then she leaned forward before speaking slowly, almost as if she were spitting out the words.

Hill: "Tell the president to come on out here. He won't find a person on the fire line who doesn't know the climate is changing. Maybe some people should get their heads out of their asses."

The big man said again, "Let's go, boss." She stared at the reporter for a full ten seconds, and then they turned and walked back to their crew. The camera swung back to the reporter's face.

Warner: "That was Beth Hill of the US Forest Service. As I said, this was a tough day on the fire line, and there are some hard feelings out here. Back to you in the studio."

The camera shifted back to the studio as Billy sensed a slight movement behind him. He cut the volume on the television.

Washington was awake and staring at him. "Family resemblance?" he asked.

Hill nodded. "Yeah, my sister."

Washington shook his head. "Figures."

Hill smiled briefly, trying to piece together how strange it was to see his sister on television in the middle of one disaster while he was deep into another one. The news story that followed on CNN was about yet another crisis, a cyclone on the other side of the world that was pounding a coastline with monstrous waves, powerful winds, and torrential downpours.

"What are you gonna do, Billy?" Between the lung cancer and the noise of the storm outside, Washington's voice was almost imperceptible now.

Billy smiled. "Well, when we get some light again, I'm going to win back that money I just lost to you." He reached for the deck of cards.

"Don't bullshit me, White boy," Washington said firmly. Billy laughed at the line, one he must have heard a hundred times in that first year on the river. He had been so cocky, just out of the Navy, and thought he knew everything about boats, waterways, and anything else. Washington always set him straight.

"I'm serious," Washington said.

Hill looked out the window at the darkness again. "I know I need to make a move, Wash. If I keep doing this, I'm never going to run out of storms."

Washington demanded, "Move to where?"

Hill sighed. "I think I'll go to California." When Washington didn't say anything, Hill added, "What the hell, I think my car will be out there."

The joke fell on deaf ears. When Hill looked back at Washington, the older man had drifted off again.

Sometime around three in the morning, the power went out, leaving the hospital with just emergency lighting. In the biggest gusts of wind, Hill could feel the building sway. He had not seen a nurse or anybody else for hours. Washington stayed asleep, his breath coming in gasps, each sounding like it could be his last. Hill sat next to him and stared out the window at the raging storm. He saw very little movement, a car occasionally venturing down the deserted streets, headlights vainly seeking safe passage. He hoped that Brooks and his family had gotten away.

When he was younger, Billy would hear about these disasters and think that he should be there. It was something about the news coverage that made these situations seem like the center of the world at that moment. Maybe he just wondered how he would deal with such a situation. Or maybe he really did want to help. Now, being in another one, he thought about how naive he had been. Reporters on television love to talk about heroes in disasters, but most people were just trying to survive and maybe help a few others along the way.

He looked at Washington and thought back to those first months of freedom after being in the military. When the barges weren't running, he drove a cab and played guitar with some bands in New Orleans for tips. Then he had moved back to California for a while. After that, he became what people now called a DT, for disaster tracker. He had worked with the Red Cross, the Salvation Army, any organization that needed help with hurricanes or fires or whatever showed up. It didn't pay much, but he did find out what it was like at the center of the world. And there was another reason he took that job. Billy realized that it had a lot to do with his father. Billy tried to come up with the reference—what was that line about the sins of the father?

Billy reached for his pack. He had been smart enough to know that he wasn't going back to the Brooks apartment, so he had packed a few things as well as the two letters he had been reading in the lobby. He started to pull them out but then realized he pretty much knew them word for word by now anyway. Having not seen his father in years, it had been a surprise when the first one showed up in his post office box a few weeks before. Indeed, that box was surely the only reason the father had found him since he had used the same one for years. Even stranger was that even though Billy had not heard from his father in years, he suddenly got another one, making it two letters in the same month. The first one was vague, something about building a modern ark and that more information was coming if he expressed interest. Billy had not done so but received the second letter anyway. And he had to admit that, suddenly, yes, he was interested, at least enough to see it.

Washington let out a long sigh and was then quiet. He never woke up again. Billy sat there for a while, making sure his friend was gone and listening to the sounds of the storm outside. Then he shouldered his pack and headed for the freight yards.

CHAPTER 3

Gateway City

The freight handlers built the train in the yard, like so many blue-collar scientists attaching more body parts to their mobile Frankenstein. They shifted and connected multicolored boxcars, laden with coal from Illinois, grain from the farm belt, and foreign goods that had come up the Mississippi River. Billy listened to the train construction from a spot in the shade of an abandoned toolshed on the western end of the yard and hoped the train would arrive before both the weather and the law. The evening weather was typical of St. Louis in the late summer, the humidity levels nearly as high as the temperatures even as sunset approached. The occasional rumble of thunder from the darkening western sky suggested that rain was inevitable. As for the law, some yard workers might dislike the fact that hoboes weren't just a ghost of bygone days and contact the authorities. Then again, Billy told himself, as usual with a cultural reference, this was St. Louis, so maybe they were all fans of Chuck Berry, whose engineers might like seeing him "sitting in the shade [enjoying] the rhythm that the drivers made." Probably not, so he stayed out of sight as he waited.

His hunch in New Orleans had been correct. Shippers wanted their goods out before Hurricane Oscar flooded the city. So there were many trains heading north. Shortly after Washington died, Billy caught one. It stopped in Memphis to change cars and then rolled on up through the day to St. Louis, getting there in the late afternoon. The city looked like it always had, the weathered gray bank towers and shiny condo buildings forming a cluster just to the west of the magnificent arch. The freight yards in St. Louis run through the southern part of downtown, so it was easy for Billy to hop off and find the passenger train station, where he used the bathroom. He then found a small convenience store, filled his water bottle, bought some apples and bread, and picked up a bottle of cheap wine. Thus resupplied, he returned to the freight yards.

Billy wasn't the only person in St. Louis that evening hoping that the approaching storm would not arrive too soon. He could hear frequent cheering from the nearby baseball stadium. Nearly all baseball games were played at night anymore as the days were just too hot. After one of those frequent cheers, Billy glanced in the direction of the stadium, just half a mile or so to the east, and could see the glow from the banks of lights, turned on in anticipation of the storm. Billy imagined thousands of Cardinals fans, perhaps wishing for a Roy Hobbs moment that would destroy the scoreboard before the lightning did.

His thoughts were interrupted by the clatter of steel coming to life. The train that had been collecting boxcars was starting to move. Soon, two large black engines came into view, pulling a long line of cars behind them. The engineer blew his whistle three times, rousing Billy to stand and stretch. The sound of tons of steel on the move increased as the train drew closer. He waited until the engines inched by, then shouldered his pack and moved toward the tracks.

Billy had hopped a lot of trains in his life, despite people saying he was crazy for doing so. Indeed, he often "caught" a train rather than using some other means of travel as it never failed to give him a thrill. Until you're standing within arm's reach of a huge mechanical monster, people just don't realize how loud the wheels are as they crunch over the iron ties. The engine bellows and the cars themselves creak as they rattle along behind like reluctant children. The smell of grease is so strong you can almost taste it. The sound is deafening, intimidating. And people always underestimate the height of the floor of the cars until they get up close. Standing on the gravel bed of the railroad ties, the cars tower overhead, rocking back and forth as if they were about to topple over, contemptuous of the precarious balance provided by two thin rails.

Coming out of the yard with a full line of cars, this train was moving slowly enough that Billy could pick his spot. Full coal cars and some empty cattle cars rolled past, then some locked freight cars, all with emblems mentioning past and future destinations such as Kansas City. He waited until he saw a light-blue boxcar come alongside, faded and rusty, but inviting with its freight door wide open. He started to jog, his feet slipping occasionally on the loose rocks until he matched the speed of the train and tossed his pack inside. He then reached up and grabbed the boxcar door with one hand and the door latch hole on the floor with the other and hoisted himself inside. It wasn't the most graceful maneuver he had ever used to catch a train, but as he rolled inside onto the dusty floor, it felt like a perfect 10 landing. And the funny thing was that a loud cheer sounded from behind him, followed by fireworks. Even if it really was for some Cardinal who had just hit a home run, Billy couldn't help but laugh out loud at the timing.

Looking around inside the car, he saw bags of grain, surely headed for the parched and hungry Western states, but for now offering the possibility of providing a little cushion for some sleep. Satisfied, he sat down in the open doorway, his legs dangling outside as the train picked up speed, and pulled the bottle of wine out of his pack. Just as the train was leaving the last section of yard, he looked up in time to see a switchman on the tracks. The yard worker overcame his surprise and started to yell something that was inaudible over the sound of the train wheels. Billy held up the bottle in salute and watched the switchman disappear behind the train, the Gateway Arch framing the city behind him. Oh well, Billy realized he would have to keep his eyes open in the freight yards down the line just in case the worker called ahead.

As Billy took a drink, the long train rolled away from the city and toward the darkening western sky. Another line from Johnny B. Goode popped into his head, the one about "leaving Louisiana for the Golden West." After a quick stop in the Gateway City, he had done just that.

CHAPTER 4

Northern Rockies

The early-September snow made Gardiner, Montana, feel more like November, but nobody in the K Bar was complaining. Instead, the place was crowded and festive, full of locals, off-duty park employees, and firefighters who were no longer needed since the snow had ended the fires. Sitting at the table just inside the front door, with a view out the window at snow piling up on the street, was the crew who had been on CNN the night before. Even though some of the other patrons were treating them like celebrities, the crew was not celebrating. One of their members was dead, one in the hospital, and the others had just received some unpleasant news.

"What the hell, boss," Frank Sanders said. Even sitting, the big man was larger than his colleagues as he leaned over the table to stare at Beth Hill.

Beth looked around at each of the seven crew members before answering. "No kidding. They fired my ass. Said you guys will be assigned to another crew before the next fire season."

Rodriguez, the Hispanic with the goatee, swore softly, "Bastardos."

Sanders said, "This calls for more of this." He uncoiled from his chair, picked up the empty pitchers, and strode to the bar.

The snow had started falling shortly after CNN did their interview. The wind shift from the north that had caught the crew on the fire line brought in a cold front. As in 1988, when an early snow put an end to those massive fires, this precipitation took care of this year's conflagration. It also provided convenient timing for Forest Service officials to take some action in response to the CNN interview. Apparently, a lot of people, including the president, weren't happy about Beth Hill's comments.

Miller's voice came through the speakerphone. "Got rid of the fire and you all in the same day, eh?" He was still in the local hospital, getting treated for the burns he had suffered to his face and right side.

Beth nodded. "Yeah, big day for them." She spoke up to make sure he could hear her over the noise in the bar. Somebody had punched up "Pancho and Lefty" on the jukebox. "How are you doing?"

Miller's voice came back. "I'd rather be there. Then again, compared to Sheffer, I can't complain."

"Right," Beth answered. "Here's to Sheffer." They all raised their glasses and drank.

"Met any nurses, cowboy?" Rodriguez asked.

Miller answered, "Nurses aren't that interested. These burns look pretty bad."

Without a pause, Rodriguez responded, "Hell, amigo, you didn't look that good to begin with."

"Fuck you, T-Rod," came the response. Some of the crew laughed.

Sanders walked back to the table with two full pitchers. Beth started to reach for her wallet, but Sanders waved her off as he gestured back at the bartender. "It's on the house." Beth looked across the room and nodded appreciatively to the bartender. Everybody there knew about Sheffer.

"So what now, boss?" Mecklenburg, the oldest member of the crew, looked at Beth.

As they all refilled their glasses, Beth pulled a couple of wrinkled letters out of her pocket and started talking. "Okay, this may sound crazy. I got these letters from my dad a while ago and have been thinking about them ever since. Long story short, he and some people are building a modern-day ark in California to save the DNA of species before they all disappear. And he needs crew."

She paused and looked around at all the puzzled expressions. "Yeah, I know. But when you read the letters, it makes more sense." She paused again. "Besides, I suddenly have nothing better to do."

She waited several seconds and then asked, "Anybody interested?"

The table was oddly quiet for a good thirty seconds. The sounds of the bar, with people talking and shooting pool in the back room, filled the air. The jukebox dialed up the next song, and in one of those odd coincidences that seem to happen so often people wonder if something or somebody else is pulling the strings, the next song that came up was the classic "Stand by Me." Beth shook her head slightly, a wry smile just barely showing. She didn't smile often, as she only did it when genuinely amused. And then, it didn't usually last long.

Not surprisingly, Rodriguez broke the silence. He was never much for quiet. "California Lindo, the land of milk and honey. Not sure I'll go on your boat, Jefe, but I'll ride out with you." He took a long drink.

Beth nodded appreciatively. That broke the ice but didn't exactly inspire the others to say yes. Other members of the crew all took turns declining, citing families or other commitments. Beth had not expected anything different, but she was surprised by what happened next.

Tyrone Green, a tough young Black guy from Chicago, said, "Why not? I'm not going back to the city."

After a pause, Miller, on the phone, followed with, "And I'm damn sure not going back on the fire line."

They all looked at Sanders. He had great respect among the crew, not the least reason being that he always thought things over before acting. This time was no exception. After nearly a full minute, he finally said, "I don't know, boss. I'll tell you in the morning."

Beth nodded. "That works. We all need to drive into Mammoth in the morning to get our paychecks and our gear. You can decide then." She glanced outside at the snow, now coming down even heavier than before. Then reaching for the pitcher, she added, "In the meantime…"

Beth got up early the next morning to get a start on the drive to California. Sanders, still undecided as to his plans, rode with her to check Miller, a large bandage covering the burnt side of his face, out of the Gardiner hospital. Then the three of them rode in Beth's pickup truck, their clothes and gear in the bed under a tarp. Rodriguez and Green followed behind on the former's motorcycle. The snow had blanketed the landscape, but plows had cleared the road into park headquarters in Mammoth. Snow would have normally made the place postcard beautiful, but ugly, scorched black earth darkened the ground that was visible and the trees that still stood were black against the white cover. Smoke still hung heavily in the air.

The truck and the motorcycle passed though the historic North Gate, climbed the hill toward Mammoth, crossed the Yellowstone River, and then stopped. A small group of vehicles had pulled into a turnoff where a short trail led down to a thermal pool in the river. Beth and her crew, curious, parked and then started down the trail, their breath showing in the early-morning air.

Green patted himself on the chest with his gloves. "Damn, T-Rod, riding on that bike is fucking cold."

"Hey, amigo, that' not a bike, it's a Harley," Rodriguez answered. "And you're lucky I don't charge you like if you took a taxi."

"At least I wouldn't freeze my ass off," Green responded.

"It's good for you, bro, toughen up for the ride to California." Then he added, "Say, maybe I will charge you for that. What do you got?"

"Shit," Green answered, "I ain't got shit…"

"Well, you better…"

"Knock it off," Sanders said as they arrived at the group looking down at the river. They followed their stares out to the hot springs, where a moose was standing, just on the edge of the hundred-degree water.

"She's been there for days," a Park Service ranger was saying. "I guess she figures that even that hot water would be better than facing more fires in the forest."

When nobody said anything, the ranger went on, "The good news is that with this snowfall, the fires are over and she should move on soon."

Several people took photos and then moved back toward their vehicles. Beth and her colleagues started to move but then stopped to wait for Sanders. He stood, staring at the moose. After a couple of minutes, they hiked back up the trail.

As Sanders climbed into the cab, he said quietly, "Count me in." Beth shook her head as she suppressed a smile. Sanders was a big, tough guy, but she knew he was a softy for animals. Suddenly, the ark made sense to him.

Miller, in the middle seat, pushed his cowboy hat back and said "Mooooooose" as if he were cheering at a Springsteen concert.

"Good," Beth answered, pleased with the company she would have for the trip.

CHAPTER 5

Great Plains

During the night, Billy's train stopped in Kansas City. The train's whistle and the smell of manure from the KC stockyards rousted him from a brief slumber on the sacks of grain. Worried that the switchman in St. Louis might have called ahead about a hobo, Billy collected his pack and, as the train slowed, hopped out, running slightly as he hit the ground to avoid falling.

The city was extremely quiet. The heat was still evident, even in the middle of the night, and a few homeless people moved around, looking in vain for a place to get some cool relief. Billy found an all-night convenience store where he used the bathroom and bought a few more supplies as well as a newspaper. He then hurried back to the yards and found a place to sit and wait. After a couple of hours, a train moved in his direction. The engines rumbled by, then a line of freight cars, and then, amazingly enough, a familiar light-blue boxcar. Billy climbed aboard again. Home away from home, he thought before catching himself; it wasn't as if he had another home somewhere else.

The train moved through the yard, over the Missouri River, and then picked up speed as it began the long trek across the Great Plains. Darkness again enveloped the boxcar, and the sky filled with thousands of stars. Sitting in the open door, Billy spotted the Big Dipper and then the North Star directly abeam of the train. He thus knew they were headed due west. Talking to himself, he recalled the liner notes to Bob Dylan's album *Blood on the Tracks* and the sentence about "the American road, all the busted dreams of open spaces, boxcars, the Big Dipper pricking the velvet night." Well, at least he had those open spaces and boxcars. As for busted dreams, he had had his share of those, too, but he didn't feel too sorry for himself. He knew that all those farmers and dust diggers out there on the dry plains during this drought could make his busted dreams pale in comparison. He moved to the corner of the boxcar again, lay down on the grain bags, and fell asleep thinking about past train trips to anywhere.

The train whistle ahead woke him up again. He didn't think he had been asleep long, as it was still dark outside. He stretched and moved to the open door. In the darkness, he could occasionally see a light come on in some farmhouse where somebody was getting ready for a very early start to the day. Another line from a song came to mind, this one from the "City of New Orleans," about how the train "rolls on, past houses, farms, and fields." How appropriate was it that the son of Woody Guthrie sang the best train song? And how appropriate to be thinking about Woody out here in the Great Plains during yet another pending Dust Bowl. Over the next hour, as he watched, with increasing frequency pickup trucks would pull out onto one of the dusty country roads, headlights illuminating the same arid land that had been there the night before. It was going to be another hot, dry day.

He ate a small breakfast of an apple and some packaged doughnuts and then decided, somewhat reluctantly, that he might as well read the newspaper to see what was going on in the rest of the world. His reluctance was immediately justified. In addition to the flood in New Orleans and the fires in Montana, several stories promised more reading on the impacts of climate change. A war between Israel and Arab states over scarce water had entered the sixth week. The death toll from a heat wave in India now exceeded three thousand. The cyclone in the South Pacific had pummeled Japan and headed for North Korea.

The entire paper was a grim reminder that the world was changing, and not for the better. Billy put it down and stared out the open door at the rising sun and the start of another triple-digit day of heat.

Maybe this time the sky really was falling. Billy thought about his father's letters and pulled them out of his pocket to read again.

July 1, 2026

Dear William:

I hope that you are well. I regret that we have had little contact in recent years but write now with a proposal.

I'm deeply concerned with the state of the world. You know as well as I do that we are now bearing the fruit of years of neglect and abuse. The impacts of climate change and the accompanying dislocations, disease, and political unrest have accelerated dramatically in just the last few years.

You may be surprised to read these words from me, as I was skeptical of the warnings for a long time. I also acknowledge that I, as you well know, contributed to these changes during my entire professional life. I intend to make some amends. I'm building a modern ark to protect the genes of thousands of species as we work through the impending crises. My next letter will provide more details.

I would appreciate your company and your help on this venture. I have sent similar letters to your sister and brother. We need crew with all kinds of skills.

Sincerely,
Oliver T. Hill
Former President, Hill Inc.

Billy looked out at the parched land baking under the sun and thought about the letter. After disagreeing with his father on just about everything he could remember, he had been surprised, pleasantly. He had heard of other efforts to save the DNA of species and even remembered seeing the idea in the novel *The Overstory*. Then he reread the second letter. It was something Oliver had written to try to attract investors.

The Ark Project

For years, biologists have warned of a sixth great mass extinction of the world's species, when more than half of the world's biodiversity will disappear in a brief period of geologic time. According to the International Union for the Conservation of Nature, nearly a quarter of all bird species, one third of mammal species, and half of all amphibian species are now threatened with extinction. Thousands of plant species as well are disappearing, faster than they can even be researched for possible benefits. Further, while speciation does create new species, that process takes hundreds of years, whereas extinction rates today are thousands of times faster than normal.

Despite some efforts at conservation, these trends have only accelerated in recent years. Scientists long attributed the loss of species to habitat destruction, overhunting, and the introduction of nonnative species into different ecosystems. Recently, however, large-scale climate change has become a dominant threat.

Therefore, in recent decades, scientists have attempted to preserve species in different ways. The most notable is the Global Seed Vault in Norway. This worthy project contains samples of nearly one million plant species in a tunnel where the temperature is maintained at below-freezing levels. While admirable, even such a place is vulnerable to terrorism or, God forbid, nuclear holocaust.

Our team has built a mobile species repository. We have purchased DNA from the Norwegians as well as from a repository in San Diego and have now collected the DNA of thousands of plant and animal species in a state-of-the-art inventory that is housed aboard a modern-day ark. Our concern now is with keeping that inventory safe. Changing climates have already motivated numerous conflicts around the globe, including recent ones in nations that possess nuclear weapons. I realize that in the event of nuclear war, no place on Earth may be safe. However, we intend to sail this ark to a remote location, as far as possible from the ravages of impending disaster.

With your help, we will build and protect a sanctuary as a refuge for plants and animals. I welcome your assistance.

Sincerely,
Oliver T. Hill
Former President, Hill Inc.

Billy folded the letters and leaned against the door of the boxcar. Up ahead, the train whistle sounded. Billy loved the sound, even though it always made him feel lonely, but he also wondered what had prompted it. Looking out the doorway, he could not see a town ahead. Nor did there appear to be any major intersection for traffic to be warned. Then, out on the plain, a solitary coyote ran by. As the coyote disappeared behind the train, Billy hoped he was heading for a family and home. Maybe the conductor had just kindly scared the animal off the tracks. Or maybe the conductor had sounded the whistle just because he, too, was alone and wanted to communicate with somebody, anybody.

CHAPTER 6

Elko, Nevada

After nearly five hundred miles on the road, Beth and her crew stopped in Elko, Nevada, for the night. They booked a couple of rooms in a hotel, ate large quantities of food at a buffet, and then visited the casino on the first floor. While Rodriguez and Green joined a poker game, Beth and Sanders and Miller sat down at a bar. The television behind the bar was showing coverage of the flooding in New Orleans from Hurricane Oscar and the growing typhoon in South Asia, but it was hard to identify with those excessive-water events in Nevada. The high desert had always been hot and dry, but in the last few years, the lack of water had intensified. Now the evidence of a drought was everywhere, from metered showerheads in the hotels to drained swimming pools. Even a glass of water at the buffet now cost money.

"Damn it, T-Rod," Beth swore quietly as she noticed a little ruckus at the poker table twenty yards away where Rodriguez was playing. As Rodriguez stood to face a security guard who had just arrived, Green glanced back at Beth with a bemused look on his face and spread his hands out as if to say he had nothing to do with it.

Beth started to get up, but Sanders beat her to it. He put a hand on her shoulder as he stood, said, "I got it," and sauntered toward the poker table.

Miller, sitting on Beth's other side, said quietly, "Just goes to show, even in a casino, T-Rod can find trouble." After a pause, he added, "Hey, Boss, check it out." He pointed toward the television.

Beth turned to look as CNN started a story titled "Modern-Day Ark." She asked the bartender to turn up the volume so she could hear over the incessant clanging of the slot machines.

The report began with a sweeping view of San Francisco and the Golden Gate Bridge. The camera then focused on a small piece of land on the eastern side of the bay identified by the speaker as Treasure Island. The land had been a Navy base, but as the reporter stated, the military had moved out and it was now the home of an entrepreneur who was leasing the dock area for construction of a ship.

A pier ran out into the bay. Tied to one side was a long white superyacht. On the other side was a much larger ship, lying low in the water, a black hull topped with a red layer and then two white upper decks. The superyacht also had three decks but looked to have been built for speed and show rather than the stability of the larger, wider ship. On the stern of the larger ship, painted in large red letters was the name *Noah*.

The sounds of cries from seagulls diminished as the reporter mentioned a Mr. Oliver Hill, and then Beth heard her father's soft-pitched voice.

"Years of work have brought us to this point, and the ark is nearly finished now. The ship is six hundred feet long, with a beam of seventy feet and a displacement over six thousand tons. When fully staffed, we'll have well over one hundred people aboard. And we've nearly finished loading enough supplies to be out for six months if need be."

The camera's focus moved from the ship to show some piles of crates and boxes still on the dock, waiting for loading. Then it came back to show Oliver Hill for the first time. He looked older than Beth remembered, of course, having not seen him in years. But he also looked different. He was thinner, his white hair longer, and he had even grown a goatee. He looked more like a casual Uncle Sam than the corporate executive that Beth knew when growing up. Oliver now dressed like an aging professor, in an open-collar light-blue shirt, ready to have some guests over for wine and cheese.

The camera focused on Oliver's face, his blue eyes bright with pride, as he resumed talking. "Most importantly, we've loaded the ark with a precious cargo. If you'll follow me, I'll show you."

He turned and began walking down the dock toward the gangway, a slight limp showing as he strode away. The reporter said something about the first look inside the ark for a television crew as she followed. As they walked, she continued talking. "In 2008, an international group constructed a seed vault in a remote arctic region of Norway to store nearly one million samples of crops from around the world. The vault has been threatened by water contamination due to ice melt from climate change. What Mr. Hill and his group are doing here is a bit different in trying to preserve all animal as well as plant species in a mobile repository that can relocate to avoid specific problems, such as water contamination."

The camera followed Hill and the reporter as they moved up the gangway to the main deck. Oliver said "Hello, Mr. Hunter" to a tall thin Native American with black hair in a ponytail and an earring. Hunter, the Indian, seemed uninterested, if not reluctant, to being filmed. The reporter commented that there were no uniforms for the crew of this ship. The guy at the bar seated next to Miller commented that he didn't know Indians could get that big.

The reporter and cameraman followed Oliver as he walked through the hatch into the interior of the ship. The passageways were narrow, lined with various pipes and painted the same gunmetal gray that one sees on US Navy vessels. Similarly, the ladders leading from one floor to another were as steep as on Navy ships. They continued moving toward the stern of the ship until pausing outside a door with a simple label of "LAB." Oliver punched in a security code on a panel and opened the door into a small foyer with dark curtains. Then he and the reporter each put on one of the heavy lab coats hanging on hooks. They then used a hand sanitizer dispenser before Oliver pushed the curtain aside.

The interior of the lab was pristine and filled with rows of gray file cabinets loaded with narrow drawers. Each section had labels at the top of the first cabinet in the row, with the first, for example, starting with "Amphibians." The drawers had subtitles, but the camera did not focus in on them, rather shifting to two people approaching.

"Good morning, Doctor," Oliver said to a middle-aged White woman, and then added, "And Mi-Sung," to a young Asian woman. Both were wearing white lab coats, and Mi-Sung was carrying a clipboard. Oliver's breath was visible in the cold air.

"Good morning, Oliver." Both women were wearing scarves and gloves.

Oliver looked back at the camera. "This is Dr. Steinberg and lab tech Lee. And this"—he gestured at the interior—"is the heart of our enterprise. We have the DNA of over one million species stored in here." He paused as the camera scanned the room.

When the camera came back to Oliver's face, he said proudly, "Impressive, is it not? You've probably heard of the Frozen Zoo?" When the reporter didn't respond, Oliver went on. "The San Diego Zoo has been building a gene bank, a collection of genetic matter from over one thousand species that are frozen in vials."

Again, there was no response from the reporter, so Oliver continued. "Well, what if something happens to that gene bank? Or God forbid, to San Diego? And the seed vault in Norway? They are already having problems." His pale-blue eyes shining, he then added conclusively, "We are a modern-day ark."

The camera then shifted to the reporter, a blonde, who looked uncomfortably underdressed for the cold air of the lab. She picked up on Oliver's line. "You mentioned God. Are you in fact playing God?"

Oliver began to smile as he thought about his response, but just as he started to speak, his answer was drowned out by the guy next to Miller again.

"Damn lunatics," he said simply.

His buddy next to him yelled to the bartender, "Hey, switch it to the fight, will you?"

As the bartender moved to get the remote, CNN finished the ark story and moved on to footage of a typhoon pounding a coastline in Asia. Beth couldn't hear the narrative anymore, anyway, as someone nearby hit a jackpot on their slot machine and the bells were even louder than the coins pouring out into their basket. People working the slots nearby cheered.

Miller looked at the crowd around the jackpot winner and said, "Is this Nero fiddling while Rome is burning?"

Beth looked back at him as she said, "Sounds like something my brother Billy would say. He's always quoting somebody."

Miller answered, "Why?"

Beth took a drink before answering, "Who knows why Billy does anything?"

Miller nodded. "Think he'll be in California?"

Beth shook her head. "Could be." She welcomed Sanders back from calming the Rodriguez situation by refilling his glass with beer.

CHAPTER 7

Sierra Nevadas

Billy made it to Nevada after Beth and her team, albeit two days later and four hundred miles to the south. After two long train rides and a couple of good days of hitchhiking, he arrived in Las Vegas, exhausted and famished. So he checked into a casino hotel, caught a much-needed shower, restocked his calories at a buffet, and had enough energy to walk the Strip in the evening before sleeping in a bed for the first time in nearly a week.

He got up early, determined to resume his journey before the heat got too intense for crossing the desert, and made a cardboard sign that simply said *SF*, for San Francisco, to improve his chances with hitchhiking. And it worked. While eating at the breakfast buffet, he strategically leaned the sign up against his table leg with the *SF* side showing. Sure enough, a couple of young guys who were also eating plates of eggs, potatoes, and pastries at a neighboring table noticed the sign and struck up a conversation. They were on their way to Yosemite and offered Billy a lift that far.

The three of them were soon crossing Death Valley on the way over to I-395 in an old Honda. Even this early, the temperature was pushing one hundred degrees, but Roy, the owner of the car, said he preferred fresh air to air-conditioning. So they had the windows cranked wide open. That made conversation challenging, especially for Billy in the back seat, but he didn't mind. He smiled at the thought of how nice it was to catch a break in Vegas. He thought of Sheryl Crow's line in "Leaving Las Vegas" about "standing in the middle of the desert and waiting for [a] ship to come in." He would not be standing in the desert with his thumb in the air, and his ship was already waiting in San Francisco.

"Anybody up for a hike?" Roy asked with a smile. He was a stocky guy with a cheerful round face and a head full of curly brown hair.

RC, an Asian with a scruffy beard and a bad hangover, wasn't tempted. "Like hell," he snarled.

Roy answered, "Right again, RC. It does look like hell out there."

Indeed, when they arrived in Death Valley, Badwater Flats shimmered in the heat. The park had broken high temperature records so often recently that the National Park Service had been forced to close the area to tourists in the summer. Even now, in September, the heat was too much for Roy, so they closed the windows and turned on the air-conditioning. That enabled conversation again.

RC looked back at Billy and asked, "So when is this ark going to sail?"

Billy couldn't see RC's eyes behind the sunglasses, but the tone was skeptical.

"I don't know, tell you the truth," Billy answered. "Hope it doesn't leave without me."

"Do they know you're coming?" Roy asked, glancing in the rearview mirror.

"Nah," Billy answered. "Until a few days ago, I didn't know I was coming. And once I get there, I don't even know if I'm going with them."

"Really?" RC asked, incredulous at the lack of a plan. He obviously didn't know Billy.

"Yeah, what the hell, I figured I could see my family, but after that…," Billy offered by way of a weak explanation. "But thanks again for the lift."

"No worries," Roy answered. "By the way, you got any weed?"

"Sorry," Billy said, feeling a bit guilty about not being able to show his appreciation that way. "But I am going to kick in ten bucks for the gas."

Roy smiled. "Hey, it's a Honda. You can make it five." They both laughed while RC pulled his hat down over his eyes and fell asleep in the shotgun seat.

Maybe because of the reference to pot, Billy suddenly had this thought of the book *Fear and Loathing in Las Vegas*. Hadn't Hunter Thompson and his Samoan attorney also picked up a hitchhiker in the desert outside of Las Vegas? If he remembered correctly, that didn't go too well for the hitcher. But he didn't worry. In fact, nearly all the people he had met when hitching were nice folks, sometimes just lonely for company and other times just willing to help someone out. These guys were just a couple of students from the University of Nevada-Las Vegas out for Labor Day weekend in the mountains.

"I could use a snooze," Roy announced. "This heat is making me sleepy."

RC didn't even pull his hat up but responded dismissively, "Don't look at me, Roy boy. This hangover is killing me."

Roy answered, "Thanks a lot, pal." Then he glanced in the rearview again and asked, "How about you, Bill?"

So Billy ended up behind the wheel as they drove north up I-395 on the east side of the Sierra Nevada mountains. And that was okay with him, as it was one of the prettiest roads in the world, with gorgeous views of the jagged peaks to the west. As he drove, he also thought of all the history here, both generic and personal. Generically, the Owens Valley provided a strong reminder of the current situation facing water users in the world. It was one of the first places in the US where people had started to understand water as a precious commodity. Today, the lands bordering I-395 baked and cracked in the hot sun, and the Owens River valley was just a dusty ditch.

In a more personal vein, Billy looked west at the peaks of Kings Canyon National Park and thought back to a week that seemed like a lifetime past. How many years ago was that when he and Teresa had done the hike up Mount Whitney? What a day that could have been. Instead, it was just a sad memory. He was nodding and mouthing the word *idiot* when he realized that RC was looking at him. The young guy had taken off his sunglasses, and his eyes were gentler than Billy had expected.

"Memories, huh, man?" RC asked, perceptively.

Billy nodded and answered, "Yeah."

RC put his glasses back on and looked over at the mountains. "So you've been up there?"

Billy nodded again, but he didn't want to talk about his own memories. "Yep. You?" When RC just shook his head, Billy went on. "Well, you see that really sharp peak back behind a little bit with the jagged edge to the south?"

RC leaned over to see better and looked.

"That's Whitney," Billy said. "Tallest peak in the continental US at 14,500 feet. What's cool is, you can climb it without any ropes or gear."

RC seemed intrigued. "That is pretty cool. How long a hike?"

"Well, you could do it in one day, but better to take some time and get used to the thin air before going up to the top."

"I've done some fourteeners in Colorado," came Roy's voice from where he had been napping in the back seat. He sat up. "Those are awesome."

"Good word," Billy answered. The car passed a sign that said "Owens River." But there was no river to be seen.

"Say," Roy said after seeing the sign, "I've heard of this. Owens Valley, right?"

When Billy just nodded, Roy went on by saying, "*Chinatown*."

RC glared back at his buddy. "What are you talking about, man? Chinatown? You blaming the Chinese again for something?"

"Hell yes!" Roy grinned. "Why wouldn't I?"

"No, he's talking about a movie," Billy defused the argument. "*Chinatown*. It's about how Los Angeles stole the river water from the Owens Valley. True story."

"Right," RC responded. "And blamed the Chinese. I can believe that."

"They didn't blame the Chinese," Roy started to explain and then, bored with the topic almost as quickly as it had come up, changed the subject while handing a CD up from the back seat. "Hey, Chinaman, how about doing something useful?"

"Fuck you, Roy," RC said while taking the tape, "but if it will shut you up, it's okay by me."

Within seconds, Grateful Dead tunes were blaring from the car stereo. Conversation was over again, at least for the moment. How these guys became fans of the Dead was beyond Billy, but he didn't complain. "Truckin'" sounded just about perfect as they rolled north.

Later, they drove by a sign for a turnoff to Mono Lake, where only a quick glance showed that what had been feared for decades had finally happened. The lake existed no longer, now just another dust pit devoid of life. A couple of miles after that, RC, now behind the wheel, turned the car west to drive up Tioga Pass Road and into Yosemite. At the entrance station, the ranger asked where they were headed.

RC answered, "The Valley. We have a campsite for the next two nights."

"Good," answered the ranger as she handed RC the park brochure. "Just remember, no fires. Everything is too dry."

"That's okay," RC answered. "We're more into water. How are the falls?"

The ranger looked surprised at the question and answered quickly, "They're spitting dust, sir." She realized she had been too abrupt. "I'm sorry, but the waterfalls are dry by July around here anymore."

RC slumped a little as he nodded. "Bummer."

They drove on. They stopped briefly in Tuolumne Meadows, where they walked around a bit to stretch their legs. Billy loved how the pines surrounding the station there gave off that wonderful mountain aroma, but as they drove on, he realized that something wasn't right. When they stopped at Olmstead Point for the view, the problem stared them all in the face. Most of the trees on the hillsides sloping down toward the Valley were either dead or dying, the green trees completely outnumbered by black stumps, leafless skeletons, or rust-colored pines.

"Shit, what's happening to this forest?" Roy asked.

"Some of it is drought," Billy answered, "but some of it's also pine beetles. I didn't know they had moved out here."

"Pine beetles?" Roy asked.

"Yeah, they bore into pine trees and kill them. They've torn up the forests in the Rockies."

RC added, "I heard about those. Story is, there're more of them now since the winters are so short and warm."

"Damn," Roy sighed.

"And," Billy continued, "some of it is fires, of course. In the last few years, whole towns have been wiped out. We aren't that far from where the town of Paradise used to exist."

"Paradise, eh?" RC responded. "How ironic."

They drove on to the intersection where the Tioga Pass Road met Highway 120 going off to the west. This was where Billy would split off and head west. Roy and RC seemed a bit sorry to lose their passenger and offered to share their campsite in the Valley. Billy was tempted but decided he should keep moving. It was midafternoon, and if his luck held, he could make it to the Bay Area by sunset. Besides, he didn't want to impose on them any more than he already had. He pulled a ten-dollar bill out of his wallet and tried to hand it to Roy when they shook hands. Roy grinned broadly and just shook his head. Then Billy tried to give it to RC, who simply said, "You might need it, man."

Without any more goodbyes, Roy and RC got back in the Toyota and drove off. Billy's faith in people, at least those who pick up hitchhikers, restored, he walked off into the woods to pee and just enjoy the quiet forest for a bit. Then he shouldered his pack, walked up to the road, and held up the SF sign. His luck continued to hold as he only waited a short while before a pickup truck pulled over and motioned for him to climb in the back.

CHAPTER 8

Treasure Island

Billy walked down the road on Treasure Island that led to the waterfront. The road was surrounded by eucalyptus and deciduous trees, but as he approached the bay and the forest thinned, the view to the west was stunning. In the early-September evening, the sun was just setting behind Golden Gate Bridge, the beautiful structure seeming to hold back the fogbank that was coming in off the Pacific Ocean. Lights in San Francisco showed on the iconic skyline. Close to shore, seagulls circled two ships, looking for any edible debris that seemed to show up whenever humans were around. The ark rocked gently in the water, tethered to the pier by thick ropes fore and aft. On the other side of the pier, a sleek, brilliant white superyacht provided a sharp contrast. Indeed, the two looked like a wide tortoise and a thin hare, both ready to leave the starting gate toward some watery goal.

Making his way to the ark, Billy noticed a parking lot on a little hill off to his left and spotted his old Toyota mixed in with cars, trucks, and even a motorcycle. Sure enough, he smiled, Brooks and his family had made it. He walked up the gangway to the quarterdeck, where a tall slim guy wearing a cowboy hat stood and picked up a clipboard off the podium.

"Evening," Billy announced himself.

"Evening," the man answered.

"I'm Billy Hill," Billy said, sticking out his hand.

The other man shook it firmly and answered succinctly, "Miller." As they shook, Billy noticed the scars on the man's hand. Then, in the dim light, Billy could see under the cowboy hat some scars on the right side of the man's face. Billy thought back to the CNN video and remembered that Beth's colleague in the hospital with burns was named Miller.

Miller looked briefly at a list of names on the clipboard and found Billy's.

"Welcome aboard," he said matter-of-factly. "They're up on the main deck." He gestured toward the ladder just a few yards away. Billy thanked him and moved on.

On the main deck, a large crowd was gathered. Over one hundred people, of all ages and races, milled about, dressed in light sweaters or sweatshirts for the arriving cool of the evening. On the superstructure of the ship, half a dozen people stood behind a single microphone and an amplifier. Just as the sun settled on the horizon below the fogbank, Oliver Hill stepped up to the microphone.

"Good evening," Oliver said and waited while the crowd stopped talking. "Good evening," he said again. "Thank you for being here on time. We gather tonight to discuss final preparations for our voyage. To get to this point has taken a lot of effort by a lot of people, and I want to introduce a few of them..."

Oliver paused as a slight commotion where the ladder from the quarterdeck connected to the main deck got his attention. As he looked that way, many others in the crowd did the same. Billy had just climbed up the ladder, looking somewhat sheepish for having disturbed the meeting. He dropped his pack and leaned against the railing.

"I'll be damned," Oliver said quietly, forgetting that the microphone was still on.

Near the ladder, James Brooks said loudly, "Hey, Billy, you made it." He walked over and gave his friend a quick hug.

Billy smiled as he released the hug and asked, "How'd that piece of junk treat you?"

Brooks shook his head. "Took some work, man, but we got here. Thanks again."

Billy started to respond but then noticed a lot of other faces staring at them.

Oliver's voice on the loudspeaker broke in. "William. I'm glad you made it. But if we could, I would like to proceed?"

"Sorry," Billy responded quickly. As he did, he looked out at others in the crowd. He smiled at his sister, Beth, who was standing nearby with some of her crew, looking familiar to him from the CNN video. Beth put a finger to her lips as if to say to be quiet and motioned toward Oliver and then back as if to say she would join Billy as soon as their father had finished.

Oliver resumed. "Thanks to all your work, we are nearly ready to sail. Let me introduce some key personnel most of you already know."

"Captain Mitchell will be the sailing master." A tall Black man, with a bit of gray in his beard, held up his right hand briefly.

"Mr. Hannigan is the first mate and navigator." A short White man, wearing heavy black glasses, waved modestly.

"Ms. Willis is the second mate and in charge of communications." A young Black woman smiled while she waved.

"Dr. Rebecca Steinberg manages our biodiversity cargo." An older woman, wearing a white lab coat, nodded quickly.

"Maria Rivera runs food supply and preparation." A short slim Latina bowed slightly and smiled. The crowd whistled and applauded. Beth's group was particularly vocal, yelling and clapping. Beth put her hand on the shoulder of another Latina woman, wearing a ball cap, as if congratulating her as well.

Oliver continued, "Dr. Harrison Smith-Garvey is our ship's doctor." A slim young guy waved his hand and smiled.

"Owen Hill is chief of engineering. He is standing over there." Oliver looked just to the side, where a tall slender man with thinning brown hair and wire-rimmed glasses waved shyly.

"Sarah Everly-Hill is an ordained minister and available for spiritual guidance. She is standing with their daughter, Annie." The woman and young girl standing next to Owen, both with red hair and warm smiles, waved at the crowd.

"And John Hunter is head of maintenance and repair." As Hunter nodded, oddly enough, the applause was joined by low hissing that emanated from Beth's group. A Latino guy wearing a purple bandanna lowered his head as if to hide, while some others in the group snickered.

Hunter, too, noticed and paused for just a moment. His face didn't change expressions as he said in a deep voice, "Head detail, Rodriguez."

"Damn, Chief," Beth's colleague with the bandanna muttered.

"Make it three days," Hunter responded. Some laughed, including the ones in Beth's group who had previously snickered.

Oliver ignored the momentary banter and resumed his talk. "You all know why we're here. Indeed, it's the reason you're here. This planet is in trouble, and it's going to get worse. And it's affecting more than just us humans. What's not clear to many of you is what exactly we're going to do about it."

Whatever shuffling and murmuring had been going on in the crowd stopped.

"In a week, we sail west. Our destination is an island in the Hawaiian chain that is only sparsely developed. We want to find a home where we are somewhat remote but also that receives enough sunlight to grow crops and power our equipment. When we arrive, we intend to build a settlement where we can preserve the species we have on board as well as possible. I will give more details once we sail. How long will we be there?" He paused. "That depends on the actions of our fellow humans, but we'll be as ready as possible. I realize this is very open-ended. Some of you may not want to make such a commitment."

Somewhere out in the harbor, another ship's horn sounded as the fog enveloped the city and the bay. Billy knew that Oliver's last comment was not directed solely at him, but then again, he couldn't help but wonder. After all, his father knew him well. And Billy found the thought of an open-ended commitment daunting.

Oliver continued, "You are welcome to leave anytime before we sail. For the rest of you, I look forward to working with you in the months and years ahead. For now, have a good evening. Tomorrow is Sunday, so we will take a day of rest and then we'll be back to work on Monday. Enjoy your day off."

The crowd on the deck was quiet for a moment as they digested Oliver's comments. Then Hunter stepped forward and took the mike. "I need two volunteers up here to move this equipment. That's you, Rodriguez, and you, Green."

"Son of a…," Rodriguez started to say but was interrupted by Green, a young Black guy, as he pulled his White Sox cap on backward.

"Damn it, T-Rod, I don't know why I hang with you, man." The crowd cleared a path as the two men moved slowly to the stage. Beth and others walked toward Billy.

CHAPTER 9

Crew

Brooks put a hand on Billy's shoulder. "Damn, Billy, glad you're here." Before Billy could respond, Janice hugged him and gave him a kiss on the cheek. The two kids, Jason and Jonah, stood by awkwardly.

"Thanks, Billy," Janice said. "You really helped us out."

Billy shrugged a bit. "Sorry about that car. It was not—"

She cut him off. "No. Seriously. You helped a lot."

James Brooks frowned as he asked, "Washington?"

Billy shook his head. "He didn't make it through that night."

"Sorry, man," Brooks answered. He noticed Beth Hill coming toward them. "Hey, I know you got people to see. We'll catch up later." The Brooks family moved off into the crowd.

Beth walked over with what was left of her group. She gave Billy a big hug, a long, firm embrace that brought back a lot of memories.

"I was hoping you would come," Beth said, with no smile but eyes as warm as the hug.

"I was hoping you'd be here as well, sis," Billy answered. "How have you been?"

Beth shrugged. "Getting by. Got rid of the husband and the job since last time I saw you."

Billy responded, "Sorry that neither worked out." He wasn't surprised about either.

"No need. He was an asshole, and my boss sucked," she said succinctly. Billy smiled, finding her brutal honesty somehow familiar and comforting. She stepped back as others stepped forward.

The huge Black man Billy had seen on CNN stuck out his hand. It engulfed Billy's as he said, "Frank Sanders. Good to meet you."

The Hispanic woman with the cap that read "Maria's Diner" then shook his hand, her grip nearly as firm as the one from Sanders, her eyes dark brown and intense. "Jessie Rivera." Billy recognized the name as the same as the head chef and was going to comment, but then he felt a hand on his shoulder and turned as he heard his brother's voice.

"Hello, Bill." Owen and Sarah had made their way across the deck. Owen shook his hand, and Sarah leaned in to give him a nice hug.

Billy's father was right next to them, peering at him with those pale-blue eyes.

"William," he said as they shook hands. "I didn't know if you would join us."

Billy nodded. "Yeah, I didn't either. Thanks for sending the letters."

Billy felt something bump his leg and looked down to see Owen's dog. He immediately bent over to rub the dog's head and was rewarded with some vigorous tail-wagging. "Hey, is this Roscoe? Wow, he looks great."

Sarah smiled. "The same. He seems to remember you." She then gestured to a cute young girl standing behind her. "And you remember Annie. Say hello to your uncle Billy, Annie."

Billy kneeled so she wouldn't have to look up at him. Annie smiled shyly.

Sanders and Rivera gestured to each other and then slipped away, obviously giving Beth and her family time to get reacquainted. But for an awkward moment, the Hills didn't exactly embrace the opportunity. None seemed to know quite what to say next. Owen was never much of a talker, and Beth didn't do small talk. In addition, they both knew that the distance between Billy and Oliver was more than just time.

Billy tried to break the ice by focusing on Annie and Roscoe. "Well, Annie, I'm glad to see you're looking more like your mom than your dad."

Sarah laughed, but Owen only offered an obligatory smile, so Billy looked at Beth. "I saw you on CNN the other day, sis. I guess some of your fire crew came with you?"

"Some," she answered quickly, as usual in short, direct bursts. "We're deck crew now."

Billy nodded. They were all quiet for a moment again. Billy was remembering why their family dinner conversations were often awkward. He glanced at Oliver again, who was studying him.

"Seems like you've built quite an operation here, Dad. It's impressive."

The pride was evident in Oliver's pale-blue eyes as he answered, "We've had a lot of help." He paused and then added, "But we do have room for another crew member."

Billy had expected that something like this was coming. "Doing what?" he asked.

Oliver answered, "While we're in port, Hunter says he could use another hand. Out at sea, we need a good helmsman."

Billy was flattered and a bit surprised. He didn't think Oliver even knew what he did when he was in the Navy, let alone remember that he had done it well enough to get a commendation. "Well, that was a lifetime ago. Not sure those skills—"

"Like riding a bike," Oliver interrupted. It was a clever line. After all, he had taught Billy how to ride. Nevertheless, Billy paused, still thinking about a possible long commitment, and not sure how to respond.

Oliver added, "We have weather coming, and the seas could be challenging. We need someone with experience."

Beth asked with a taunt, "You scared, Billy?"

Billy chuckled. He thought of all the times the two of them had teased each other with that challenge when they were kids, so many times that "the memory was worn," as the singer John Prine would say. He looked at all of them as they waited for an answer, and then back to Beth as he gave her the same response they had always used when growing up.

"Not enough." He and Beth were always proud of the ambiguity in that response. It could mean that it was no big deal to take the dare or that the dare needed more challenge before it would be worth it. Either way, he liked the answer, because it delayed him having to give them any final decision.

Before anybody could push Billy for a more definitive answer, another group walked up. They were led by a large man, as tall as Oliver, but much heavier, wearing a big cowboy hat, not beat-up like Miller's, but more like something you would buy in a hunting store at a premium price. He stuck his hand out and gave Billy a shake.

"Hello, Uncle Henry," Billy said. "I wondered if that was your ship parked next door."

"Damn right it is, boy," Henry said in a loud voice. He always did talk loudly. In fact, he did pretty much everything loudly. "Here, I'll let the rest of the family say hello as well."

A tall slim woman in a beautiful evening dress that seemed a bit out of place among the rest of the crowd reached out her hand. "Hello, William," she said quietly. She was probably half Henry's age and pretty, although, at least to Billy, she was wearing more makeup than she needed. He could smell her perfume as they shook gently.

"Hi, Helen," Billy answered. "Nice to see you."

Again, before he could say more, the third member of their party stepped forward and stuck out his hand. Richard Hill was tall like his father, but as thin as his stepmother, Helen. He had blond hair and pale-blue eyes like his uncle Oliver, but the eyes were not as gentle as Oliver's.

"Cousin," he said. They shook hands lightly.

"Richard," Billy answered and then scrambled for something else to say. "Congrats. Last I heard, you had graduated from Harvard."

"Harvard, yes," he responded proudly. "And Yale Law." His blue eyes sparkled. "You're behind."

"Behind what?" Billy answered, brusquer than he intended. The two had never really gotten along.

Oliver intervened diplomatically. "It has been a while since the two of you saw each other."

Henry jumped on his brother's comment. "That's right. Just what the hell have you been doing, Billy? We haven't been able to keep track."

It felt to Billy like one of those questions you get asked where the person asking isn't all that interested in the answer, so he kept it short. "Just staying out of trouble, Uncle Henry." Billy quickly changed the subject to one which he knew his uncle preferred. He gestured in the direction of the pier and smiled. "I saw that name *White Diamond* on the yacht and figured it was yours." Henry Hill was one of the biggest almond farmers in the country, if not the world, and his brand was White Diamond. Admittedly, it was also a good name for a sparkling white ship.

Henry grinned broadly and pushed back his cowboy hat. "She's a beauty, ain't she? I knew Oliver was up here doing something, so we figured we would sail up here to see for ourselves."

Oliver said graciously, "I'm glad you did, Henry. And you know where we're going, so you're free to join us out on the seas if you want."

Henry patted his brother on the back. "You never know, brother, you just never know."

The conversation turned to small talk, and after a while, Oliver, Owen, Sarah, Beth, and Billy agreed to get together for dinner the next day to catch up. Then Beth walked Billy below to get him situated in some quarters. They found an empty bunk in the forecastle in the berthing area with the other male deckhands. Beth said her quarters were farther aft, with some other single women. Oliver was old-fashioned enough to have segregated the genders.

Billy stowed his gear in the locker next to the bunk and fought off any feelings of nostalgia for such a berthing situation. Then the two of them worked their way back topside, where the deck was dimly lit only by ship lights. A few persistent stars were fighting their way through the fog. Some people were still out, talking quietly in small groups. Beth waved at her colleague Rivera and the woman who had been introduced as the head cook. Rodriguez and Green, having apparently finished the work detail with Hunter, leaned on the aft railing. Miller, no longer on watch on the quarterdeck, was sitting on a bollock and strumming a guitar. A woman standing next to him was playing the violin. Another guitar hung in a stand next to her.

"You looked good on CNN," Billy said sarcastically. "Stinks they fired you for it."

Beth nodded. "So does shit, brother, and you know as well as I do that it flows downhill."

Billy looked back at his sister, who he had not seen in years, recalling just how feisty she could be. "So that's when you decided to come out here? And do this ark thing?"

She nodded. "Yeah, I already had Dad's letters, but I hadn't decided."

"And you brought your crew?"

She nodded. "A few of them. The others said we were crazy."

Billy laughed a little. "Funny, I heard that too."

"Then again"—she looked at him pointedly—"you haven't signed on yet?"

Billy avoided answering, getting some help when Sanders walked by on his way to join Rodriguez and Green. Miller, in between songs, let out a long "Mooooose" call that brought laughter from the two at the railing. Sanders shook his head and called back to Miller. "Up yours, Cowboy." Miller just grinned.

Billy asked, "What's that about?"

Beth smiled slightly as she answered, "Sanders decided to come along only after we saw a moose in trouble in Yellowstone."

"Animal lover, huh?"

"Yeah, he looks rough, but he has a heart of gold." Beth paused. "He used to play pro football but tore up his knee, ended up in the Forest Service. He's been on my crew for five seasons."

"How about the others?"

"Green's the youngest. Just joined us this year. Tough kid from Chicago. He got in trouble and had to choose jail or community service. He joined us as a temp and then stayed."

Out of their hearing, Rodriguez said something that cracked up Green and Sanders.

Billy asked, "What's his story?"

Beth shook her head slightly. "Tomas Rodriguez. He's something else. He's always screwing up or cracking up. I never know which is coming, but he's in his third season with me, and I'm glad to have him."

Billy looked over at the musicians. "And that's Miller on the guitar, right? I met him on the quarterdeck."

She nodded. "Yeah, we're standing watches down there. We call him Cowboy, as he's from somewhere in western Canada. Been with me four seasons now."

As if on cue, Miller, with just a touch of an accent, said loudly enough for those nearby to hear, "Here's one from the Great North, eh?" and started playing the Ian Tyson classic "Some Day Soon." The woman on the violin joined him on the chorus when she wasn't offering some nice backup on her instrument.

"Who's the violinist?"

"Susan Harris," Beth answered. "One of the tech people. Has a teenage daughter."

Beth looked at Billy and said, "Hunter's now on the quarterdeck, but I'll have to relieve him at midnight, which means I'm heading down to the rack soon to get some sleep. So, brother, if you want to play a little guitar, I'm sure they wouldn't mind."

Billy smiled at his sister already looking out for him. "You sure you don't mind?"

Beth was already walking away as she answered, "Hell no."

Billy walked over, glanced at the extra guitar and then at the violin player. She nodded slightly as she kept playing. When they finished the song, Billy asked, "Okay with you guys?"

Miller answered simply, "Free country."

Harris added with a nice smile, "What do you like?"

Billy thought for a moment and then answered, "Everybody likes Dylan, right?"

Miller nodded and started strumming the chords to "You Ain't Going Nowhere." He was being accommodating as it was an easy song and Billy could pick it up quickly. Besides, somehow the lyrics seemed appropriate, at least for the moment.

They played well into the night.

CHAPTER 10

Sisters

Billy woke up early the next morning. Not only was he sleeping in a cramped birthing space with a bunch of snorers, but his body was also still on a different time zone, and he was famished from a long day on the road and nothing to eat the night before. In addition, he wanted to get some much-needed exercise. Slipping out of the berthing area as quietly as possible, he resisted the vengeful temptation to wake Rodriguez, who was snoring like a freight train. The rest of the ship seemed quiet, not surprising, given that this was a Sunday and a day of rest. Moving past the berthing area where Owen and family were sleeping, Billy heard a noise. Roscoe, his tail wagging, ambled out of the space and, after an ear rub, followed Billy aft.

As they arrived in the mess hall, a television mounted in the corner was playing CNN. Billy heard someone else moving around in the kitchen, but before he could see who it was, he paused to watch the last of a story about the cyclone in Asia. The volume on the TV was down low, so Billy could only see the graphics, which showed the projected path of the storm as moving east, across the Pacific toward Hawaii and the West Coast of the US.

"Buenos días. You are the other Hill boy?" The Mexican accent was strong.

Billy turned to see Maria Rivera standing behind him, wearing an apron and another Maria's Diner ball cap. She looked to be just a bit older than the other Rivera woman, her eyes surrounded by a few wrinkles, but they were still dark and pretty.

"Yes. I'm Bill. Or Billy, if you like." He shook her hand, noticing yet another firm grip. As she reached down to pet the dog's head, Billy added, "And this is Roscoe."

She said fondly, "I know Roscoe, and he will get the usual." Roscoe wagged his tail in anticipation. "As for you, Bill, or Billy, even if you cannot decide that, maybe you can decide what you like for breakfast."

"Oh, I didn't mean to cause you to do anything. Maybe just an apple or—"

She cut him off. "A vaquero burrito? Eggs, bacon, ham?"

Billy smiled. "I can see why you got the most applause last night."

Maria smiled appreciatively and moved back to the galley.

An hour later, Billy was digesting a tasty burrito, and Roscoe a bowl of something. They had finished their breakfast, said hello to Brooks on the quarterdeck, and then departed the ship, walking past the stern, where the name *Noah* shone in bright paint. The morning was nice and cool, although the clouds on the horizon promised weather to come. Instead of taking the road back up toward the highway, he and the dog took a trail through a forest of coastal pines and eucalyptus trees, savoring the fragrance of both. As they moved to the interior of the island, Billy found a grove of deciduous trees. Not surprisingly, they were species often growing near water, mostly sycamores and cottonwoods, and while they didn't have a lot of color in the leaves, there was some yellow and golden brown. And autumn was close enough that when the breeze came in off the bay, the trees swayed and sent down the gifts Billy always appreciated.

He ran around in the grove, chasing the falling leaves, even catching a few. Roscoe ran with him for a bit but then, tiring of the game, lay down in the shade. Billy had just managed to catch a leaf and let out a little exclamation of "Yes!" when Roscoe got up, tail wagging, and walked back toward the trail. As Billy watched him, the dog approached the Rivera woman from Beth's crew, standing on the edge of the clearing, wearing her Maria's Diner ball cap, black running shorts, and a baggy gray T-shirt. She was watching Billy with a bemused look on her face. As Roscoe neared, she, too, seemed to know him well enough to reach down and scratch his back. Roscoe obliged with a vigorous wag of his tail.

Looking at Billy, she asked, “Catching many?”

Billy tried to suppress the blush he knew was coming to his face. “Mostly chasing,” he answered.

She nodded slightly and said in a neutral tone, “Sounds like life.”

Billy wasn't sure how to respond, so he kept it light. “Yeah, maybe a little less serious.” He saw a hint of a smile on her lips.

“Of course,” she answered. “How does it work?”

“Well…,” he started to say, and then a big green sycamore leaf circled down and he went for it. And missed.

She suppressed a giggle. “Do we keep score?”

He gave her a serious look. “Absolutely not.”

Soon she was chasing as well and laughing at the surprising difficulty of the game, just like everyone else Billy had ever taught the fine art of leaf-catching to. Roscoe wandered back to his spot in the shade and lay down, somewhat bored with the strange games of human beings.

The humans, on the other hand, kept at it for a good twenty minutes before pausing to catch their breath.

“It's Jessie, right?” Billy asked.

“Si.”

“You work with my sister, Beth.”

“And you, Billy Hill?” she asked. “What do you do?”

Billy smiled a little. “Well, so far, I've played some music, had a great breakfast, and went for a walk. By the way, your sister is quite a cook.”

“The best,” she answered, pride evident in her dark-brown eyes as she smiled.

Roscoe got up and walked to Billy, doing those little circles a dog does to say he was ready to get moving.

Billy glanced at Jessie's outfit before asking, “If you're running back, want some company?”

She looked back at him, the smile with just a bit of a taunt now. “Are we keeping score on this one?”

He nodded. "Sure."

Without a word, she started running back up the trail toward the ship, about two miles back to the west. Roscoe took off after her, and Billy picked up the rear. Other than dodging the occasional root, the trail was excellent for running, and Billy soon caught his stride. The trees flashed by as he closed the gap on her. The dog was well ahead of them, his tail flying out behind him. As Billy got closer, he admired Jessie's form. She was obviously in good shape, and her motions seemed almost effortless. He remembered a phrase someone had used before to describe another woman with whom he used to run: 0 percent body fat. But he noted with some satisfaction, there was a small circle of sweat on the back of her gray T-shirt. At least he was making her work.

Billy pulled up next to her after a mile, both continuing their pace. "To the bay, then?" he asked in between breaths.

She barely glanced at him before saying, "You're on." And then she kicked up the pace a notch. He hustled to keep up.

After several minutes, they emerged from the forest and the ship came in view, behind it the bay. Billy could see a few people milling about on the pier. Several reached to greet Roscoe as he arrived ahead of the humans. As he and Jessie got within a hundred yards, Billy summoned some energy and launched a sprint. He went by her, but his lead was short-lived. She matched his sprint and then some, soon getting ahead of him by five feet, and then ten. The people on the pier saw the two of them coming and stopped what they had been doing to watch. Some of them began to yell encouragement, all of it for Jessie, of course. Rodriguez pulled a green bandanna off his head and began to wave it as if it were a finish line.

Billy found one more burst of speed and just about caught Jessie before she matched it. She went past the bandanna ahead of him by five feet and raised her hands in a mock celebration.

Billy had a sudden thought and couldn't resist. He kept his pace and ran right by her and the others, gasping out, "We said the bay."

He ran down the sand and plunged into the water, diving under head first. The water was shockingly cold, so he surfaced almost immediately. As he did, he was rewarded by laughter behind him on the beach. Roscoe barked and then jumped in and swam to Billy, an excited look on his face as he realized the water was not calm. Billy picked up the dog and then looked back to see Jessie and Rodriguez both shaking their heads, as if disgusted by his antic. But her smile was reward enough.

CHAPTER 11

Penance

The members of the Hill family gathered for dinner on Sunday in the mess hall. The ark had just one mess hall so that everybody, from officers to children, ate together in the same room. The Hills ate after everybody else so that they could take over one of the dozen long tables. Oliver sat at the end, Beth and Billy on one side, Owen, Sarah, and Annie on the other. Roscoe lay on the floor nearby. Other members of the crew passed by as they finished their meals and took the trays up to the front of the room, but they left the family alone during the conversation.

As they were finishing up their meal, talk of the weather and an approaching storm prompted Beth to tease Billy. "I heard you couldn't wait to get wet, so you went for a swim, Billy?"

Billy answered, "I couldn't resist. The ocean was there. I was there—"

Beth interjected, "An audience was there."

Annie looked up from her plate. "Was it cold, Uncle Billy?"

"Yeah, Annie, it was cold"

"So why did you do it?"

Beth backed up her niece. "Yeah, Uncle Billy, why did you do it?"

Billy ignored Beth and smiled at Annie. "I guess I would ask you the opposite question, Annie. Why not do it?"

Annie didn't miss a beat. "Because it's cold."

Beth laughed briefly. "Ha! Take that, Uncle Billy."

Owen joined in. "Annie, you'll soon learn that your uncle Billy does lots of things worth questioning."

Sarah frowned at him. "Owen."

Owen answered, "I don't mean anything by it. I just don't know any other DTs."

Annie looked puzzled. "What's a DT?

Sarah answered for Billy. "It stands for *disaster tracker*, honey. Your uncle Bill went to where storms hit, and tried to help people."

Annie shrugged. "What's wrong with that?"

Billy smiled again. "Take that, Brother Owen."

Owen held up his palms as if asking "Who, me?" before responding, "Again, I didn't say anything was wrong with it. I just..."

Sarah put her hand on her husband's arm. "I think it's fine." She paused as she looked at Billy. "I'm glad...we're all glad you're here."

Billy answered, "Thanks, Sarah. I'm sure people are glad you're here as well." He paused and then continued, "Are you the only official religious person on board?"

"Yes, but remember that I am Unitarian," she answered and continued with a line she had obviously used before: "We believe in at most one God, so we get along with just about everybody."

Billy's answer was sincere. "Well, you certainly do."

Sarah nodded gratefully. "We've hardly seen you since you lost Teresa. I was hoping—and it's none of my business—but I was hoping you would have found someone after her and settled down somewhere."

Billy shrugged. "I got better at finding storms than finding someone else." He fidgeted a bit, uncomfortable with the attention, but then thought of a clever segue. "And it seemed like we were never going to run out of storms." He glanced at Oliver.

Oliver looked back at his son, knowing it was not an innocent comment. "And we won't either, William. And that's why we're here, isn't it?"

Billy pushed on. "What I'm wondering is something I've been wanting to ask you ever since I got your letters, Dad. What happened to you?"

Oliver looked puzzled by the question. "What do you mean?"

"Well, what you said in those letters wasn't exactly what you would have said five years ago. Or ten. Or…"

Owen said gently, "Take it easy, Bill."

Beth seconded Billy. "No, Owen, I want to hear this too."

Oliver looked around at all of them and rubbed his chin before answering. "Fair enough. You deserve an answer." He paused to collect his thoughts. "Do you know what I did after your mother's funeral?"

When nobody answered, he went on. "I went to Africa. I wanted to hunt an elephant. I didn't think much about it. I just wanted to get away and do something. Feel like a man again."

Billy started to interrupt. "As if hunting an elephant—"

Beth put her hand on his arm to tell him to be quiet.

Oliver went on. "Well, I did it. I shot a big bull, a beauty. And that evening, we camped nearby, one of those fancy trips with big tents and fine dining. And we got out the wine, expensive stuff, of course." He closed his eyes, as if remembering. "But that night, the bull's mate showed up. She didn't charge our camp. Nothing that dramatic. She just stood nearby, and she moaned. And the next day and the day after, she moaned. And nights. You may not know that elephants only sleep a couple hours a night. I do now." He shook his head slightly. "I don't know if she ever left. She was still there when we did."

Everybody at the table remained silent. Annie looked like she was going to cry.

Oliver went on. "Do you know how smart those animals are? When people used elephants for labor in Africa, they would work them during the day and then let them roam at night so they could graze and be ready for the next day's work. So to save time for the next morning, at night the people put bells around the elephants' necks so that they could track them more easily. You know what the elephants did? They used their trunks to scoop up mud and shove it into the bells to keep them quiet."

Oliver smiled a little. Beth and Billy were stunned. They had never heard him talk like this before.

Oliver's smile disappeared. "It didn't work. People would find the elephants anyway and put them back to work, and when they did, the calves were left to fend for themselves. Most of them didn't survive. And those, well, in retrospect, those were the good days. The days before people started killing elephants just for their tusks. And today, you can't even find an elephant in most places. Even if they survive the other animals and the hunters and the poachers, they don't have much habitat left. So..."

"Wow," Billy exclaimed.

Oliver looked back at his son, his pale-blue eyes bright. "I learned, William. I went back home after that hunting trip with my souvenir tusks, and I couldn't get that elephant's moaning out of my head. And I started reading. And I talked to people. And I learned. And I realized that what we've done to elephants is just the tip of the iceberg. How we've treated animals is unforgivable. Just like what I did to that elephant and his mate. Unforgivable."

The room was so silent they could hear a pin drop. Oliver looked down at the table and collected his thoughts before looking up again and continuing. "And now, on the largest scale, what we're doing to the climate has terrible consequences for elephants and other species. Not just animals but plants too. Thousands of them will disappear before Annie and her generation even see them."

None of them said anything. Annie was crying now, very quietly. Her mother reached over to rub her back. The rest of the family looked at one another and then back at Oliver. Billy thought back to all the years they had shared a house and couldn't remember, even imagine, having a conversation with his father about a subject like this. And yet Billy still had this little nagging doubt, the kind that comes from all the conventional wisdom that people never change, not really. But when Oliver looked up, his eyes said that conventional wisdom was wrong.

Oliver looked around at all of them and then finished, "So we built an ark."

There was a long moment of silence at the table. Sarah continued to rub Annie's back. Owen looked down at his plate, as if not sure what to say next.

Billy said again, much more quietly than the first time, "Wow."

Sarah finally said, "Thank you, Oliver."

Oliver nodded and then smiled a little as he looked around the table. "I didn't mean to ruin your appetites. William, I've never seen you not finish a cookie before."

Billy realized he had a half-eaten macadamia nut cookie in his hand. He smiled sheepishly as he said, "You're right. And these are delicious."

Sarah, sitting next to Billy, said, "Would you like mine, Bill?"

Before Billy could answer, Owen got the subject back to the ark. "So how many crew have we lost since your speech last night, Dad?"

Oliver thought for a moment and then answered, "As far as I know, an even dozen people decided this adventure was not for them."

Owen nodded. Beth slowly turned to look at her younger brother. "How about you, Billy? You with us?"

Billy looked back at her and let out a breath. The others looked up and were now staring at him as well. He tried to deflect.

"Uh, yeah, like I said, these cookies are delicious, aren't they?"

The others didn't laugh at his feigned diversion but instead continued to look at him and wait for his answer.

Billy started, "Okay. Let me first say that's quite a story, Dad, and I truly appreciate what you're doing. What you're all doing." He looked around at the others and noticed Owen shake his head slightly, surely sensing what was coming. Sarah looked down again. Beth and Oliver stared at him, waiting for him to go on with an answer they now anticipated.

Billy continued, "But it sounds like you guys are committing to the long haul. And you know me and chasing horizons. So I guess I'm not ready…"

Beth didn't even try to hide the disgust in her voice. "When are you going to be ready to commit to something, Billy?" She stood and picked up her tray. "Ah, what the hell, do whatever you want."

Owen added, "He always does."

Sarah tried to calm her husband down. "That's enough, Owen." But when Billy didn't say more, they, too, got up to leave.

Nobody said anything else for a moment. In the awkward silence, Billy tried to think of something to add, something that would justify his answer or even something to change the subject but came up with nothing. He hoped Beth might use their old line on him again about being scared, but she didn't say anything else as she left. Owen and his family, too, walked toward the front of the room. As they went by, Sarah tapped Billy sympathetically on his shoulder briefly. Oliver sat just a moment longer with Billy and looked at him, the disappointment evident in his eyes, and then he, too, moved away from the table.

Billy sat alone for a minute longer and then realized that the Brooks family and the Rivera sisters were all sitting at nearby tables, trying not to stare at him. He finally got up and carried his empty plate to the front of the mess hall. Not knowing what else to do, he made his way up to the main deck and walked down to the stern of the ship. He sat down on one of the bollocks that held a large rope securing the ark to the pier. To the west, the sun was just starting to settle down over San Francisco and the Golden Gate Bridge, the Pacific Ocean stretching out behind. To the east, Billy could see the vehicles going over the Bay Bridge.

After a few minutes, someone walked up behind him and grasped him on the shoulder. Billy looked up to see James Brooks smiling at him. Brooks handed him a set of car keys and then leaned against the ship's railing.

"I'm guessing you might need these," Brooks said quietly. "By the way, your duffel bag is still in the trunk."

Billy shook his head slightly. "Man, word spreads fast. Like we always used to say, you can't keep a secret on a ship."

Brooks nodded. "I figured something was up. We saw you guys talking at dinner." He paused. "Your family didn't look happy about it."

Billy frowned. "That's one way to put it." He looked back at Brooks. "How about you guys? You staying? Could be a long time away."

Brooks looked toward the ocean. "We're staying. Janice likes the idea less than I do, but we're going to give it a shot."

Billy stared at him. "Why?"

Brooks thought and then smiled. "I could say it's because of the food." They both laughed, and then Brooks got serious. "I don't know, man. Seems like a chance to do something that might matter."

Billy nodded but didn't say anything for a moment as he looked beyond Brooks toward the Bay Bridge. Then he started talking again. "You remember the setup back in boot camp?" Billy and Brooks had both done military duty, albeit in different branches at different times. "I know we both did boot camp in San Diego, and I remember how the Navy was in one place and your Marines were on the other side of the fence."

Brooks looked puzzled. "So?"

"Well," Billy went on, "your base was in between our base and the airport. Seriously. And when any of us stood watch in the middle of the night, it was awful lonely. We could look over there and see planes landing and taking off, going on to other places, good places, any places better than boot camp."

Brooks smiled. "Yeah, I remember."

Billy smiled slightly. "No wonder so many of our guys jumped that fence and tried to make it over to the airport. We heard stories about how your guys—"

"More than stories," Brooks interrupted. "We would catch you Navy pukes and beat the crap out of you before sending you back." He smiled. "No offense."

Billy smiled back. "None taken." He admired Brooks. The man had done his time in the Marines, serving a tour in Afghanistan, and had then come back and made a life for himself.

Billy's smile disappeared. "Looking at those cars out there on the bridge, JB, I'm feeling like that again. The Navy was a commitment for a few years. This? Where this ark is going, who knows, man? This could be for life."

Brooks nodded sympathetically. "You sound like Janice, so I know what you mean. But hey, Billy, you ended up liking your time in the Navy, right?"

Billy nodded. "Yeah, but I always knew it would end. This? I just don't know."

They were both quiet for a minute. The sun settled lower out to the west while traffic on the bridge looked even busier than it had before as people turned on their headlights. In between the ark and the bridge, in the forest on the island, birds talked to one another as they made their ways to their homes for the night.

Brooks stuck out his hand. "Good luck to you, Billy."

Billy stood and gave Brooks a hug instead of a handshake. "You too, JB. Take care of your family."

Brooks walked off and left Billy alone on the deck.

CHAPTER 12

The Rubicon

As Billy came out on deck early Monday morning, the storm's arrival on America's West Coast was imminent. The contrast between the bright sunrise in the east and the heavy clouds on the western horizon was dramatic. He wanted to get moving before the storm arrived, but also leave the ship without goodbyes. But he did have to leave by way of the quarterdeck, where someone would be on watch, so his departure would not be completely undetected. As he walked up, he saw Jessie Rivera in jeans and a jacket, the Maria's Diner cap pulled down on her head. She was looking out at the forest still dark in the dim predawn light.

Billy tried to be cheerful. "Nice morning for a run, eh?"

She looked back at him without expression. "I wish." She took her hands out of her pockets and took a small bag off the podium. "We thought you might be leaving, so my sister packed you a sandwich." Again, Billy was reminded that nothing stays secret on a ship for very long. No wonder the "Loose lips sink ships" line became famous.

He was touched by the gesture. "Wow, that's awful nice. I don't know how you knew."

Jessie looked at him, her dark eyes unreadable. "We couldn't help but notice your family gathering yesterday."

Billy nodded. "Yeah, that didn't go too well."

Jessie handed him the sack and said matter-of-factly but also without any tone of judgment, "We all have to do what we have to do."

"Thanks, Jessie," Billy answered as he stuffed the bag into his pack. "And please tell Maria thanks as well."

He wasn't sure why, but he stood there for another moment, like he wanted to hear something else. She waited. Just to finally say something, he asked, "So how many have left by now? Still a dozen?"

Jessie looked at the clipboard on the podium. "Si. No more overnight. You will be number thirteen."

Billy frowned. "Thirteen. Bad luck."

Jessie answered quickly, "I hope not." It came out fast, as if she had not been able to check herself. But the tone was warm and genuine. She smiled at him, very slightly.

Billy was surprised at the catch in his throat as he mumbled, "Thank you." He turned and walked down the gangway, suddenly in a hurry to get off the ship and away. He hiked up the hill to the parking lot, found his old car, popped open the trunk, and dropped his pack in next to the duffel bag that held the rest of his clothes. He then sat in the front seat for the first time in over a week and rolled down the window to take in some of the morning air.

The car smelled familiar. And to Billy, it felt like a ticket to freedom. A mile or so to the east, cars and trucks rolled along on the Bay Bridge, moving slowly in the traffic early on a Monday morning, going to different places and for different opportunities. He leaned his head against the back of the seat, thought about where he might go next, and promptly dozed off. He slept just long enough to have a dream. He dreamed of the dog the family had when he was growing up, a little stray they had unimaginatively named Brownie for his colors. The dog and Billy did a lot together, but Billy never could teach him how to swim. In his dream, they had been camping by a river, and Billy was packing up when he suddenly couldn't find Brownie. Then he looked in the river and there he was on the other side, dog paddling to stay afloat. Brownie didn't seem panicked, but he was looking for a place to climb out. Billy dived into the water to save him, and that was when he woke up.

He heard thunder in the distance. As he opened his eyes, lightning lit up the inside of the dark cloud bank to the west, beyond the Golden Gate Bridge. In the foreground, the ark rocked on the bay waters. Thirty seconds later, more thunder rolled onto the island. Thunderstorms had historically been rare in the Bay Area until the last few years, but with the changing climate came different weather patterns. This storm looked unusually ominous, and Billy was sure that it marked the arrival of the typhoon that had devastated Asia.

Billy felt hungry, so he got out, opened the trunk, and reached inside his pack to get the sack Jessie had given him. He found not only the sandwich Maria had made but also something wrapped inside one of the mess hall's napkins. He unwrapped it, finding one of the macadamia nut cookies from the previous day's dinner.

"Sarah," Billy said quietly as he shook his head.

Whether it was because of the food gifts, Jessie's smile, his dream, or something else, Billy suddenly started having second thoughts about his decision to leave. The silver lining to his lifelong inability to commit to things was that he had developed a system for thinking through big decisions. As he ate his breakfast, he started going through the arguments for and against staying with the ark.

On the side of leaving was the one that had driven his decision the day before, his freedom. Billy had always loved his freedom, some said to a fault, and after the pandemic of 2020, he had savored it even more. He did what he wanted, when he wanted. The car reminded him of that. All he had to do was turn the key and he was off and running. Giving that up for some long commitment that could last years was intimidating.

On the other side of the ledger were several things. The food made him think of the good people on board the ark. He and his family had obviously not been close over the years, but they were at least trying now. And the other people on the ark, well, they had welcomed him on board. And he realized, while he took another bite of the sandwich, that they had fed him for two days. Further, Billy knew he could be of some help. With large storms, ships often fare better being out at sea, where they can ride over big waves, rather than being buffeted while tied to a pier. But ships need someone who knows how to steer. Infamous shipwrecks, like the sinking of the ocean liner *Andrea Doria*, had resulted from incompetent helmsmen. And he knew he could steer as well as anybody.

Plus, he admitted to himself that while he wasn't convinced that the whole endeavor was necessary, he did admire what Oliver and the people on the ark were doing. Thinking about Oliver's story from dinner the day before prompted him to recall a Barry Lopez line from the book *Arctic Dreams* that "one of the oldest dreams of mankind is to find a dignity that might include all living things." Maybe his memory of Brownie was his own version of that dream.

All those were good reasons to stay, but ultimately, Billy concluded with a simple plan. The ark would likely sail out of the harbor for a few days to ride out the storm and then return to finish whatever other preparations were needed. He could repay their kindnesses with a few days of steering the ship, training others to do so, and then come back and move on. He could get the car and join those folks over on the Bay Bridge driving off to wherever. It was thus a chance to do something right, without a lot of cost. And if he didn't do what he could to help now and something terrible happened to the ark, he knew how he would feel. Because he had felt it before. Guilt is a powerful thing, and he had enough of it already without hanging more of it over his head.

So Billy decided to go back to the ark. In the weeks and months after that, he thought many times about that exact moment. Billy would never claim that his decision to go back to the ark was like the apostle Paul converting to Christianity while on the road to Damascus. Nor would he compare himself to Julius Caesar crossing the Rubicon River on the way to becoming the emperor of Rome. He couldn't do either because he wasn't being spiritual or heroic. He was taking the easy way out, doing the decent thing while still preserving his long-term options. He stood, picked the duffel out of the trunk, took one last look east at the traffic on the Bay Bridge, all those people free to go wherever they wanted, and sighed out loud. Then he started down the trail to the west and back to the ark. Little did he know that Rubicon Rivers can show up in lots of times and places, even on a little hill on an island in San Francisco Bay.

CHAPTER 13

Loading Dock

Billy returned to the ark the same time the storm arrived. In one odd way, the timing was fortuitous as the storm allowed him to just slip back quietly. The scene looked like a computer graphic-generated image of a massive storm moving in on a city in a disaster movie. The skyline of San Francisco was barely visible, being swallowed by a dark bank of clouds crackling, with frequent lightning bursts and rolls of thunder. Massive waves crashed against the seaward side of the ark, spray coming over the gunwales and soaking the decks. The ship strained at the ropes tied to the bollocks as if trying to escape the clutches of the pier and get out to sea.

Billy saw Beth and her crew lined up at the pile of stores still on the dock. Beth saw him arrive but just glared at him for a moment, unwilling to acknowledge his return. The others were in a single line that stretched from the pile to a motorized conveyor belt that stretched up the ark's gangway. Billy jumped into the end of the line nearest the ship, behind Rodriguez, Jessie, and Brooks. They teased him with mild recriminations.

"Welcome back, Billy," Brooks said. "Good trip?"

Jessie, her face barely visible under the Maria's Diner hat, chimed in, "He must have gotten hungry."

Hunter interrupted them with a shout from the top of the gangway. "We're ready on top! Get that shit moving!" He had assembled another group to unload and put the supplies under the roof of the hangar bay.

Billy threw his pack and his duffel bag onto the moving conveyor, assuming he could find them later. At the head of the line, Beth used a hunting knife to cut the ropes on the tarps, and Sanders started the first box moving just as the rain started to fall.

As Brooks handed Billy the first box, he said, "Storm reminds me of New Orleans." He added, "Glad you could join us."

Billy shook his head. "Yeah, I couldn't miss all this fun."

"You have a strange idea of fun, helmsman," Rodriguez grunted as he hefted a heavy box.

"You deckhands talk too much!" Hunter yelled from back on deck. "Move it!"

They settled into a rhythm, moving bags of potatoes, boxes of canned goods and dried milk, and other items. As they worked, the storm came in with intensity, wind and rain pelting their faces. Thunder and lightning rolled across the bay. Billy was soon soaked from rain as well as sweat, but the exertion felt surprisingly good, the manual work an odd relief after his mental exercises about leaving.

Then another person joined them. A husky guy with a broad weathered face hustled up to the crew, carrying an acetylene torch welding kit. He gestured behind him at the *White Diamond*, yelling, "We borrowed this yesterday!"

The newcomer set the kit on the conveyor and then called to Beth. "Name's Reese. Can I give you a hand?"

She nodded, and Reese fell in line behind Billy. With the extra pair of hands, Beth saw an opportunity. She yelled to Sanders, "Let's double this up, Frank!" She moved deeper into the pile to cut the ropes on more boxes.

Sanders yelled over the wind at Miller, "Get up here, Cowboy!" Miller climbed onto the pallet behind and to the left of Beth, with Sanders on the right. Both commenced getting boxes started as the others formed themselves into two lines with Green, Rodriguez, and Jessie behind Sanders, while Brooks, Billy, and Reese got behind Miller. They were instantly doubling the passage of goods to the conveyor. Of course, there was more space between each set of hands, so they had to do little jogs with the loads.

"Pronto, you gringos!" Rodriguez yelled as he ran a box back to Rivera.

"Who you calling gringo?" Jessie snarled as she dumped the box on the conveyor.

"You should work that hard, Rodriguez," Hunter's voice sounded from above.

"Caramba, Chief, give me a break!" Rodriguez yelled back.

Hunter answered, "You get a break when you finish."

"I thought she was in charge," Reese said with a smile, glancing up at Beth.

Rodriguez swore, "Damn Chief always thinks he is. Someday..." He started to suggest what sounded like a different plan.

"All right!" Beth yelled back for all of them to hear from where she had moved to the next pallet. "You heard the man. You want a break? Let's finish this." She picked up the pace. Sanders and Miller matched it, and the lines started to compete.

Brooks let loose a little laugh as he nearly threw a package. "Here you go, Billy," he said. "Ain't like New Orleans anymore."

Billy laughed a little, the sound drowned by a huge clap of thunder right on top of them. He felt the stress in his forearms, but no way was he going to ask for a break. Once, he struggled with a heavy box, but Reese moved up to grab it as if it were no problem.

They were all breathing hard and soaked with rain, but nobody slowed down as the adrenaline was really pumping. As Beth, Sanders, and Miller waded deeper into the piles, Green and Brooks moved up to shorten the distance between the pile and the lines. To compensate, the rest of them had to cover even more ground.

Sanders called out, "Now we're rolling."

Rodriguez answered back, "Rapido, amigos."

Billy noticed a smile under the brim of Jessie's hat. She caught his look and gave him a little nod. They were both breathing too hard to say anything. Indeed, nobody spoke for several minutes while they diminished the piles. The boxes moved so fast up the conveyor that a new pile began to appear at the top of the gangway. Then they could hear Hunter yelling at the people up there to pick up the pace.

"Take that, Chief!" Rodriguez yelled at him. The crew on the dock all chuckled, the laughs coming short between their panting for breath.

The pile on the final pallet dwindled down to a few boxes. Then, as she started a big one up the line, Beth yelled, "Last box!" When it got to Reese, he dumped it on the conveyor and slapped Billy's open hand. The others pounded one another on their backs.

Just then, as if on cue, they heard the foghorn from the *White Diamond*, signaling that the yacht was about ready to pull out. Reese looked that direction and then back at Beth and her crew. "Got to go," Reese said.

"Thanks!" Beth yelled.

Reese gestured out to sea. "Maybe we'll see you down the line," he called back as he took off running for the yacht.

"Hey, helmsman!" Rodriguez grinned at Billy, using his green bandanna to wipe some of the rain off his face. "You can do shit jobs with us deckhands anytime."

Billy smiled back, knowing that might be the warmest welcome back he could expect. "I think I'll look for an inside job," he answered.

Some of them laughed. Beth shook her head slightly, smothering a smile, still angry that her brother had left in the first place.

Then, as if he had heard Billy, Hunter called down from the deck, "Helmsman, they want you on the bridge."

CHAPTER 14

Windows of Heaven

A deafening crescendo of thunder told everyone on the ark that the storm was on top of them and the need to get underway was urgent. As Billy hustled forward through the ship to get to the bridge, the wave swells were rolling the ark at least ten degrees each way. Bouncing off the bulkheads in a passageway, he nearly collided with Sarah, carrying Roscoe in her arms, and Annie.

"Hey, Sarah, thanks for that cookie," Billy offered.

Sarah smiled. "I'm glad it helped you decide to stay with us."

Billy smiled back. At least one member of the family was happy to have him back. "It did. But this is going to be a wild ride. You guys be safe."

"You too," Sarah said and then added, "Windows of heaven, Billy."

Billy paused, thought, and then responded, "Genesis." Sarah smiled back at him. It was the first time they had played a certain little game with each other in years. Billy was no biblical scholar, but he knew enough passages that Sarah would quiz him on occasion. He was proud that he had recalled this one from the Noah story.

As she kept walking, Sarah called after him, "All the fountains of the deep were broken up, and the windows of heaven were opened."

Billy moved on to the bridge. As he entered, Captain Mitchell was talking into the voice tube. "What's our status, Owen?"

Billy heard his brother's voice on the other end as he answered from the engine room, "Ninety percent. We'll be ready."

"Good," Mitchell answered. "We sail in ten." Oliver was sitting in a captain's chair at the front of the bridge. He gave Billy a slight nod, apparently not that surprised that his restless son had come back. Hannigan, the navigator, was examining a chart of the harbor with Second Mate Willis. A radioman stood by, waiting for orders.

Captain Mitchell walked over to Billy and stuck out his hand. "Helmsman, right?"

"Bill Hill, Captain." They shook hands briefly. Mitchell's dark, weathered face and gentle eyes reminded Billy of Morgan Freeman.

"Good," Mitchell answered as he pointed to the wheel, the old-fashioned kind with pegs, oddly out of touch with the rest of a bridge that looked modern and high-tech. As if reading Billy's mind, he added, "Don't worry, it's more up-to-date than it looks." Next to it, the lee helm, used to adjust the speed of the ship, looked just functional compared to the impressive wheel. Hannigan pulled Mitchell over to the chart table.

One look at the controls made Billy realize that Mitchell was right about things being up-to-date, as the meters and dials in front of the helm were high-tech. The lee helm was quite simple, with two handles, obviously suggesting that the ark had two propellers. The twin screws would make the vessel more maneuverable. Billy gripped the spokes of the wheel. It felt comfortable in his hands, as if his tour in the Sixth Fleet had just ended.

He thought back to his first days on board the light cruiser and initially feeling more than a bit intimidated by the idea of steering a 550-foot-long vessel. Then he got good at it. And his confidence grew over time to the point that he savored a call to battle stations since it meant he would be back on the helm, where he felt competent. Billy was not one of those people who was good at just about anything he did. Much as he liked sports and music, he knew he was never going to be a professional baseball player or a concert guitarist. And he knew why. He was never dedicated to any one thing enough to develop any expertise, but instead restless in his pursuits, always eager to try new things well before he perfected any. But the Navy forced him to become adept at steering a ship.

"You got it?" Mitchell was back next to him.

"Yes, sir," Billy responded, the *sir* coming back automatically from his Navy days.

As Billy looked around, he remembered something else he had always enjoyed about being a helmsman. You had the best view on the ship. While many other sailors toiled belowdecks, like in the boiler rooms or the galley, the helmsman looked out the windows of the bridge. That view was often impressive, even inspiring. Today, the view was daunting. The bow of the ship pointed toward the darkest part of the storm that now obscured San Francisco and everything else in the bay. Lightning punctured the sky at an alarmingly high frequency. And huge waves were breaking over the bow. He noticed Oliver looking back at him.

"Does it feel like old times, William?" he asked.

Billy nodded. "For better and for worse."

Oliver gave him a confident little smile and looked out the window again. The rain was coming down in sheets now, pelting the bridge windows. Ah, Billy thought, just another of the benefits of being a helmsman, being out of the rain. A particularly large wave crashed over the bow, and the ship shuddered.

Mitchell spoke into a walkie-talkie. "Hunter, you read me?"

They could hear crackling on the other end, and then Hunter's deep voice. "Captain?"

"What's the situation?" Mitchell asked.

Hunter answered back, "Dock is cleared. We're bringing in the ropes and securing the gangway."

"Good," Mitchell responded.

"Aye." Then, before Hunter lifted his finger off the Speak button, they could hear something bang loudly off the ship, probably a swinging gangway. Hunter yelled, "Get your back into it, Rodriguez!"

Mitchell put down the walkie-talkie and picked up the 1MC with which to communicate to the whole ship. He paused for just a moment and then, pressing the button, spoke into the mike.

"All hands, this is Captain Mitchell. A large storm is on us. We are going to general quarters now and intend to depart within a minute." He paused and then continued calmly. "You know what to do. Let's do it well." He pulled the alarm for general quarters.

Even without being able to see it, Billy knew what was going on below. Hunter and the deckhands were releasing the ship from the dock. Owen and the engineers were bringing the ship up to full steam. The radio operators were sending out messages to other ships to let them know the ark was getting underway. Susan Harris and others in the intel center were scanning the radars for contacts in the harbor. Maria Rivera and the cooks were stowing all the food and kitchen supplies for launch. Others were doing the same in their spaces. Given the different ages of people, some people were obviously working with the kids and animals to make sure they were ready to sail. Billy felt the adrenaline coming up through the rest of the ship and into his own blood. He gripped the wheel tighter as the ark was released from the pier.

Hunter's voice came over the walkie-talkie. "We're clear, Captain."

Captain Mitchell picked up the 1MC again and spoke into the mike. "Underway. Shift colors." He put the mike back in place and then flicked a switch to turn on the ship's running lights. Then he looked back at Billy.

"We'll get a lee helmsman in a moment, Mr. Hill. For now, we'll come to all ahead one-third," he said as he pushed both levers forward a notch to send the signal to the engine room. Then he added, "Steer course two-five-zero."

Billy answered, "Two-five-zero, aye." The ark lurched forward, as if happy to finally be free of the pier, and then responded to his turning of the wheel.

And that was when Billy really felt that surge of excitement that he always had when a ship left the dock, and he was on the helm. He figured it was like the feeling that engineers get when their train leaves the station, or a pilot when the plane leaves the ground. All that power getting underway and being a part of it is invigorating. And to be steering such a machine is downright thrilling. But it also requires focus. Unlike a train on rails, ships are often bouncing, both forward and back, as well as left to right, in even small waves. And the waves on this day were anything but small. With ropes unattached, the ark's rocking was instantly more noticeable. Billy focused on the course dial.

The bridge became crowded as the deckhands all moved up from below to take their general quarters stations. Miller took the spot on the lee helm and nodded to Billy to let him know that he knew the basics. The lee helm is straightforward, just moving the levers forward and back, but it does need to be done quickly and sometimes separately for each handle to use each propeller. The forward speeds range from ahead one-third to ahead two-thirds to full to flank. At flank speed, the ark was built to achieve twenty-seven knots. Beth, Rodriguez, Jessie, and Sanders, all wearing foul-weather gear and binoculars around their necks, moved out onto the bridge wings, trying to peer through the fog and rain to make sure the ark was not approaching any other ships. Brooks and Green stood next to Hunter, ready to help wherever needed, although both were already looking a bit queasy.

As the ark moved away from the pier, Mitchell issued a series of orders, skillfully using both screws to turn the ship quickly, forward on one and reverse on the other, and degree headings to steer. He ultimately called for all ahead two-thirds and a course heading of 270 degrees (due west on a 360-degree circle).

As the ark moved farther out into the bay, the rocking intensified. Green, his face nearly the color of his name, stepped out on the port bridge wing for a moment, surely to vomit his lunch into the bay. Well, Billy thought smugly, that was yet one more benefit of being a helmsman. It's like when you drive a car to avoid getting carsick. He had been seasick before, but never when he was steering a ship.

Slowly, Golden Gate Bridge came in view through the rain for just a moment and then disappeared again. Beyond that was the Pacific Ocean and, almost certainly, much bigger waves. As they passed Alcatraz Island on the port side, they could all just barely see the waves crashing on the rocky shores. The captain had been looking for the landmark and maneuvered the ark around it. Shortly after that, they passed underneath the bridge and into the Pacific, and as expected, the wind and the waves increased substantially. The waves were now running twenty to thirty feet high. The ark rode over them well enough, the wide hull providing some stability, but as it dropped into the troughs between, it squirmed and Billy worked to keep it on course.

"Green water over the bow, Captain," Willis, the second mate, called. Big seas sometimes appear green, and these waves were large enough to be drenching the forecastle and the front of the bridge. Billy wondered how many people below were getting sick as well as scared.

Mitchell shifted the course direction slightly to take the waves head-on and the speed to all ahead full. Just then, the radio crackled, and the operator, Grimaldi, turned the volume dial. The voice sounded far away and came through only intermittently.

"Rogue wave conditions here," the voice said and then added coordinates. It concluded with urgency, "Issue tsunami warnings onshore."

Mitchell immediately looked at Hannigan, the quartermaster, who was already plotting the coordinates on the chart. "Location?"

Big ocean storms were nothing new. History was filled with stories of massive storms, from Homer's *Odyssey* to the wrecking of the Spanish Armada in the sixteenth century to recent disasters like the El Faro in 2015. But in the twenty-first century, the frequency and intensity of storms had all increased due to the warming of ocean waters from climate change. And even the hardiest sailor could get caught in one that was truly intimidating. Waves can run more than fifty feet tall, some much higher. Occasionally a ship gets hit by an ESW, short for an *extreme storm wave*. Some call them rogue waves because nobody knows where they come from or what they're going to do, but a few have been documented at over one hundred feet high. Indeed, large waves capsize dozens of ships and boats every year.

After just a few seconds, Hannigan answered, "Forty miles west of us, Captain."

They all did the math in their heads. The tsunami was probably moving at over one hundred miles per hour, and the ark was sailing directly into it. Billy figured ten minutes, maybe twenty at most, until they hit some monstrous waves. He had been in a tsunami once before. Rather than just one big breaking wave, a tsunami will produce a series or what some call a wave train that can last up to an hour and could literally flip ships. And the sound, with gale-force winds howling, was terrifying.

Mitchell, as calm as if he were reading about Noah to his grandkids, said, "Issue the warning, Mr. Hunter."

Hunter reached for the 1MC and pressed the Speak button. "Attention. Large waves approaching. Secure all loose items and personnel. Brace for heavy rolls."

Billy pictured people belowdecks moving as best as they could in the rocking ship to secure pots and pans in the galley, supplies in the storerooms, parents with their kids.

Mitchell spoke again. "Bring in the hands from the bridge wings."

Green and Brooks moved to call in their comrades. As they opened the bridge doors, the wind and the driving rain poured through. They all hustled into the bridge, soaking wet, Rodriguez quietly muttering profanities. Brooks and Green pulled the hatches shut behind them.

While the others shook the water off their rain gear like wet dogs, Beth walked behind Billy and touched his back slightly, whispering, "You scared, Billy?" Billy couldn't help but smile, not only because she had forgiven him enough to say something, but also because of what she said. He answered quietly, "Not enough."

Even though it was late afternoon, the sky turned pitch-black. The darkness enveloped the ship, and on the bridge, only the dials for the radio and the helm and the radar provided lights. When the sea was visible, it appeared white as foam, and the froth from breaking waves was everywhere. The deckhands stood quietly, trying to look ahead through the bridge windows. The ark plowed ahead like this for a couple of minutes that seemed like a couple of hours. They couldn't even hear the engines over the sounds of the storm battering the outside of the ship with winds that howled like banshees.

"Hill and Miller," Captain Mitchell said calmly, "I need all your attention so we'll hit these waves dead center. Everyone else should stay quiet so they can hear my orders."

"Aye," Billy and Miller responded simultaneously. They all knew the waves were coming and that getting crosswise could be disastrous.

From his vantage point at the front of the bridge and decades of experience spotting them, the captain saw the large waves before any of the rest of them could.

"Course two-six-zero," he called back.

"Two-six-zero," Billy answered and adjusted the helm.

"All ahead flank, both throttles."

"All ahead flank," Miller cranked the two handles ahead. The ark's screws dug in, and the ship responded almost immediately. The others on the bridge were grabbing whatever they could to hang onto. Billy spread his legs wider to increase his balance.

Then the waves, coming from slightly south of due west, were on them, much larger than any they had experienced. These were at least forty feet high. The ark took the first one head-on and climbed it like a train going up a hill. They crested.

"All ahead full," Mitchell said and added, "Maintain course two-six-zero."

Again, they both repeated the orders, and Miller dialed back the speed. The ark slid down the back side of the wave, as if dropping into a trench. Billy focused on the dial in front of him and kept it as close as possible to the 260 mark. They moved on to more waves, as if on a watery roller-coaster ride. Mitchell cut back the speed on the crest of the larger waves only to increase it again before starting to climb, like a bicyclist does before tackling a big hill. He also called out occasional slight course changes as the buffeting waves tried to twist the ship. The storm hammered the ship relentlessly, as if insulted that any vessel would challenge it.

And then they were into waves that approached fifty feet.

"All ahead flank," Mitchell said, still calm.

"All ahead flank," Miller answered and pushed the levers as far forward as possible.

The ark climbed one of the monsters and moved on gamely. It was working hard. Billy was so focused at keeping the ship on course that he completely forgot everything and everyone else nearby. At some point, somebody lost their balance behind him and fell to the deck, but Billy didn't even look back to see who it was. Nobody was saying anything other than the captain and himself and Miller.

"All ahead full," Mitchell said again, and Miller dialed back the speed as the ark slid over a crest.

Then they all caught a glimpse of something ahead, a rogue wave so large that when they were in the bottom of the trough, you couldn't see the crest. It had to be nearly sixty feet high.

"Sweet Jesus!" someone exclaimed quietly.

"All ahead flank," Mitchell called out. "Stay course two-six-zero."

"Aye, flank," Miller called back and thrust the handles forward. The ark picked up some speed at the bottom of the previous wave and then started to climb. Billy fought the wheel as the wave tried to turn the ship sideways. They all knew that even the slightest turn sideways would roll them over.

Miller patted the lee helm and whispered under his breath, "Come on, baby, you can make it."

Suddenly, others were talking as well, urging the ship onward or even praying out loud. There was no reason not to. Behind Billy, Green was saying "Go" over and over. Rodriguez was muttering something in Spanish. They climbed. They could all feel the ark slowing down as the ship fought gravity and the pull of the wave. But they kept moving up the side of the liquid wall.

As they approached the top, Billy couldn't help but smile, scared but also exhilarated. He chuckled very slightly. Miller heard him and whispered, "Damn right. We got this." The ark seemed to almost pause just before the crest, time nearly standing still as the wave took one last shot at toppling this persistent intruder.

Then they were over the top. As the bow started downhill, the stern came nearly out of the water as the propellers sought purchase on the downside of the wave. Then the screws got a grip on the water and the ship had some control again.

Glancing up from the dial, Billy could see the next wave, and it wasn't nearly as big. Miller exhaled loudly. Even Captain Mitchell sounded relieved as he said, "Back it off, Miller. All ahead full. And stay the course, Hill."

Miller, grinning, answered, "All ahead full, aye," and pulled the throttles back a notch.

"Aye, two-six-zero," Billy responded.

Behind them, Hannigan said with a sigh, "Thank God!" Others joined in with their own cheers. Billy felt a congratulatory tap on his back and, still focused on the dial, glanced back to see Beth. Jessie was standing right next to Beth, looking back at him with a relieved smile on her face. Billy looked ahead again and then over at Miller, and they both just nodded at each other.

Then Mitchell looked back at Billy and Miller from the front of the bridge for just a moment as he said, "Good work, you two."

They still had waves to cross, but they all relaxed just a bit. Within a few minutes, the waves had diminished considerably. The rain began to let up, and then they could see the sky in the west starting to clear. Hunter picked up the 1MC and announced, "Stand down. I repeat, stand down. Report any damages to the bridge."

The ark plowed on like its crew, tested but undeterred.

CHAPTER 15

With a Bang

The mood on the ark after the storm was ebullient. The ship had proven itself seaworthy in challenging conditions. The crew was proud of having survived their baptism by typhoon. The only casualty from the storm was Second Officer Willis, the person who had fallen during one of the largest waves and broken a wrist, but even she was laughing it off as a "rookie" mistake. Billy, personally, felt a sense of accomplishment in that he had now helped his family and friends and could move on without guilt or remorse. On the return trip to California, he could train replacements on the helm. Indeed, Miller was already filling in now while he took a break.

In the meantime, though, Billy realized he was enjoying the company of the people on board. They had gathered in the mess hall to celebrate their maiden voyage with tacos and tequila. Most of the crew was there, although a few people were still feeling seasick. Indeed, at one point, Susan Harris hurried to the hatch opening out to the deck with her daughter, Naomi, in tow, the latter's face quite pale. Billy sat at a long table with the other deckhands as well as Brooks and his family, laughing at a story Jonah Brooks was telling about getting tossed out of his bunk when the ship came down in one of the troughs.

Jonah was funny enough on his own, but the deckhands added to it with their own comments about Billy's driving. Jessie Rivera started it by fingering Billy as "the one who was steering," to which Jonah looked at him accusingly and said, "You?"

Rodriguez piled on, "Si, amigo, and he's the best driver on the ship."

Jonah's face fell.

Sanders added, "We're in for a long trip, kid."

Before Billy could even try to defend himself, Oliver stood up from his nearby table and held up his glass of tequila.

"If I might interrupt," he started and then waited for the room to quiet down. "I propose a toast to all who helped get this precious cargo away from danger." Oliver continued standing. He looked directly at Billy and graciously gave a different assessment of his son's driving than Jonah was getting. "Including those who remember the things they learned in their youth."

Billy smiled gratefully as he pushed back from the table, stood, and looked at Oliver before speaking. "And to those who continue to learn new things." Oliver smiled back, not offended by the meaning within the toast that perhaps only the Hill family appreciated.

Just then, the hatch from the deck opened and Grimaldi, the radio operator, walked into the room. He moved purposely toward the radio in the galley and turned it on. Oliver and Billy both continued standing, waiting silently. On the radio, a commentator was talking, saying with considerable anger in his voice, "This is what happens when you have trigger-happy blowhards leading nations with nuclear weapons. All it takes are natural disasters to set things off."

Another voice objected, "Come on, you can't blame the president for the storm."

The first voice responded, "The hell I can't. You elect people that deny the climate is changing, and then you get massive storms like—"

Before he could finish, a loud, emotional voice interrupted. "We break in with more news of missile strikes…" And then the radio deteriorated into static. The members of the crew all looked at one another, confused.

Oliver stared at the radioman. "What else did you hear, Mr. Grimaldi?"

Grimaldi, his expression grim, was about to answer when an explosion sounded in the distance, a sound like none of them had ever heard before. Just then, Susan Harris opened the hatch and, her face flush and her voice breaking, said, "You need to see this," as she motioned outside.

They all followed Susan out to the main deck, where Naomi was standing, looking back toward the eastern horizon with her mouth wide open as if in shock. They looked in the direction she was staring at a mushroom cloud billowing up into the sky, back in the direction of San Francisco. Nobody said anything for a moment. Then, Sarah said very quietly, "God help us all."

Then another cloud appeared. Seconds later, they heard the explosion. Then another cloud was visible, south of the first two. And they heard another explosion.

Americans used to say that they would all remember where they were when Neil Armstrong walked on the moon or when the Twin Towers came down on 9/11. From here on out, anybody still alive, Americans or not, would know where they were at that moment. Several people sobbed. Others started openly crying. Oliver was standing next to Billy. He spoke quietly, recalling the previous toast. "And then there are those who did not learn and never will."

Billy felt a lump in his throat. For just a moment, the T. S. Eliot line came into his head about the world ending "not with a bang but a whimper," and he wondered if Eliot had been wrong. The world was now apparently engaged in nuclear war, and if it was coming to an end, it would not be with a whimper.

CHAPTER 16

To Be

The world had not ended, but the enormity of what had happened settled down on the ark like a black cloud of death. Everyone was stunned and saddened but also frustrated in the lack of information about the extent of what had happened. Most communication channels had been destroyed, although some stayed online long enough to provide bits of information. As best as the crew could figure, the world had spiraled out of control so fast nobody could stop or even slow the destruction. Analogous to the ark story in the Bible, human behavior had prompted an unleashing of terrible weather that produced severe consequences. North Korea, a nation desperate for food and water and then heavily damaged by the massive typhoon, launched missiles against South Korea. While the world scrambled to respond, militants in Pakistan took the opportunity to take over that country's nuclear arsenal and attacked India. India counterattacked with a nuclear strike. Diplomacy, long a dying art, was left out in the cold of nuclear winter as other nations, including China, Russia, and the US, joined in with their own strikes. Billions of people were dead or dying from explosions and radioactive fallout.

Like most of the crew, Billy got little sleep that night. He had a chance to get some rest, thanks to Miller and Jessie, who both learned the essentials of handling the helm and the lee helm. The three of them set up a rotation. Miller took the 8:00 p.m. to midnight shift, then Jessie from midnight to 4:00 a.m., and Billy had the sunrise shift. So at 8:00 p.m., Billy went down below, where he tossed and turned for a while before finally nodding off for a few hours. Then, he woke up at three and decided he might as well go up and relieve Jessie.

When he got to the bridge, he muttered something to the effect that perhaps she could do better than he had with sleep. Jessie nodded sympathetically and went below. Billy took over on the wheel. Sanders, the other deckhand on duty, stood over by the port bridge wing. He acknowledged Billy briefly and then went back to his own thoughts. Hannigan, out on the bridge wing, was also quiet. Hunter came up to relieve Sanders at four, but he and Billy only nodded at each other. Once, Billy thought he heard a faint explosion in the distance, somewhere well behind the ark. Billy knew his personal issues were incredibly insignificant in the larger context, but he thought about them briefly. He knew well that he was not going back to California, at least not anytime soon. His unwillingness to commit to the trip was suddenly a moot point.

The bridge remained nearly silent until a little before 0600. Then, Maria Rivera walked onto the bridge, kindly carrying a pot of fresh coffee and some cups. She set them on the chart table and left quietly. A minute later, Rodriguez showed up to start his shift as the duty boatswain. Even he was subdued and seemed content to just stand quietly, sipping on some coffee, but before he could even finish his cup, Hunter handed him a walkie-talkie and told him to hike around the decks to check on any damage from the previous day's storm.

A few minutes later, just before sunrise, Miller walked on the bridge. He, too, was early for his shift but said he also had been unable to sleep much. The weariness in his eyes, just barely visible under the pulled-down cowboy hat, was evident as he offered to give Billy a break so he could go below for some breakfast. Billy had started to head off the bridge when the walkie-talkie in Hunter's hand crackled to life. It was Rodriguez.

"Chief, we got a guy with a gun on the fantail. Get down here, pronto!"

Hunter answered, "On my way," and glanced at Hannigan. The first mate waved him on and said he would alert the captain. Hunter motioned for Billy to follow him. The two went straight to the arms locker and each pulled out an AR-15 rifle. Billy had not handled one before, and he was surprised at just how cold and light it felt in his hands. He hoped he would not have to use it. They then ran down the main deck toward the fantail.

When they arrived, Rodriguez had his hands in the air, one of them holding the walkie-talkie. He was twenty yards in front of a tall thin man with heavy black glasses, standing at the very stern of the ship. The man had an odd, unsettled expression on his face and was waving a pistol in the air in little circles. Behind him, the sun was just starting to come up in the east, the sky a bloodred color as the sun's rays reflected off the clouds of dust and particles left over from the explosions.

The pistol-waver was talking in a loud, frantic voice. "We have to go back. Those people, all those people…" The eyes behind the glasses darted back and forth. He obviously noticed Hunter and Billy arrive with the assault rifles, but he didn't seem at all surprised. Even when Hunter leveled the gun in his direction, it did not upset him more than he already was; rather, he seemed to expect it. But he did stop talking for a moment.

Hunter looked at Rodriguez, who said simply, "His name's Myerson. I don't know—"

Myerson interrupted. "We're going back."

Hunter stared at Myerson and said bluntly, "There's nothing to go back to."

This only seemed to agitate Myerson even more. He waved the pistol menacingly as he yelled, "How would you know?"

Hunter simply said, "We all know."

Myerson grimaced, not wanting to accept the assertion. He shifted the pistol to point it at his own head. "Either we go back or I'll kill myself right here."

Billy didn't know what reaction Myerson hoped to get but doubted it was the one he received. Hunter responded coldly, "Your call."

Billy had no idea what would happen next, but he felt like he needed to do something. He handed his rifle to Rodriguez, who welcomed having something in his hands other than just a walkie-talkie. Billy glanced at Hunter, who gave a slight nod as if to say, "Go ahead and try." Billy held out his hands palms up to show that he was not a threat and took a couple of small steps toward Myerson.

He spoke quietly. "How about we go get a cup of coffee? Talk about this?"

Myerson looked at Billy and stopped waving the gun for a moment. He looked surprised at the offer, and Billy figured that was a good thing, so he kept talking. "We're all shocked by what's happened. But all we have now is this ark. Maybe all the world has is this ark. We have to keep going." Billy didn't have time to think about the irony of the comments for his own reluctant commitment.

Myerson shook his head vigorously and then narrowed his eyes. "You're a Hill, aren't you? It was your family that dragged us out here."

Billy answered, "We didn't know this was going to happen." He gestured toward the east. The sun was just starting to show, a dark blotch about to crawl up into an ugly red sky. "And goodness knows, I sure didn't plan on being here."

Myerson glanced behind himself in the direction of Billy's gesture. When he did, Billy also looked around and realized that some others, including the captain and the ship's doctor, had arrived. Above them, on the flight deck that looked out over the fantail, some other people had gathered to watch. Billy realized he had put himself in the middle of a situation over which he had no control. He had no formal training in negotiation and wasn't at all sure what to do next. He was relieved when Susan Harris walked up and started talking in a soothing voice.

"You don't really want to do this, Lee," she said. "Let's put the gun down and go below. I need you in the computer center."

Myerson's tone shifted from anger to sadness. "I can't do that, Susan. This is over. We're kidding ourselves if we think we can live through this."

Susan answered, "We're breathing. If we're breathing, we have hope."

Myerson was not swayed and nearly spit out his next line. "There's no hope. We should go back and be with the people we love."

Captain Mitchell's voice sounded from behind Billy, "There's no one back there, son. We have to move on."

Dr. Smith-Garvey added, "We can talk about this, Lee. Let's all think about it a bit."

Myerson's eyes darted back and forth from Mitchell to the doctor and then back to Billy and Susan. "Not me. I make my own choices."

His line sparked a thought in Billy, as usual a cultural reference. He knew it was a Hail Mary pass, if you will, but since nobody else said anything for a moment, he gave it a try. He figured that if he kept Myerson talking, that meant he wasn't shooting. And maybe somebody else could think of something.

"I don't know you, Lee, but I bet you're well educated."

Lee nodded dismissively.

"Probably read a lot, right?"

"So?" Myerson demanded angrily.

Billy pushed on. "Shakespeare?" He noticed Susan and the doctor also looking at him, puzzled.

"What?" Myerson demanded. "Shakespeare?"

"Me too," Billy went on. "You know the famous scene in Hamlet? You know, the 'To be or not to be' speech?"

"What of it?" Myerson asked.

"It's a load of crap," Billy answered. "Suicide's a load of crap, a gutless way out. The answer should always be 'To be.' Otherwise, what's the point?"

He knew it was a reach, but Billy hoped it would give the troubled man something to think about. And at least for a few seconds, it seemed to work. Myerson didn't respond immediately but instead seemed to be considering his options. The ark bounced roughly in the choppy waves. Nobody else spoke for thirty seconds.

But then, a cruel twist of fate intervened. Behind Myerson, back on the eastern horizon, a dark cloud arose. Billy grimaced because he knew what was coming, and seconds later, the sound of another explosion reached the ark. Nobody on the fantail knew what caused it, probably another nuclear blast, but the effect was immediate. Hearing the sound, Myerson glanced behind him and then, almost in slow motion, turned around with a dark smile on his face. He lifted the pistol to his mouth and pulled the trigger. The force of the blast knocked him over the low guardrail and down into the wake of the ship.

Billy and the others all raced to the guardrail, only to see Myerson's body floating back toward the carnage in the east. They were all stunned into silence, and nobody said anything for nearly a minute. Dr. Smith-Garvey then looked at Billy and patted him on the back before walking away. Susan Harris, sobbing quietly, turned away. Captain Mitchell said quietly, "Good try, Mr. Hill." He walked away with his arm around Susan's shoulders.

Suddenly, only a few people were left on the fantail. Hunter and Rodriguez, still holding the rifles, both stared at the body floating off into the distance. Rodriguez muttered quietly, "At least there's no cleanup."

Hunter looked from the body to Billy and then said, without any judgment, "Shakespeare, huh?" He and Rodriguez then turned and walked away.

Billy continued to stand at the guardrail, staring at the floating body, now just barely visible in the early-morning light. He felt a hand on his back and looked over to see Beth. Standing next to her was Jessie. Both looked sympathetic, but neither of them said anything.

Billy shook his head slightly. "I thought I had him."

Beth patted his back lightly as Jessie said quietly, "He was gone before you got here."

Billy looked at each of them and then back at the ocean. The mushroom cloud spread in the distance. The ark continued to sail west, away from Myerson and what was left of their former world.

CHAPTER 17

Gone

Myerson's suicide added even more gloom to the ship. When people moved around at all, they did so quietly. Those who had to work to keep the ship running did their jobs, indeed some of them finding some relief in the mundane efforts of routine duties. Billy, Jessie, and Miller took shifts on the helm and lee helm, varying the rotation so each could get some sleep, as the ship continued to steam west.

Late in the afternoon after Myerson's suicide, Miller came up to the bridge for the 4:00 to 8:00 p.m. shift. Knowing that the ship was due to have a memorial service that evening, Billy offered to stay on the helm so that Miller could attend. But Miller said he had no interest. So Billy joined the rest of the nonduty crew on the main deck at sunset. Oliver, Sarah, and Captain Mitchell stood at the same spot where they had held the planning meeting just days before. They waited patiently for people to gather until Oliver said, "Thank you all for coming. I've asked Sarah to say a few words to start."

Sarah began to speak. "We gather today to recognize the tragic events of the last two days. I don't have the words to express our sorrow. And our prayers cannot bring back all those we have lost. We also do not have the body of our own Lee Myerson to commit to the sea but only the memory of the time he spent with us. As I have no words, I ask that we all consider our own thoughts and memories in a moment of silence."

Sarah bowed her head and stood quietly. The crew, many of them also bowing their heads, some holding hands, was silent. The flags on the mainmast fluttered softly in the breeze coming from the west, while the ocean's waves lapped at the hull.

The crew remained quiet as Sarah resumed speaking. "I do not pretend to know what you believe. We are people of many faiths or even none. So I will not tell you what to think. But I will tell you what I think. The book of Isaiah talks of a time when the foundations of the earth will be shaken and the earth, to quote, will be 'utterly broken down.' I don't know if this is that time. But I do know that, for us at this moment, we will go on. We will go on, and we will know better days. To quote another passage in the Bible, Psalm 51 says, 'Make me to hear joy and gladness, that the bones which thou hast broken may rejoice.' And someday we shall." She looked out at the crew and then stepped back.

Oliver continued, "Thank you, Sarah. Indeed, our memories are all that we have for so many that we have lost. We will take them with us as we continue our mission, a mission that is now even more urgent than before. We have no radio contacts at this point, but we will continue to monitor all frequencies. We do not know who or what is still out there. We have not even heard from the *White Diamond*, although we told them our planned course when we were back at Treasure Island. We, of course, hope that they and others have survived. But it may well be that we are now the hope of the world. I ask that we all keep that in mind as we go forward." He paused, looked at all the crew, and then stepped back.

Captain Mitchell took the microphone and spoke briefly. "We are proceeding on a due westerly course. Our immediate goal is Hawaii, nearly two thousand nautical miles away. If we average twenty knots, we should get there within the week. In the worst scenario and we find the islands uninhabitable, we will move on. We are fully provisioned with food and water and not in need of any assistance." He stopped and looked around at the crowd. "I know this is hard, but all we can do is to do all we can. As this service ends, we will thus resume our regular duties."

As Mitchell, Oliver, and Sarah backed off from the microphone, people in the crowd stood a bit longer, some with tears in their eyes or on their faces. Many left quietly. Others exchanged hugs or shook hands. Billy, standing on the side of the crowd, started to walk away, quite willing to be alone with his own thoughts. From attending so many other funerals, Billy knew he was okay if left alone but much more affected when made aware of the feelings of others. But then Sarah saw him and came over to give him a hug. Sarah was followed by Owen and Annie and then Beth. After they moved on, James and Janice Brooks walked over to embrace him briefly. Billy felt a lump in his throat and tried to move off again, but this time the Rivera sisters walked over and each gave him a quick hug. Billy knew that they did not know him well enough to hug him out of affection but rather just out of concern for another human being, and the humanity of the gesture was quite touching, so Billy, now feeling more emotion than he expected, finally slipped away.

He walked back to the fantail to think and stared out at the ocean. The salty sea air felt somehow reassuring. The wind was minimal, and the sky mostly clear. Moderate waves bounced the ark as it continued to plow along. The only other noises were the ship's engines, offering a steady, almost-comforting purring. In the darkness off the stern, the moon and the stars started to appear in the eastern sky, oblivious to what had happened to the planet that was making another trip around the sun. Billy thought about what Oliver had said; for all they knew, they were now alone in the world.

As a disaster tracker, Billy had resigned himself to tragedies, and he felt less susceptible to being overwhelmed by them than many people. He had seen so much death. And as someone who was always better at saying "Goodbye" rather than "I'll stay," he was less sentimental about some things than others. He knew this was not a virtue, but he also knew that a hard edge could sometimes help him cope. But then he suddenly thought of Roy and RC and wondered if they had still been in Yosemite when the bombs hit. And they were just two people. Thoughts of disaster started filling his mind. Billions of people, animals, birds, all of them had been killed in a moment of time. Everything from schools to hospitals was destroyed. Humans had always worried about the end of the world, and now it seemed to be closer than ever.

The enormity of it all hit him. As usual, Billy tried to mentally escape into cultural references. The song "Eve of Destruction" popped into his head, and he began to subconsciously sing the chorus. And then he thought of another reference. In the book *Cities of the Plain*, a young cowboy asks an aging cowboy what he has learned over the course of his long life, and the older guy looks at the younger one and says, "When something is gone, it's gone." The finality of the thought was overwhelming. Billy considered praying, but his mind couldn't focus as he didn't know where to begin. He tried to think of a silver lining but came up empty, other than the fact that they were still alive. And all those emotions Billy thought he had buried were still there, and they started to bubble up. He suddenly had to catch his breath. He even felt a bit shaky on his feet, so he grasped the railing on the fantail to steady himself. And as the ark moved on, he tightened his grip.

PART 2

The Ocean
September 2026 – November 2026

Tonight, all is silence in the world
as we take our stand.

—Bruce Springsteen,
"Jungleland," in *Born to Run*

CHAPTER 18

Arkonauts

As the ark sailed on, the crew wondered if they were the only ones left in the world. Billy thought of Springsteen's line about "silence in the world" and felt a certain awe as well as trepidation. He knew that, at some point, they would need to find someplace to make their own stand.

Someone came up with the name arkonauts, and it stuck. Not only were they on an ark, but since the venture started in California, where gold miners had been called argonauts, it also seemed clever enough. And people were quite willing to use the term referring to themselves except for when they wanted to tease someone for doing something questionable, by dropping the second *a*. Teasing increased in the days after the memorial service, in part because they had no choice but to get along. The other reason for the improving morale was that they had hope. Specifically, as they sailed toward Hawaii, they hoped to find that other people had indeed survived.

They also established an onboard routine to focus on their jobs instead of constantly thinking about what was, or wasn't, going on in the rest of the world. The routine was like that on most working ships. The three officers (Mitchell, Hannigan, and Willis) rotated so one was always on duty. Many in the crew, such as the lab techs and supply people, kept regular, daytime hours. Others in the crew worked whatever hours were necessary. For instance, Maria and her staff in the galley prepared meals and made sure that food and coffee were available to those who worked all hours. The deckhands and

Owen's boiler techs worked four-hour shifts to ensure that vital functions on the ship were always manned. The oncoming shift would show up fifteen minutes before the hour, every four hours, to provide transition. Each shift had a nickname, such as the midwatch from midnight to 4:00 a.m. In addition to working the shifts in their rotation, the deckhands also had responsibilities for all the maintenance, cleaning, and fire protection on the ship. Consequently, they liked to say that the boiler techs kept the ship running but the deckhands kept it working. Hunter, Beth, and Sanders split up the oversight of the deckhands, again one of them always being on call.

Fortunately, even though they had not had time for a shakedown cruise, the ark was ready for work. The labs holding the collections of species DNA were secure and kept at cool temperatures. With the superstructure covered in solar panels, the ark generated all its own power, more than enough electricity for daily use, with some left over to charge the batteries in the hold as storage. The high-tech desalination system constantly filtered ocean water to provide plenty for drinking, showers, laundry, and sanitation. The vast holds contained enough food stores for at least six months. Finally, the ark had some amenities, such as a small gym and a library with books and movies. The only problem areas were communication and computer systems, still inoperative after the nuclear explosions.

Even without the computer systems, the arkonauts knew their location for a somewhat-ironic reason. They used a combination of what sailors refer to as dead reckoning and celestial navigation. Most of the time, they would reckon their location by simply multiplying speed of travel by time on a planned course. They would then check those dead reckoning plots periodically with celestial navigation, a technique that mariners have used for centuries. With a sextant, navigators can "shoot" the sun or certain stars at specific times and then, using tables in manuals, plot exact locations. Thus, in a world that had developed enough technological capability to destroy entire nations, navigation now depended on a process that predated steam engines.

Knowing their exact location and maintaining their route was important for several reasons. First, they wanted to be as efficient as possible. Second, Oliver had shared their planned route with Henry Hill so that if the *White Diamond* was still afloat, they might stay in touch. Third, before sailing, Captain Mitchell and his officers had wisely collected as many pilot charts as they could find. Pilot charts are the equivalent of maps of the sea, divided into manageable squares. They include all the readings and data that have been collected by other sailors over the centuries on depth, currents, wind, and weather.

For celestial navigation to work, the chronometer must be accurate. Therefore, typically one person on each ship is responsible for winding the chronometer and other clocks on board at a designated time each week. That became one of Billy's jobs. So three days after they sailed, he made the rounds to all the clocks on board. He liked the clock-winding job as it gave him a chance to meet many others in the crew and learn firsthand of their varying personalities. On his first trip to the engine room, for instance, Owen welcomed him, but his chief assistant, a crusty old Black Merchant Marine sailor named Carter, merely growled. Billy understood. Guys like Carter didn't get to see much other than warm, smelly boilers, thus spawning the John McPhee line "Join the Merchant Marine and glimpse the world." On the other end of the scale, his first trip to the galley netted him a fresh-baked cookie from Maria Rivera.

Billy's other work responsibilities were split between manning the helm and working with the deckhands. Thus, he spent most of his time cleaning and maintaining the decks, heads (bathrooms), and other common areas on the ship. Not surprisingly, he preferred to be on the helm and was happy to be designated the chief helmsman for challenging situations like storms. All the deckhands were expected to know how to handle the ship for routine sailing so that they could rotate. Therefore, Billy trained the others in the relatively straightforward techniques of manning the helm (for steering) and the lee helm (for speed). He thus scheduled a few minutes with each of the ones who had no experience as well as just a couple of minutes with Miller and Jessie, who already knew the basics. Billy was happy for the chance to get some sense of his colleagues.

Glen Miller was a quick study and learned the nuances of the steering devices easily. He needed so little additional training that Billy tried to engage him in other topics, such as guitar-playing, but Miller, to his credit, kept his focus on ship-handling. He was also circumspect about his past. Given that he was rarely without his battered cowboy hat, his nickname was logical. When Billy asked where he was from, Miller said, "Alberta. I started working on a ranch when I was about twelve." As he was Canadian, the word *about* sounded more like "a boot," of course. Miller wasn't unfriendly, but he was laconic.

Tyrone Green also showed an affinity for the steering instruments. As Beth had said, Green was a young guy from the south side of Chicago, again not unfriendly but still reserved toward strangers like Billy. Like Miller, he didn't say much about his past either, but he did mention that getting on a Forest Service fire crew was his ticket out of a bad situation. When Billy asked if the war had him worried about family back in Chicago, he responded bluntly, "Anybody back there is on their own." Okay, then.

James Brooks was a bit more nervous about the responsibility of driving the big ship, so Billy made sure to tell him that he would only be doing it when they were just steaming. Hearing that, Brooks relaxed. Brooks was a lot more forthcoming with concern about the rest of the world than were Miller or Green and said Janice was distraught, having left family back in Memphis.

Trying to teach Tomas Rodriguez was more challenging. He had a quick wit, so Billy knew he could learn, but getting him to focus was something else. He was cocky, claiming at one point, "I've driven everything on wheels." When Billy answered that this was not on wheels, Rodriguez responded, "Even better, amigo. No flat tires." He was so confident that after a little training, Rodriguez wanted to talk about nearly anything else. Billy quickly realized that Rodriguez was one of those people who act like they know what you are going to say before you say it and then move on to whatever point they want to make.

Like Miller, Jessie Rivera had also already had some time on the helm, so she and Billy scheduled a very brief session where she could ask any questions. She instantly impressed him by the questions she asked, such as the benefits of using twin screws instead of just one for steering. After a while, she was asking questions about propulsion and steerage that were beyond Billy's capacity to answer. Unlike all the other trainees, she also peppered him with questions about his experiences, asking, for example, how steering this ship differed from the one he had steered while in the Navy. Billy couldn't tell if she was asking to become more adept at the job or because she really was interested in his past, but he flattered himself thinking that it was the latter. When they finished with the time allocated, Billy's training schedule was done and he passed the wheel off to Green, who had the next shift.

As he and Jessie left the bridge, Billy joked with her that if she wanted to hear more sea stories, they could go get a cup of coffee in the galley. He was rewarded when she said, "Sure." So they went below together.

CHAPTER 19

Coffee Break

When Billy and Jessie moved down to the galley for some coffee, Maria joined them. Being midafternoon, the place was nearly empty other than the members of Maria's crew, who could be heard working in the kitchen. The conversation was a bit awkward at first as they didn't know one another well, but Billy quickly found himself enjoying it.

Maria, still wearing her apron, asked Billy about the training. "Did they learn well?"

"I think so," Billy answered. "Of course, one of them said he didn't need any training."

Maria nodded. "Tomas?"

Billy wasn't surprised that it was an easy guess. "Yeah, but he'll be all right."

Jessie said, "We do have a mix of people on this ship."

Billy smiled. "Yep, and we're all stuck with one another." He thought of something and added, "A famous British sailor once said, 'Being a sailor is like being in a jail with the chance of being drowned.'"

Both the sisters just stared at him. "Does this feel like jail to you, Billy?" Jessie challenged him.

Billy realized that his joke had fallen flat. "No, I didn't mean it that way. I just…"

"Don't worry, she likes to tease." Maria let him off the hook and then glanced at her sister. "And how did she do with the training?"

Billy was happy to answer honestly. "The best. She learns fast."

Maria stated proudly, "Si, she asks many questions. She would have done well at university."

Billy asked, "That didn't happen?"

"No, she came to work for me. We had family to support."

Jessie added quickly, "Well, I learned a lot there too."

Billy, always too willing to use some cultural reference that others might not know, mused out loud, "Rich man goes to college, poor man goes to work."

They both looked at him, puzzled. "What?" Maria asked.

"Sorry," Billy answered. "It's a line from a song. I have this habit of using quotes when I can." Feeling a bit embarrassed, he changed the subject quickly. "Was there other family back in the States?"

Maria responded, "There were some left. A brother. Primo carnal…how do you say, cousins?"

Jessie looked at Billy. "What about you, Billy? Your family seems to all be on this ship."

He chuckled slightly before answering, "Yeah, it's funny. We haven't been together for years, and now we're pretty much all here."

"But you were almost not here?" Jessie prodded.

He nodded. "Almost." He wasn't sure what to say next, so he took an easy way out by remembering what Jessie had said to him about getting more food when he had returned to the ark. "I came back for some more of your sister's cooking."

Both sisters smiled at that, and they all relaxed a bit. As Maria took another sip of her coffee, Jessie took off her Maria's Diner cap, and a pile of black hair fell loose. She shook it out gently. Billy stared long enough that Maria noticed.

Now with her own little teasing smile, Maria asked, "And what about a girlfriend, Bill or Billy? Did you leave one behind?"

Jessie joined in. "Yes, Bill or Billy, I heard sailors have one in every port?"

They stared at him, their dark-brown eyes showing a hint of mischief, waiting for an answer. He fidgeted a little before saying, "Well, I wouldn't exactly call those girlfriends."

They both smiled, understanding the little joke.

Maria said, "Aha. You must tell more."

Jessie added, "Yes, you promised sea stories."

He shook his head and said, "Hey, those are port stories."

Jessie faked a frown before responding, "Is that what we call a cop-out?"

They both seemed to be enjoying making him squirm. Just then, John Hunter emerged from the kitchen and walked over to their table, dough all over his hands. He looked from Maria to Jessie and then to Billy before saying quietly, "Break's about over, right, Shakespeare?" Billy couldn't tell how serious he was.

When none of them answered right away, Hunter said simply, "Go ahead and finish your coffee," and then sauntered off.

Maria looked at each of them and explained Hunter's presence in the kitchen by saying, "He likes to help making the bread."

Jessie added quickly, "That's not all he likes." She winked at Billy.

Maria's pretty face blushed a little as she smothered a smile. She then shifted the attention back to Billy by demanding, "Well, Bill or Billy, we are waiting…and what is this Shakespeare?"

Billy couldn't blame her. He found the Shakespeare reference amusing, although he assumed it had nothing to do with the fact that Don Henley, at least, had referred to the author as Billy Shakespeare. He answered, "Ah, I tried to use Shakespeare on Myerson. It didn't work."

Maria let that answer go but persisted with the previous question. "Anyway, we are still waiting for your answer on the girlfriend."

Billy thought about continuing the light banter but, for some reason, gave an honest answer. "I was engaged once. It didn't work out."

They both paused as if he would say more. When he didn't, they didn't push him. Jessie took a drink of her coffee and said simply, "They often don't."

He looked back at her, tempted to ask if that was the voice of experience, and simply asked, "Oh?"

She finished her coffee and set the cup down before answering, "Another time. As the man said, break is over."

They both thanked Maria for the coffee, and all three of them went back to work.

CHAPTER 20

Porpoises

Owen, Sarah, and Annie began a habit of taking a walk on the main deck before dinner. On the third day after they left California, the sea was calm and a gentle breeze ruffled the flag on the stern. When they paused to lean against the railing, on the fantail Roscoe lay down next to them on the deck.

Annie was pushing her parents to explain what had happened to the world. "So they're gone?" Her tone verged on angry as she was not getting an answer she liked.

Sarah tried to defuse it. "Well, honey, we don't know if they're gone. But we won't be able to find out for a while."

Annie responded, "But Daddy said the nucular bomb—"

Owen corrected her, "*Nuclear*, Annie."

Sarah continued, "Like your father says, Annie, we don't know how extensive the damage was from the nuclear blast—"

Annie persisted, "But if they're gone, where did they go?"

Sarah tried, "We just don't know, sweetie. Some people think they go to heaven. Some aren't sure about that. Some say they come back in another form. Maybe even an animal."

Annie now looked more puzzled than angry. "An animal?"

Owen held his hands out, palms up, to say he didn't have an answer.

Annie continued to stare at her mother until she explained, "We believe things, but how can we really know until we die?" Even as she said it, Sarah realized that it was not what someone might expect from an ordained minister. Then again, she was not big on dogma.

Annie nodded slightly, oddly satisfied with the uncertainty and having forced her parents to admit they didn't know everything.

In the background, someone yelled, "Porpoises!"

They all looked to the starboard side of the ark, where they saw a group of porpoises a short distance away. As they watched, the porpoises swam closer, some occasionally leaping out of the water as if performing.

Annie exclaimed, "Wow!"

Owen, also looking out at the porpoises, said, "See, Annie, the nuclear war didn't kill everything."

Sarah grinned. "It sure didn't." She looked away for a moment and glanced up to the deck above them. She said quickly, "Look at Mr. Sanders."

Owen and Annie looked up to Sanders standing there, a mop in his hand, staring out at the porpoises. The big man looked thrilled, a wide grin on his face.

Annie said proudly, "When I come back, I want to come back as a porpoise."

Sarah and Owen both chuckled slightly.

"Sarah?" Owen asked.

Sarah thought for a moment before saying, "I want to come back as a bird, so I can fly over and see everything."

When nobody else spoke for a moment, Roscoe stirred. Noticing people looking off the side of the ship, Roscoe rose up slightly to look in that direction. Not seeing anything other than the usual waves, he lowered his head with an audible sigh and closed his eyes to go back to sleep.

Owen looked down at Roscoe and said quietly, "I want to come back as a dog."

Annie started giggling as Sarah laughed out loud.

CHAPTER 21

Meditation Interrupted

Beth sat quietly in her bunk. She had developed a fondness for meditation and relished the fact that, at least for the moment, she finally had the peace in her berthing space to practice. Her berth-mates, Susan and Naomi Harris and Irene Doyle from the galley crew, were all out this evening, watching the movie on the mess deck.

She tried to focus on her breathing to get into a meditative state but was having trouble. Her brain was far from silent, rather bouncing from one topic to another even as she was trying to quiet it down. She thought about the things they had been doing to make up for the fact that the ark had not had a shakedown cruise, especially those for which she was responsible. Logically enough, Mitchell had put her in charge of fire preparedness. A decade on the fire line should have taught her a few things. So earlier that day, she and the other deckhands had inventoried the fire equipment. It all checked out fine, but she knew they needed to do a drill. Her brain then moved on to the larger context. The world seemed to have gone to hell, but they didn't go with them. Why was that? And were they really the lucky ones? Beth pushed her thoughts aside and resumed counting her breaths.

Having finally reached double digits, she had just started to relax when there was a knock on the door. She opened her eyes to see Sanders stick his head into the room. He said something about a poker game in the deckhands' berthing area and then left. Beth considered her options. She wasn't feeling particularly lucky, but she wasn't doing well with meditation either. She got up to go try her chances.

CHAPTER 22

Contact

"Contact off the starboard beam," Brooks called from the bridge wing. Everyone on the bridge looked eagerly in that direction. Captain Mitchell stepped out to the wing, raised his binoculars, and announced, "It's the *White Diamond*."

Oliver said, "So Henry stayed on the path we discussed after all." Oliver was a bit surprised at that but also happy to know that other people, including his brother, had survived the war and the typhoon.

With the radio still not operative, the two ships moved close enough to communicate using visual signals with flag semaphores. Grimaldi, the radioman, stood on the bridge wing with Oliver and exchanged messages with a tall woman with short blond hair on the yacht, who stood next to Henry Hill. In short, Henry invited his brother to use the ark's pilot boat to come over for lunch and to catch up.

So a short time later, a group of six made the trip over to the *Diamond*. As the chief helmsman, Billy was designated to drive. In addition to him, Oliver, and Mitchell, they needed deckhands to help with the boat, so Hunter told Jessie and Rodriguez, his favorite "volunteer," to come along. To Billy, the thirty-foot boat felt quite different from the ark, but the seas were mostly calm, so after some study of the controls, he motored them over to the yacht with no trouble.

Reese, the *White Diamond* deckhand they had met days before, lowered a rope ladder, and the arkonauts climbed aboard. "Welcome to the *Diamond*," he said and shook each of their hands as they came onto the quarterdeck. His grip was strong, like a vise.

Hunter said quietly, "Thanks for your help loading back on Treasure Island."

Reese smiled as he answered, "Sure, boss man."

Richard Hill walked up. He looked like he was heading for Wimbledon, dressed in white shorts and polo shirt. He said nothing by way of greeting other than, "You all can follow me." He then added, "Not you, Reese."

Reese grunted, "Aye," as he tended to the ladder.

As the rest turned to follow Richard, Hunter said quietly, "I'll stay with the boat."

Oliver seemed about to encourage Hunter to come along, but before he could say anything, Rodriguez responded, "Good idea, Chief. I'll eat your share." The comment drew a frown from Hunter but a chuckle from Reese.

Then Richard climbed the ladder to the second deck, and the others followed. Along the route to the stateroom, they walked by the tall woman who had operated the semaphores.

"Good work with those flags," Mitchell said. "It's a lost art."

The woman nodded silently as Richard said dismissively, "That's Reichardt. She can't talk."

They walked into a beautiful stateroom, where Henry and Helen were waiting with food already on the linen-covered table. Billy immediately felt underdressed and out of place. Not surprisingly, the food was excellent, and Henry and Helen were gracious enough. They shared stories about the storm and their respective rides. But the conversation was less easily digested when it turned to a discussion of the war. Billy found his uncle's view of recent events unrealistic. He and his family recognized that a war had occurred but somehow seemed to think that the effects were localized. Indeed, Henry mentioned how, after their trip to Hawaii, they would be eager to return home to see if there had been any impacts on his farm.

"It's a big, wide world, Oliver," Henry said at one point. "North Korea can go to hell for all I care."

"I think they already have," Oliver countered. "But this involved much more than Korea."

Henry snorted back, "Hell, brother, we'll be partying on those Hawaii beaches in a few days and forget about all this shit." He poured himself another drink.

The others pretty much let the brothers talk. Helen occasionally voiced her support of her husband, and Billy once interceded to second his father's assessment of the nuclear consequences, drawing a snide look from his cousin. For his part, Richard seemed more interested in bragging about the yacht and its amenities. So after the meal, he showed the visitors around. The yacht was indeed pristine and luxurious, but at least to Billy, Richard's attitude seemed snobbish, if not condescending. Billy knew he could be defensive about things like that, so he mostly ignored it, but he couldn't resist responding at one point.

Rodriguez, who had, as promised, eaten Hunter's share as well as his own, made some comment about the "great chow, amigo." Richard reacted by saying they had a world-class chef on board and then added dismissively, "I'm sure you haven't eaten that well in quite some time."

"We appreciate the dinner, Richard," Billy answered, "but don't worry, we have a damn good cook on the ark as well." That prompted a nice smile from Jessie.

Billy also noticed that his cousin took much more interest in Jessie than in the rest of them, even speaking to her in Spanish at one point. Billy suddenly wished he had taken his Spanish classes in school more seriously. But he also appreciated that Jessie did not seem all that impressed. And he was flattered when Jessie returned his compliment of her sister with one of her own directed toward him. They were on the bridge, and Richard had just introduced their chief helmsman, a Frenchman named Charles Perreau, adding that he had crewed a yacht in the America's Cup.

"He steered us through that storm with no problem," Richard stated.

Jessie answered, "Fortunately, we have a good helmsman ourselves."

Anyway, it was that kind of visit, and nobody seemed too sad to see it end. After a couple of hours, Oliver thanked Henry and offered to have them over to the ark, an invitation to which they did not commit, nor did they seem that interested. Oliver and Henry did agree to try to keep each other in sight as the two ships sailed toward Hawaii. As the visitors from the ark came back to the quarterdeck to disembark, Hunter and Reese were both just standing by the ladder, quiet, as if neither had spoken since the others had left them. Their handshake suggested differently, however.

CHAPTER 23

Potatoes

As the ark's crew settled into a routine, Billy resumed an old Navy tradition of catching a nap every day after lunch. He and his shipmates used to joke that if someone wanted to attack a US Navy vessel, the time between 1230 and 1300 would be ideal as sailors were sound asleep, scattered all over the ship. On this day, he found a quiet spot on the fantail where a warm sun, a light breeze, and the gentle rocking of the ark put him out for fifteen minutes.

Before going back to his cleaning duties, he stopped by the galley. Maria Rivera had been baking cookies during lunchtime, and he hoped she might part with one before he went back to work. He found both Rivera sisters in the galley, aprons on and their dark hair pulled back, peeling potatoes.

"Hello, ladies," he said, happy to see both.

"Buenos dias, William," Jessie answered. "Did you enjoy your nap?"

"Yes," he answered somewhat sheepishly. "In the Navy, we call that a nooner since it's right after lunch."

"In the rest of the world," Jessie responded, "we call that a siesta."

Billy was about to make a smart remark about the rest of the world sleeping for hours during the day instead of just a nap when Maria interjected.

"William? I thought it was Bill or Billy or Shakespeare. You have too many names." She tossed Billy a potato. "I will use Guillermo."

Billy caught the potato and laughed. He had always liked the name Guillermo, but he particularly liked how she pronounced it with the emphasis on the middle syllable. He certainly liked it better than Shakespeare and the reference to his failed attempt to stop a suicide, but his irritation had not prevented the nickname from catching on among the deckhands.

"That works. And thanks for the potato," he answered, "but I was really hoping for a cookie."

"I know you were," Maria said. "You must earn it."

Billy said, "Deal," as he stepped farther into the galley. He picked up a paring knife and started peeling, something he had learned how to do whenever he got in trouble back in his Navy days and got assigned to kitchen duty. Not surprisingly, then, he was good at it. And as he started peeling, he was rewarded with impressed looks on the faces of both sisters.

"Bueno, Guillermo," Maria beamed. "You have skills."

Jessie put her peeled potato in the bowl and picked up another before adding, "Si, peeling potatoes, playing guitars, taking naps, and steering a ship."

Billy grinned. "There might be others."

Jessie smiled a little as she said, "We can hope."

"Ah," he answered, "let me show you." He picked up two more potatoes and began juggling the three of them.

Jessie smothered a giggle and then added with a little frown, "Then again, some people are so hungry they don't play with their food."

Billy answered, "Don't worry, I learned with rocks, not potatoes."

Maria watched them to see if more banter was forthcoming. When none came up and they went back to work, she restarted the conversation.

"Guillermo, last time we talked about having your family on board. But not your madre. Was she alive when the war came?"

They had all resorted to calling it the war.

"No," he answered succinctly, "she died a while ago."

"What happened?" Jessie asked and then instantly realized the abruptness of her question. "If you don't mind me asking."

"No, it's okay," he answered. "My parents divorced when we were young. Oliver always had some big deal going on and never had much time for a family. So he didn't fight very hard when my mom got custody. She didn't have anywhere near the money he did, but she wanted us anyway and not his money. And her having custody was okay with us as we were certainly closer to her than to him." He paused as he finished one potato and started on another.

"She was a grade school teacher in a little town in Northern California. She and I were close. Seemed like Owen was always into mechanical things, and Beth was an athlete who discovered boys early. I was restless during the days, but at night I liked to sit with her and read, so she got me into all kinds of stuff." He paused again.

"Like Shakespeare?" Jessie asked.

"Yeah, Shakespeare, Steinbeck, Melville, all the classics. Even the Bible."

"The Bible?" Maria said, sounding somewhat surprised, while grabbing another potato. Their pile was growing.

Billy understood her surprise. He wasn't exactly a man of the cloth. "Yeah, we weren't real religious, but she liked some of it."

Jessie asked, "Like what?"

Billy was learning that, with Jessie, logical questions would not go unasked. "Well, let's just say that I knew the ark story before I got on this ship."

They both just smiled at that, so Billy continued. "One summer, in fire season we had a big one in our area. You know how California was—dry, hot, ready to explode. At some point, state officials said to evacuate. But with budget cuts, there weren't enough people to enforce it. And they had their hands full anyway."

Billy paused for just a second. Both sisters were watching him closely.

"We should have left. Beth said so. She and I were still in high school and at home with Mom. Oliver was gone, and Owen was at college by then. The neighbors left, and we should have. But Mom was stubborn. She said something about having fires all the time and why leave for this one. I…well, I was seventeen and feeling like all teenagers did, like nothing could hurt me, so I…"

As he paused, Jessie reached out and touched his shoulder. "It's all right, Billy. You don't have to finish."

But he wanted to finish. "It's okay," he continued. "When one of the big trees came crashing down on the house, that was it. We knew we had to go. So we jumped in the truck and drove through the flames to get out. But we all inhaled a lot, Mom more than either of us. We got to a shelter, but by then she was in bad shape. She only lasted another day."

"I'm sorry, Guillermo," Maria said quietly as she stepped around the table to give him a hug.

Jessie reached over to squeeze his shoulder and added, "It was not your fault."

Even though he wasn't sure that was true, he appreciated how perceptive they were in trying to make him feel better.

Just then, the ship's bells rang twice to indicate that it was one in the afternoon. Lunch hour was over.

Billy finished his story. "So after the funeral, Beth joined the Forest Service. Makes sense, right? Fight fires." He dropped his potato on the pile. "And I turned eighteen and joined the Navy."

He looked at each of them and smiled a little. They both waited, graciously allowing Billy to be the one to finish the conversation. He finally said, "Well, I guess we have to do something other than peel potatoes this afternoon."

"Si, I suppose so," Jessie answered. She peeled off her apron and pulled on her Maria's Diner cap.

Maria smiled. "Gracias to you both, for the potatoes and for the company. I am glad we have each other. We will do well."

"Mi hermana," Jessie said with a smile as she patted her sister on the back. "Always the optimist."

Billy knew it was time to get back to work, but he was surprised at how reluctant he was to leave. He stood there, a bit awkwardly for a moment, as if he was going to say something else. When he didn't, Maria shoved a plate of cookies at him and said, "Okay, Guillermo, you earned that cookie."

CHAPTER 24

Approaching Hawaii

On the last evening before the ark reached the Hawaiian Islands, Miller, Susan Harris, and Billy sat on folding chairs on the fantail and played music while the sun settled down on the ocean. The clouds on the western horizon suggested the potential of land and created a glorious scene of red and purple hues.

In between songs, Billy looked around at his shipmates and thought about how comfortable they had become with one another. Owen and Sarah stood nearby with the Brooks family, talking while watching the kids chase Roscoe around the deck. Beth and Sanders were in a serious discussion with the doctor and Mi-Sung from the lab. Closer to the stern, the Rivera sisters and John Hunter and the Smith-Garveys were standing together and talking quietly.

"Hey, cowboy," Rodriguez called from where he had been talking with Grimaldi. "Got anything from somewhere other than Texas?"

Some people laughed. Miller's only response was a slight shake of his head, his face impassive under the cowboy hat. Billy silently admitted that they had been playing a lot of country songs, and most of them slow at that.

"How about one from Jersey?" Billy offered and started strumming the A and D chords to Springsteen's "Glory Days." Miller and Susan picked it up quickly. Indeed, after the second verse, the two of them did a back-and-forth on guitar and fiddle that would have made the E Street band proud. After the third verse, many of the people on the fantail sang the chorus. They finished to a nice round of applause and mock shouts of "Bruuuce" from some. Billy stood and gestured grandly at his partners, announcing in his best Springsteen voice, "Soozie Tyrell Harris on fiddle and Cowboy Miller on guitar." They both just shook their heads but also couldn't help but smile.

"Well, all right, then." Miller looked out at the people standing nearby as he asked, "You all want to sing?"

He started playing the Eagles's "Already Gone." It's an easy song with just three chords, so Susan and Billy jumped on it. They both chuckled when Miller changed the chorus from "I'm already gone" to "We're already gone." They took turns on the three verses, and Billy followed his up with a harmonica break that went on a bit too long, but nobody seemed to mind. As he finished up his solo, he looked out at the crowd and noticed Beth waving at him. She pointed to herself and mouthed the words "I'm already gone" as she walked toward the bow. Billy silently guessed where she was going.

The trio did the final chorus twice so everybody who wanted to sing could. Few didn't. When they finished and people were clapping, Miller waved his cowboy hat at Billy and said, "And that's Shakespeare Hill on harmonica."

The musicians paused, trying to think of what would be appropriate to play next. The sun in front of the ark was down now, but the reflections on the bottoms of the clouds were still magnificent. The sea continued to roll gently, only occasionally showing a whitecap on top of a small wave. Out of the corner of his eye, Billy noticed Green, with his White Sox cap on backward, stroll onto the fantail to join Grimaldi and Rodriguez by the port railing. Billy had guessed correctly. Green had been on duty on the bridge, and Beth went up to relieve him so he could enjoy some of the party. Billy thought proudly, no wonder her crew loved her.

Susan started sawing her violin like a fiddle, back and forth, again between three simple chords. Billy smiled as he recognized the song. Miller growled the first line, "I saw a Chinese werewolf with a menu in his hand…" And they were off and running on "Werewolves of London." When they hit the chorus, Billy had never heard so many people, in so many different voices, trying to howl.

People were giggling like kids and prodding one another to join in. And the real kids were trying hard to get Roscoe to show them all how to really howl.

It felt good to feel good again. Billy suppressed a premonition that the good feelings would be short-lived and kept playing.

CHAPTER 25

Oahu

The morning after the impromptu concert, nearly everybody on board other than those on duty stations gathered again in the same area of the ship. The ark was within ten miles of Oahu, on a direct course to Honolulu. Even this close to the island, they still had no radio communication, and the clouds over Oahu were tinged with an odd orange color that only added to their trepidation. As eager as the arkonauts were to see land, they slowed the ark and approached the island with caution.

Oliver stood with Captain Mitchell, John Hunter, and Mi-Sung Lee in front of the crew and outlined a plan. While stating that their preparations had anticipated the possibility of nuclear war, Oliver also acknowledged the fact that the crew might not be completely protected. More specifically, he was concerned about the levels of radiation in case Hawaii had been hit by nuclear attack. That was a real possibility, given the presence of military installations on the islands. The ark had gas masks for everybody on board, but only a dozen of the most high-tech hazmat suits.

"Nevertheless," Oliver continued, "we need to find out what we're dealing with, so here is our proposal. Rather than take the ark close to shore, where we might be affected by radiation, we'll use the launch. A small crew wearing hazmat suits will go in as close as possible to get some visuals and to assess the radiation."

A murmur went through the crowd.

"What about the *White Diamond*?" Griffiths, the supply chief, asked.

Oliver paused before answering. "We contacted them via semaphore. They declined to assist but will await our report."

Someone snorted derisively.

Oliver gestured at the others standing with him as he went on. "Chief Mate Hunter has volunteered to lead the trip. Dr. Lee has offered to accompany him to take the necessary radiation readings. At the first sign of increased levels of radiation, Mr. Hunter has orders to turn around. We don't want to take any risks." Oliver paused and then continued, "But we do need some volunteers to handle the boat."

Billy said, "You'll need a helmsman." Hunter nodded. It was an old habit for Billy, volunteering without much thought. The irony in this case was that was how he had ended up in the Navy and learned to be a helmsman.

In the following silence, Rodriguez muttered to Green, "Hazardous-duty pay for suckers."

Hunter responded, "You'll do, Rodriguez." As Rodriguez swore, Hunter went on, "We need two others."

Owen started to raise his hand, but before he could speak, Brooks said quietly, "I'll go." Janice glared at him, but before she could say anything, Oliver said, "Nobody who has children. Thank you anyway, Mr. Brooks." Owen also lowered his hand.

After letting that ominous warning digest for a few seconds, Jessie spoke up. "I don't have kids." She avoided Maria's glare.

Beth started to follow with "What the hell…" but was cut off by Carter, the veteran boiler tech in stained dungarees. "You might need an engineer."

Within an hour, the six "volunteers" were bouncing toward shore in the launch at a clip of twenty knots. Hunter stood next to Billy on the helm, both peering ahead silently. The other four sat quietly, deep in their own thoughts, on the benches in the hold.

Then Rodriquez, never one to stay quiet for long, tried to break the ice. He tapped Carter on the arm and said, "I'm from Mexico, amigo. Where you from?"

Since nobody had spoken for quite a while, the sound of the question caught their attention, and they all looked at Carter, who stared back at Rodriguez for several seconds before answering brusquely, "Why, you writing a book?"

Billy smothered a chuckle at the tone of the response, but he felt a little sorry for Rodriguez.

"Ah, forget it," Rodriguez muttered resignedly and was silent again.

A few quiet minutes later, they could see the faint outline of land underneath the orange clouds. "Land ho," Billy said quietly. The four in the back stood to peer ahead.

Hunter said, "Rivera and Rodriguez, I want you in your suits and out on the wings with those viewfinders. Tell us if you see junk that we should avoid."

The wings of the launch were small, but they were equipped with high-powered viewfinders that swiveled on stands, much like those on the bridge wings of the ark. Hunter continued, "Mi-Sung, get your suit on and get that radiation counter ready. Carter, stand by."

As they neared Oahu, the mountains, looming behind the beaches, came into focus. It was an iconic view, one that Billy remembered from movies such as *From Here to Eternity*. And Billy had always thought it looked inviting, if not seductive, but not so on this day.

"Crap at one o'clock," Rodriguez called out from the starboard wing. Billy swerved slightly to port to dodge it. It was mostly pieces of wood and plastic, including things that could foul the boat's screws.

Hunter spoke quietly. "Slow to ten knots, Shakespeare." He added to all of them, "Gas masks on tight." They all checked the straps on their masks. Billy suddenly realized that what they were not seeing were any gulls or seabirds that are often harbingers of approaching land.

Hunter looked at Mi-Sung and motioned her to go out on the starboard side, behind Rodriguez. "Talk to me, Mi-Sung."

She walked out, peered at her counter, and said quietly, "Good so far."

Jessie called back without looking away from her viewfinder, "Small boat off the port bow." The others could soon see the shape of what was left of a fishing vessel.

Billy brought the launch a bit to starboard to avoid it but also stayed close enough that they could see. As they passed it, nobody was visible on board, a small ghost ship floating on the Pacific., the breeze rippling through the tattered sails. Billy felt a little chill in his spine. They were now within a mile of shore.

Hunter said, "Back it to five knots, Hill." He followed with, "Mi-Sung?"

She answered quickly, "Still okay."

They continued for another minute, and then out of the corner of his eye, Billy noticed Jessie look down from the viewfinder for just a second as if to collect herself. Then she looked at the others before saying, "You'd better see this."

Rodriguez added from the starboard wing, "Here too."

Hunter stepped to the port wing quickly and stooped to peer through Jessie's viewfinder. Carter moved to starboard, where Rodriguez backed off to let him and Mi-Sung look. As Mi looked away, she shook her head slightly as if in disbelief and then stared back down at her instrument. Billy tried to not guess at what they were seeing and instead focused on the seas ahead.

Hunter, his expression revealing nothing, came back into the cabin and put a hand on the wheel, jerking his head toward port to tell Billy to go look. Billy relinquished the wheel and stepped to the wing. As Jessie moved to let him see, Billy thought he noticed tears in her eyes. Even that did not prepare him for what he saw. The shoreline at Waikiki was devastated. Where once had stood tall buildings and hotels were now just hollow shells of twisted metal and broken glass. Below them, the beach itself was strewn with dark objects that, once his eyes had focused, Billy realized were bodies. Some were in groups, as if they had huddled together, and others lay alone, in grotesque positions, some half in the surf, rocking back and forth in the waves.

Billy backed away from the viewfinder, stunned, and looked at Jessie in disbelief. Tears were now rolling down her cheeks. He fought back a lump in his throat as they reached for each other to hug briefly.

From the starboard side of the boat, Mi-Sung said quietly, "Mr. Hunter, we have readings." Billy hustled back to the wheel so Hunter could go to the starboard wing.

Hunter took one look at the radiation counter and said firmly, "All stop." Billy reluctantly slowed the launch. His instinct was to continue toward the beach, see if they could help anyone, as if he were a disaster tracker again, but conflicting thoughts were running through his head. Could they really help? Would it be a fool's errand?

On the bridge wing, Hunter looked at the radiation instrument one more time, looked back at Billy, and ordered, "Turn it around." And as if he knew what Billy was thinking, he stared to make sure the helmsman had heard him. He said brusquely, "Ten knots, Billy. Let's get out of here."

Billy spun the wheel, increased the speed, and they headed back out to sea. As they pulled away from Oahu, Hunter stood with Billy, looking ahead, while the others stayed on the wings for several minutes, casting glances back toward the island, as if hoping they would see something other than what they had.

Then Jessie, Rodriguez, Mi-Sung, and Carter all came in and moved slowly into the well behind the steering area. They stripped off the masks and the hazmat suits. Quietly, they all sat down on the benches, trying to digest what they had seen. Not surprisingly, nobody felt like talking.

"Kick it up to twenty," Hunter told Billy quietly.

They traveled in silence for quite a while, the only sounds being the motor and the launch bouncing over the waves.

"Texas." The voice from the hold broke the silence. Billy and Hunter both looked behind them at Jessie, Rodriguez, and Mi-Sung, who were all looking at Carter. The engineer paused and then, staring at Rodriguez, added, "I'm from Texas."

Rodriguez stared back at Carter for several seconds and then nodded before saying, "Figures." Jessie grinned as Carter just glared back at Rodriguez.

Then Mi-Sung said quietly, "South Korea."

And they all, even Carter, laughed just a little bit.

CHAPTER 26

Different Plans

After Oahu, Billy drove Oliver over to the *White Diamond* for a consultation. People on both ships had seen the devastation, albeit from farther away than had Billy and the others on the launch.

"Damn, Oliver, that was some ugly shit!" Henry bellowed. He, Helen, and Richard sat at the dining table in the stateroom with Oliver and Billy. There was no food this time, but there was an open bottle of bourbon on the table and some glasses.

"I know," Oliver said calmly. "We thought it would be bad, but William and the launch got in close enough to check the radiation readings—"

"Bad shit!" Henry interrupted. "Looked like a scene out of hell."

Helen looked at Billy intently. "How high were those readings, William?"

"High enough that we were glad to have hazmat suits," Billy answered. "We turned around as soon as we got a reading—"

Again, Henry interrupted. "We turned around too, boy, and saw enough before then." He took a drink and then added, "We got to get the hell out of here."

Oliver and Billy paused, unsure what that meant. After a moment, Oliver spoke. "And go where?"

"Well, back to the good ol' USA, brother. Of course."

Oliver shook his head. "Look, Henry, you saw those mushroom clouds. You know missiles surely hit at least the cities. And the radiation…"

"We don't live in a city, Oliver. Thank God! We're going back to the ranch." Henry smiled proudly. "And we'll be damned glad to see it."

Again, nobody spoke for a few seconds.

Then Helen said calmly, "We think you should turn the ark around and come with us." Her mouth formed a smile, but her dark eyes did not change.

"What?" Oliver seemed stunned. Billy realized this was going to be an intense conversation and reached for the bottle to pour himself a drink.

"I'm quite serious, Oliver," Helen said, belying the smile.

"Why?" Oliver asked.

This time Henry responded, trying to sound more reasonable than before. "We have a couple dozen people on board this beauty, Oliver. A few of them are my business associates, but a lot of the others are just deckhands." Billy glanced at Richard, who looked back with the same fake smile his mother was showing.

Henry went on. "If things have been disrupted back in the US of A, as you say they will be, or wherever we go, we'll need some people along with us to resettle and repopulate. We don't have all the skills on board that you do, and we'll need doctors, carpenters, and such."

Helen added, "In addition, of course, we would enjoy your company."

Henry, realizing he should have said that before, added, "That's right, of course. That goes without saying."

Billy knew his father could see bullshit when he heard it too, so he gave him credit for remaining calm as he said, "And what about the species?"

"The species?" Henry reacted quickly. "Well, hell yes, we'll find a place for them too. They're going to be worth big money someday."

Both Oliver and Billy reached for their glasses at the same time. After a drink, Oliver said succinctly, "That's not our plan."

Henry demanded, "Well, what is? You got to give up on Hawaii, brother."

Oliver tried to keep his tone matter-of-fact. "There are other islands. We're steering toward the Big Island to look. If that doesn't work, then—"

"Shit," Henry interrupted again. "Horseshit! You're gonna see the same crap on all these islands. And if there are any people there, they don't know how to rebuild."

Helen joined in. "Back home we have roads and buildings. Infrastructure. People. Civilized people. Law and order."

Billy found their attitude disturbing but tried to emulate his father's calm demeanor as he said, "There are other places to check. As you said once, Uncle Henry, it's a big, wide world." His imitation of his uncle's comment from the previous meeting came out harsher than Billy intended, so he added, "Maybe we should just go different ways."

Richard said angrily, "You should watch your tone, cousin."

Billy was ready to jump back at his cousin, but Oliver put a hand on his arm. His lifetime of negotiation and bargaining showed. He waited a moment to collect his thoughts and then spoke quietly.

"Here's my suggestion, Henry. We will steam toward the Big Island as planned. I encourage you to stay with us. You may like it. I worry about you going back to the mainland so soon after the nuclear blasts. Staying out here a little longer won't hurt, right?"

Henry took another drink, looked at Helen for a moment, and then back at Oliver before speaking. "Okay, brother, we'll try it, but as your son said, we may then go a different way."

CHAPTER 27

Trawler in the Fog

The attack came just before dawn. The morning was warm and humid, a hint of rain in the air, and a thin layer of fog lay on the ocean. Billy was on the sunrise shift with Second Officer Willis, Sanders, Rodriguez, and Green. The latter two were on the bridge wings, watching for debris or boats since the ark was near land. Just before six, Green called out, "Port bow, one thousand yards."

Willis, her broken arm in a sling, moved out onto the wing, carrying binoculars in her good hand. She peered through the fog in the direction Green had pointed the viewfinder. After focusing, she picked up the megaphone.

"Who goes there?" Willis called through the megaphone. "Identify yourself."

Nothing was visible for several seconds, but then a boat started to appear out of the fog. It was some sort of large fishing trawler, about a hundred feet long. It was moving toward the ark and closing fast.

"Identify yourself," Willis called out again but got no answer. She turned to look at Sanders, concern on her face. "Go to battle stations, Mr. Sanders." And then added, "And call Hunter and available hands to the arms locker."

When the trawler was two hundred yards away, Willis called out again but got no answer. As the trawler closed, Billy could almost make out the faces of the people on board. They looked to be mostly young men and women, a mix of Whites and native islanders.

Rodriguez came in off the starboard bridge wing and stood next to Billy. "Que pasa?" he asked quietly.

Before Billy could answer, the trawler swung to starboard to parallel the ark's port side and closed to within fifty yards. Billy could see the people on board gathering up ladders and long bamboo poles with hooks attached to the ends. They were apparently looking for the lowest part of the ark.

"They intend to board," Willis called out. She turned back from the wing and came back on the bridge. She put her good hand on the wheel. "I'll take the wheel, Mr. Hill. I need all of you on the port stern to repel boarders. I'm no help down there."

Rodriguez and Billy hurried out to join Sanders and Green on the port bridge wing. With Sanders in the lead, they hustled down the ladder to the main deck and began to run along the port side of the ark toward the stern. The deck was slick from the mist, and Billy almost fell once but grabbed the guardrail and kept running. He had a bad feeling in his stomach. The intruders were so quiet that Billy was sure they meant harm.

As the four of them approached the fantail, they could see one of the intruders climbing on board. Sanders ran straight to him, dodged a wild swing with a pole, picked the guy up, and threw him into the ocean. Other intruders placed a metal ladder to hook the lower railing on the deck of the ark. Green slid, as if going into a base, and caught one end of the hook. Billy followed his lead, slid, and caught the other end. They tried to lift it, but one man was already climbing up, so the ladder was heavier than they had expected. Rodriguez, having found a pole somewhere, reached over and pushed the man off the ladder. Green and Billy picked up the ladder and tossed it back down below. Then they spotted a second boat, just off the stern of the ark, smaller than the trawler, bobbing in the water, with a dozen people on board, looking for a way up.

With nobody there to stop them, the intruders quickly had a ladder up on the stern and were climbing up onto the deck, carrying bats, poles, and axes. And they were no longer quiet but now calling to one another and yelling wildly. Sanders hurried to them, knocked one down, and started wrestling with another, but he was outnumbered. Rodriguez ran that way with his pole. Green and Billy got up and moved to join the fray.

The action was a blur. One of the boarders came at Billy with a bat. Billy ducked, and the swing went right over his head. Billy used a move he had learned from high school wrestling and went for the attacker's legs. The move surprised the invader, enabling Billy to push him over the side of the ship. Just yards away, Green was wrestling with another guy on the deck. Suddenly, Green cried out "No!" as a knife went into his chest. As Green lay on his back, his assailant reached up to stab him again when Billy heard a shot from behind them. The shot took Green's assailant full in the chest, and he toppled over.

The shot stunned everyone for a second but was quickly followed by a rapid succession of bursts of gunfire. Hunter, Beth, Jessie, Miller, and Brooks were all moving toward the fantail, firing the AR-15 assault rifles that had been stored in the small arms locker. The attackers who had made it on board dropped like bowling pins. Beth ran to the port railing, near Green, and leaned over to fire on those trying to climb up from below. She had a look on her face that Billy had never seen before, calm but also furious. Brooks, familiar with assault rifles from his time in the Marines, went to the stern of the ship, where Sanders stood with blood pouring from a gash on his left shoulder, and leaned over the railing to spray bullets on the boat that had tied up there.

Then the firing stopped, only moments after it had begun. Smoke and the smell of gunpowder hung in the air. Billy moved immediately to Green, getting to him the same time as Jessie. Green's White Sox hat was crooked on his head, and his black T-shirt was covered in blood. Billy ripped off his own T-shirt and pushed down on the wound in Green's chest, trying to stop the bleeding. Dr. Smith-Garvey hurried over, picked up Green's arm to check for a pulse, and shook his head, saying simply, "Sorry." He moved over to help Rodriguez, who was down on his side, blood coming from a gash to his leg.

Billy, stunned, looked at Jessie and then around to try to understand what had happened. He could see a few swimmers making their way back to the fishing trawler that was already starting to pull away. Then he noticed that many in the ark crew, having heard the alarm, had gathered on the flight deck overlooking the fantail to look down at the carnage below. They were silent, obviously shocked. He glanced off to the starboard side and was surprised to see the *White Diamond* fairly close at hand, people on the bow watching with binoculars. They must have heard the gunfire.

Then Beth walked over from the railing, carrying a smoking AR-15. Jessie and Billy, both still kneeling over Green, looked up at her as she knelt and stared into Green's lifeless eyes, hoping in vain to see them move. The fight had lasted less than five minutes but a lifetime for one of their colleagues.

CHAPTER 28

Funeral at Sea

The fog of the early morning turned into a light rain as the crew of the ark gathered on the fantail and the flight deck. Green's fellow firefighters wrapped their friend in a flag, laid the body on a slab of wood, and stood at each of the four corners. They looked like they had been in a battle. Sanders, a large bandage on his arm, was wearing Green's White Sox hat. Rodriguez, his leg wrapped, was solemn as he looked past the body and out at the ocean. Miller's face was barely visible under his cowboy hat as he stared down at the flag-wrapped body. Beth's face was wet, the rain mixing with a few tears.

Oliver broke the silence gently and offered a few words. "We gather to bury one of our own. Most of us didn't know Mr. Green that well, but what we did know was good. He worked hard, he never complained, and he was certainly game for this endeavor. We will miss him."

Again, they were quiet. They could hear the waves breaking on the hull of the ark. Beth looked at her sister-in-law and asked, "Sarah, could you say a few words?"

Sarah looked back at Beth, nodded, and collected her thoughts before speaking. "I, too, did not know Mr. Green well, so I encourage others to say more if they would like. I will say this: according to a story in the Bible, when the people of Jerusalem were threatened, one answered the call by saying to the Lord, 'Here am I, send me.' Tyrone Green also heard a call that needed answering and said, 'Here am I.' God bless his soul."

Several people in the crowd said "Amen" quietly.

After a few moments, Sanders said simply, "He was a good kid."

Then Beth cleared her throat and spoke. "Just last week, Green told me thanks. I asked him, 'For what?' and he just smiled. I knew. He came from a tough world, but…" Her voice caught for a second, but she pushed on. "But he tried to make it better. You can't ask for much more than that." As she stopped, Sanders, standing on her side of the slab, reached over with his good arm and patted her softly on the back.

And then there was silence, except for the sounds of the rain hitting the steel deck and the waves. The entire crew waited until the four remaining members of Green's fire crew were ready to let him go.

Beth nodded to the other three, and all four bent to pick up the corners of the slab. Rodriguez said very quietly, "Adios, amigo," as they lifted it and slid the body into the sea.

CHAPTER 29

New Crew

After the service for Green, people milled about on the fantail in small groups, quietly talking. Small pools of water lingered on the decks from the rain, but the sun came out and began evaporating them and burning off the mist. Suddenly, they heard Brooks yell from the starboard bridge wing, "Boat off the starboard beam!" His voice was followed by Hannigan on the speaker system calling, "Mr. Hunter to the arms locker." Hunter swore, "Not again," as he moved to get the guns they had stored from the morning's battle, followed by Miller, Beth, Jessie, and Billy.

The rest of the crew moved to get a better look at the boat that was now heading toward their starboard side. It was a beat-up fishing boat, powered by a small motor in the back with a torn sail hanging loosely off the mast. As it closed, they could see a young man in a tattered white shirt standing and waving a dirty towel. A woman sat on the floor of the boat behind him, holding something in a blanket.

The deckhands came up from the arms locker, carrying the rifles. As they pointed them at the approaching boat, Hunter said firmly, "Hold." Their emotions were raw from the morning, and Billy, for one, wondered if things would go badly quickly.

Then the man in the fishing boat called out, "Help." He was thin and dark-skinned, perhaps an islander from nearby, and looked to be in his early twenties.

"Hold your distance!" Hunter yelled back. "What do you want?"

The man in the boat cut the motor, and the boat bobbed in the waves. "We need help," the man called again. "Our baby, she is sick." The woman in the boat shifted the blanket to reveal a young child.

An awkward silence followed. Billy wondered what that meant. Had she been affected by nuclear fallout? Was her illness something that they should avoid bringing on board? Was it just a trick to get closer? Or did they really need assistance? Hunter looked to Oliver, who stood nearby. Oliver looked back at Hunter, then back at the boat, and then at Dr. Smith-Garvey.

Oliver asked, "Doctor, can you check them?"

"Of course," Smith-Garvey said reassuringly. "Bring them around to the stern of the ship and we can check them for radiation levels. If they're okay, we'll take them to the clinic for any needed treatment. I'll get suited up." He moved to go down below.

Hunter motioned to the boat to move to the stern. Once there, the deckhands secured it and dropped a rope ladder. Dr. Smith-Garvey returned in a hazmat suit, climbed down, and checked the young family. Fortunately, there were no signs of radiation contamination, so the doctor then led the new arrivals back up the ladder onto the deck. Beth and Billy helped the doctor move the family down to the clinic.

Billy soon felt that they had made the right decision by picking these people up. The guy kept trying to express his appreciation in broken English, and the woman kept nodding gratefully. But the baby was the one who really got to Billy. At one point, she looked up at him with deep-brown eyes and smiled. Here was a little girl who had surely been through hell and was now being shuffled by strangers into a strange place, and yet she smiled. He was glad that they were on board. Beth and Billy left them with the doctor and came back out on deck to find a serious discussion taking place.

"It's clear to me…" Rodriguez was talking. He was seated in a deck chair, his wounded leg propped on a box. There were twenty or thirty people standing around on the flight deck. When neither Beth nor Billy said anything, Rodriguez continued, "Pretty damn clear to me that this area is enfermizo."

"If that means it ain't safe, I'm with you, T-Rod," Sanders said, the bandage around his arm red from blood. The two of them looked tired and angry.

"We don't know that, Mr. Sanders," Susan Harris responded. "If these people aren't contaminated, there may be other islands here that are not affected."

Irene Doyle, the cook, backed her up. "Right, there are plenty of islands nearby. Some of them might be safe."

"Then again," Rodriquez responded quickly, "they might not be."

"With all respect, Mr. Rodriguez," Jordan Smith-Garvey jumped in, "there are people on these islands who we might be able to help. I don't think we can just sail on."

"The hell we can't," Rodriguez answered.

Griffiths jumped in. "There is a concept in philosophy called lifeboat ethics. And it surely applies in this situation." He pulled off his glasses to wipe the ocean spray.

"Lifeboat what?" Sanders demanded.

"Lifeboat ethics," Griffiths answered, putting his glasses back on for effect. "A lifeboat can only take on so many survivors. If it's overloaded, it will swamp and all will be lost. So you can only help so many."

A pause followed while the others digested the thought. Then Rodriguez welcomed his new ally. "Si, I'm with the professor."

Dr. Smith-Garvey came up from below. He looked around at all of them before saying quietly, "You all should know. The young woman is four months pregnant. All of them should be fine with some nourishment."

Just then, a flock of birds flew overhead, moving south. Billy saw them and wondered about the direction. Flying now made some sense as it was late September and a season for migration, but then again, the Hawaiian Islands were north of them, so where would migratory birds be headed? As the birds disappeared, he noticed Oliver. He had been standing quietly, listening to the discussion, but he seemed to be following the birds as well. He looked down from the birds and caught Billy's gaze. The tiniest of smiles appeared on his lips, and he then gave Billy a quick wink before looking back at the rest of the group. He took a step forward and cleared his throat before talking.

"These are all valid opinions and worthy of more discussion and deliberation. For now, however, I think I know just where we should go to rest for a while and consider our options. I will put my thoughts in writing and make a formal recommendation to all of you." He looked around once more and then started walking toward the bridge.

The group watched Oliver walk away and realized that no other explanation was immediately forthcoming. Obviously, the discussion was over. As they started to split up, Billy looked after Oliver, who was mounting the ladder behind them. He glanced back at Billy, the little smile still on his lips, and nodded briefly.

CHAPTER 30

New Directions

Within an hour after the discussion on the deck, Oliver posted this directive on the bulletin board in the galley:

September 30, 2026

I have now instructed Captain Mitchell to set a course for Pitcairn Island in the South Pacific Ocean. I offer this plan as a recommendation, subject to your approval.

Pitcairn has numerous attributes as a port of refuge:

1. *The island is remote, thereby reducing the chances of conflict, such as what we saw in Hawaii.*
2. *Unlike Hawaii, there are no military installations on Pitcairn, and thus it was likely not targeted in the nuclear conflict.*
3. *Pitcairn is inhabited, but by less than 200 people. Hopefully, these people will welcome our arrival.*
4. *Pitcairn is mild and lush. Historically, it receives 70–80 inches of rain each year.*

5. *Pitcairn has enough elevation to avoid problems from sea level rise due to climate change.*
6. *Pitcairn is ecologically rich and has been recognized by the World Heritage Convention for impressive biodiversity. Some of you noticed birds flying south from Hawaii. They were going to use Pitcairn as a rest stop on their migrations.*
7. *One more, somewhat-ironic reason to use Pitcairn as a refuge is that we are not the first to do so. In 1789, mutineers from the HMS Bounty settled on Pitcairn in a dramatic attempt to escape the British naval authorities.*

Thank you.

—Oliver Hill

CHAPTER 31

Sunset

After the long day, Billy sat by himself on a gear locker on the starboard side of the ship and watched the ark bounce along on the moderate ocean waves. The sun hovered above the western horizon, oblivious to the tragic events of the preceding day.

His thoughts were grim. He barely knew Tyrone Green, and it was hard to digest that he was gone. Billy also thought about the people from the trawler that they had killed. They had given the arkonauts no choice, so Billy didn't feel guilty, but then again, he wondered, How much choice did those people have? Their world had been torn apart, and they were desperate. He took some solace in the fact that, on the same day they had killed some desperate people, they had also rescued others from a perilous situation. Finally, of course, in the broadest sense, if the situation was so desperate in Hawaii, what was the rest of the world like?

Just then, Jessie Rivera came walking up from the stern of the ship. She was moving slowly, her hands in the pockets of her shorts, perhaps lost in thoughts like those Billy had been having. Without the usual baseball cap, her dark hair hung down to her shoulders and blew in the gentle breeze. She spotted Billy on the gear locker and approached, her expression neither warm nor cold but rather one that suggested she understood why he was sitting there, with just the setting sun for company. She reached the locker and stood silently.

Billy looked in her dark eyes and saw some moisture there. He didn't know if it was from sea spray or tears, but he shifted on the locker and held out his arm to indicate a space for her. After a brief pause, she sat down. They both looked back out at the sea and the sun now halfway below the horizon. After a few seconds, Billy felt her hand patting his gently. He turned his hand over to grasp hers. They sat quietly until the sun was gone and darkness began to envelop the ark.

CHAPTER 32

A Welcome Visitor

Beth Hill was also deep in thought that evening. Her cabin-mates were quiet too. Susan Harris was sewing a patch on her jacket, and her daughter, Naomi, was reading a book. Irene was out. Beth sat and tried to meditate, but her brain kept thinking about losing Green. He had only been with the crew for a season, but Beth liked him, liked him enough to wonder if she had done the right thing by bringing him along. Then again, he wouldn't have lasted if he had stayed back in the States either. *Damn pirates,* she concluded. No wonder Sanders and Rodriguez were so tense when that other boat had shown up.

They heard a knock on the door. Beth looked up and said, "Come on in," as she guessed who it was before the door even opened. Sanders leaned in, his big frame filling the door. He was wearing Green's White Sox cap, and a white bandage on his arm showed under the T-shirt. He nodded at the other cabin-mates and then Beth before asking quietly, "You okay?"

Beth stared at him and shook her head back and forth slightly before answering, "No."

Sanders waited, unsure what to say. In that moment of silence, Susan looked at her daughter as she said, "Hey, Naomi, let's go see what movie is showing in the mess hall."

Naomi looked puzzled as she answered, "I've already seen it."

"I haven't," Susan answered and gestured at Beth and Sanders.

Naomi looked at her mom and then at Beth before answering simply, "Oh, right." She set her book on her bunk and stood. Sanders backed out of the doorframe to let them walk out.

"Thanks," he said quietly as they passed. He then looked back in at Beth.

"You?" Beth asked.

He shook his head slightly.

She shifted on her bunk and said quietly, "Come on, then."

He turned off the lights and settled in next to her.

CHAPTER 33

Betrayal

Billy and Oliver went over to the *White Diamond* the next day to inform Henry of their new plans. Later, as Billy had time to reflect, he realized that what happened should not have been that surprising. From the Cain and Abel story in the Bible to Cal and Aron in *East of Eden*, brothers have been perceived as capable of the most devious betrayals.

As soon as he and Oliver arrived in the yacht's stateroom, they realized something was strange. In addition to Henry, Helen, and Richard sitting at the dining table, Reese and another guy were standing at the end of the room. And they had pistols on their belts. Reese seemed uncomfortable, unlike the extroverted, friendly deckhand they had met before. The other guy, tall and thin with greasy black hair and restless eyes, looked quite comfortable. The smudged name badge on his work shirt read Wilkes.

"So, Oliver, we saw your shootout with the natives," Henry started before his brother could even sit down. "Still glad you visited the Big Island?"

Oliver was surprised at the tone. "No. But that could have happened anywhere."

"My point exactly," Henry pronounced. "It could, and it will, as long as you hang out around these damn islands. And then you take on more of them?" Henry had obviously seen the ark pick up the people in the small boat. "Just what the hell are you doing?"

Oliver answered immediately, "They needed help. You would have done the same."

Henry snorted derisively. "Like hell we would. We want nothing more to do with this place or any of these people." He pointed his finger at Oliver. "And you shouldn't either. So where are you going now?"

Oliver hesitated before answering, "Our plan is to go south, to Pitcairn Island, where it's unlikely there would have been any nuclear activity—"

Henry cut him off abruptly. "Pitcairn? Might as well be Shitcan Island." Helen smirked, and Richard giggled. Neither Oliver nor Billy realized at that time the potential cost of making their plans transparent.

"Let me tell you what we're gonna do," Henry continued. "We're going back to the US of A, just like I said we would."

Oliver responded, "I'm sorry to hear that, Henry, as I don't think it's a good idea. But—"

"Bullshit!" Henry bellowed, standing. At this, Reese and Wilkes pulled their pistols and pointed them menacingly at Oliver and Billy, who both instinctively backed up.

Henry went on. "Here's what's gonna happen. You two are going to follow these boys aft to show you your new quarters. Then Billy is going back over to the ark to tell your crew what's going on and to pick up some clothes for you. And then he's coming back here. And then the ark is going to follow us back to California."

Oliver started to ask, "Why do you want us—"

Again, Henry interrupted. "We want your company. And we want your cargo."

Then Helen added, "And we're looking out for you as well."

Billy started toward Henry, but Oliver reached out and stopped him. His voice carried an anger that Billy had not heard before. "You have no right—"

"No, brother," Henry answered. "You give us no choice."

"The hell you say," Oliver responded. "This is more than betrayal. This is theft. And kidnapping." He glared at Henry, and then Helen and Richard. The latter two turned their eyes away. "You're wrong. You're dead wrong."

Henry gestured to Reese and Wilkes, who moved forward with their guns. Reese said, as calmly as he could, "Let's go now," and gestured for Oliver and Billy to follow him. Wilkes moved around behind and prodded Billy in the back with the gun. Billy turned to respond, prompting a glare from Wilkes as he thrust his pistol in Billy's face.

Again, Oliver intervened. He put his hand on Billy's shoulder and said calmly, "Come on, son." They both continued to glare at Henry as they followed Reese out of the room with Wilkes trailing behind.

Reese led them down the main deck toward the stern. They paused at one small room with an open door, and Reese motioned for them to look inside. "This is where one of you will stay when the other is in the boat." The tiny room had a toilet and a sink and a small bed. Before they could even ask, "What boat?" Reese led them farther aft.

Tied off the stern was one of the two rowboats the *White Diamond* carried. It was about twenty feet long, partially covered with a roof in case occupants got stuck at sea.

Reese said, "We don't have a jail on board, so one of you will be in here at all times." He paused, obviously not proud with what he had to say next. "We'll tow it behind us. One of us will be here to shoot you or cut it loose if anybody tries anything."

Oliver and Billy were both silent, stunned.

Wilkes smirked as he said, "So don't try anything, old man." He moved toward Oliver to push him into the boat. Billy moved in between them.

Reese said quietly, "Back off, Wilkes," and put out his arm to stop his colleague. "I'm sorry, Mr. Hill, but you need to get in the boat, and I'll lower you down. Billy can relieve you when he gets back."

CHAPTER 34

Stars

The stars were the best thing about being in the lifeboat. On his second night in the makeshift prison, Billy lay on his back and looked up at the night sky. The stars were brighter and more numerous than a van Gogh painting. The lifeboat was obviously older than the yacht, but functional, with crude row benches along each side. On each row were cheap plastic cushions that provided minimal comfort for sitting or sleeping. A little roof covered the stern half of the boat, providing some relief from weather. Henry's people had removed the motor and the oars, leaving only a water container, an old blanket, and a beat-up pillow.

When Billy wasn't in the lifeboat, Oliver was. Their other prison cell was the small room on the yacht that did not have a view of the stars but did have a toilet. Plus, the stewards always brought in leftovers from meals so Oliver and Billy wouldn't starve. Whenever either was in that room, the deckhands would lock the door, so neither of them had seen any more of the yacht or met any of the other passengers besides the four deckhands that had been assigned to be the wardens. Oliver and Billy also barely saw each other, only when they were switching spaces.

Billy was trying to minimize the amount of time Oliver had to spend in the rowboat, exposed to the elements and not beneficial to his father's health. So Billy would limit his own time in the cabin to just a few hours a day to use the toilet, eat some food, and catch a nap. Then he would pound on the door until one of the wardens led him back to the rowboat to relieve Oliver. Oliver always objected, saying he could stay longer, but even the wardens knew it was better to have the older man in the cabin.

Billy, of course, preferred the nights to the days. Spending days in the bottom of a rowboat was as tedious as it sounds. On one of her shifts, Reichardt, one of the wardens, brought him a tattered copy of *Moby-Dick*, and that provided a diversion. The boat got quite hot in the afternoon, and the sun was relentless, so it was helpful to at least have the little roof. The nights were much cooler, so the blanket was essential. And being down by the water at night, he could sometimes hear odd noises, including fish swimming nearby. Billy could also look off to the starboard side and see the running lights of the ark as it steamed along in parallel. Henry's orders had been that the ark would always be in sight but never so close as to allow Oliver or Billy to communicate with their shipmates. When Billy lay down again, the lights of neither ship were visible, and other than the hum of the *Diamond*'s engines, it was almost peaceful. And he loved the stars.

Billy thought about what had transpired. On the day of the betrayal, while Oliver stewed in the lifeboat, Billy drove the launch over to the ark to explain Henry's plan and pick up some spare clothes. People on the ark were predictably angry.

"What about ramming them?" Rodriguez, on the helm, asked.

"They would just shoot him," Billy answered.

"We have arms. How about we pull alongside and...," Beth started.

"They always have a guard on Oliver," Billy answered. "And they're armed as well."

Mitchell was as calm as always. "We can't do anything now. But they will let their guard down at some point."

Billy and Beth went below, collected some clothes and toiletries for him and their father, and then met back up by the launch. When they got there, the deckhands were holding the launch for him and the Rivera sisters were waiting as well, Maria holding a small bag with some sandwiches. As always, word had traveled fast on a ship.

Maria handed Billy the bag as she said, "Don't forget, Guillermo, one is for your father." He smiled back.

Jessie gave him a quick hug, saying quietly, "Take care of yourself as well as your father, Billy."

Beth, still seething, swore, "We'll fix this soon, brother."

Then she and the other deckhands helped him load up and get underway again.

When Billy got back to the yacht, Reese and Wilkes were waiting on their quarterdeck. The latter, cigarette hanging from his mouth, looked at the bag of food and sneered, "Brought us something to eat, huh, boy?"

Billy snarled back, "Too good for you."

Reese stepped in again. "You just ate, Wilkes. Now, tie this thing up."

Reese then led Billy back down to the rowboat to relieve Oliver. And for the record, yes, he did give his father one of the sandwiches.

Two nights later, as he lay in the boat, looking at the stars, Billy heard voices from up on the deck where the rowboat was tied. He always heard the guards when they changed shifts. They did so every four hours. They all had their own personalities. Reichardt was quiet, of course, but courteous. Wilkes, on the other hand, was the opposite. He would greet Billy as he came on his shift with some taunt, and he always ended his shifts with a poor imitation of Arnold Schwarzenegger saying, "Hasta la vista, asshole." Billy guessed he thought he was being funny. Wilkes was followed by a Polish guy named Syszmanski, or Ski for short. Billy couldn't tell how much English Ski spoke. Instead, he would often sing. And as they were in Polish, Billy couldn't tell if they were sailing or drinking songs. And sadly, Ski wasn't as good a singer as he thought he was.

And then there was Reese. He and Billy had started with small talk, where they were from and stuff like that, but the conversations moved on from there. Reese was curious about the ark and what they were doing out here and why they didn't want to go back to the States. Billy found himself enjoying the conversations. This night was no different.

After Sysmanski left, Reese called down, "How you doing in there, Billy? Heard enough Polish music for a while?"

Billy smiled. "Enough for a lifetime." After a pause, he added, "Good stars tonight."

"Beautiful," Reese answered. After a minute, he added, "Glad it's not too rough out here for you and your dad." The seas had been calm, thankfully.

"Yeah, I would have to rely on my sea legs."

"Fleet sailor?" Reese asked.

"Light cruiser. Three years. You?"

"Sixteen years."

"Sixteen years? Damn, you might as well have done the twenty." The military had long offered retirement benefits for anybody who lasted twenty years on active duty.

Reese laughed briefly. "Hell, I'm no lifer." After a moment, he added, "I punched out an officer and got booted."

Billy laughed too. "He must have really pissed you off."

Reese paused before he answered. "He told me to do something that wasn't right. So I didn't do it." And he left it at that.

Billy settled back on the bench, unsure if he was going to get some sleep or resume the conversation. Reese waited patiently. A shooting star passed quickly through the Big Dipper.

CHAPTER 35

Sacrifices

On the third day that he and Oliver were hostages, after a quick lunch, Billy was escorted by Reichardt back down to the lifeboat. As they approached, he could hear his father and Reese stop talking. Reese looked at his watch and said, "You are way early." Reichardt gestured at Billy.

"Hey, this lifeboat isn't good for my dad, and it doesn't make any difference to you guys which one of us is in there."

Reese looked at Reichardt and then Oliver and Billy. "Ah, what the hell. Climb on in. Mr. Hill, you can climb out."

Oliver, in the bottom of the lifeboat, hesitated. "If it's all the same to you, Mr. Reese, I would like to stay and talk to my son a while."

Reese shook his head. "You know the rules, Mr. Hill. You two are supposed to be separated."

Oliver smiled. "What are we going to do? Overpower the two of you?"

"Besides," Billy added, recalling his conversation with Reese from the night before, "it's just a rule."

Reese looked at Reichardt, who held out her hands as if to say it was his call. "Okay," Reese said, "but only for a few minutes. And if anybody else comes down here, one of you gets out immediately."

"Fair enough," Oliver responded.

Billy settled on the bench opposite his father. Despite Billy's efforts to minimize his father's time in the lifeboat, Oliver's face was looking haggard from the cramped conditions and the lack of sleep. But his blue eyes remained bright.

"I know what you're doing, William," Oliver began, "and I appreciate your sacrifice."

Billy shrugged as he looked around inside the lifeboat. "No worries. It's not so bad out here."

"It's not so good either," Oliver answered. He glanced up at the guards who were standing on the deck above, leaned in to Billy, and lowered his voice. "I did want to tell you, son, that if you get a chance to get away, do not hesitate. You might find an occasion to cut this boat loose and—"

Billy stopped him. "When we go, we're going together, Dad."

Oliver smiled in appreciation. "I knew you would say that, William, but I want you to understand something. It's not just you that I worry about. The ark should not continue to follow us."

Billy shook his head. "The ark won't leave without you. You know that."

Oliver objected, his voice rising slightly. "I worry that if the lab is exposed to any radiation, all our work will have been in vain."

Billy pushed back. "I understand. But the people on the ark won't."

"They have to," Oliver said forcefully. "Let me ask you something: What do you think of when you hear the word *forest*?"

Billy answered quickly, "Trees. A group of trees."

Oliver smiled slightly. "That's what most people would say. What I used to say. Did you know that trees, even trees of different species, communicate with one another and cooperate to care for the entire forest?"

Billy nodded slightly. "I have heard stories like that."

Oliver shook his head briefly. "It's not just stories, William. In recent years, scientists have done formal experiments that show trees, especially mature trees, share resources such as water and use them to nurture younger or more vulnerable trees as well as plants, completely different species. A forest is not just a collection of trees, you see. It's an organism itself, a fantastic one with diversity and sharing."

The intensity of Oliver's eyes had increased along with the urgency in his voice. Billy glanced up at the deck, saw a shadow from Reese, and wondered if by now he, too, was listening.

Oliver paused and stared at Billy. "This is not just idle musings from an old man, William. It is a fundamentally different view of the world than the one that dominated my life. I always thought the world was one of competition, where we fought over whatever resources were out there. I behaved accordingly. Most people did. My brother still does. But don't you see? Nature is different, and we can learn from that. And we can benefit from that."

Oliver coughed briefly and then finished. "I can die. We all die someday. And my day is closer than most. But entire species should not. And if that's the sacrifice that I personally make, I'm at peace with it."

Billy was quiet as he tried to think of a possible response. But before he could say anything, Reese called down to them, "Better break it up, guys."

Oliver reached out and put his hand on Billy's arm as he stared into his son's eyes. Billy finally nodded to indicate that he understood. Then, with a satisfied smile, Oliver got up slowly and limped over to climb the ladder out of the lifeboat.

CHAPTER 36

Adrift

On the fourth day of the hostage situation, Reese had the morning shift. He relieved Syszmanski, which also meant relief for Billy from Polish singing. But this time was different. After Ski walked off, Reese looked around to make sure no one was in hearing distance.

Then he called down quietly, "You know Morse code, Billy?"

"At one time I did," Billy answered, puzzled.

"Well, brush up," he said, tossing down a large flashlight. "Open it." Inside with the batteries was a small piece of paper with Morse code signals, dashes and dots, for the letters.

"Okay," Billy said, unsure as to why.

"When it gets dark, call Hunter. Tell him, 'Watch Reese.'"

Before Billy could answer, he heard voices coming near. Reese started talking to Wilkes, who had wandered by. Billy started studying.

That night, while Syszmanski was back on watch, Billy started flashing the light in the direction of the ark. He flashed "Hunter" again and again. He wasn't worried about anybody on the yacht seeing the light as it was pointed away. But he did start to worry about using up the batteries. And he worried that a long response from the ark might tip off the guards.

Finally, he got a response. It was short, just three long dashes and then a long, short, long. They were the letters *O* and *K*.

"Finally," Billy muttered quietly. Then he sent, "Watch Reese."

Again, he got a quick *O* and *K*. Billy was sure the people on the ark had been watching and knew the shift rotation of the guards.

His anticipation for Reese coming on watch at midnight grew. Oliver was looking worse each time Billy saw him, and when he talked, he coughed. Billy, too, was feeling the effects of exposure, lack of sleep, and sheer boredom. Finally, Reese came on duty, relieved Syszmanski, looked down at Billy in the boat and then at the ark. He called down, "Time to go." He opened his jacket briefly and used his flashlight to illuminate himself that someone watching from the ark could see, and only if they were watching him closely.

Reese paced around for a bit, then sat on the bollock, and then paced some more as if he were restless. After a few minutes, Reichardt walked up. That was strange in that she wasn't due to come on watch until the sunrise shift, starting at four. Even stranger was the fact that Oliver was with her, a blanket wrapped around his shoulders. She handed a pack down to Billy and then helped Oliver climb down into the boat. Billy got his father settled onto one of the rows. Oliver appeared as confused as Billy, but they were both quiet. Then, Reichardt climbed down into the boat with them and simply held up a finger to her mouth to say to continue to stay quiet. She started untying the boat to the bollock. Billy moved to help her. Then Reese came down the ladder himself as the ropes came loose. Suddenly they were adrift. The lifeboat, no longer tethered to the mother ship, bounced in its wake. Water from the waves splashed over the gunwales and into the bottom of the boat. Within seconds, the name *White Diamond* on the stern of the yacht faded from sight.

Reese looked at Oliver and Billy and said, "Now we'll see if your man Hunter has been paying attention." He pulled a flare gun out of his belt, where it could have been seen by someone on the ark with a viewfinder or binoculars when he had opened his jacket, pointed it to starboard, and fired. When it exploded ten seconds or so later, it was well over the ark. It illuminated the ship but nothing around it, including the lifeboat half a mile away.

Reese gestured at Reichardt. "Linda's got the next watch. They won't notice we're gone for nearly eight hours." He and Reichardt both looked proud.

Oliver and Billy both smiled. "I'll be damned," Billy said involuntarily. He patted Reese on the back and repeated, "I'll be damned."

Reese laughed a little. "Yes, you will be, Billy, if your mates don't figure out what that flare meant."

They all laughed, but it was true. If people on the ark had not been paying attention or watching Reese, the lifeboat could be drifting out on a vast sea for a long time. Reichardt noticed Billy's grin disappear and opened one of the packs. She held up two more flares.

Oliver reached over and shook her hand and then Reese's. "You know, when mutinies happen, the mutineers usually take over the ship, not just a lifeboat." He smiled.

Reese nodded. "I know, Mr. Hill, but this was the best we could do."

Oliver answered, "I'm just glad to be free, regardless of the circumstances."

Billy echoed his father. "We really appreciate you two getting us out of that situation."

Reese laughed briefly. "Better save that until we find out where it got us."

They drifted for a while, all of them straining to hear a sound other than the lapping of waves on their boat. They were again surrounded by stars and the moon, just now rising on the eastern horizon. Then, somewhere out in the darkness they heard a long, low moaning sound. They all cocked their heads as it sounded again.

"Whale," Reese said calmly.

When he didn't continue, Billy asked, "By the way, what is your first name?"

"Michael," he answered. "My friends call me Mike."

"So, Mike and Linda," Billy said as he looked at both the yacht's former deckhands, "why help us?"

Reese paused for just a moment before answering. He looked at Oliver and said, "I heard what you said about forests, Mr. Hill. Not sure I believe all of it, but I would like to." He then looked at Billy. "And as I told you, Billy, I do what I'm paid, but not when it's not right." He gestured with his thumb at Reichardt. "Same with Linda."

The whale's moan was answered by another, and then seconds later by another.

CHAPTER 37

Rescue

"So, Mr. Hill," Reese said, "I guess Reichardt and I will be looking for work." For a rough-looking guy, Reese often smiled as he talked, in part because he was frequently saying something humorous.

"You're hired," Oliver said. "But call me Oliver."

Reese nodded. "Okay. I won't call you boss. That's Hunter, right?" Reese grinned.

Oliver nodded before answering. "He does take charge."

"I haven't seen a lot of Indians in my time at sea," Reese said. "How did he end up here?"

"It's a long story." Oliver started coughing.

Reichardt reached over with one of the water containers, and Oliver took a drink before saying, "Thank you. I would like to know how you ended up here, with my brother. Both of you."

The lifeboat continued to drift as Reese thought about his answer. They were keeping an eye out for the ark, confident it would not run them down in the dark.

Reese started, "Well, you know, you bounce around. Being a sailor ain't exactly a trade that leads to some nice job. Like I told Billy, I worked for Uncle Sam for a while, and then I was in Folsom for a stint."

Billy couldn't say he was surprised that Reese had been in prison.

Reese continued. "Then the Merchant Marine. That's where I met Reichardt. One day we saw this fancy yacht moored near our ship, so we walked over and started talking to people. Your brother offered us jobs. And the pay was a lot better than what we were getting for the shit work we were doing for the Marine." He paused again before continuing. "We didn't know he was an asshole. No offense."

Oliver shook his head. "None taken. He wasn't always."

Just then, something bumped the rowboat. In the darkness, it was hard to see anything, but Billy thought he saw a dorsal fin. "Damn," he said quietly. "Shark."

They all shifted to try to see in the water. The moon, up now, gave them a little light, but they couldn't make anything out more than ten feet from the boat.

Billy said quietly, "I hope they're coming and paying attention."

"Let's give them another hour," Reese answered.

An hour later, when they still had not seen the lights of any ship, they fired off another flare. For just a moment, the sky lit up like a starburst firework on the Fourth of July. Then it became dark again. Even inside the boat, they could barely see one another's faces as they grew silent, each of them surely thinking about the vastness in which they found themselves. It was intimidating. Billy thought about the stories he knew of people adrift on the ocean, like the men of the USS *Indianapolis* who spent days and nights at sea after their ship had been sunk by a submarine, and had some small sense of just how terrifying that must have been.

Finally, around three in the morning, Reichardt pointed back in the direction they had drifted. Sure enough, she had spotted a light. Reese and Billy both stood in the bottom of the boat and gripped the small roof, peering ahead. Slowly but surely, more lights came into view. And then they could see a searchlight sweeping the water ahead of the ship. They looked at one another and grinned.

They waited until the ark grew near and then fired off the final flare to show their exact position. Minutes later, the ark pulled alongside and the deckhands threw down ropes to pull the lifeboat next to the ship. Even in the darkness, Billy could see that the railing was lined with familiar faces as he climbed back on board, *Moby-Dick* stuck in one back pocket and the flashlight in the other.

Their shipmates greeted them like they had been gone for weeks. And to Billy, at least, it felt like they had. He savored the hugs from Jessie, Maria, and Beth. Even Sanders gave him a big bear hug. Then Billy introduced Reese and Reichardt, who both stood by awkwardly.

Hunter walked over to Reese.

"I'm glad you were paying attention, boss," Reese said, sticking out his hand.

Hunter gripped his hand and nodded. "Good plan," he said simply.

Billy noticed something new. All the men on the ark, at least the ones standing around near them, had grown or were in the process of growing beards. Even Owen had one started, and Billy had never seen one on his brother before.

"You guys look a little different," Billy commented.

Owen answered simply, "Solidarity, bro."

Billy instinctively reached up to rub the four days of growth on his face and smiled. What the heck, it was an old Navy tradition anyway that sailors grew beards while on a cruise, but he still appreciated the gesture.

Oliver, standing nearby with a blanket over his shoulders, looked at Captain Mitchell and said so all could hear, "Let's go get our launch back."

CHAPTER 38

Recovery

The ark caught up to the *White Diamond* just as the first streaks of dawn started to light the sky. Mitchell drove the ark up behind the yacht, within fifty yards. Maneuvers like this could be dangerous, but the seas were like glass this morning.

As the ark accelerated slightly and slid up alongside the yacht, Billy was standing down on the main deck with the other deckhands. Normally, he would be on the helm for something like this, but Miller had proven himself quite competent. And Billy would have other duties soon. Spread along the rail with him were the other deckhands, several cradling an AR-15. Oliver and Mitchell were above them on the port bridge wing, also quietly staring across the fifty yards of ocean while sipping on cups of coffee.

At a little after 0700, one of the stewards on the *White Diamond* emerged from the galley, carrying a pot of coffee, and started walking toward the fancy stateroom. The steward suddenly noticed the ark sailing alongside and then, looking closer, saw people, many of them armed, lined up and staring back at him. He dropped the coffeepot, hesitated, picked it up, and then hurried forward to the stateroom.

Reese, standing next to Billy, muttered quietly, "Showtime."

Sure enough, after just a few moments, Henry, in a bathrobe, and another man in an officer's uniform came out on their starboard bridge wing and looked in the direction of the ark. Henry had obviously just been roused from bed, his hair disheveled and his robe open down the chest. Billy could read lips as Henry said, "What in hell's name?" Then the *White Diamond* captain hurried back inside their bridge and sounded their general quarters alarm. He came back outside and handed a megaphone to Henry. Helen and Richard, also in bathrobes, followed.

Henry held the megaphone up to his mouth and tried to sound defiant. "We have guns too, Oliver."

Oliver didn't respond to Henry but instead leaned over the bridge wing and called down calmly, "Mr. Hunter."

Hunter leveled his AR-15 at the yacht and loosed a burst that shattered the morning stillness as well as the windows of the stateroom. Everybody on the *Diamond*'s bridge wing flattened on the deck. When they slowly stood again, some shaking off broken pieces of glass, they looked terrified.

Neither Oliver nor Henry said anything for nearly a full minute. People on board both ships came out on their respective decks to see what had caused so much noise. On the yacht, Helen said something to Henry, and then she and Richard retreated inside their bridge. Wilkes, Syszmanski, and another member of the yacht crew came out on deck, wearing pistols, but, seeing the AR-15s pointed their direction, made no move to pull them.

Henry, his face flush, called out, "Okay, Oliver, you've made your point. What do you want?"

Oliver paused and then responded in a calm voice that did not reveal the anger he was surely feeling. "We want three things. First, we want our launch back. Stop your vessel and Billy will bring your lifeboat back to you and get our launch and our gear." He paused to make sure that registered and to look at the other people who had come out on the yacht's deck.

"Second, anyone on board the *Diamond* that wants to sail with us is welcome. If you go back to the States with Henry, you are sailing with a man who is willing to kidnap his own brother to get what he wants. And you are sailing into danger. You can come back over in the launch with my son."

He coughed briefly and then finished. "Third, I saw a dozen cases of fine rum in your stateroom when you abducted us five days ago, Henry. You can send that over with the launch."

Several of the deckhands on the ark chuckled. Henry's face reddened as he scanned the faces of the people who were laughing at him. His scan stopped when he spotted Reese and Reichardt, and his eyes narrowed in anger as he figured out how his hostages had escaped.

He called out on the megaphone, "Reese, you and Reichardt, you'll never work in the shipping industry again."

Reese waited just a moment and then yelled back, "Hey, Mr. Hill…go fuck yourself!"

The ark's deckhands all broke up laughing. Billy thought back to the war cry from the Ukraine resistance during the Russian invasion, how it was appropriate then and now.

There wasn't anything else to say. The *Diamond*'s crew stopped the yacht. Billy, Reese, and Reichardt climbed back into the lifeboat with Hunter and Beth, both armed with AR-15s. They rowed over to the yacht, where Sysmanski and Wilkes lowered a ladder for the ark's hands to climb aboard. Billy, Reese, and Reichardt went below to collect their belongings as well as Oliver's, while Beth and Hunter moved to the launch. As they all returned to the launch, it was obvious that nobody else on the yacht was taking Oliver's offer to transfer to the ark. But the launch did get some new cargo. Syszmanski and two of the stewards brought the cases of rum down to the deck and began loading them. Billy noticed a little smile on Ski's face. He was, of course, humming a Polish drinking song.

One incident occurred just before the launch returned to the ark. As Billy moved to board the launch, Wilkes stood in front of him on the quarterdeck, a sneer on his face and the usual cigarette hanging from his lips. Billy, resigned to the fact that this guy still wanted a confrontation, shook his head slightly, then said in his own poor Schwarzenegger imitation, "Hasta la vista, asshole."

Wilkes's sneer turned angry, and he swung his right fist. Billy had never done well in the few fights he had been in, but he had learned how to react. So he ducked the swing and, using the fact that Wilkes was now off-balance, grabbed the extended arm and pulled. Wilkes tumbled over Billy and off the quarterdeck, down into the sea ten feet below. The splash seemed to stun everyone nearby for just a moment.

Then Billy heard laughing from his colleagues and clapping coming from the ark. Reese and Reichardt pulled him up off the deck. Beth and Hunter patted him on the back. Then all five of them climbed into the launch and pushed off as Syszmanski lowered a rope to fish Wilkes out of the ocean.

Billy and his shipmates returned the launch to the ark and removed the rum as well as their own belongings. They then watched the yacht sail east while the ark turned to the southwest. They hoped they would never see Uncle Henry, his family, or the yacht again.

CHAPTER 39

Crossing the Line

Three days after splitting from the *White Diamond*, the arkonauts marked a special occasion. The interim had allowed them to get back into a routine. Oliver was exhausted and still had his cough, but he benefitted from a lot of rest. Billy recovered quickly, in part because his colleagues made sure he didn't serve any night watches and thus could get some needed sleep. The crew got Reese and Reichardt involved in ship duties. Reese had been a machinist mate while in the Navy, and the ark had plenty of things that needed maintenance, so he went right to work. Reichardt was a capable deckhand, so she worked into that rotation.

On the day of the special occasion, at the end of the lunch hour, Captain Mitchell used the ship's speaker to call for the entire crew to report to the main deck. Upon arrival, they found a long table on which sat several large pitchers and cups from the galley. Captain Mitchell and Engineman Carter stood at one end of the table, both in costume. Mitchell wore an artificial long white beard and a captain's broad-brimmed hat turned sideways. He held a pitchfork upside down to look like a trident. Carter wore the traditional white Dixie cup that Navy sailors had used for centuries, and a black eye patch. He also carried a makeshift cat-o'-nine-tails, three ropes tied together each with several knots. Reese stood at the front of the table, a red bandanna wrapped around his head and a black vest with no shirt on underneath so that the entire array of tattoos on his arms was visible.

"Avast, pollywogs," Mitchell announced as the crew began arriving. "Line up for your rations."

"You 'eard King Neptune. Get in line, you limeys," Reese snarled as he lined people up at the head of the tail.

Billy and Jessie and Maria had walked up from the galley together and were at the front of the line. As Jessie and Maria looked puzzled, Billy started to explain to them that *limey* was an old nautical term for seafarers who consumed lime juice to avoid scurvy.

"Si, but what are they doing now, Guillermo?" Maria asked.

Billy suddenly realized the answer. "Of course. We just crossed the equator. Sailors have always marked that with some initiation."

Jessie looked troubled. "Initiation. Like what?"

Billy smiled as he teased, "Oh, could be anything, like dunking the uninitiated from the yardarms."

When Jessie and Maria both frowned, Billy chuckled and suggested other possibilities, like keelhauling.

Reese interrupted him. "You find this funny, Mr. Hill? Nobody crosses the equator on this ship until you have a taste of King Neptune's grog." He gestured back to the cases of rum they had pilfered from the *White Diamond*. Several bottles had already been opened and placed on the table.

"Aye," Carter said, relishing his part as he waved his prop in the air. "Rum or a taste of the cat-o'-nine-tails."

By this point, nearly all the crew had gathered, with curious smiles on their faces. They began to line up behind Billy and the Rivera sisters.

Mitchell bellowed, "You'll have your chance, Mr. Carter, but we want to be fair. Are there any other shellbacks out there?" He waited and then continued, "Ms. Reichardt is also a shellback and took the helm so that you other swabbies can all be initiated."

Nobody stepped forward. Apparently, the captain, the old boiler tech, and the two Merchant Marine sailors were the only ones on board who had ever sailed over the equator before this day.

"All right, then," the captain said. "Let us begin."

James Brooks interrupted. "What about the kids?" Jamal and Jonah were standing next to him and Janice. Jonah looked mystified, if not terrified, by the whole scene.

"Hold your tongue, knave, or you'll get a taste of the cat," Carter snarled, raising his ropes. He looked like he meant it.

"Easy, Mr. Carter," Neptune intervened. "It's a fair question. We've prepared a special mixture of the grog for the young pollywogs." He winked at Brooks, who started to smile but hid it from Jonah.

"Ready the grog, Mr. Carter," Neptune ordered. "And start moving them along, Mr. Reese."

"Aye, sir," came Carter's answer as he poured some drink into the cups.

Reese, too, was enthusiastic. "Step right up, laddie." He pushed Billy slightly in the back.

With nobody else looking too eager, Billy stepped forward and took a substantial drink. He almost gagged. Traditionally, grog was three parts water and one part rum. Carter's grog was basically just rum, with a tiny bit of water. Carter shot Billy a wicked, semitoothless smile.

"That'll do, Shakespeare. Move along," Carter said. Billy handed the cup to Jessie behind him, who took a swallow and then shook her head as if trying to make the taste go away.

"Aye, wench." Carter smiled again, savoring his role. "We need strong lasses in this crew."

Jessie passed the cup to her sister behind her. Maria smiled and took a drink, coughing a little after she swallowed. Carter and Reese both grinned like maniacs.

After drinking, Billy and the sisters moved to the other end of the table, where they stood behind Neptune to welcome their fellow shellbacks. Soon the line was moving along, with individuals showing their personalities. Oliver acted as if it were a wine tasting, holding the cup beneath his nose to get the aroma and then swishing the grog around inside his mouth. After swallowing, he nodded approvingly and said something about "a nice, woodsy taste." Oliver's granddaughter, Annie, grimaced as if the grog was the worst thing she had ever tasted, even though the "special mix" for the young pollywogs was nothing more than colored water. Owen, long a teetotaler, showed almost the same expression as his daughter when he got his taste of the real grog. Sarah and Beth looked at each other like kids about to jump into a pool at the same time and then drank simultaneously. Doc Harrison and Jordan Smith-Garvey each held up a cup and poured into the other's mouth to drink. Sanders took a full drink and smacked Carter on the back to show his approval. Miller also took a full drink, pushed back his cowboy hat, and exclaimed, "Damn, that's good."

Not surprisingly, the funniest response was from Rodriguez, who was in line behind Miller. Like his colleagues, he took a long drink and then, beaming at Carter, pronounced, "Bueno, amigo." But unlike the others and rather than coming over and joining those who had been through the ritual, he slipped back around to the end of the line to go through again. When he got back up to the table a second time, the other deckhands were all watching. Reese and Carter both acted like they didn't notice Rodriguez coming through the line for a repeat but then each grabbed an arm and wouldn't let him drink.

"What should we do with this one, King Neptune?" Reese growled. "He's trying to get an extra ration of grog."

"Aye, so he is, Mr. Reese," Neptune answered. "What say you, Mr. Carter?"

Carter leered at Rodriguez. "I say we give him the cat." He started to loosen his whip.

Hunter, standing nearby, said loudly, "Flog him." He looked ready to do it himself.

When Rodriguez looked to his colleagues for sympathy, Sanders said simply, "Cheaters get what they deserve."

"Works for me," Miller said, his face completely unsympathetic.

"Cat with nine tails," called Jonah Brooks.

People laughed at his pronunciation and then started chanting, "Cat! Cat! Cat…"

Rodriguez played his part. While Carter and Reese continued to hold him, he acted like he was devastated that his mates were turning on him and then looked at Beth as if she would help him out.

Beth teased, "And after the flogging, how about we make him walk the plank?"

That became the next rallying cry. People chanted, "Plank! Plank…"

Finally, Neptune relented. "My decision is this: Mr. Rodriguez, you will pour grog for everyone else who wants another portion before you can have your own."

The crew applauded the decision and stepped back up to the table, where Rodriguez began filling cups again. The ceremony was complete. The arkonauts stood around, having their drinks and congratulating one another on becoming shellbacks. They had crossed the equator into the southern hemisphere.

CHAPTER 40

Fundamental Choices

In the evening after the equator ceremony, many in the crew relaxed out on the main deck. The setting sun illuminated the sky with a dark-orange hue, and a mild breeze felt refreshing after the heat of the day.

Owen was talking to Sarah and Annie about the ship. "All the systems are good. The solar panels are great. The engines run like clocks. The desal [desalination] plant is working like a charm." Owen smiled proudly before continuing. "And when we get to Pitcairn, we can do full checks on all of them."

Annie looked up at her father before asking, "How long will we be in Pitcan, Daddy?"

Owen looked down at her. "That's Pitcairn, honey. And we don't know how long. Some people live there, and we don't know if they'll welcome us or not."

"Will Aunt Beth and Uncle Billy fight those people also?

Owen answered, "Let's hope not."

Annie persisted, "Why do people fight?"

Neither parent responded for a minute. Annie waited for a response. Roscoe, too, looked up as if he also wanted an answer.

Sarah knelt to look at her daughter before responding. "Sometimes bad events happen, sweetie, and people lose things they had and they feel desperate. Or they want other people's things and they try to take them, like the people on the trawler."

"And the people on the yacht," Owen added.

Annie wasn't satisfied. "But we killed the people on the other boat. So why didn't we give them those things instead of killing them?"

Owen answered brusquely. "They didn't ask us, so we didn't have a choice." He paused as he regretted his tone. Nobody said anything for thirty seconds as the waves from the choppy seas slapped against the hull.

Sarah continued, "Those people were trying to take our things and hurt us. Your aunt and uncle and the others were just defending us."

Annie looked resignedly back out at the ocean. "There should be more stuff so everybody has enough."

Sarah kept trying. "Right, but sometimes there are just too many people that want the amount of stuff that's available. What people need to do then is either increase the stuff, reduce the number of people, or discuss how to divide what they have. But the people on the trawler and the yacht did not even try to talk to us."

Annie said, "Guess we showed them, didn't we?"

Sarah continued, "That's why we hope the people on Pitcairn are willing to talk and share."

Annie answered, "They'd better be, or we'll make them."

Sarah sighed. "Well, I like to think that most people will do the right thing. But even some philosophers say that humans will always resort to fighting."

Both Sarah and Annie looked at Owen, as if expecting his input. Owen shrugged and then noticed his brother and Jessie approaching. "Hey, I'm just the engineer…let's ask your uncle Billy. He reads all kinds of stuff."

"Ask him what?" Billy said with a smile as he walked up. Jessie bent down to say hello to Annie and scratch Roscoe's back.

Annie smiled shyly. "Hi, Jessie."

Billy bent down as well. "Did you have a question for me, Annie?"

Annie looked puzzled and said, "I forgot."

Owen followed up. "You're getting off easy, brother. It was about philosophers."

Billy stood to answer. "Which?"

Sarah answered, "Ones who say the world is a violent place. Like Hobbes."

Billy nodded in assent. "Yes. He said that if you left people in nature, they would turn on one another and life would be 'nasty, brutish, and short.' Grim stuff."

Sarah agreed. "Yes, it is. I did a sermon once that discussed how philosophers compare Hobbes to Rousseau. As grim as Hobbes was, Rousseau said that people in nature would be noble savages."

Billy nodded. "Right. And that argument was why so many of us in school had to read that book *The Lord of the Flies*."

"Lord of what?" Owen asked.

Billy answered, "Yeah, it's about a bunch of kids on an island who become savages and turn on one another."

Sarah, relishing the conversation, added, "Yes, but there was a recent book about a group of kids who got isolated on an island for over four years and did quite well. I used it in the sermon. Real life was more optimistic than the fictional version."

"I love it," Jessie said, always relishing new knowledge.

Owen started to ask his daughter if she understood, but she was playing in a puddle on the deck. So instead he turned to Billy again. "What do you think, Bill?"

"Well…" Billy paused. "I guess I think there's both kinds…"

Owen interrupted as he thought out loud. "Like Dad is Rousseau and Uncle Henry is Hobbes?"

Billy liked the comparison. And he liked that Owen was engaging him, even if it often sounded like a challenge when he did. Billy felt like Owen had been warmer toward him since the *White Diamond* incident and guessed that his brother appreciated what Billy had done for their father while they were hostages. He responded, "Yeah, that sounds about right."

Owen still wasn't satisfied. "Then again, here we are after a nuclear war. Seems there are a lot of Hobbesians out there…or were."

Billy remembered how his brother could be like a dog with a bone when he got ahold of a serious subject in a conversation. As he thought about whether he agreed with the latest assertion or not,

Jessie helped him out. "That's true, Owen, but then we are still here too, right? And we are still trying to do good."

Sarah nodded. "That's right, Jessie. Or at least that's what I want to think."

Jessie looked at Sarah. "I'm sure that was a great sermon, Sarah. I've been wanting to tell you that I appreciated your comments at both the services we have had."

Sarah smiled. "Thank you, Jessie."

"And I wanted to ask you something about your eulogies, Sarah," Billy started and then thought for a moment. "Both were from the book of Isaiah, right?"

Sarah's smile widened. "Good for you, Billy. I thought you might catch that."

Jessie looked at each of them, seeing their interaction on biblical references for the first time. "So you know the Bible too, Billy?"

Billy blushed a little. "Nah, not so much. I heard that line 'Here am I' in a movie."

Owen chuckled. "That I believe."

Jessie, too, smiled. "You do remember those movie lines, don't you?"

Sarah reached out to pat Billy on the arm. "That's all right, Billy. However you learn things is good with me."

Billy nodded appreciatively. "Thanks, sis. And don't get me wrong. They were good comments, but I hope you don't have to refer to Isaiah's doom and gloom again too soon."

"You and I both," Sarah answered. "I would rather use him to talk about turning swords…"

"Into plowshares." Billy finished the thought, drawing a mock round of applause from his sister-in-law. They all stared at him until Billy went on. "That was in another movie."

Sarah and Jessie laughed.

After a moment, Owen brought them back to the immediate moment. "And speaking of movies, we're heading to the mess hall to see what's on tonight. Want to join us?"

Billy and Jessie looked at each other, and then Billy answered, "Thanks. Maybe in a bit. We're going to keep walking for a while."

CHAPTER 41

Esqueletos

Billy and Jessie took another lap around the deck and then stopped to sit on the starboard gear locker again.

Billy said, "I was hoping we would end up here."

She answered immediately, "Me too."

He felt a little rush of excitement inside, realizing how much he appreciated that she wanted to be with him.

"How was your afternoon?" he asked. "After the ceremony, that is?"

"Quiet. I saw you sleeping out on the quarterdeck."

Billy nodded. "Rum does it to me every time." He smiled to make sure she knew he was kidding.

"You looked very relaxed."

He chuckled a little. "Oh, I'm a good sleeper. Anytime, anywhere, as the saying goes."

"You must have a clear conscience."

He didn't know if she was prying or not, so he hesitated.

She pushed on. "No esqueletos? You know, skeletons?"

He smiled. He loved how the Spanish rolled off her tongue while the English had an accent. "Well, I have a couple. Then again, who doesn't?"

She looked puzzled. "What does that mean?"

He thought for a moment and realized she wanted a serious conversation, not some clever banter. He also realized that he wanted her to like him, so he eagerly tried to push some positives.

"I've made plenty of mistakes, some big ones, but I don't cheat. I don't steal. And I don't lie."

"I like that." She paused. "But it doesn't explain the skeletons."

He hesitated again. He remembered something he had realized before, that she was one of those unselfish people that gets you talking about yourself before you have a chance to ask about them. She looked at him for nearly half a minute and then, to her credit, realized he was struggling to answer. She smiled. "My sister says I sometimes ask too many questions."

He shrugged and smiled in return. "No, the questions are good. I'm just not good with the answers."

She nodded briefly before asking another one. "You didn't really intend to be here, did you, Billy?"

He tried to dodge the obvious implication. "Well, I figured it would be good to see the family, so…"

"You know what I mean," she persisted. "You were leaving the ark and then ended up out here with no way to go back. And then you were…on the *White Diamond* and on your way back to California, and now here you are again."

She was looking at Billy like she was seeing right through him. "Yeah," he answered. "I've been thinking about that."

She continued to look at him. "So?"

He nodded. "Okay. I told you that for the last few years I've been moving around, helping after disasters." He paused and then pushed past the censor that was checking his willingness to come clean. "I didn't do that kind of work because I'm a saint. I always liked the changes. I like moving on from one thing to another. And I'm just not good at staying with something. Anything."

She waited a moment to see if he was going on, and when he didn't, she asked the obvious question. "Why?"

"Changing all the time makes me feel like I'm not letting things catch up to me." He hesitated for a moment and then added, "I sometimes say that eternity is somewhere out there, just over the next horizon."

Jessie wasn't impressed with his pop philosophy. "Well, the only horizon I see is right here, Billy," she said quickly. "And you're committed to this now."

"I was thinking about that when I was on that lifeboat. Just sitting out there at night and staring up at the stars." He hesitated.

She waited, so he went on. "It seems like often decisions are made for us by things that happen. You know, stuff happens and it affects you. Stuff happened and I ended up on this ark. And then stuff happened and I ended up on that yacht. And you know…" He realized he was babbling a little, still forming his own thoughts even as he spoke, but he kept going. "I told you about my friend Washington in New Orleans?"

She nodded.

"When he was dying, he gave me some advice. He said, when you find something you like, you dig in and hold on to it. You embrace it."

He hesitated again, and she continued to look at him, silently demanding more.

He asked, "You know the difference between bad times and good times? The best thing about bad times is that you don't mind that time is moving so that they will be over. Like that pandemic, I couldn't wait for 2020 and 2021 to end. But good times? The worst thing about good times is that you hate to see time moving, so you try to grab onto them when you can. But in both cases, time just keeps moving on."

She still didn't say anything, determined to make him finish his thought. The phrase "Give a man enough rope and…" popped into Billy's head, but he ignored it.

He went on. "In other words, I get restless when I think about time passing."

Jessie said quickly, "You can't outrun time, Billy."

He nodded. He appreciated again just how perceptive she was and that she was giving him an honest reaction. "You're right. And I'm here now, and I'm committed to this, at least at this point. I like my family. They're good people. I missed them when I was on that damn yacht. And funny, I felt closer to my dad when we were both over there than I have in years, and yet we barely talked to each other."

She interjected, "You did a good thing for your father on that yacht, taking his shifts in the boat. Reese told us."

Billy started to say, "Well, Reese—"

She interrupted again, "He likes you. So does Reichardt. They would not have helped you otherwise."

"Good." Billy found himself wanting to finish his thoughts. "I like what we're doing on this ark. It's nice to think about helping some things before they get destroyed for a change. And I…" He paused and looked directly into her eyes. "I like some of the other people that are here too."

She smiled just a little and couldn't resist teasing him. "Is that what I am, Billy? Some of the other people?"

Billy squirmed a bit. He knew that he had never been able to hide his feelings when he wanted someone to like him. He also realized that she knew it, and yet he liked that she did. He realized that meant he was starting to trust her.

He went on. "Give me a break. I'm trying to figure this out." He paused, but she waited, not letting him off the hook. "Let me put it this way: I liked that hug you gave me the other day when I was going over to the yacht."

Her smile widened, but she didn't say anything, so he kept going. "It helped me as I lay there in that rowboat, thinking."

The sun sat on the horizon, like a big orange ball that was starting to leak and sink in the water. Billy realized that the conversation had opened him up like a book and that it had been focused way too much on himself. He looked for an out.

"So yeah, I'm here, and I'm okay with that. What about you, Jessie? Why are you here?"

She thought for a moment before answering. "I, too, like how we are trying to save the plants and the animals."

As she paused, Billy joked, "Yeah, I suppose now there are millions of esqueletos out there." He realized it was a pretty weak joke, but it did let him get the conversation back to where it started. He used the segue. "So you have esqueletos of your own?"

She frowned a little at his poor Spanish and then looked toward the ocean. She soon seemed deep in thought. Billy figured that like a lot of unselfish people, she was less comfortable talking about herself than about others. While she was thinking, a breeze from the ocean blew some of her hair across her face and covered her eyes. She pushed it away and looked back at him.

"Yes, I do," she finally answered. "But none that keep me awake at night."

When she didn't go on, Billy pushed a little more. "Come on, Jessie, you spent a lot more time thinking about that answer than giving it."

She studied him closely before answering. "Okay, Billy, but you and Maria are the only ones on board who will know this story. I don't quickly trust most people." He appreciated that she was starting to trust him.

"My full name is Jessica Sierra Rivera."

"It's a pretty name."

"Gracias. Maria's full name is Mariposa Rivera. No wonder she prefers Maria, si?" She paused. "You know, Sierra and Mariposa are in a certain part of California, so you can probably guess my little brother's name."

What was left of the sun hid behind a little cloud on the horizon as he thought before answering, "I'm guessing Yosemite…"

"Bueno. Yosemite Rivera. He always went by Yosi, or even Jose when other kids teased him."

She went on. "My parents were migrant farmworkers in that area. They worked and worked and finally saved enough money to buy a little house in the town of Mariposa, just outside of Yosemite. They loved that place. They had nothing else, but that was okay because they loved being there. So when we kids came along, they wanted to…how do you say?"

"Commemorate?"

"Good. Yes, commemorate, so they gave us those names." The last part of the sun popped out again and hit them both in the face. The western sky was now a beautiful shade of red.

"When the climate changed, so did their work. The drought went on for year after year and destroyed many farms and many jobs. The years when it did rain, it rained hard and flooded everything. Too little or too much. One of the books I read in school was *The Grapes of Wrath*. Do you know that book?"

"Of course. One of my favorites," Billy answered.

"Ah, si, your mother." He was impressed that she remembered his comment about his mother encouraging him to read. "That book could have been about us. My parents had to travel farther and farther away for work. Usually, my dad would go and my mother stayed, but sometimes we would all go. It just wore them out. One night, after a full day of work, we were driving back to Mariposa when my father fell asleep and drove off the road. We hit a tree. It killed them both on the spot."

Billy heard a catch in her voice, and he put his hand on her shoulder. "I'm sorry."

She continued, "It was many years ago. Maria was only fifteen, but she was the eldest. She went to work and tried to keep us in school. Then she met a man who said he would take care of us, so we moved in with him. He was a decent man most of the time, but when he drank too much tequila, he would—"

Billy suddenly had a bad feeling about where this story was going, so he interrupted. "You don't have to tell me this if you don't want…"

"No, I will finish. One day when I was fourteen, I found a gun in his truck. I took it and hid it. The next time he started to hit Maria, I pulled it out and told him to stop. He was furious. He came at me. And I killed him."

She lowered her head and took a deep breath. Billy patted her gently on the back and looked out at the sun now settling into the ocean. "They put me in a facility for two years."

Billy suddenly remembered her reaction to his joke about a sailor being in jail with a chance of drowning by asking him if he thought the ship was like jail. She really knew.

Jessie continued. "Then Maria turned twenty-one and took custody of me. That was almost twenty years ago." She looked full at

Billy. "She and I are five years apart in age, but we are very close. So when she asked me to come along, here I am."

"I understand," Billy answered quietly and then added, "I'm glad you are."

Neither of them said anything for minutes. The colors in the western sky turned brilliant shades of pink and dark blue and then started to fade to darkness.

He wondered if it was too soon to make a clever remark but then figured that if nothing else, it might make her feel better. "So you do have an esqueleto in your past. Literally."

He was rewarded with a little smile. "Si, but as I said, I do not lose sleep over it."

CHAPTER 42

Leadership

In the week following the equator crossing, the arkonauts resumed a routine of working, standing watches, and relaxing. For the deckhands who weren't on watch in the evenings, relaxing often meant a poker game. Beth Hill didn't always play, but she did enjoy the camaraderie, a nice name for a lot of trash talk.

This evening, Rodriguez was giving Miller a hard time because the Canadian couldn't seem to win a hand. Finally, Sanders interrupted. "Why don't you just shut up and deal, T-Rod?"

Miller let Sanders know he appreciated the support by making the "Mooooose" sound.

"Easy, big guy," Rodriguez answered. "I'm just making sure Cowboy knows I've got his next paycheck." He did have a pile of chips in front of him.

"As if," Miller said simply, always a man of few words. Obviously, none of them got paychecks, so talk was cheap.

Jessie chimed in, her eyes barely visible under her cap. "If that's all it takes to get you to shut up, Tomas, you can have my paycheck too."

Beth and Sanders both laughed.

"I'm starting on you next, senorita," Rodriguez answered as he shuffled the cards. "In fact, senoritas are wild in this hand. Ante up or shut up."

The one other person in the room was Hiluka, the islander they had rescued from the small boat. Captain Mitchell had assigned him to the deck crew to replace Green. For the moment, Hiluka, who they were already calling Luke, just watched, and Beth was trying to figure out how to get him involved.

Then Hunter walked into the compartment. Beth didn't know if he had heard T-Rod's trash talk or if he noticed the pile of chips in front of him or if it was just habit, but his first comment was predictable. "I need one volunteer…that's you, Rodriguez."

"Maldecir, Chief," Rodriguez responded instantly. "I'm on a roll."

"I don't give a—" Hunter started to say before Beth interjected.

"He really is on a roll, Hunter. I'll go."

Rodriguez looked up at Beth as he said, "Gracias, Jefe, gracias."

Hunter didn't respond at first but stood watching the hand play out. Jessie, with two jacks and a queen (or a senorita as Rodriguez called them), took the pot and winked at Hunter as if to say thanks for interrupting T-Rod's winning streak.

"Some roll," Hunter said with a smirk.

Beth stood and gestured for Hiluka to take her spot. She pointed at her small pile of chips. "That's about ten dollars' worth, Luke. Don't let T-Rod cheat you."

Rodriguez answered, "Hey, I'm so good I don't need to cheat." He started shuffling again. "So, Luke, you know how to play this game?"

Hiluka answered earnestly, "I learn fast."

"Bueno," Rodriguez answered as he dealt him in. "You're in, amigo."

Hunter muttered quietly, "This could get ugly. Let's go."

Hunter and Beth left and worked their way aft to the gun locker that contained the AR-15s used in the trawler fight and a few rifles and pistols other members of the crew had brought along. Hunter explained briefly that he wanted to make sure that all the arms were ready, as they didn't know what to expect on Pitcairn.

As they started working, Beth noticed a long case, like those holding a rifle with a scope, in the corner of the arms locker. "Didn't know we had one of those on board."

Hunter glanced at the rifle. "It's mine. Never know when something like that might be useful."

They started taking apart the AR-15s and cleaning them.

Hunter said quietly, "It's good we got your brother back."

Beth smiled a little. "Yeah, he can be useful."

Hunter snorted slightly. "I've also been meaning to tell you, I'm sorry about Green. He was a good worker."

Beth had not expected the remark but appreciated it. "Thanks. Good company too." After a pause, she added, "He's not the first I lost this year."

Hunter looked at her briefly, his dark eyes unreadable. His hands kept working, quickly, adeptly.

She continued, "Yeah, we lost a guy on the fire line in August."

"How?" he asked.

For just a second, Beth thought of the old Western movies that had Indians using that word all the time, but she resisted trying to make a dumb joke. She wondered if Billy would have shown the same restraint.

"Fire blew up on us. Bad weather forecast."

Hunter stopped cleaning for a moment. When Beth looked up from her piece, he was staring back at her.

"That why you quit?" he asked bluntly. Somehow, he seemed to know that there was more to her answer, and he was giving her a chance to vent if she wanted. She didn't.

"They fired me more than I quit," Beth answered. "Besides, this is fun."

Hunter almost smiled and went back to cleaning the piece in front of him. After a minute, he said, "Your men followed you out here?" He answered his own query. "Impressive."

She shook her head slightly before saying, "Hard to know why. I keep getting them killed." She was surprised that she had said it. Obviously, Green's death was more on her mind than she realized.

"Not your fault," he said succinctly. He barely even paused before saying, "And I can tell you why they follow you."

"Oh yeah?" She realized that she really wanted to hear the rest of it.

He answered quietly, "They follow you because you care about 'em." He went back to cleaning.

She thought for a second. "You mean like doing this job so T-Rod can keep on his winning streak?"

Hunter nodded slightly. "Yeah, like that. And like getting the new guy in the poker game."

Beth saw the opening to talk to him about something that had been on her mind. "What's the deal with you and Rodriguez?"

Hunter thought for a minute. "I didn't say that caring about them is always the best approach."

Beth persisted, albeit gently for her. "With all respect, I think you ride him too much." When he didn't answer, she asked, "How come?"

Hunter finished one of the rifles, set it aside, and picked up another before speaking. "Two reasons. One, I've known guys like Rodriguez all my life. On the rez, in prison, on this ship."

Beth resisted interrupting to ask about those hints to his past, so he continued.

"They do the song and dance, tell a few jokes. But when it's time to work, they're always missing or cutting corners."

Beth shook her head. "I don't think that's right. Rodriguez bullshits a lot, but when there's something that needs doing, he'll do it. I know, he's been with me in some tough spots."

Hunter hesitated and then said, "All right."

Beth appreciated his response and his tone, so she pushed on. "And two?"

Hunter answered matter-of-factly, as if they were discussing how to take apart the rifles. "It's good for him."

"What? Why?"

"Rodriguez is a guy who doesn't like bosses. But he does like you. He doesn't really want to have two bosses that he likes, but he does like having one that he doesn't." He paused. "That way he works harder for both of us."

While Beth let that digest, something from a Forest Service training session popped into her memory, something about type A and type B bosses. Too bad she fell asleep in the session and didn't remember much of it. She also recalled how Rodriguez had nearly been kicked off the fire crew in his first year after a disagreement with another boss turned physical, so she knew there was some truth in what Hunter said.

She nodded as she said, “Okay, that may be right.”

Hunter didn’t gloat or push the point as some people do when they get a concession in a conversation. Instead, he surprised Beth. He looked at her with just a slight hint of mischief on his face and then used her term: “Besides, it’s fun.”

Beth chuckled at his clever sense of humor as she admitted, “Yeah, it is kinda funny sometimes.”

Hunter smothered a laugh. “Tell you what? I’ll only ride him when he’s got it coming or when he’s working for me, not when he’s working for you. Does that work.”

Beth nodded. “It works. Thanks.”

As they continued cleaning, she realized how the conversation had evolved. They had started by talking about how her guys respected her leadership, but by the time they had finished, she had gained respect for his.

CHAPTER 43

Midwatch

"Wake up, Shakespeare!" Sanders said as he shook Billy's shoulder. "You got midwatch. I'm not letting you go back to sleep again."

Billy croaked, "Okay, I'm getting up."

Sanders waited as Billy swung his legs out over his bunk. Across from him, Rodriguez, in the top bunk, and Miller, in the bottom, were both snoring loudly.

Sanders shook his head as he looked at his colleagues. "I don't know how you can sleep in this racket anyway." He looked back at Billy. "I brought you a cup of coffee, but I put it over there, so you have to get out of bed to get it." He gestured at the card table ten feet away.

Billy stood, wobbly at first, and said, "Thanks, Frank. I'll be up."

Sanders nodded, shook his head at the snorers, and then left. Billy drank some of the coffee, pulled on his clothes, and then, also shaking his head at the cacophony of sound coming from his neighbors, headed out of the berthing area.

All sailors dread the midwatch, from midnight to four in the morning. The best you could say for it is that it's the quietest time on board and thus conducive to deep thoughts. But for most, midwatch is just another term for sleep deprivation.

Billy took the outside route up to the bridge to enjoy a quick look at the stars and to let the salty air invigorate him. He noticed the decks were slick from waves breaking over the side. That was unusual. Other than a couple of storms, the seas had been mostly calm since they started moving south. On this night, though, modest waves from the west rocked the ark slightly from starboard to port and then allowed it to bounce back. As Billy approached the bridge, he smiled a little, knowing that Jessie would be on the helm. They had been getting together most evenings for a walk on the deck or to just sit and watch the sunset, but she had been on watch the previous evening. Billy admitted to himself that he had missed her.

She greeted him from her spot on the helm with a little nod when he came on the bridge. "You look great," she said sarcastically.

"Yeah, right. Thanks," Billy answered, also sarcastically. He nodded at Sanders, silently thanking him again for his wake-up call. Billy's arrival on the bridge was followed almost immediately by Officer Hannigan, who was there to relieve Officer Willis, and Hiluka, who would serve as messenger. When they were just steaming along, the midwatch required only three people—an officer of the deck, a helmsman, and a messenger who could do any needed errands and wake up the next watch.

Hannigan and Willis exchanged their information and standing orders. Then Sanders and Willis both went below to get some sleep. Hannigan confirmed the orders with Billy, who was then on the helm, and then told Luke to step out on the bridge wing with him, where he said he wanted to explain some things about being a lookout. Jessie lingered on the bridge as the others departed.

The bridge was mostly dark. Bright lights interfere with night vision, so they were using only low green lights that illuminated the chart table, the radar stand, the helm's course dial, and a mercury gauge on the bulkhead behind the helm that showed the degree that the ship was rocking.

Billy, happy that Jessie had stuck around to say good night and wanting to keep her there for as long as he could, said quietly, "Hey, let me show you something we used to do on the midwatch on my ship." He gestured at the mercury gauge and said, "Watch that."

As the next wave from the west rolled the ship slightly to port, Billy swung the wheel hard over to starboard. When the ark rolled back, it came over to starboard more than it had with the previous wave, a modest increase from ten degrees to twelve. Then he did it again with the next wave, and the roll increased from twelve to fifteen.

Jessie started to smile and said, "Knock it off, Billy." But Billy knew she didn't really mean it. They both glanced out to the bridge wing, where Hannigan and Luke were deep into conversation, oblivious to whatever their helmsman was doing.

"One more time?" Billy asked as the next wave came in from the west. Jessie giggled briefly as Billy spun the wheel again.

Before the ark rolled back, Billy said, "We used to get my ship up to twenty-five, thirty degrees. Turn some chairs over in the berthing areas. Guys falling out of their bunks. People yelling at me when I got off duty because they knew the seas weren't that rough." Jessie smothered a laugh as the ark rolled to just over twenty degrees.

"Stop it, Billy Hill," she said firmly and put her hand on the wheel to keep him from cranking it over again. "I'm leaving."

"Okay, okay," Billy relented. "I'll stop it if you'll stay a while longer."

She smiled but shook her head as she released her grip. "Sorry, helmsman, you're on your own."

Then she was gone, and Billy was left by himself on the bridge. Keeping the ship on course required some attention, but not so much as to preclude other thoughts. Billy let his brain wander. Being somewhat alone reminded him of his nights in the lifeboat and just how lonely that felt. But he wasn't lonely anymore. He felt good about his family. He felt good about the crew. And he felt good about Jessie. He liked their habit of getting together in the evenings. The more they talked, the more comfortable Billy felt. Jessie was the most inquisitive person he had ever met and was always asking questions, about all kinds of stuff. Sometimes he knew the answers, and sometimes he didn't, but he admired her appetite for learning, and his ego got a nice boost when he was able to teach her something. He knew there were many things she could teach him as well, but he also knew he wasn't as good at asking questions as she was. He told himself to do better in the future. But he still had this persistent self-doubt. Did she like him, or was he just flattering himself? And she didn't open up to emotions easily. How careful should he be?

Movement behind Billy broke his reverie. Oliver stepped onto the bridge, wearing only shorts, sandals, and a T-shirt instead of his usual slacks and polo shirt. His white hair was sticking up in places, like he had just gotten out of bed. "How's the coffee?" he asked, after clearing his throat. There was always a pot ready on the bridge, like on any ship. The quality depended on who made it, of course.

Billy glanced over at the chart table, where it sat. "Decent, better than the usual swill some of these clowns make." Oliver shuffled over to the pot. Billy noticed Hannigan and Luke pause in their conversation and look back into the bridge. Seeing who it was, they resumed their own conversation.

"Want some, William?" Oliver asked from the chart table.

"Sure. Throw some sugar in there, please. Thanks."

Oliver made the cups, handed one to Billy, and then sat down in his chair at the front of the bridge.

"Couldn't sleep?" Billy asked.

"No, it seemed like the ship was taking some rolls up here, and I wanted to see if the seas had roughened." Billy was glad his father couldn't see his guilty smile.

Oliver went on. "Besides, I find myself enjoying the freedom to get up when I want and just wander." He paused and then asked, "I suppose you would, of course, rather be asleep?"

"Yeah, it's hard to like the midwatch." He thought for a moment and then asked, "Did you ever read *The Good Shepherd*?"

When his father shook his head no, Billy went on. "It's a classic in Navy literature that was made into a movie. Anyway, the exhausted captain refers to 'typical midwatch depression.'"

Oliver responded, "You don't seem depressed, William."

Billy answered, "Nah, I'm good. Glad to be off that damn yacht. But speaking of that, I wanted to tell you that I've thought about what you said about forests and would like to read those studies if you can find them."

"I'll get them for you," Oliver said. He was quiet for a moment as he sipped his coffee. "You always were a reader. Like your mother. More like her that way than your brother or sister."

Billy was silent, so Oliver went on. "What are you reading now? Still *Moby-Dick*?"

Billy chuckled slightly. "Yes, but in my defense, it's a long book."

Oliver responded, "And a good one for you."

"Because we're at sea?"

"No. Because it's about searching and wandering. Like you, William."

Billy wasn't sure what to say to that. "Well, I think it was just what Reichardt had available."

"I suppose so," Oliver answered. "Thanks to her. And to Reese." He took another drink and then continued. "We haven't had much chance to talk since our time on the yacht, but I want you to know that I appreciate what you did for me."

"Well, I think we were all just trying to get through that." Billy paused. "And we didn't kill anybody, although I think we would have if we had to."

Oliver was quiet for a moment before responding. "I just don't understand Henry. We were never that close, but I didn't think we were that far apart either."

Billy sipped on the coffee and then changed the subject. "Are you hopeful about Pitcairn?"

Oliver nodded. "Hopeful, yes. Are you?"

Billy responded, "I thought you might go for Australia. Personally, I always did want to see that place."

Oliver shook his head. "My thought was that Australia was likely a target in the war."

Billy got to the question he had wanted to ask for quite some time. "On the day we lost Green, I caught your glance after we noticed that flock of birds flying south. Did seeing that really convince you to suggest Pitcairn?"

Oliver thought for a moment. "They may have been godwits. Did you know that godwits hatch in Alaska each year and then fly to French Polynesia? Remarkable."

Billy stared at his father. His mind was thinking back to some of their arguments back in the days when Oliver had so little respect for animals that he hunted them for trophies. His father had been a man who couldn't tell the difference between a robin and a starling, a man whose only thought upon hearing the word *cardinal* was of the Catholic church. And now here he was, identifying birds, telling stories about elephants, and recommending readings about forests.

Oliver looked at Billy and smiled slightly. "I thought they might have a good idea by flying south."

Billy shook his head slightly before responding. "Well, I'll admit that answer surprises me."

Oliver seemed to be pleased with that result. "Birds know where to go for land and for water."

Billy answered, "No, I meant that you would make a decision based on that. That's taking quite a chance."

Oliver stood, took one more look out at the dark ocean in front of the ark, and then back at Billy, before saying, "Sometimes, William, as you know, you have to take a chance." With that, he drained his coffee, walked to the chart table, and set the cup there.

Billy was still digesting the comment when Oliver added, "With directions, with choices, with people." He winked at his son.

Billy was puzzled. Was his father trying to tell him something? About him? About Jessie? Billy had wondered how many people on board knew that he had been meeting with her. Every sailor knows that it's hard to keep secrets on a ship.

Oliver stared at Billy for a moment, seemingly happy with the fact that he had surprised his son and frequent critic in past years into silence. "Thank you for the conversation, William. We should do it more often."

As he left the bridge, Billy thought to himself, again somewhat surprisingly, that he hoped they would.

CHAPTER 44

Rest Day

One Sunday, Oliver called for a day of rest. Only essential duties, like standing watch, continued. He and Captain Mitchell scheduled three voluntary activities.

The first was a generic spiritual service. Sarah recruited Miller, Susan Harris, and Billy to play some music. They came out early to rehearse a couple of songs she requested and found a fine morning, with a beautiful sunrise over a calm ocean. Nevertheless, Billy worried that, given the various beliefs and nonbeliefs among the crew, the service might get low attendance, thus disappointing his sister-in-law. He was therefore pleasantly surprised when nearly everyone who was not on duty, from the captain to the deckhands, showed up. He estimated over a hundred people in the crowd on the main deck.

Sarah started by easing any concerns of proselytizing, saying it would be a generic service that gave them all a chance to think and, if they wanted, to pray. Then, as if to prove it, she had the musicians play the Joan Osborne song "One of Us." When Susan began singing, "What if God was one of us, just a slob like one of us…?" people laughed and smiled. Sarah then thanked the band and began speaking.

"As you can tell, this will not be your traditional church service. I won't be offering Communion, and we won't be passing any collection plates." Some laughed. "But we will take the opportunity to say thanks for what we have and to share our fellowship. I will ask you all to take a moment of silence to think about whatever you want, to remember those who are gone, and to say thanks that we are still here on this beautiful morning." She paused and lowered her head. The crowd was silent. For a minute, the only sounds were the ark's motors humming along and the ocean water as it gave way to the ship.

"Thank you." Sarah broke the silence. "As you all know, we have met several times now as a group. Unlike the ceremonies we have had recently, I don't want to focus on who we have lost and what is behind us, but rather on what may lie ahead. We are, to use an obvious pun, sailing into uncharted waters." And she was off and running. She talked about their situation and how similar it was to the ark story in the Bible. She reminded everyone of the part of the ark story that is often forgotten. God made a covenant with Noah and his family and promised that he or she would not again loose another devastating flood on the earth but rather would leave people to their own behavior to determine their fate.

"Some people may be tempted to blame God for what has happened in recent days, but God, if he or she does exist, did not create this current version of a disastrous flood on the earth. He or she did not invent nuclear weapons. He or she did not create our dependence on fossil fuels. He or she did not tell people to elect and rely on false prophets. No, we know who was responsible for these things, and it was not God." She lowered her voice and looked out at the crowd. "Some of you may know the famous Pogo cartoon that was used on the first Earth Day in 1970, where the punch line is…"

Billy and several others in the crowd smiled, knowing what was coming. Sarah paused as she noticed the reaction and then continued.

"Say it with me, those of you who know it. We have met the enemy, and he is us." She nodded to appreciate the chorus of voices. "Well, so it is again. It's up to you whether you believe God exists. But even if he or she does, what happens from here on out is not up to God. It's up to us. We have another chance. And starting with what happens next week when we arrive at Pitcairn, let us do it right this time." She looked out at the crowd. "Thank you all for listening."

The audience gave a hearty round of applause. Sarah appeared surprised, even a bit embarrassed at the response, and put her hands out to end the applause. She then gestured at the musicians.

"I've asked Susan and Cowboy and Billy to play one more song. I ask that you think about what might happen if we don't do this right. John Prine wrote this about a place that no longer exists." The band played "Paradise." By the second chorus, many in the crowd were singing along.

The service then ended, but people stayed on deck to continue talking and greeting one another. Susan came over and again thanked the musicians, but they demurred, thanking her instead. Others came up to thank Sarah.

"Excellent," Jessie said.

"Just right," Maria agreed.

Hunter looked at Billy and, with a straight face, added, "And she did it without Shakespeare." Billy laughed briefly, always unsure how to take Hunter's sense of humor.

Six bells sounded, indicating it was 11:00 a.m. Jessie said, "I have to go relieve Reichardt. She's in the tournament."

Billy answered, "Right. In fact, she's playing me." He paused and then smiled. "Then again, maybe you shouldn't go so she'll forfeit."

Jessie smiled. "But of course, you don't want to win that way, Billy."

Maria added, "Si. And you don't need to win that way, Guillermo." She patted Billy on the back. "I must go prepare lunch."

As Jessie's departure suggested, the second activity of the day began at eleven. Oliver had created a chess tournament for the first thirty-two people to sign up. He rounded up four chess sets on board and then randomly assigned all entrants to single-elimination games. He also offered up one of the bottles of expensive rum from the *White Diamond* as the prize.

Billy and Beth and Owen, who had all been taught by Oliver, were among the first to enter. They were also among the first to be eliminated. Billy's tournament was quick and painless. Reichardt checkmated him in under twenty minutes. The silver lining, as far as he was concerned, was that, since she could not speak, there was no trash-talking. Instead, he just received a hearty handshake and a gracious smile and then went on his way. Billy quickly found his siblings, who had been similarly dispatched.

"I guess we showed them, didn't we?" Billy asked Beth and Owen.

Owen shook his head as he looked over at Oliver finishing off his opponent. "Yeah, maybe the old man didn't teach us all his tricks."

Beth started to answer, "Or we have met the enemy…" She paused so the others could help her finish. "And it is us."

Billy soothed his bruised ego by telling himself that he would therefore have more time for the third activity of the day. That activity was unusual, but it was also logical given that the ark was steaming near the equator in the middle of a bright, clear day, with the air temperature running nearly a hundred degrees. Captain Mitchell stopped the ark's motors, letting the ship drift, and announced swim call. What made it unusual was that this just didn't happen out in the ocean very often. Billy had experienced it only a couple of times when he was in the Navy, and both times, many in the crew were shocked. Captains typically just didn't want to use the time or risk the crew with something so frivolous. Besides, most people don't like swimming in the ocean. The vastness, the depth, and the possibility of predators make it risky, if not somewhat terrifying. You can't touch the bottom like in the backyard pool.

But because the ship was stopped and nobody had to be on watch, everybody on board had the opportunity to overcome those fears, and some literally jumped at it. Before anybody took the leap off the starboard side, the deckhands lowered a net and a Jacob's ladder so that swimmers could climb out whenever they wanted. The one other preparation involved Hunter, who volunteered to stand watch with his long rifle in case anyone spotted sharks. Then off they went. Reese, Rodriguez, and Billy agreed to jump together to get things started, and then, no surprise, Rodriguez stopped just as the other two leaped. Reese and Billy hit the water at the same time, and as soon as they did, Billy wondered if it was such a good idea. Even south of the equator, the ocean water was extremely cold. And salty. Nevertheless, they were soon joined by the delayed Rodriguez as well as Beth, Jessie, Brooks, and a few others. They swam and splashed each other to try to get their bodies adjusted to the temperature, but that was more ambitious than successful.

Others joined them in more dramatic ways. Naomi Harris performed a graceful dive from a handstand that was worthy of a much wider audience but at least earned applause from her mother and others watching on deck. Frank Sanders followed with a massive cannonball. Then, as the swimmers and those on deck watched, Luke climbed out on the yardarm, holding the radar until he was perched as high on the ship as one could be and still be over the water. He then did a perfect flip into a dive that finished with a no-splash entry into the ocean that would have earned him a ten score in the Olympics.

People applauded. Reese, floating next to Billy, said, "I don't think I'll be doing any dives. I wouldn't want to show him up."

Billy said, "Right, me neither. He must come from somewhere with cliffs."

Reese answered, "Yeah, let's go with that."

Shortly after that, those still left in the water climbed back up the net or the ladder. As they got back on deck, they found Hunter watching, his rifle cradled in his arms. He gestured toward the ocean. Looking closely, they could make out a dorsal fin slicing through the water.

"Damn, Chief," Rodriguez said angrily. "When were you going to warn us?"

Hunter said simply, "Sharks got to eat." As Rodriguez just stared back at him, Hunter walked away with a satisfied look on his face.

Later that afternoon, the chess tournament got down to the serious contenders. A substantial crowd, large enough to necessitate moving out of the mess hall and setting up a couple of tables, gathered. The final four participants were Oliver, Reichardt, Doc Harrison, and Miller. The prize bottle of rum perched on a stand nearby with some glasses.

Reichardt and Doc Harrison had the first match. They both started quickly, taking several of each other's pieces, but then, apparently realizing that their opponents knew what they were doing, slowed down. Each of the final moves required quite a bit of thought. And of course, neither of them said anything. Finally, after nearly an hour of playing and over fifty moves, Doc Harrison looked at Reichardt, smiled, leaned forward, and tipped over his king, knowing that he was beaten. She reached across the table and shook his hand.

Oliver and Miller took even longer, eyeing each other warily like veteran players at a poker table. Oliver studied Miller with his pale-blue eyes and occasionally made some comment like, "Interesting move, Cowboy," that may or may not have been gamesmanship. Miller, inscrutable under his cowboy hat, didn't say a word but would stare at Oliver after each of his moves, as if daring him to take a challenge. Late in the game, when each of them only had a few pieces left, they seemed to relish each move, both even chuckling at times at the other's strategy. After just over an hour, Miller finally muttered, "I'll be damned," as he stood and removed his hat to salute his opponent.

After a short break, the final match between Oliver and Reichardt was excruciatingly slow. Billy had played enough chess to know that each player was thinking several moves ahead, but still, their patience was impressive. After they had played an hour or so, Maria Rivera came out from the mess hall and announced that dinner was ready for anyone who wanted it. Nobody moved. Even she stayed, coming over to stand with Billy and Jessie as they watched quietly. And then, after another half hour, Oliver made a mistake. You could almost see the light come on in Reichardt's eyes as soon as Oliver lifted his hand off his piece. She moved her queen immediately. Then Oliver saw the imminent checkmate. He frowned briefly, backed his chair, stood, and bowed slightly. Reichardt grinned broadly as she stood and bowed back.

The spectators applauded and then moved to congratulate the participants. Billy patted his father on the back. Reese gave his colleague a big bear hug. Oliver took the bottle of rum off its perch and passed it to Reichardt, who held the bottle aloft, opened it, and took a shot. She then reached for the glasses and started pouring for any interested takers. It was a good ending to a good day.

CHAPTER 45

Sunrise Shift

The morning after the rest day, Beth and Jessie were both on the morning shift, from 4:00 to 8:00 a.m. It's not as onerous as the mid-watch, but it's a tough way to start a day as you don't get to go back to bed after you finish. But Beth was glad to have Jessie's company. She always seemed to be interested in everything and, on other occasions, had gotten Beth talking about firefighting, the Forest Service, living in the Rockies. And it was easy for the two of them to talk as the bridge was otherwise empty, with Captain Mitchell and Willis out on the bridge wing, shooting stars for navigation.

Jessie, too, was pleased that Beth was on duty, as she had something on her mind. "I want to talk to you about your brother," she said, glancing away from the steering gauge in front of her. Beth leaned against the lee helm next to her.

"Which one, Owen or Billy?" Beth teased.

"You know which one."

Beth grinned. "Okay, what do you want to know?"

Jessie began slowly. "I think you know I am cautious about men."

"Smart woman," Beth said instantly.

"But Billy and I have been getting to know each other." Jessie paused. "And before this goes much further, I want to ask you if this is a good idea."

"For him or for you?" Beth asked.

"For both of us," she answered instantly.

"Right answer," Beth responded and took a drink from her coffee cup. As with other conversations, Beth appreciated Jessie's directness. Beth knew that she had had trouble with men in the past, yet another reason they could relate. And she didn't blame her for looking for a reference. In fact, she was flattered Jessie would ask her, Billy's sister, for an honest answer.

"What you see is what you get with Billy," Beth began. "He's one of the most honest people I've ever met, so if he seems to like you, well, then, he genuinely does."

Jessie nodded. "He seems to, but I wasn't sure."

"Come on, Jessie."

"Okay, I know that he does." Jessie couldn't hide a little smile as she said it. "I think he also trusts me. He told Maria and me about your family, and your mother. I'm sorry you went through that too."

"He told you that story, did he?" Beth asked quickly. "He really does like you."

"Si," Jessie responded and then sighed. "But he has other things inside that he has not shared."

Beth hesitated. "Teresa?"

"Si."

Beth nodded. "He'll have to tell you about that. That's not my call." She paused.

"I understand."

"He's taken some shots." Beth paused and then continued, "Then again, I suppose we all have."

"Yes, we have," Jessie answered.

Beth collected her thoughts before continuing. "Here's how Billy handles those shots. He deals with bad news and then moves on fast. He wasn't always that way. When he was a kid, he took stuff hard. Made him quiet. Even a little shy."

"Billy?"

"Yeah, no kidding. Something changed him. Might have been growing up. Or losing Mom. Or the military. Or Teresa. Or this disaster stuff he's been doing." Beth found herself trying to understand it even while she was talking. "In fact, I think he started doing the disaster stuff because of this part of him. Whatever. But he has this thing about time…"

Jessie looked over from the gauge to Beth and said, "He talked about that some, but I still don't understand."

Beth tried to answer. "Don't get me wrong. I'm not saying he doesn't have feelings. But he doesn't stay down long." She thought for a second. "Let me put it this way: Billy is the guy who will choke up at a funeral but then dance at the wake, if that makes sense."

"Why does he do that?"

Beth thought before answering. "He's restless. Billy has this appetite for life that just never seems to quit. He hates to see anything die, but then he wants to get on with whatever is left. Or help others get on with it. He just wants to move on to something else. It's like he has to keep moving or he'll feel like he's wasting time. He even has that odd saying about chasing things over the next horizon."

"Yes, he said something like that the other day," Jessie said. She didn't say anything else, so Beth took another sip of her drink. Light from the rising sun was just starting to appear off the port side of the ark. Whether because of the coffee or the conversation, Beth found herself going on again.

"Maybe this is helpful, I don't know, but his appetite is something you should know about. He won't hold back. He wants to get as much as he can out of anybody and any situation. And then…" She paused, not sure she wanted to finish. Beth loved her brother and knew he was interested in Jessie.

Jessie sensed her hesitancy and pushed her to go on. "Okay. He said something like that the other day, that he tries to…how did he say…embrace good times. But we all do, yes?"

Beth smiled. "I like that word, *embrace*. Yeah, that's Billy. I'll give you an example. We didn't get together much after Mom died. But we all came back to California when Owen and Sarah got married. Billy had been working for some whitewater rafting company up by Sacramento. So that weekend, he and some of his coworkers got us some rafts. Have you ever seen the Yuba River?"

"I have never seen it," she answered.

"Well, the Yuba has big rapids when the water level is right, and one of them can be a killer. It's called Maytag. You know, like the washing machine, because it will churn you up, particularly this big hole in the river that can swallow a raft." She looked at Jessie, not sure if she was following. "A hole is like a low spot in the river behind a big rock."

Jessie waited patiently and adjusted the wheel to stay on course.

Beth continued. "So we ran Maytag and tried too hard to dodge the hole and ended up flipping two of the rafts. People swimming all over the place. Really embarrassing."

Jessie asked, "Anyone hurt?"

"Just pride. So at the bottom of the rapid, we collected everyone, and then Billy got this idea that we should strip one of the boats, carry it up to the top of the rapid, and run it again, this time going right for the hole. You know, so we would have to row ourselves out. Crazy, right?"

Beth couldn't help but grin a little, remembering. "Only he didn't think so but instead was calling for volunteers and yelling at us to decide as it was getting dark and a storm was coming."

Jessie smiled a little. "You went with him, didn't you?"

Beth chuckled slightly. "Yeah, I and his friend Teresa and two other suckers. While Owen and Sarah and Oliver and everybody else looked at us like we were insane. They watched us carry the raft back up to the head of the rapid. And then they got their cameras ready to roll."

Jessie said, "I can almost picture it."

"Yeah, it was something. We hit that hole dead center, and the raft perched up on the downstream wave. Up there, it either flips over backward and we're in big trouble or we pull ourselves over the top. The five of us were leaning over the bow so we could dig the paddles into the water, waves pounding all around us, and we were pulling with everything we got. And I glanced over at Billy, and get this, he was laughing."

"Ha!" Jessie started to laugh and smothered it. They both glanced over at the bridge wing, but the officers out there had their minds on the stars.

Beth continued. "Right. He was so excited that he was laughing, like he'd never been so happy. It was funny at first. And we all couldn't help but laugh for a moment. But the odd thing was that Billy kept laughing. I think he was paddling just enough as if he wanted to just stay there on that wave forever. The rest of us had to get serious and lean in to pull us over the wave."

"This is a great story," Jessie said.

Beth had another drink of coffee before finishing. "You know, I will admit this. Pulling on the paddles and laughing, I've rarely felt more alive. We were probably up there for twenty seconds, but it felt like twenty minutes. Kind of like really good sex."

Jessie giggled again and nodded. Beth looked back at her and smiled also before she went on. "If it had been up to him, we'd still be up there." She looked directly at Jessie to make sure she got the point.

"That's Billy," Beth said.

Jessie looked back at her and asked, "So he is, how do you say, a thrill-seeker?"

Beth shook her head. "Not exactly. He's a seeker. He seeks moments like that, but they don't have to be dangerous. He also savors moments that aren't what you would call thrills, like dancing or playing his guitar."

"This is all good, si?"

"Sure, we all like good times." Beth was still trying to put the rest of what she wanted to say in words, so she hesitated and sipped the coffee. "But here's the thing with Billy. He hates to see the good times end. Like being on that wave. You know how some people start to get impatient about life when they turn fifty or sixty. Like time becomes more precious then and they hate to let it slip away. Billy didn't wait for fifty. He's been that way since, well, since Mom died. He was seventeen then, and do you know how long he waited before leaving to join the Navy? One week. Hell, the body was barely cold."

Jessie waited.

"The best word I can use to describe Billy is what I said before: he's restless. He's the most restless person I know. Once the event is over, he moves on. He moves on from bad events quickly. He even moves on from good events quickly. Hell, he moves on from everything quickly. He gets impatient and thinks that there is always something better, so he'd better move on to find it." Beth paused before finishing. "I'm glad we got him off that damn lifeboat. He must have been going crazy."

"Me too," Jessie said and then was quiet, deep in thought.

Beth looked at her and hesitated. She didn't want to screw anything up, but she also didn't do false advertising.

"Restless even explains Billy's thing for quotes. He seems to have a quote for everything. That's because he knows a little about a lot of things, like the Bible and Shakespeare and whatever. But he's no expert on those things. It cracks me up that they're calling him Shakespeare. His mind was always as restless as the rest of him, so he just learned a little about a whole bunch of literature. And restless is why he's decent at a lot of things but not great at any of them. He's good at steering a ship only because the Navy made him do it. Restless is also why he didn't have a permanent job before all this shit. It's why he didn't even have an address. It's why his family hasn't seen him in years. It's why he almost didn't come with us. And it's why I don't know if he would stay with us if he had a choice…"

Beth paused as she realized Jessie was staring at her, waiting. She chose her final words carefully. "And it's why he's never committed to someone."

Jessie continued to stare at Beth and then nodded slightly before looking back at the gauge in front of the helm.

Beth wondered if she had said too much. "Look, Jessie, I love my brother and I like you, and I can tell he likes you. But since you asked, I want you to know, there may come a day when you guys have to make a decision, and there are no guarantees as to what he'll do. So getting close to him will be good in a lot of ways, but it will also be a challenge."

Jessie waited nearly a full minute before answering. In the silence, Beth looked around and noticed the predawn light starting to illuminate the clouds in the eastern sky.

Finally, Jessie said, "Good things always are."

Beth smiled. She worried that they would both get hurt someday, but she liked Jessie's attitude. And Beth decided right then that she would do what she could to help. Then they both were quiet as they watched the sun peek out from under the clouds.

CHAPTER 46

For Now

On the evening before the ark arrived at Pitcairn, Billy and Jessie sat on the starboard gear locker again. They did not have the usual red sunset, but rather a sky filled with clouds and occasional rain showers. Not surprisingly, the ride on the ship was rougher than normal as the ark bounced over the swells created by a wind from the southwest.

Billy was telling Jessie about the book Oliver had loaned him about cooperation between trees. Jessie had plenty of questions, and some of them were tough. Billy was trying valiantly to address them, and Jessie enjoyed seeing him struggle to come up with an answer. Billy got a reprieve when they were interrupted by visitors, first the odd pair of Oliver Hill and John Hunter.

"William. Jessica," Oliver said in greeting as they walked up.

Jessie responded, "Hi, Mr. Hill. Hi, John." Hunter just nodded.

Billy thought the timing was fortuitous and sought his father's assistance. "Jessie was just asking me about how invasive species affect the cooperation of trees in the forest."

Oliver smiled, pleased that his son was pursuing his suggested reading. "That's an excellent question, Jessie, one that the book addresses, so I'm sure William will come up with a satisfactory answer."

Billy shook his head. "Gee, thanks a lot, Dad."

Oliver chuckled. "We do have a question for you, William, and thought we might find you here."

"Okay," Billy answered, again being made aware that his liaisons with Jessie were no secret.

Oliver continued. "My reference material indicates that the harbor at Pitcairn may be rough. Mr. Hunter suggested we put some extra weight in the bottom of the launch for ballast. Perhaps that will make it more stable."

Billy nodded. "Could help. As long as we spread it evenly."

Hunter and Oliver both nodded and were about to walk off when Owen and his family came walking up, their arrival announced by Roscoe. The dog ran up to Billy, barking and looking for the usual back scratch.

Billy obliged and then couldn't resist living up to his nickname, saying, "Ah, yes. Dogs bark at me as I halt by them." He glanced at the others and focused on Hunter, who had bestowed the nickname. "That's from Shakespeare."

The others paused. Then Hunter responded, "*Richard the third*."

Billy's jaw dropped open as Jessie, Owen, and Sarah all just stared at Hunter. Oliver, seemingly not surprised at all, just smiled knowingly.

Hunter looked very satisfied as he said by way of explanation, "I read a lot while in prison. And King Richard reminded me of somebody."

None of them had time to ask any of the obvious questions, such as why he was in prison, because Oliver and Hunter, both looking quite content, moved on.

"Wow," was all Billy could say. He had thought he was being clever with the quote, but he had been clearly upstaged.

Owen sounded sympathetic as he admitted, "I would not have expected that."

Sarah smiled. "Why not?"

Owen nodded, understanding the point. "Yeah, I guess so."

After that, they, too, walked on, leaving Billy and Jessie by themselves.

"So, Billy Hill, if you didn't want to be called Shakespeare, you won't get rid of the nickname that way," Jessie said.

"Yeah, who knows, maybe we should be using it on Hunter." He sighed. "Oh well, I've been called worse. As they say, call me anything but late for dinner."

"I'll stick with Billy," Jessie answered. Her expression turned serious. "And, Billy, I do have another question. It's from our conversation the other day about esqueletoes."

Billy had expected more questions about forests but was not surprised that she wanted to resume a discussion that had ended without all questions being answered. He tried to deflect with another stupid joke. "What is this, the Hispanic Inquisition?"

She ignored the joke. "No, I want to be serious. I don't mean to pry, but if we are going to get close, we need to understand each other."

Billy, like his sister, did admire her directness.

"Your sister and I had the sunrise shift this morning, and we had a good conversation," Jessie said.

Billy thought of Beth's directness. No wonder the two of them were becoming friends. He fidgeted and tried another deflection. "I'm reminded of a line in the movie *Body Heat*, when the suspect asks if he should have his lawyer present."

"No, and stop screwing around," she said. "It was all good. She loves you." When Billy didn't respond, Jessie went on. "She loves you, and she respects your privacy. So she did not tell me what happened to you and your friend Teresa."

The ark bounced as it hit a large wave head-on. Jessie, realizing the bluntness of the question, looked at Billy before continuing. "And if you do not want to tell me, I will not push you, but I am telling you that I would like to know."

He appreciated that she cared enough about him to ask. "Do you want the abridged version or the whole story?"

Jessie stared at him. "What do you think?"

He thought for a moment. "Teresa was like you in a lot of ways—smart, honest, tough, independent. Maybe she didn't ask as many questions."

His little joke fell flat. She stared at him, waiting.

"Okay, after the Navy and the barges on the Mississippi, I was back in California for a while. I got a job teaching school in the East Bay. Social studies. You know, Shakespeare, the Bible, all kinds of good stuff." Billy smiled as he looked at Jessie. "You didn't think I just remembered those quotes from reading them once, did you?"

Jessie smiled slightly, patiently.

"Teresa had gone to medical school and was doing her residency at Berkeley. Her brother Ed was one of my colleagues at the high school where I taught. He set us up because he knew we liked to do a lot of the same stuff on days off, like hiking and rafting and camping."

Jessie said, "Beth told me the story about the river, the Yuba?"

"Yeah, I bet she did." He chuckled. "I love white water. It's playing in nature, on nature's terms."

"Like leaf-chasing, right?"

Billy was pleased she had made the connection. "Yeah, like that."

She waited.

"We did stuff like that when we could, mostly on weekends. She moved in with me shortly after the Yuba trip." He smiled, thinking about it. "And it was good. You know how some people say living together will let you know if you should make it permanent."

"Si," Jessie answered. "You learn a lot."

He looked back at her. "Sounds like you did?"

She sighed. "I learned enough one time to move out after one week."

"Maybe you should be talking here…" He tried.

"No." She looked at him. "This is your turn. Continue."

"Yes, ma'am," he answered. "When Teresa was finishing her residency, she got two job offers. One was to stay there in the Bay Area. The other was in New York. It was a tough decision. The New York offer was a good one, but she liked California too. I didn't really want to move to the big city right then, and I knew that I could tip the scales toward staying if we…"

As he paused, Jessie interjected, "Made a commitment?"

Billy nodded and then went on. "Have you ever hiked up Mount Whitney?" When Jessie shook her head, he continued. "It's the tallest mountain in the continental US at 14,500 feet. And you can hike it. You don't need ropes or any of that stuff."

She tried to keep him on point. "Okay?"

"But I didn't want us to just climb it." He looked back at her. "What better place to get engaged than the top of the continent?"

The rain picked up, the drops coming down on the deck and on the small roof that covered the gear locker. Puddles began to form just in front of their feet.

"Yeah, I even bought a ring. I told Eddie what I was going to do, but I didn't tell Teresa, so I could surprise her. We made great time going up. When we stopped at the base camp halfway up for the night, we were so excited about the coming climb to the summit that neither of us slept a wink. The moon was full, and at that elevation, the light was so bright we played cards without even a flashlight."

He paused. For just a second, he thought of the aborted conversation he had with RC about Mount Whitney on the drive along the Sierra Nevadas just months before.

Then he went on. "We were really wired, so we started climbing again well before dawn. I remember how Teresa changed the 'burning sunlight' phrase to 'burning moonlight.' I thought it was clever. Anyway, we made the summit well before noon. And the view up there…well, it's indescribable. We felt, literally, on top of the world. We had started so early and moved so quickly that we were the only ones on the summit. A perfect spot, right?"

Jessie waited. The rain pounded down on the little roof over them so hard it almost sounded like hail. She asked quietly, "You didn't do it, did you, Billy?"

He shook his head and stared off into the rain before looking back at her. "No. I carried that ring back down the mountain." He tried unsuccessfully to make a wry smile. "In fact, later I thought I could write a country song with that as the first line. Something about how the ring came down the mountain in my pocket instead of on her finger."

Jessie's thoughts were unreadable. "Teresa learned later from her brother that I had planned to propose on top of the mountain and didn't do it." He paused. "At that point, we knew it was over. She moved to New York without me."

Jessie nodded briefly before saying, "But you could have stayed in touch. Or at least visited?"

"No. I kept saying I would, and I intended to when the school year ended in June. But then that damn pandemic came." He felt a catch in his throat. "Killed her."

"Oh no." Jessie reached out and put her hand on his shoulder. "I am sorry. That was a terrible time, especially for doctors. And in New York."

"Yeah, front lines. She was one of the first to go." Billy paused again. "I couldn't help but think that if I had…well, she would not have gone and she…"

Jessie squeezed his shoulder. "You cannot blame yourself for that. That virus…"

Billy nodded slightly. "I know. Still…anyway, that was when I went to work for the Red Cross and started doing the disaster tracker stuff. And I kept doing it and eventually ended up all the way back in New Orleans. Funny how things worked out."

Jessie waited. Billy knew there was another issue. As did she. "But you know, I just never did even ask her to stay with me."

She asked directly, "Why not?"

He looked around and then down at the puddle by their feet. "There's the big question."

After a long moment of silence, Jessie tried to help. "Your proposal would have been a great moment, but then, maybe she was not the right person after all."

He smiled at her, understanding that she was trying to let him off easily. And he wanted to tell her how much he appreciated it. "Thanks." He also knew that he needed to finish the thought. "But when I'm honest with myself, even if she had been the right one, I didn't do it."

He paused. And she waited. So he went on. "Hell, just ask my family. They've seen it before. They saw it when I left them right after

Mom died. They saw it when I quit jobs. They saw it with Teresa." He looked at her. "And they saw it at Treasure Island when I started to leave the ark."

Jessie thought about how Beth had said nearly the same thing and how siblings really do know each other. She said simply, "It is hard for some to commit to things. Harder for some than for others."

He continued to stare at her, not really having anything else to say. "How did you get to be so smart?"

After a long moment, she answered, "I ask a lot of questions."

But she didn't ask the next question. And he wouldn't have been ready to answer it anyway. Both were silent for nearly a minute, and the only sounds were the heavy rain and the waves on the hull of the ark.

"Well…" She finally spoke. "I, too, understand being careful with emotions, but we are here now."

Again, he realized that she could have made this a lot harder on him. He smiled at her. "I like it here now."

She looked back at him with that little smile that seemed to suggest so much more as she said, "That will have to do, then."

He knew then that there would be a reckoning one day. But as she said, they were there at that moment. They leaned toward each other to kiss. Before she did so, she said very softly, "For now."

PART 3

The Island
November 2026 – January 2027

In a world of steel-eyed death and
men fighting to be warm,

Come on in, she said, I'll give you
shelter from the storm.

—Bob Dylan,
"Shelter from the Storm"

CHAPTER 47

A Wary Reception

After weeks at sea, the arkonauts were thrilled by the sight of mountain peaks emerging from low-lying clouds. And as the ark neared Pitcairn, they could see lush green forests and wave-washed, sandy beaches. Still, as inviting as the island appeared, they had no idea what kind of reception they would receive.

The ark had gone to general quarters for their arrival, so the bridge was crowded. In addition to Oliver and Captain Mitchell, Navigator Hannigan was working the charts for the approach and Second Mate Willis was watching the short-distance radar screen for local contacts. Billy was on the helm, and Miller on the lee helm. Beth and Brooks were scanning the sea to port, while Jessie and Luke looked to starboard. Sanders and Rodriguez were down on the forecastle, armed with the AR-15s, just in case they were needed.

As excited as Billy was, he also felt the usual tinge of regret at the end of a voyage. Journeys always had a simplistic virtue to him. All your focus was on the present, so time almost seemed to stand still. And people had bonded, whatever their backgrounds, during the voyage. Billy thought of the quote from Mark Twain that "travel is fatal to prejudice, bigotry, and narrow-mindedness."

Willis called from the radar screen, "Something moving. Just separated from the island, Captain." On the radar, a boat would look like a tiny blob splitting off from a much larger one.

"Got it," Beth called from the port-side viewfinder. "Welcome party. We've got four, make it five people, on a powerboat heading our way."

The captain stepped out on the wing to follow her stare and asked as he focused his binoculars, "Are they armed?"

Everybody on the bridge waited. Then Beth answered, "I see rifles."

The captain continued to look as he spoke. "Slow speed to all ahead one-third. We don't want to seem threatening. Nevertheless, Mr. Hunter, take two others to the arms locker, gear up, and reinforce the forecastle."

Hunter called out, "Rivera, Brooks, with me." The trio hurried off the bridge.

Mitchell and Oliver used binoculars to watch the speedboat approach. The people on board, three men and two women, were armed with old repeater rifles. When they got within fifty yards, the boat slowed and then hovered, bouncing in the waves. For a full minute, a burly, bearded man studied the ark with binoculars. Then he lowered his binoculars and raised a megaphone.

"My name's McLeish. Who are you, and what do you want?" The accent was either British or Australian; Billy never could tell the difference.

Captain Mitchell raised his own megaphone and called back, "My name is Mitchell. We're looking for a harbor to rest. We mean no harm."

McLeish called back, "You radioactive?" The tone was neither hostile nor friendly.

Captain Mitchell responded, "No, we've been careful." Then he added, "Are you?"

McLeish answered immediately, "No. How about the COVID?"

Mitchell called back, "No. And you?"

McLeish answered, "No, mate. That's why we live here." Billy smiled.

Mitchell and Oliver could see one of the women on the boat talking on what looked like a walkie-talkie, presumably to someone onshore.

Finally, McLeish called back, “I see you have a launch. Is it seaworthy?”

“That’s affirmative,” Mitchell called back.

McLeish responded, “Use it and follow us to shore. Just four of you. No guns.”

CHAPTER 48

Adamstown

The trip from the ark to the shore took nearly an hour. The currents swirled in the harbor, and the tides were strong, waves crashing on the hull of the launch as it followed McLeish's boat into the small port. Hunter, as promised, had put extra weight in the small boat for ballast, and it seemed to help, but Billy still had to focus. In addition to him and Hunter, Oliver and Dr. Steinberg were going ashore to explain the mission to the Pitcairn residents.

Billy was so focused on driving that he didn't take a good look at the island until they had tied up to the pier. When he finally did, the beauty of the place nearly took his breath away. The shores were sandy and wide. Behind them, the jungle was dense and green all the way down to the beach. In the background, the mountains stood impressively tall, with puffy white clouds hanging on the peaks.

After both boats were tied up, McLeish's colleagues, glancing warily at the new arrivals, walked up the pier, while McLeish himself approached the launch. "Welcome to Adamstown." He introduced himself again. He reminded Billy of what an island version of Santa Claus might look like, from the full white beard to the large belly. Again, his tone was not overly friendly, but his handshake was firm. To Billy he said simply, "Good work with those currents, mate. They can be tricky." He followed that by saying, "Follow me."

Hunter didn't move, stating bluntly, "I'll watch the launch." It was a smart move to have an escape option in case anything bad happened. For the others, though, the sensation of walking on dry land again was anything but ominous. Instead, they all instantly noticed that there was no rocking from waves. Billy pulled off his work sandals and let his toes grip the sand.

McLeish noticed and smiled through his beard. "Been out a while, eh?"

"Over a month," Billy answered. "This feels great!"

They followed McLeish into a waiting electric cart, and he shuttled them up a dirt road leading away from the pier. The dirt had been smoothed from years of usage and frequent rains, so the cart kicked up very little dust. As they rode, Billy heard birds in the surrounding forest but was unable to spot any of them. They stopped at a modest hut on the edge of a row of tidy wooden buildings and entered a small but orderly room that looked a bit like an office, with a desk and chairs and an overhead fan cycling slowly. As they settled in, the door stayed open behind them, letting the humid tropical air come inside.

An elderly woman, her gray hair pulled back in a bun, rolled forward in a wheelchair to greet the arrivals. "I'm Helen Turner, the governor of Pitcairn Island." Her accent was identical to that of McLeish. "We don't mean to be inhospitable, but one can't be too careful these days."

After the visitors introduced themselves, Governor Turner talked a while about the island. She explained that some of the residents, including her, were direct descendants of Spencer Christian and the *Bounty* mutineers. Christian and his group had burned the *Bounty* so that they would not be tempted to leave, and they then survived despite some bitter infighting until British ships tracked them down. While several of the mutineers were hauled back to England in chains, a few others managed to stay on Pitcairn. Over the centuries since, the numbers of residents fluctuated, even dropping to near zero at one point when some residents were convicted of sexual abuse and sent to prison in New Zealand. The Pitcairn residents were still officially subjects of the British crown, but they were also self-governing. Turner stated proudly, "We are the world's smallest democracy." She finished by saying that she was eager to hear the story of the ark and why they were here.

Oliver and Dr. Steinberg thus explained the history of the ark and the goal of saving species. As they talked, Billy's gaze strayed out the open door to the road outside the hut. A variety of people wandered by, looking in to see these new arrivals or stopping to talk briefly with McLeish, who still sat in the driver's seat of the cart. They seemed to be a mix of Anglos and Polynesians, all casually dressed and apparently healthy enough. Just as Billy was wondering if they had been touched at all by the nuclear war, Governor Turner began discussing that very subject.

"We typically have shortwave connections with the outside world, but we heard only preliminary reports of conflict and then all our communication ceased. Normally, we also have two or three ships of tourists arriving each month, but we have had none for weeks. We are therefore at least as intrigued with you and what you can tell us about the rest of the world as you are with us."

"I'm afraid we don't know much more," Oliver answered and then added, "but we fear the worst."

The governor sighed and nodded. "So they've finally done it, the fools." As she paused for several seconds, the only sound was that of the waves pounding on the shore. Then she looked back at the visitors and, with a wry expression, said, "And yet they said we were foolish to stay on this island. Little did they know. Even if Pitcairn weren't out of the line of fire for their bombs, this place is a wonderful refuge. We have elevation and are thus less susceptible than other islands to the rise in sea level resulting from climate change. We have our own food and our own water system. We..." She stopped, seeming to realize that she had started to boast, and then said, "I applaud your intentions to save the species. Your plans may have been changed by recent events, but your assessment of the need to take action has certainly been justified."

"Thank you," Oliver said simply. He and Dr. Steinberg waited. They knew the next move was hers.

She finally smiled slightly. "You're welcome to anchor in our harbor for a few days and figure out what you want to do next." She then added a comment that was warm enough but also included a warning not to take their hospitality for granted. "We'll enjoy having some visitors for a bit."

CHAPTER 49

The Waterfall

Billy was getting restless. They had anchored the ark a couple hundred yards offshore, safe from any danger of running aground. People were eager to get on dry land again and to explore the island, but the Adamstown residents asked that they not all come ashore at once. So Oliver set up a rotation whereby one-half of the crew was allowed shore leave each day. And someone had to shuttle them in and out to shore in the launch. Billy's role was thus predictable.

At first, he enjoyed the job. The currents and tides were tricky, especially during the occasional afternoon thunderstorm, and Billy was proud of his growing skill with the small craft. He also enjoyed the chance to talk to all the other crew and passengers as they shuttled in and out for their island visits. But by the third day he was starting to regret his own lack of time on the island. People came back with stories of sandy beaches, interesting residents, and thick jungle forests.

One of those stories came late on the second day, when he was bringing back the Hill and Brooks families. Annie told her uncle Billy about a hike they had done just north of the settlement along a river to a waterfall that made the "best swimming pool ever." Jonah Brooks called it "awesome!" Knowing that kids could exaggerate, Billy looked at the parents, and they nodded in agreement. His interest in the waterfall increased even more on the third day. Jessie rode in with him, but as she disembarked at the dock, she couldn't resist teasing Billy that she was going to use her day off to search for "the famous waterfall." Billy mumbled a "Lucky you" before he had to return to the ark for the next load of passengers.

So he was grateful that afternoon when his sister made him a nice offer. Beth rode in to the island with a group just after lunch, but then she lingered, busying herself tying the boat to the pier with one of the ropes as the others disembarked. When it was just the two of them on the pier, she said, "So, helmsman, why don't you take the afternoon off?"

"Wish I could, sis," he answered.

She answered confidently, "I can handle this boat."

Billy was tempted. But then he glanced at the puffy white clouds building up behind the mountains to the west for another afternoon storm. "I don't doubt that, but the chop in the bay during the storms—"

Beth cut him off. "I can take a load before any storm hits. And if we get a storm, the boat can stay at the dock until it passes." She paused and then continued, "Or until you get back."

He didn't answer for a moment while the launch just bobbed in the water. Beth noticed him glancing toward the north end of the beach, where the trail to the waterfall reportedly existed.

"You scared, Billy?" Beth taunted. It was their old line, but this time he couldn't help but wonder if she knew Jessie had gone that way earlier.

He smiled and answered, "Not enough." She stared at him as if to say to get going.

After giving Beth a couple verbal instructions for the boat, Billy climbed onto the pier. He glanced back at her to say thanks, and she just waved him off.

"Don't get lost," she said as she sat down in the pilot chair and put her feet up on the steering console.

Billy hustled onto the beach and turned north. He took off his sandals to feel the sand and surf under his feet. He had barely been on land since they arrived three days before, and it felt great. The waves crashed in on the shore, scattering a few gulls and terns. The air smelled of salt, of course, but other smells, greener and more tropical, wafted down from the jungle. Within a few minutes, just as Annie and others had said, he found a modest stream coming out of the mountains and flowing down to the beach with a little trail alongside. He put his sandals back on, hurried onto the trail and into the jungle. As he walked, the palm trees that had lined the edge of the beach were quickly surrounded by ferns and bushes of all shapes and sizes. Soon, the vegetation was so thick he lost sight of the mountains and clouds in the distance. Unseen birds made all kinds of noises, although it wasn't clear whether they were objecting to or welcoming his arrival.

Billy heard voices. He looked ahead through the brush and saw Rodriguez and Reese coming down the trail, wearing only shorts and sandals and carrying their shirts. Both were wet, as if from swimming. They saw Billy coming and paused on the trail as he arrived.

"About time you got off that boat, man," Reese said.

Billy answered quickly, trying to be coy, "Yeah. I hear there's a good swimming hole up this way."

Rodriguez answered, "Yeah right, amigo, a swimming hole." He grinned at Reese and then back at Billy before adding, "It's just up ahead. Don't get in too deep." They both laughed. It was obviously not an innocent line, and Billy was beginning to wonder if everybody on the ship had some idea about what he wanted to do with his day off.

Before Billy could say anything in response, Reese put his hand on T-Rod's back, as if pushing him down the trail, and said as he passed, "Have fun, Billy."

Billy continued up the trail. Fifty yards farther on he heard water falling and knew he was close. The trail continued to parallel the stream, the clear blue water moving along fast enough to create little ripples and rapids. Then, as he emerged into a small clearing, he froze in his tracks and stared at one of the most beautiful sights he had ever seen.

The jungle opened as the trail led straight to a sizable pool formed by a gorgeous waterfall on the western side. The water fell from about twenty feet high and thus made considerable noise as it splashed into the pool. On a flat rock on the northern side of the pool, twenty yards from where Billy stood, Jessie sat with her back to him, her day pack sitting nearby. She was completely naked and had obviously just been swimming, the water drops still visible on her back as she combed out her wet black hair. Her body was impressively athletic, a narrow waist and relatively wide shoulders. Billy could see the muscles in her back as she lifted the comb over her head. He felt his blood pumping. And it was not from hiking the trail.

Billy stood and watched, not at all sure what to do next. He heard a clap of thunder off to the west. And then, even though he was sure that he had not made a sound, Jessie shifted to look back at the trail. She didn't seem at all surprised that he was there but instead just stared back at him, confidently, as she continued grooming. He stood transfixed. A light rain started to fall.

"You found it, Billy Hill," she said calmly, "the famous waterfall."

He swallowed before he spoke. "I didn't really come up here for the waterfall."

She smiled as she put down her comb, stood, and said, "Neither did I." She dived into the pool.

Whatever doubts Billy had before about her feelings vanished. He shed his clothes as fast as he could and dived into the water. It felt mild from the heat and the warm rainfall as he swam her direction. When he came up for air, she was on him and giving him a full hug. He could feel the strength in her body.

She whispered, "C'mon," and led him under the waterfall to the little space behind it, between the cascade and the rock wall. The rocks there were smooth, flattened over the centuries from the falling water. Billy lay back as she pushed him down and climbed on to make love.

Afterward, they lay on the rock without moving, listening only to each other breathe and to the sound of the falling water. They could look through the waterfall to see raindrops hitting the pool.

After a full minute, Billy said simply, "Wow!"

"Wow is right!" Jessie answered.

He shifted slightly so he could look in her brown eyes and then started singing very quietly the old Van Morrison song, "Hey, where did we go, days when the rains came…" Jessie smiled. Billy skipped some lines to get to the chorus. "Blah, blah, blah...you're my brown-eyed girl."

She feigned disappointment. "You should sing the whole thing or forget it."

"Okay, then, I'll forget it."

She laughed. He lay back and thought for a moment about how this day had developed. He said quietly, "Thank goodness for my sister."

Jessie responded immediately, "Sisters can be very helpful."

Billy suddenly realized that even though he had not even explained what he was referring to, she knew. He was as elated as he was surprised. Her dark eyes met his.

"So you and Beth—"

She cut him off with a kiss before saying, "Seemed like we would never get some time off that ship together."

Billy lay back, feeling incredibly content. He said, with just a touch of sarcasm, "Well, now that we know this spot, this island isn't missing much of anything, is it?"

Jessie nodded slightly, but then her expression turned serious as she answered. "Winters. I always loved winters in the mountains."

Billy remembered. "You're right. And we will miss them."

"What do you miss, Billy?"

Billy thought for a moment about all the things he knew they would all miss, from sporting events to libraries, but he went for a simple answer. "Train whistles. I loved the sound of train whistles in the distance."

Jessie looked at him and smiled slightly. "Feeling restless again, are you?"

"No," Billy answered. "I just always thought that sound was haunting. Most lonesome sound in the world." He looked at Jessie. "You realize, of course, that there is a line in a song about it."

"Of course," Jessie answered with a sigh.

"Yes, a song by Woody Guthrie's granddaughter. How appropriate is that?"

"Okay," she prompted.

Billy answered, "The line is, 'Freight train whistle taught me how to cry.'"

Jessie looked at Billy with a quizzical smile. "Are you feeling lonesome, Billy?"

Billy smiled broadly. "Not today, I'm not. That's why it would be so nice. Now I could hear a train whistle when I'm not feeling lonesome."

Jessie just shook her head as she leaned over to hug him again.

They stayed at the pool until the storm passed and the sun came out again. They then came out from under the overhang, took a quick dip, and crawled out on the rocks to dry off enough before getting dressed. They headed back down the trail and along the beach toward the pier. The sun dropped down onto the mountains to the west.

"Another pretty sunset," Jessie said quietly. Billy thought of the evenings sitting on the gear locker and smiled in return.

Approaching the pier, they could see the launch bobbing in the water. Beth was sitting on the dock, her legs folded underneath and her hands out in front, meditating. She heard Billy and Jessie coming and stood up. As they neared, she didn't say anything. Beth and Jessie nodded at each other.

"Hey, where is everybody?" Billy asked, noticing that no one else was around.

"After the storm, I took everybody else back to the ark," Beth said and then looked at them with a raised eyebrow. "Ship's meeting."

"Oh yeah," Billy muttered. "I completely forgot."

"As did I," Jessie added. "I'm sorry, Beth, that we are making you miss it as well."

Beth smiled a little. "What was that line in the movie? I'm not really missing it."

All three laughed.

Billy said, "I owe you big-time, sis. I'll pay you back somehow."

She answered quickly, "Well, you can start by taking your job back." She tossed him the key to the ignition of the launch.

CHAPTER 50

A Plan for the Season

The ship's meeting had already started by the time Billy slid the launch up next to the ark. As he often did with meetings, Oliver had scheduled it to start at sunset, in part because so few among the crew were wearing watches anymore. Thus, just as the last rays of sunlight illuminated the higher portions of the ship's superstructure, Oliver stood near the ladder leading to the bridge and faced the crowd.

Using a megaphone, he started speaking with a "Good evening" and then waited until people quieted down. "We have had a good visit to Adamstown. I hope you all have enjoyed the town, the island, and the hospitality of the residents. I certainly have."

Just then, the crowd on the side of the deck closest to land shifted slightly as Beth, Jessie, and Billy climbed up from below. Billy looked a bit sheepish, as if hoping nobody would notice them trying to slink quietly into the back of the gathering. It didn't work. Reese shot Billy a knowing smile. Rodriguez nodded as if to say they weren't getting away with anything. Maria Rivera, standing near Hunter, shook her index finger a little in the air to let Jessie know her older sister was keeping an eye on her. A little smile belied the feigned concern, however.

Oliver either did not notice the late arrivals or decided to ignore them as he continued. "I appreciate, and the Adamstown residents appreciate, how we've all been on our best behavior."

"Yeah, wait until they see what we're really like," Rodriguez muttered. Some laughed. Hunter scowled at him.

Oliver went on. "Therefore, they have suggested the following. North of where we are now, on the other side of the harbor is the site of a larger settlement that was abandoned years ago. Some residents took Captain Mitchell, Mr. Hunter, and me down there yesterday. Some buildings as well as a pier are left, albeit in bad shape. Their suggestion is that we settle in there for the season. That would allow us to weather in during monsoon season and stay close by, but not too close to them, while we get used to one another."

"How bad is bad shape?" Sanders asked.

"Fair question, Mr. Sanders. It will take some work," Oliver answered. "The pier is long, and damaged. But the bay there is deep, so once the pier is restored, we could tie up the ark. Some of the building foundations will be useful. Between that and the prefab building materials on board, we can get some housing together before the monsoons come in late November. As we all know, with the climate changing, we can expect some pretty rough storms."

"How would moving ashore affect the species?" Susan Harris asked.

"Thank you, Susan," Oliver answered. "Dr. Steinberg assures me they are fine where they are, but she would also welcome a facility onshore should the situation offshore deteriorate."

Griffiths asked, "What are our other options?"

Oliver paused to collect his thoughts. "Of course. Governor Turner tells me that there is another bay on the other side of the island if we wanted to get some distance from them, although it's a rocky shore. She also pointed out that Henderson Island is not too far away, where there was once another settlement. Alas, there is little fresh water there, but we could use our desalination system. Finally, we could take to sea again and head north to try to get calmer winter weather." This prompted some murmuring in the crowd.

"How bad is the weather likely to be?" Janice Brooks asked.

From the other side of the gathering, Carter, who seemingly had experienced everything at sea, said brusquely, "Bad."

Reese added, "And monsoons can be really bad at this latitude."

Miller muttered, "This island's sounding better all the time."

Griffiths demanded, "What does Adamstown want from us?"

Oliver was ready with his answer. "Several things. First, our company. There are fewer than one hundred residents on Pitcairn. There are obvious reasons to worry about that. Second, for electricity, they depend partly on diesel generators. That fuel is dirty and will be hard to come by. Owen suggested that we may be able to help them further develop some alternative sources of energy. Third, they like us being here for protection, if needed."

This prompted considerable discussion in the crowd. They all knew that other people might show up, uninvited, someday. After letting people have some time to talk about the options among themselves, Oliver called for a vote. It was unanimous. They would stay on Pitcairn, at the abandoned site, at least for the coming season.

"I'll inform them of our decision." Oliver smiled and concluded, "We thought this would be the outcome. They've invited us to a welcome party tomorrow evening."

CHAPTER 51

Welcome Party

The name of the ship, the *Bounty*, that brought the first humans to Pitcairn was ironic, given the natural bounty on the island. Fresh water was abundant. Available food included pineapples, coconuts, and bananas. The bay was teeming with fish. Indeed, the British government had established the Pitcairn Islands Marine Reserve in 2015 as one of the largest marine protected areas in the world because of the abundance and diversity of sea life. In addition to these naturally occurring foods, the residents had imported some chickens and dairy cows. Further, the soil was conducive to some crops, and the residents had cultivated potatoes and vegetables. They also had an impressive bee colony and had even exported honey to numerous other nations.

Thus, when the arkonauts arrived in the late afternoon for the welcome party, they found long tables laden with food and grills loaded with fresh fish from the bay. Nor did they arrive empty-handed but brought pots of stew that Maria and her cooks had made, as well as bottles from their liquor locker.

Throughout the late afternoon, Billy enjoyed ferrying boatloads of his shipmates, all in a festive mood, from the ark to the settlement. He particularly enjoyed his final load of guests as it included the Rivera sisters, both wearing simple white cotton dresses, Maria in sandals and Jessie in cowboy boots. Billy felt fortunate to be going in their company. Not only were they great companions, but they also both looked beautiful. He imagined it was how he might have felt if he had taken the prom queen to the prom, that is, if he had even gone to the prom, let alone known the prom queen.

As he finished his duties and tied up the launch, McLeish greeted him with a tankard that he thrust into Billy's left hand as he shook his right. The first swallow revealed McLeish's beer to be as strong as his grip. Billy nearly coughed, a reaction that seemed to please McLeish. He clapped Billy on the shoulder and said cheerily, "You do good work with that dory, mate. The bay can be tricky." Billy had thus received his first indication that it might be a long night.

Not surprisingly, the party started slowly. Most people were settling for familiarity at first, arkonauts standing around with one another while the residents either busied themselves with preparations or just talked to their own neighbors. But like with most parties, the drink and food broke the ice. The residents were curious about where the visitors were from and for any news from the outside world, even from before the war. And the visitors had lots of questions for the residents, about the island and their lifestyle.

Billy loaded a plate of food and sat down with the Rivera sisters, John Hunter, and a couple from the island named Allison. Maria and Jessie were full of questions about the food, which the Allisons were happy to answer. Hunter was quiet but much more relaxed than usual. He even gave a little autobiography to the Allisons, telling them briefly about the Sioux reservation near the Black Hills and how he had chafed at reservation life. Coming from him, it was nearly a soliloquy. Billy, too, was quiet as he savored the food and provided the cheap man's compliment by stuffing himself.

The sunset was, as always, beautiful and lit up the mountains with a soft orange glow. Even with over two hundred people in the plaza, the waves could still be heard crashing on the shore. Billy tried to take it all in and then noticed, just beyond the unlit bonfire, a gazebo-type structure with some things under wraps. He took a guess and asked the Allisons if those were covered musical instruments.

"Oh yes," Mrs. Allison responded. "We have concerts most every Saturday evening."

Billy nodded. "What night is this?" He truly had no idea.

She smiled. "Well, this is Saturday, of course, Mr. Hill."

Billy immediately excused himself and went to collect Miller and Susan Harris. Those two needed no persuading to join Billy on another run to the ark to get their instruments.

An hour later, the trio from the ark gathered with the Pitcairn musicians on the stage of the gazebo. The locals welcomed the new players as they uncovered their own instruments. They included a young Polynesian named James, who revealed a rudimentary drum set. A middle-aged woman named Lisa sat down at a little piano. She also had an accordion in the stand next to it. An older guy named Reed proudly showed off his stand-up bass. Billy guessed they must play a lot of jazz, but whatever it had been, now they had six musicians and no idea about what they might play in common.

So they started with simple songs, ones with only three or four chords, and with which most people were at least somewhat familiar. For instance, some Dylan songs were easy and catchy. Then they started trying more challenging material, like from the Beatles and the Rolling Stones. The Pitcairn residents were, after all, British subjects. Nobody else at the party paid much attention at first, perhaps sympathetically understanding that the musicians needed some time to sort things out.

After the sun went down, the party grew livelier. The residents lit the bonfire, and that got at least as much attention as did the band. Occasionally, some people would stop by the gazebo to listen or watch, but then they would go back to the fire or their own conversations. As far as Billy was concerned, that was fine, as the musicians were still getting used to one another and, as he admitted to himself, for the first hour or so, the music was more enthusiastic than impressive. At some point in the evening, Rodriguez and Reese began mixing up drinks with Henry Hill's expensive rum and some pineapple juice and passing them out to anyone who stopped by their table. Billy would have hardly noticed except that between songs one time, Jessie strolled up and offered him a sip of hers. He was not shocked to find that it was a bit heavy on the rum. And McLeish kept wandering around, refilling mugs with more of his homemade brew. After a while, the conversations and the laughter were getting significantly louder.

Then Billy started thinking that, objectivity be damned, the band was starting to sound good. Feeling confident, he got out a harmonica and led the group into “Key to the Highway,” a straightforward, twelve-bar blues song that the others in the makeshift band picked up right away. The rhythm from the bass and the drums added so much that he felt his own feet tapping. But they didn’t let it stop, several doing breaks on their own instruments. By then, the Rivera sisters and quite a few others were standing near the stage, swaying with the rhythm of the song. When the band finished, they got a nice round of applause. Billy celebrated with another swig of the rum and realized that not only was he feeling the joy of playing with others; he was also getting buzzed.

“Hey, you Yanks must know some Chuck Berry,” Reed said from behind his bass. It was a smart call and a natural follow-up to the blues song.

Miller responded, “Hell, I’m Canadian, and even I know Chuck Berry.” He started playing “Johnny B. Goode.” If there is a universal rock song, that’s it. So the band jumped on it. Miller did an excellent break on his guitar, and Billy, channeling the Michael J. Fox scene in the *Back to the Future* movie, even did a little duck walk, earning some laughs from the crowd. They finished to an ego-filling round of applause.

As the band paused for just a minute, Billy looked around. The sunlight was gone, and the stars were starting to appear. He could hear the bonfire crackling away and the waves hitting the beach in the background. People were talking and laughing. And he got one of those feelings when a moment is there that you want to savor without it going by too fast. He tried to embrace it and freeze it in his memory.

Then McLeish yelled as he raised a tankard, “Don’t stop now, you’re starting to sound decent!” People laughed. When nobody else volunteered a song, Billy knew exactly what he wanted to play.

“Here’s a song from one of your countrymen,” he said and began strumming G and C chords, then G and D chords. Over and over. Then, looking at Jessie standing in front of the stage, he started singing:

Hey, where did we go
Days when the rains came
Down in a hollow
Playing a new game

Jessie smiled and shook her head back and forth. Maria looked from her sister to Billy and then back again and, even without knowing the back story but figuring there was one, smiled as well. The band picked the song up at a nice, fast tempo.

Laughing and a running
Skipping and a jumping
In the misty morning fog
Well our hearts were thumping
And you my brown-eyed girl…

Miller, Susan, and Lisa all joined in on the chorus:

Do you remember when…
We used to sing
Sha-la-la…

Lisa sang the second verse with gusto. And when the band hit the chorus again, Billy couldn't resist. He leaned his guitar against a post, stepped off the stage, and stuck out his hand to Jessie. She took it and let him spin her around. At first, others around them cleared a little space for them, but they had only taken a few steps when others started dancing as well. James and Janice Brooks showed they had done this before, even as their kids backed away, at least acting as if they were embarrassed. Maria Rivera pulled Hunter out of the crowd and forced him to start swaying to the beat. Sarah did the same with Owen. Soon, all over the plaza people were dancing.

As the band stretched out the song, Jessie looked as happy as Billy felt, so he swung her around even more vigorously. Miller sang the first verse again, and after everybody sang the chorus, Susan Harris did a violin solo that was as catchy as anything Billy had ever heard to that song. Jessie and Billy were moving so fast to the solo that they bumped into Mi-Sung Lee and Rodriguez, who were also dancing wildly.

"Bueno amigo!" Rodriguez shouted over the noise.

Billy tried to look around even as he was dancing. A bit removed from the wild scene in front of the stage, the Allison couple was slow-dancing together gracefully. Near them, Beth and Sanders were also slow-dancing, not quite so gracefully. On the other side of the plaza, Oliver was dancing with Dr. Steinberg near Governor Turner as the latter clapped along in time in her wheelchair.

After a twirl, Jessie pulled Billy in close and, over the music, whispered in his ear, "You still haven't finished singing that song to me."

He looked back at her and whispered, "Someday." Then they joined the line of dancers that was making its way around the bonfire.

The band wisely followed up with all kinds of good dance songs, everything from "Shout" to "Twist and Shout." Then Lisa picked up the accordion and started playing duets with Susan on the violin, Cajun music like you might hear in the Bayou. With James on the drums, Reed on the bass, and Miller on guitar all providing rhythm, it was infectious. Billy, knowing his limitations on guitar and loving the alternative anyway, continued dancing with Jessie.

Ultimately, the band went on for hours, reminding Billy of a Springsteen concert. And everybody seemed to have a great time. Goodness knows, after all that had happened in the world, they all needed it. After the music finally ended, people started drifting away. Governor Turner and the other Adamstown residents said their good nights and headed to their huts. The musicians all promised to do it again sometime and packed away the instruments. Those feeding the bonfire let it die down.

In the bay, the running lights of the ark were visible, and Billy realized that at least some people needed to get back out there. So he and McLeish both chugged down some coffee and threw water on their faces to the point where they felt sober enough to make runs in their small boats. Jessie rode with Billy to give whatever help she could. Oliver, the families, and most of the crew all returned to the ark. But after several runs by both boats, upon returning to the island, Billy and Jessie and McLeish felt like their work was finally finished for the night.

McLeish started to walk away toward his hut and then looked back at Billy. "Good party, mate. You're welcome to sleep on the island if you want."

Billy nodded and looked around at who was left onshore. Beth and Sanders were standing by what was left of the bonfire. "We're staying," Beth said simply. As he dropped one more log on the embers, Sanders glanced over near the gazebo, where Rodriguez was stretched out on a table. "T-Rod's not going anywhere either." Reese walked past, mumbling something about "sleeping on dry land," and headed toward the jungle. There were a few other stragglers sleeping in the beach chairs or under some of the trees, and nobody seemed to be interested in any further rides to the ark until the morning.

Billy asked Jessie quietly, "What do you want to do?"

Jessie glanced at the ark floating in the water, then at the folks settling down near the bonfire, and finally back at Billy before answering, "Waterfall?"

Billy laughed, but before he could answer, she added, "Just kidding, Billy. How about the beach?"

So they grabbed a tablecloth for some cover and walked a short distance away from the fire down onto the sand near where the waves were pounding on the shore. They lay down on their backs and pulled the tablecloth over themselves like a blanket. Looking up, they could see the stars were so thick that it was hard to pick out constellations, but the Southern Cross was big as life.

"You know the line in the Steve Stills song about seeing the Southern Cross for the first time?" Billy asked.

Jessie murmured as if to say yes.

"Well, there it is," he added. Billy knew she was tired, but he was still wired and not ready to go to sleep. He thought about the party and how, for the first time since the world had blown up, they had all just cut loose for a whole evening. Should they feel guilty for forgetting all the tragedy for a while? Was that wrong? An answer came to mind. Maybe it was the length of their playing reminding him of Springsteen, or maybe it was because they did a couple of his songs, but for not the first time that night, Bruce's lyrics came to mind.

He asked, "You want to know my favorite Springsteen line?"

Jessie rolled over so she could rest her head on his chest, mumbled "Si," and closed her eyes, only partially interested.

"Ain't no sin to be glad you're alive."

She smiled a little, opened her eyes to look in his for just a second, then closed them again and fell asleep almost immediately.

"Yeah, well, I thought it was profound," Billy said out loud even though nobody else could hear. And at that moment, he realized something. Whatever their skeletons, whatever their sins, whatever the sins of the world, they were still here, with another chance. He let out a deep breath. He had not felt that good in days. Weeks. Years. Maybe ever. All the deaths and losses and tragedy only made it even more true. He was glad to be alive.

CHAPTER 52

Settling In

The arkonauts went to work building a new home on Pitcairn Island with enthusiasm. After being at sea for weeks, they had a lot of pent-up energy. And many of them, particularly the families, wanted to sink some roots. Finally, they knew they needed to move quickly as monsoon season was coming. They had no shelters, no source of electricity on land, and only a few months' food supply on the ark to supplement the island's natural bounty. They wondered just how many bananas they could eat before they became more necessary than desirable.

As planned, they moved a few miles away from the Adamstown settlement to create their own space. The new location was as gorgeous and benign as Adamstown. The mountains were even closer to the sea here, and because of less activity in this area, the forests grew nearly to the waterline. Past visitors had carved out a clearing just off the beach that had, since those early settlers left, grown over somewhat with vines and small plants. The trees nearby were bulging with fruit. Near the clearing, a creek flowed down from the mountains into the ocean, providing a source of fresh water that required simple boiling before drinking. Finally, the bay nearby was full of fish, suggesting the possibility of fresh protein every night.

Oliver's foresight in hiring became evident when he split the crew into teams. Beth and what was left of her fire crew went to work restoring the pier. Hunter led a building group that included Brooks, a good carpenter, and a Chinese civil engineer named Bao Ling, who had considerable construction experience. Owen and his engineers as well as Reese, the machinist, began building new solar panels with the materials they had brought. Their intention was to get the panels up in their area while also helping the Pitcairn residents expand their solar supply at Adamstown.

The food crews worked on preparation as well as supply. Every day, Maria and her galley crew put out supplies, such as bread for people to make their own breakfast and lunch, but they stopped each afternoon to prepare dinner for everyone. Jordan Smith-Garvey took charge of planting. Jordan, a horticulturalist, knew how to grow crops such as potatoes, carrots and even corn in salty water. A family from India named Sirpathia had expertise in growing rice. A Japanese couple named Misumo began a hive to produce honey. Luke and his wife, Hari, not surprisingly, were experts in island fishing and began training others. Somebody started an orchard to grow apples and oranges. Finally, the Adamstown residents kindly traded their new neighbors some cows and chickens in exchange for help on their energy infrastructure.

Others worked on projects that suggested a certain permanence to the settlement. Doc Harrison set up a small clinic. Janice Brooks and Susan Harris claimed a spot in the clearing and began a little school for all the kids while their parents were working. And thinking somewhat ahead, Oliver and Captain Mitchell began drawing up a charter of self-governance for the community.

Billy's job was predictable. The currents in the new location were as tricky as, if not more than, where they had anchored down by Adamstown. In fact, the early settlers here had abandoned this spot precisely because it was so difficult to get ships, or even boats, in and out. A reminder of the potential for disaster lay in the water just a quarter mile north of their location, a shipwreck that dated back to the early settlement. Thus, Billy's job was to run the launch, ferrying people back and forth to their jobs from the ark to the settlement as well as others, such as Owen and his solar crew, to Adamstown.

One benefit of not being at sea was that nobody had to stand watches in the middle of the night, so all the arkonauts got onto the same schedule. Because of the pending monsoon season and the need to hurry, they developed a routine of working six days a week. They did take time in the evenings to relax, swim, take walks, or when it wasn't raining, watch another of the supply of movies projected on a screen on the fantail after dark.

Billy relished those evenings. Every night after dinner, he would load up the launch with any takers and go into shore for an hour or two. Jessie usually accompanied him, and they would go for a walk on the beach or a swim in the waves, sometimes with others, but often just the two of them. The island invigorated all his senses. He loved the sound of the waves crashing on the shore, the sight of the sun going down behind the mountains to the west, the taste of the salt in the ocean air, the aromas of the sea and forest both nearby, and the feel of Jessie's hand in his. He avoided saying it out loud, but he couldn't help remembering the Eagles song that once you call a place paradise, you could "kiss it goodbye." Occasionally, he would have some sense of foreboding that this idyllic lifestyle couldn't last forever, but he would shove it aside and savor the time at hand.

CHAPTER 53

Progress

After a full week of work, the whole crew took a day off on Veterans Day. It was a pretty day, a blue sky punctuated with puffy white clouds that reminded Billy of what was referred to as a Simpsons sky from the opening of the cartoon TV show. Nearly everyone wanted to get ashore, so he spent the morning shuttling people on the launch. He and Jessie planned to take the last group, one that included his family, into shore and then relax. While waiting for them, Billy read the memo that Oliver had sent around.

Date: November 11, 2026
From: Oliver Hill and Captain Joseph Mitchell
Subject: Governance Proposal

Captain Mitchell and I, with input from numerous residents, offer the following proposal for self-governance in our settlement.

Governing body. A board of trustees will be elected to office, consisting of three members serving staggered terms so that we have continuity in the event of replacement. The first set of trustees will serve terms depending on the size of the vote. The person receiving the most votes will serve a four-year term. The second highest will serve three years. The lowest will serve two years.

Elections. Elections will be held on the first Tuesday of each November. We will hold our first elections next month and then, after two years, every November. All people over eighteen years of age will be eligible to vote.

Basic freedoms. In accordance with the US Constitution, we hold freedom of speech, religion, and assembly to be essential.

Dispute resolution. All disputes and alleged violations of the common law will be heard by the board of trustees for resolution. Resolution requires a simple majority. The trustees will consider the establishment of a court of law for future resolution.

This is a draft, subject to amendment and revision. We welcome all suggestions.

Billy finished it and looked at Jessie with what must have been an odd look, as it prompted her question.

"Is there a problem? It made sense to me."

He hesitated and then said what was on his mind. "Well, it makes sense, but I'm just not sure where all this is headed."

"What does that mean?" she asked.

"I guess I worry a little about what people might want to do to this place. You heard Griffiths earlier…"

Just then, Owen, Sarah, Annie, and Roscoe showed up and climbed down into the launch, wearing swimming suits, carrying towels and a beach umbrella they had found somewhere. After all the "Good morning" greetings and a couple of hearty back scratches for an excited dog, Billy fired up the motor and started the launch toward the shore.

Sarah began talking. "Ah, our first day off in a week. Feels good, doesn't it, Annie?"

Annie answered, "I liked sleeping in this morning."

Sarah said, "Didn't we all? Even your daddy stayed in bed until breakfast." She looked at Billy and Jessie. "You two probably didn't sleep in, did you? Nice of you to be running folks into the beach."

Jessie answered, "I slept a little later and missed the first run. Billy got up early." She glanced at Billy. "Maybe that's why he's so feisty today."

Billy knew she was goading him but took the bait. "I'm not feisty…I was just saying…"

Jessie teased, "You sure didn't look happy with your father's proclamation."

Oliver perked up and looked back at Billy from the front of the boat. "Is there something wrong with the proposal, William?"

Billy answered, "No. The proposal's fine. I'm just not sure where all this will lead. We're changing this island, and maybe…"

Owen weighed in. "It sounds to me like we walked into something here. What's the matter, Bill? You don't like democracy?"

Billy, trying to not sound defensive, answered, "I have nothing against democracy. As the saying goes, democracy is ugly but still better than any other form of governance. No, my problem—"

Owen interrupted. "Oh, great. Here it comes."

Sarah intervened. "Let him talk, Owen. I want to hear it."

Billy continued. "Setting up government, putting up houses, clearing land, it all feels like—"

Owen interrupted again. "Progress?"

Billy answered, "Okay, progress. Civilization. Whatever you want to call it. On a trip earlier this morning, Griffiths suggested—"

Owen, obviously relishing the prospect of an argument, cut him off again. "What would you do, Bill? Go back to sea and leave the island to the jungle?"

Oliver, with a smile, added, "I can't say that I've seen you turn down any bananas or coconuts, son." Owen laughed. Billy even smiled.

"Okay, here's the thing," Billy responded. "This morning, Griffiths suggested we build a road to go from our settlement all the way back to Adamstown." He paused to let that sink in.

Jessie finally said, "That must have been on the first run, as I had not heard that before. I don't think I like it either."

Owen wasn't as troubled by the idea. "There is some logic there. We could run a path down along the boundary between the beach and the forest. Start narrow—"

Sarah stopped him. "Spoken like an engineer, Owen. Yes, we can do it, but is it a good idea?"

Billy was happy to suddenly have some allies. "I'm just saying that we should be careful how much we change things here."

The conversation paused as the launch approached the pier. Billy drove past the spot where work was ongoing and pulled in next to the intact portion. Jessie jumped off the bow with the rope and secured the boat.

As she disembarked, Sarah said, "Nice driving, Billy."

Annie added, "Yeah, nice driving, Uncle Billy."

As Billy shut off the motor, he answered, "Thanks, guys. Let's hit the beach."

Annie looked puzzled. "Why?"

Owen explained, "He just means let's go to the beach, Annie."

Annie still looked puzzled. "Why doesn't he say that, then?"

Sarah, leading her daughter up the pier, answered, "You can ask him, honey. He's going with us."

Annie yelled, "Hooray!"

They all walked up the pier and into the clearing. Sarah began testing Annie by pointing to the different piles of lumber, the fruits of the labors of Hunter's construction crew, and asking her what building would be in each spot.

Sarah finished, "So there is still a lot of work to do."

Owen added, "Yes, but they are making progress."

Annie responded innocently, "This is progress?"

Billy broke out laughing as he answered his niece. "Now that's an interesting question, Annie."

Owen, too, wasn't ready to drop the conversation. "Always the eco-zealot, eh, Bill?"

Billy answered, "I'm not saying we shouldn't change things. I'm just saying it's worth thinking about how much."

Oliver nodded. "That's a fair point."

Annie was less convinced. "I don't know what you're talking about, Uncle Billy."

Owen added, "There you go, Uncle Billy. Why don't you explain it?"

Billy started to respond, "Okay. See, Annie, the thing is that until now this place has changed only when nature changed it, but now..."

Annie interrupted him. "Look, there's Aunt Beth." She pointed toward the beach, where Beth and her colleagues were putting up a large tarp on poles for some shade. "Come on, Roscoe, let's go over there."

Jessie patted Billy on the back. "Nice try, Uncle Billy." They all followed Annie.

As they approached the beach, the deckhands finished their shelter. Miller lay down in the shady sand with his cowboy hat over his eyes. Beth welcomed Annie with a big hug. And Roscoe ran straight to Sanders, who picked the dog up in both arms and let him lick his face. Rodriguez was dribbling a soccer ball, adeptly, on the hard-packed sand, where high tide had wet the beach earlier.

As Billy approached, Rodriguez kicked him the ball. When Billy misplayed it, Jessie took it, dribbled around Billy to the delight of Rodriguez, and then passed the ball back.

"Gracias, senorita," Rodriguez said as he took the pass. He sent it once again to Billy, who did a better job of receiving it this time and then passed it to his brother. They soon had a little game of the brothers against Jessie and Rodriguez.

It was no contest. Billy and Owen weren't very good, whereas Jessie was and Rodriguez was impressively skilled. After a few minutes of humiliation, Billy held up his hands and said, "No mas." Even if nobody else caught the reference to a famous boxer who once called it quits in the ring, Billy was prouder of it than he was of his playing.

Jessie graciously shook hands with both Owen and Billy, but Rodriguez was, at least for the moment, more interested in talking trash. He raised his hands in triumph and proudly exclaimed, "Viva

Mexico!" Owen shook his head and moved over to sit with Sarah and Beth in the shade of the tarp.

"Be nice, Tomas," Jessie scolded him.

Rodriguez couldn't resist more teasing as he looked at Billy. "It's called football, Shakespeare. And the whole world has been playing it since the nineteenth century."

Billy looked at Rodriguez, held up a finger, and said, "Watch this."

He ran down the sand and dived into the surf. He swam out about thirty yards, popped up out of the water, and then kicked furiously to catch the first big wave coming in to shore. He nailed it. He stretched out flat, like a board, and rode it all the way into the beach. When he emerged, Jessie gave him a round of applause.

Billy walked up the beach to the two of them and said to Rodriguez, "It's called surfing, T-Rod. And they've been doing it on these islands since the eighteenth century."

The people sitting under the tarp all laughed. Rodriguez smiled and nodded, saying, "Touché, amigo."

Jessie grinned. "You do have other skills, Guillermo." Billy thought back to their earlier conversation and smiled back. She nudged him. "Can you teach me?"

Billy nodded. "Come on." They ran down the sand and dived into the ocean.

CHAPTER 54

Monsoon

Monsoon season in the South Pacific runs from November to April. In the year the arkonauts arrived on Pitcairn, the first big storm happened to arrive on what would have been Thanksgiving Day back in the US. The arkonauts had been planning on having a big meal that day to celebrate, but the storm ended those plans.

In the morning before the storm arrived, Roscoe and the other animals all seemed restless, as if somehow aware they would need to seek shelter later. Their behavior seemed odd in that the day had started like most others, but the animals proved prescient. By that afternoon, the clouds had grown and darkened, the bottoms bulging with moisture. Lightning lit them up frequently, like at a balloon glow when the pilots light their burners to heat the air inside the bags. Thunder rolled in on waves from the mountains.

Realizing that this was going to be a large storm, families and animals moved into the few secure shelters that had been built and tied down everything else as best as they could. And then the crew thought about what to do with the ark. They had three options, none of them optimal. The first was to tie it up as securely as possible to the mostly finished pier. The problem was that a secured ship buffeted by a storm can do tremendous damage to the vessel and to the pier. The second option was to anchor out in the harbor and hope for some protection from the surrounding mountains. Sailors use the term *hurricane holes* to refer to natural shelters, but Bounty Bay was not an ideal candidate as there was substantial space between the mountains and the water, thus allowing large storm surges. The third option was to set sail with a skeleton crew and face the storm at sea. This has an obvious downside for those on board, but being underway allows a ship some space away from a dock or a coastline and gives the crew the chance to steer the ship into the waves to avoid capsizing.

After deciding on option 3, a skeleton crew sailed the ark out into the darkening ocean. They were several miles off the coast when the full force of the monsoon hit in the middle of the night. Although the waves did not reach the epic size of the ones they had encountered after leaving San Francisco, the ship nevertheless rode up and down thirty-footers like a car on a fiendish roller-coaster ride. And with few people and no freight or supplies on board, the ark had very little ballast and rode like a cork. The personnel on the bridge all stood with their legs spread apart for balance and gripped whatever they could to stay upright. What also made the storm so intimidating was the rain, heavy and relentless. Given that it was the middle of the night, the darkness and the torrential downpour made it impossible to see much outside of the bridge except when the lightning bolts struck nearby. When that happened, the scene lit up briefly with an ominous glow that showed only the nearest waves, towering over the ark like skyscrapers over a car on a city street.

Assuming there were no other ships with which they might collide, the crew focused solely on the waves. It took all the captain's concentration just to give directions to Billy to keep the ship as perpendicular to the waves as possible to hit them head-on and to tell Miller on the lee helm when to throttle up to climb out of some of the deepest troughs and throttle down when they were sliding down off the peaks. When Miller cranked the handles on the lee helm, Owen and his colleagues in the engine room had to respond immediately. These efforts went on through the night, up and down the heavy seas, with waves crashing over the forecastle and slamming into the bridge.

Then something quite unexpected happened. After a couple hours of the carnival ride, oddly enough, they started to enjoy it. Deep in the bottom of one of the troughs, after the captain gave an "All ahead flank" order and Miller cranked the lee helm handles forward, Rodriguez said out loud as the ark started to climb, "Ride 'em, Cowboy." Miller, embracing the moment, brought out some good rodeo slang, saying as the ark crested, "Let 'er buck." Billy and Rodriguez laughed. Billy expected Captain Mitchell to tell them to knock it off, but then he surprised them.

Deep in the trough after sliding down that wave, Mitchell said with a straight face, "Let 'er rip, Cowboy." Miller, flattered that the captain even knew his nickname, chuckled as he cranked the handles forward. The ark climbed. As they crested again, this time the captain simply called out, "Whoa," and Miller, now laughing out loud, brought the handles back to full speed.

As they slid down into another trough, a flash of lightning showed a huge wave ahead, so tall they couldn't see the top. Captain Mitchell, still in rodeo mode but also mixing his metaphors, told Billy, "Right reins to 280 degrees, Shakespeare." Billy smothered a laugh as he repeated the order and shifted the rudder.

As they started to climb out of the trough, the captain said simply, "Give her the spurs, Miller." Miller cranked out the all-ahead flank order on the lee helm. And then, as they crested the wave, Mitchell followed up with another "Whoa, baby." They did it again on the next wave, with only minor variations on the orders. Billy glanced at Jessie, who gave him a puzzled look. Beth, Hunter, and Sanders in the back of the bridge were all just shaking their heads in disbelief. Who would have expected this from their normally taciturn captain?

For whatever reason it happened, this odd entertainment went on for a good half hour before the captain returned the bridge to the normal decorum and they rode out the rest of the storm with more typical behavior. As the waves started to subside, Billy looked over at Miller, who whispered quietly, "Go figure." Billy didn't know why it had happened. Maybe the captain thought it was a good way to release tension. Maybe he was feeling less formal since he was the only officer on board. Maybe he had confidence by this point that his crew knew what they were doing. Or what the hell, Billy concluded, maybe he just wanted to have some fun.

CHAPTER 55

Pilgrims

Wild as the monsoon ride was, the crew's night was not over. The ark had nearly returned to Pitcairn when the skeleton crew first knew something was unusual. The seas had calmed some, but the rain continued to come down heavily, so they couldn't see much and were relying on the radar images of the shoreline to sail back to land. Beth, peering at the screen, suddenly called out, "Captain, we have an object just off the coast by Adamstown!" They all went silent.

Captain Mitchell moved from the front of the bridge to look. After just a moment, he said calmly, "Darken ship, Mr. Hunter. We have another vessel in the harbor."

Billy instantly thought of his uncle Henry. Nobody had talked about him or his yacht in the past few weeks, but Billy remembered that his father had told Henry where they were going and had often wondered if that had been a mistake. He felt a sense of foreboding.

They drove the darkened ark into the harbor and anchored out nearly a mile from Adamstown. Leaving just a few people on board, the deckhands grabbed the few weapons still on board, climbed into the launch, and headed into shore. Billy steered the boat close to the beach north of Adamstown, where they tied it up. They waded ashore in the predawn darkness and started hiking along the shoreline toward Adamstown. With the rain hanging over the area, the night remained dark enough that they could barely see more than a few yards ahead. Having moved most of the arms ashore, they had few weapons. Hunter and Sanders each carried an AR-15. Beth and Miller had pistols. Rodriguez, Jessie, and Billy had nothing.

As they neared the town, Hunter held up his hand to signal a stop. They gathered in a stand of palm trees and peered ahead. Through the rain, they could just barely make out the shapes of some of the outlying buildings. Adamstown was very quiet and dark, with just one exception. The glow from a fire in a fireplace seeped out of the building near the beach that the residents used as the mayor's office. Billy imagined hostages, perhaps the mayor, being held by the intruders, or worse.

"That's the office," Billy whispered.

"Okay," Hunter answered. "That's our target."

After a pause, Rodriguez asked, "If there's a fight, what do we use? Bad language?"

Hunter glared at Rodriguez for just a second. Then he surprised them all by handing T-Rod the AR-15. Hunter then pulled a large bowie knife from his belt and held it in front of him. "Happy now?" he demanded.

Rodriguez tried to look as agreeable as possible. "Anything you say, jefe."

Hunter headed up the muddy road toward the town. They all moved as quietly as possible as they closed in on the building. When within ten feet of the front door, they paused. Hunter and Sanders looked at each other, nodded, and then moved quickly. Hunter swung the door open, and Sanders entered the room, the assault rifle at the ready. The rest piled in behind the two.

Four men sat at a table in front of the fireplace, coffee cups in hand. They all turned to look at the intruders, completely shocked at their entrance. The only one Billy recognized was Archie McLeish, who looked as stunned as the others. For just a moment, nobody moved.

Then McLeish's face broke into a wide grin as he raised his hands. "Stand down, mates," he said quickly, suppressing a laugh. "And I'll introduce you to my nephew." He gestured at a toothy young blond guy sitting across the table, who raised his cup of coffee in greeting. Everybody relaxed.

Within a couple minutes, they were all drying by the fire, warming up with cups of coffee, and comparing stories. The new arrivals on the island were a crew on an Australian nuclear submarine named the *Darwin* that was now anchored in Botany Bay. In addition to Archie's nephew Reggie, the other two newcomers were Captain Decker and another officer named Gibbons. The ship had been doing maneuvers under the Antarctic ice when the war broke out. After coming out from under and getting no communications, they realized that the world had changed completely. In addition, they had a crew member who was too sick for their limited medical staff. Not knowing where to go, Reggie had remembered visiting his uncle on Pitcairn as a boy. Like the people in the ark, the Aussies took a chance with this possible port of refuge.

Realizing that his other colleagues were not exactly loquacious, Billy filled the Aussies in on the ark story. He did so succinctly as they were all exhausted and in serious need of sleep. He even resisted the temptation to point out the irony of the fact that the two ships now anchored near a town named after Adam were named *Noah* and *Darwin*. He was sure that nobody else would be that interested, at least not this night. He himself felt so tired that he was starting to think that if they didn't move soon, he could fall asleep right there in front of the fire.

Captain Decker recognized their weariness and, in his strong Australian accent, did a good job of finishing the conversation. "I want to point out that the *Darwin* is completely provisioned, so we won't be a burden. I would like to meet with your captain as soon as possible," he said, and then, as if he realized that sounded a bit dismissive, he added, "Of course, perhaps all my crew could meet with all of you again, once we've all had a chance to rest."

Billy offered, "I know that Adamstown has a doctor, but we also have a doctor with us. I can bring him over in the launch tomorrow if you want another perspective on your ill sailor."

"We would appreciate that, mate," Decker responded.

McLeish then gestured at the rifles leaning against the wall and said, "And you don't have to bring those guns next visit." He then added with a grin, "But we do appreciate you Yanks showing up ready to help."

They all shook hands as the ark crew walked out of the building. They trudged back down the beach to the launch just as the sun was trying to peek out from behind the dark clouds in the east. As they walked along the beach, the morning air smelled clean and refreshed by the storm. Trailing behind the others, Jessie reached out and patted Billy's back. He smiled back at her, relieved that this morning had turned out much better than it might have. They later referred to the new arrivals as the pilgrims because they came on Thanksgiving. But the arrival of these pilgrims, as had those on North American shores, had made all the current residents remember that there was a larger world out there. And it could show up on the island at any time.

CHAPTER 56

Ararat

As November stretched into December, the pilgrims, the Australian arrivals, settled in on Pitcairn. Sadly, their sick crew member, Fitch, passed away before Doc Harrison could even see him. But the rest of the crew needed rest and recovery, and the Adamstown residents were happy to have them. Captain Decker, true to his word, made sure that the *Darwin* sailors lived almost entirely on their own rations and that they were not a burden at all to the existing residents. Quite the contrary, they proved to be valuable assistants and brought considerable technology as well as know-how to several projects, such as a simple but functional walkie-talkie system between Adamstown, the *Darwin*, and the ark settlement.

The arkonauts also continued to work on their own projects. Beth's crew finished the pier and proudly tied the ark to its pilings. Hunter and the carpenters finished enough shelters, several of them in the form of barracks, that everyone could now sleep inside rather than on the ark or camping on the beach, whenever they wanted. The food crew began to see early signs of producing some vegetables and potatoes from the gardens. The residents held elections and made Oliver, Captain Mitchell, and Maria the first trustees. They also set aside a little plot in the jungle to the west of the settlement for a small cemetery and, although lacking either bodies or ashes, put up crosses for Tyrone Green and Lee Myerson. Finally, they also named their new settlement. Though most of them were not overtly religious, the name for the place was an obvious choice once Sarah suggested it. According to the biblical story, Noah's ark ended up in the mountains of Ararat. So one day in mid-December, Sarah and Owen posted a sign that simply read, "Welcome to Ararat."

CHAPTER 57

Christmas

On Christmas Day, the Hill family gathered in Oliver's hut for a holiday meal. After they finished a brunch of oatmeal, eggs, and toast, they all sat at the table, sipping on coffee.

Annie looked at her mother. "Look at what Aunt Beth gave me." She held up a small wood carving in the shape of a dog. "It looks like Roscoe."

Sarah answered, "That's great, honey. Why don't you give Roscoe his present?"

Annie picked up a short rope and extended it to the dog. Even if he had been hoping for something more edible, Roscoe seized it eagerly. They then began a tug-of-war that pulled them away from the table.

Beth asked, "So how many showed up last night, Billy?"

"We took over eight people, right, Owen?"

Owen added, "Yeah, and a couple dozen from Adamstown were already at the church."

Oliver asked, "Did they do much of a service?"

Owen glanced at Sarah. "It was nice. They asked Sarah to say a few words, and then we went out and did some caroling."

Oliver persisted, "What did you speak about, Sarah?"

Sarah said quietly, "No surprise, a version of the Christmas story."

Billy responded, "You're too modest, Sarah. It was good. It was the usual story, but from the perspective of the shepherds and why they were so excited."

"And?" Oliver asked.

"Hope," Billy answered. "It was all about hope. Like for all of us."

Sarah nodded gratefully. "Thanks, Billy."

Beth asked, "Any *Darwin* sailors show up?"

Owen answered, "Four. One was that big guy, Lyle. Man, he has a voice."

Billy chuckled. "Yeah, I asked him to join in with us next time we play." He reached for his cup of coffee as he added, "Then you won't have to listen to me as much anymore."

Owen nodded. "It is a season of blessings."

Sarah ignored her husband's jab as she noticed something hanging off Billy's neck when he reached for the coffee. "Say, Billy, that's a nice tooth."

Billy showed off a large black shark's tooth on a string. "Thanks, Sarah. Christmas present from Jessie."

Sarah answered. "Aw, you should have asked her to come along."

"I did," Billy answered. "She's doing Christmas morning with her sister. We'll get together later."

Beth said, "And we assume you got her something, brother."

Billy smiled. "Funny. I gave her a necklace of little shark's teeth strung on a fishing line. We didn't even know we were doing gifts, let alone nearly the same thing."

"Must be love," Beth teased.

"I should be so lucky." Billy stood and started to collect dirty dishes.

Sarah stopped him and grabbed the plates. "Let me get those, Billy. Call it my contribution to breakfast. Those were good eggs you and Owen made."

Beth stopped her. "Come on, Sarah. We know you made dessert." She took the plates from Sarah and moved toward the sink.

Oliver changed the subject. "So, Elizabeth, I note that you did not attend the service. Any particular reason?"

Beth shook her head. “Not really.”

Oliver continued. “Hmmm…seems odd that your brothers went but you didn’t.”

“Then again,” Billy defended his sister, “I didn’t see you there either, Pop.”

Oliver was undeterred. “Don’t worry. I don’t mean anything by it. I just think it’s interesting that an engineer, a man of science, has such views while others don’t.”

Owen took the bait. “What views?”

Oliver showed a mischievous smile. “You must believe in God, son.”

“Why, because I went to church on Christmas Eve?”

“Well, then, do you?”

Owen paused before answering. “I believe that a man named Jesus Christ lived a couple thousand years ago, maybe born on this day, and taught us a lot of good things. Those are things that Sarah teaches. And things Annie should know.”

Sarah looked at her husband proudly.

Beth looked over from the sink, where she was rinsing the dishes, and said, “I used to believe in God. I figured he got things started and then turned things over to people.” She shook her head. “He sure took this last year off.”

Billy added, “Make that the last fifty years.”

Owen answered, “God didn’t make this mess. We did.”

Oliver responded, “Exactly. Thus, we’re here.”

Beth turned back to the table. “That reminds me of something, Dad. I saw a newscast of an interview with you when I was in Nevada, headed for California. A reporter asked you if you were playing God. Then somebody switched the channel and I never did get to hear your answer.”

Oliver smiled. “Would it have mattered to your decision to join us?”

Beth answered, “No, I’m just curious.”

Oliver paused, and in the silence, Owen said, “Funny, I am too.”

They all stared at Oliver. Oliver looked around before answering, "Let me put it this way: I felt like we needed to step up in God's absence."

"And then what?" Billy pushed. "We step up and then God will help us?"

Beth added, "Like they say, God helps those who help themselves?"

Sarah brought a plate over to the table and uncovered it to show some cookies. Then she said, "Do you know who said that line?" She looked around. "Ben Franklin. Many people use that quote, but it isn't even in the Bible."

"Really?" Beth asked.

"Yes. So I find it interesting when people think God helps them with something when they ask for it, like winning a football game." She paused before continuing, "Personally, I think what happens is up to us."

Billy nodded and then said, "This is quite a conversation for Christmas morning. Some might call it ironic."

Beth reached for the plate as she said, "Ironic, hell, I just want some of those cookies."

CHAPTER 58

New Year's Eve

To celebrate the new year and to show off their new settlement, the arkonauts invited the Adamstown residents and *Darwin* sailors to Ararat. Maria's crew grilled a pile of fish and made some huge pots of stew. Others constructed long tables and benches down by the beach. Billy and others set up a stage for the musicians. Then the visitors started showing up, bringing food, drink, and musical instruments.

Unlike the welcome event in Adamstown, this party did not take long to get rolling. People were more comfortable with one another now, and they wasted no time consuming food and drink and then moving on to revelry. In addition, the band sounded better than before. Lyle, the baritone from the *Darwin*, joined along with another *Darwin* sailor who played the saxophone. They started with some holiday music, but that quickly gave way to songs you would hear in a roadhouse.

As the music picked up, the party started to take a dangerous turn. The band was deep into a catchy version of the Chris Isaak song "Wrong to Love You" when some inevitable tension surfaced. Rodriguez was dancing with one of the female sailors from the *Darwin*. As Billy watched from the stage, he saw another *Darwin* sailor go to them and either ask to cut in or just said something that T-Rod didn't like. The two of them exchanged words and then a couple shoves. Within a few seconds, three other *Darwin* sailors moved toward Rodriguez. Billy watched as Sanders shouldered his way through the crowd to get to his buddy. By the time the big man had arrived at the confrontation, the band and the other dancers had all stopped. Billy put his guitar in its rack. As he moved to get off the stage, somebody threw a punch and the little melee was on.

Billy hurried to the fracas, his adrenaline fueled by alcohol as much as a certain loyalty to his crewmates. He got to the fight the same time as Hunter and Reese, who shot Billy a wicked little grin. They jumped into the scrum, and within seconds Billy was rolling around in the sand with some guy from the *Darwin* who was at least as drunk as he was. Billy doubted either was going to do much damage, but they never really had a chance to find out.

A shot from a pistol stunned everyone. Billy and his opponent stopped fighting, as did the others. They all looked toward the sound of the gun to see Captain Decker with his pistol in the air and an oddly bemused look on his face. Several *Darwin* crew members were standing behind him. Decker looked at all the brawlers and then focused on Hunter, who was sitting on top of a sailor, who looked relieved to have someone stop the fight.

"This is quite a party, Mr. Hunter," Decker said calmly. "How would you like it to go from here?"

Before Hunter could answer, Rodriguez started to speak. He and the other original combatant both had bloody lips but no other apparent harm. "Hell, Capitan, we were just dancing and then—"

His *Darwin* opponent interrupted. "Who do you think you are, Yank? Ms. Evans is one of us."

Rodriguez started to answer, "I don't care if she's the queen of England. She wanted to dance—"

Hunter cut him off. "Shut up, Rodriguez." He looked back at Decker, who was smiling at the line about the queen. In fact, Ms. Evans and most of the *Darwin* crew were also smothering laughs at the irreverent reference.

Hunter's face was expressionless. "Your call, Captain Decker." Billy looked around at the crowd and figured the arkonaut combatants were willing but were also outnumbered.

Decker, too, looked around before responding. "We just came to have a good time, mate."

Hunter stood and said, "Good, let's do that, then." He stuck out a big hand.

The *Darwin* sailor paused for a second and then took Hunter's hand, allowing himself to be pulled to his feet. Everybody relaxed. As if on cue, Miller, still onstage, started playing "Friends in Low Places." Billy laughed at the same time as his counterpart from the *Darwin*. They shook hands, and Billy headed back toward the stage. Before he had even picked up his guitar, Miller was into the first chorus, and people from all around the stage were joining in.

The music was infectious, and the dancing got more and more enthusiastic. At one point, Billy and Jessie were part of a line of people bouncing around the big bonfire, singing like you might see in an old Western movie. Later, Billy couldn't even remember what the song was, but he did remember that the participants included Ararat residents, Adamstown residents, and *Darwin* sailors. And they were dancing together. Rodriguez was back with Ms. Evans. Archie McLeish was swinging Irene Doyle around. Reggie McLeish was dancing with Naveena Sirpathia, the eldest daughter in the Sirpathia family. Billy concluded that the party was a success.

After a couple hours of playing, the band took a break. Billy was standing at a table with Jessie, enjoying their drinks, when he noticed a few of the older residents either heading to their huts in Ararat or catching a ride with Archie McLeish back to Adamstown. But a lot of others stayed and kept eating and drinking. Then, as the band started to move back up on the stage to resume playing, Beth and Sanders walked behind Billy as he poured Jessie a drink.

He overheard Beth saying, "So, Moose, you want to fight, dance, or fuck?"

Billy's head jerked up as he reflexively strained to hear the response without looking back at them.

Sanders answered matter-of-factly, "We already had a fight. And I don't much like dancing."

"Good," Beth said simply. "Let's go."

Billy, with a puzzled look on his face, looked at Jessie, but she was already smiling back at him, shaking her head slowly as if to ask him why he was surprised.

"Well, I didn't know…," Billy started to answer.

She leaned closer and said, "Just pour the drinks, Billy."

The rest of the night was a blur.

CHAPTER 59

Ships

Billy dreamed of a bear. The animal was right next to him, sniffing around his head, his breath warm. He remembered reading sometime that if a bear comes that close, you should try playing dead, so he didn't move. But the animal persisted, nuzzling his ear with a cold, wet nose. Then Billy thought he heard a giggle and wondered if he really was dreaming or lying someplace, half-awake. Before he opened his eyes to see, the animal licked him on the chin and then the cheek. The giggling was joined by laughter.

Billy heard Owen's voice. "Good dog, Roscoe."

Then Sarah said, "Okay, Roscoe, that's enough."

But Roscoe persisted and continued to lick Billy's face. Billy shifted to scratch the dog's ears and get him to stop licking. In doing so, Jessie shifted as well to get her head off Billy's chest and started to open her eyes to the morning light. She and Billy were stretched out on the beach, only partially covered by a tablecloth.

Annie stopped giggling and asked, "What's wrong with them?"

Her father answered, "They got stinking drunk last night."

Annie asked, "What does that mean?"

Her mother answered this time. "They had a big party, honey, and some of them overdid it."

"Ya think?" Owen asked derisively.

Annie leaned in to see her uncle's face, and Billy reached up and grabbed her. As he pulled her close, she giggled again.

"Hey, Jess, look who woke us up. What should we do with her?"

"Hmmm," Jessie answered. "Do you think she's ticklish?"

Annie said "No," but she also squirmed to try to get away, thus revealing the truth.

"Let's find out," Billy said. While Billy held Annie close, Jessie reached over and started tickling her ribs. Annie started giggling and then laughing. Roscoe jumped in and started licking Annie's face. Annie got to laughing so hard she almost sounded like she was in pain and twisted to get away. Billy finally let her go.

"I call that a yes," Jessie concluded.

"Yes," Billy said, "and that's what we'll give her whenever she wakes us up."

As Annie backed away, Billy and Jessie sat up just in time to see Maria walking up with a coffeepot and a handful of cups.

"Buenos dias and happy New Year," Maria said. "Would you like some coffee?" She began pouring.

Owen said, "I think Billy may want the hair of the dog."

Annie asked, "Hair of Roscoe?"

Billy reached up for the cup. "No, coffee sounds better."

Taking her cup, Jessie smiled at her sister. "Mi Hermana. She is a saint."

Billy added, "Gracias, Saint Maria." He took a full swig of the coffee and then looked around. The bonfire was still smoldering, with a half-burned bench sticking out of the ashes. One of the new tables had been upended and left on the beach, now partly submerged in the waves. Chairs, plates, and containers were strewn about like there had been an explosion. Other people, in addition to Billy and Jessie, were lying where they seemingly fell or passed out. Several of the band members lay next to their instruments, as if they played until they collapsed.

Billy looked back at Maria. "So what all happened?"

She shook her head. "Ah, Guillermo, what didn't?"

Billy took another drink and looked around again. Rodriguez, who had been lying flat on his back on the sand, sat up with a pained expression on his face. Miller, on the stage with his guitar, pulled off his cowboy hat, looked out at the rising sun, then pulled his hat back over his face as he lay down again. Hunter and Reese pulled what was left of the bench out of the fire and sat down on it like they could barely move.

Billy said softly, "I guess we'll have to build some new benches."

Owen responded, "We're lucky you clowns didn't burn the whole place down." He continued to look around and then stopped as his gaze settled on the harbor.

"What is that?" He squinted. "Ships." He then yelled, "Two ships in the harbor!"

People all over the beach came to life as they stood up to see. A moment later, Captain Mitchell's voice sounded from the loudspeaker on the ark. "Battle stations. Essential crew to the ark. All other personnel to the shelter."

What had been a quiet morning exploded into a flurry of activity. Maria took the coffee cups and gave her sister a quick hug as she stood. Owen said goodbye to Sarah and Annie and took off running toward the ark. Oliver came out of his hut, shouting into the walkie-talkie for Adamstown to pick up. Hunter started calling for the deckhands as he ran toward the pier. Beth and Sanders emerged from somewhere and hustled toward the shelter housing the rifles.

Then Billy heard a voice from near where the band had been set up, calling, "Billy, Billy Hill." It was Lyle from the *Darwin*.

"Over here," Billy called. He suddenly realized that Lyle and his shipmates who were still at Ararat needed to get back to the *Darwin*. He looked at Jessie, who realized the same thing and just said, "Go." She gave Billy a quick kiss and then went running after Hunter toward the ark.

Lyle and half a dozen *Darwin* shipmates hustled up, followed by Reggie McLeish, who came running from the area of the family huts. They looked as ragged as Billy felt. Reggie started to say, "Billy, we have to get back..."

"I know. Let's go," Billy answered and then ran toward the launch tied up on the pier.

They had the launch underway in less than a minute, bouncing over the waves toward the site where the *Darwin* had been anchored near Adamstown. Lyle got on his walkie-talkie and was immediately in touch with someone on the sub.

"They're coming this way, Billy," Lyle said, his voice ripe with urgency. "We can intersect and transfer."

"Great, we're at full speed," Billy answered. "The binoculars are there." He pointed at their holder by the console.

Reggie picked the glasses up and started scanning for the sub. He then looked at the ships entering the bay from the east.

"Sun's blinding, but I see four ships." He peered into the binoculars. "Looks like a cruiser and two gunboats. And what the hell? A yacht?"

Billy's brain was racing. A yacht? He had frequently worried that Henry might track them down. Could it be?

"The cruiser is staying out," Reggie said.

"They're afraid of running aground," Billy responded. "They don't know these waters."

"Not the gunboats," answered Reggie, still looking through the binoculars. "They're coming." He swung the glasses back toward Adamstown and then called, "There's the *Darwin*."

Billy pushed the yacht out of his mind and focused as they closed quickly, the sub also moving at high speed. Within a minute, he had pulled the launch up next to the conning tower on the sub, where the *Darwin* sailors had thrown a cargo net over the side. The Aussies piled out of Billy's boat and jumped for the cargo net. "Thanks, Billy!" Lyle yelled as he moved to disembark. Reggie called out, "Good luck, mate."

Billy heard something that sounded like a large firecracker in the distance, and then another. Water splashed on both sides of the sub. Whoever the intruders were, they were shooting. Billy put the launch in reverse. More shots were heard, and a spout of water shot up in the air just off the sub's bow.

As he sped away, Billy could hear Captain Decker's voice on the sub's loudspeaker, "Dive, dive!" Billy glanced behind him. The Aussies had gotten all their crew aboard, pulled up the net, and were submerging rapidly. He then looked back toward the gunboats, and his heart skipped a beat. One was closing on the submerging submarine, but the other had turned his direction and seemed to now be pursuing him in the launch.

A water spout went up thirty yards behind his stern, and then another just twenty yards behind as the gunner started to correct the range. Billy began to swerve the boat. At full speed and with the waves in the bay, he feared that he might roll the little craft, but then again, that would beat taking a direct hit. When the launch was within a thousand yards of Ararat, he saw that the ark was underway. Captain Mitchell had maneuvered it so that the bow was facing the approaching gunboat, providing less of a target than if it were broadside. And figures were scurrying about on the bow, Billy's shipmates. A shell exploded just off the port beam of the launch, showering Billy and the deck with water. He swerved right and then came back just in time to miss one off the starboard beam. The gunboat was about five hundred yards behind.

When Billy had cut the distance between the launch and the ark to two hundred yards, he could see his shipmates on the forecastle. Jessie and Beth were waving at him to hurry. They were all holding weapons, the AR-15s from the gun locker. Then Billy noticed Hunter settling down on the superstructure of the bridge, carrying something that looked much longer than the assault weapons.

Billy cut his speed only when he was in the shadow of the ark. And as he nestled the launch in on the starboard side, he could hear the gunfire from his shipmates. The gunboat was still at least a hundred yards behind him, so he doubted the efficacy of the AR-15s at that distance, but at least his shipmates had pulled the fire off him as people on the gunboat were firing their small arms at the ark rather than at Billy's launch. The gunners manning the cannon on the gunboat had also shifted their target from the launch to the ark. Their first couple of shells flew past, just missing the exposed hull. Then they started to zero in.

CHAPTER 60

Battle in the Bay

On the ark, the skeleton crew scrambled to face the assault. With Miller replacing Billy on the helm and Brooks on the lee helm, Captain Mitchell maneuvered the ark to get away from the pier and to face the oncoming gunboat, thus presenting a smaller target. Hannigan, Willis, Reichardt, and Hiluka were all on the bridge, ready to help out with messages or anything else where needed. Beth, Jessie, Rodriguez, Sanders, and Reese were all on the forecastle, armed with the only weapons they had, the AR-15s. After watching Billy flee the gunboat, they stretched out prone to reduce their own vulnerability. Even so, one of the bullets from the approaching gunboat grazed Jessie's left arm. She grimaced as Beth reached over to wrap some cloth around it to stop the bleeding. Then they began firing at the gunboat as it came within a hundred yards.

The fire and the noise from both sides intensified, but eventually the gunboat backed off a bit. The ark's AR-15s were not designed for long-range accuracy, and the gunboat's crew was smart enough to move to about five hundred yards away from the ark, where they were beyond range but could still pound away with their own three-inch cannon. After a couple near misses, a shot from the cannon hit the port side of the ark's bridge, shook the ship, and ripped out the bridge wing.

On the forecastle, Beth and the other deckhands couldn't know the damage to the bridge, but they knew it was not good. Beth suddenly had a bad feeling that they were severely outgunned. Then she heard something else, a noise from above them up on the roof of the bridge. The sound was different, neither the rat-a-tat of the AR-15s nor the loud boom of the gunboat's cannon, but a sharp, resonating crack like she would hear when lighting hit a tree in the forest. After the first retort, she saw one of the guys at the gunboat's cannon bounce backward as if he took a vicious punch to the stomach. Beth looked up and saw sunlight glinting off the barrel of Hunter's long rifle sticking out where it was just barely visible. She remembered the conversation weeks before at the gun locker.

"Hunter," she said out loud.

Hunter's long rifle boomed again, and another guy at the gunboat's cannon slammed backward into the bulwark and then fell forward, toppling off the deck and into the bay. Then there was another shot and a third guy fell to the deck, writhing in pain. That took care of the gunboat's cannon crew. Hunter shifted his aim to the bridge wing, where the invaders stood stunned, as if still not sure what had happened. Hunter's next shot knocked one of them off the bridge as he fell to the deck below.

"Damn, Chief," Rodriguez, lying next to Beth, said quietly in amazement.

Hunter shifted his aim to the shooters on the forecastle of the gunboat. His next shot knocked another guy off the ship and into the bay. The men on the forecastle started to scramble for cover behind the anchor housing.

Reese exclaimed, "This is like Crazy Horse at the Little Bighorn!"

Hunter shifted his focus, fired again, and glass on the bridge window blew out. Then he pumped another shot into the bridge. Beth couldn't even tell what Hunter was seeing in there, but then again, she wasn't looking through his scope.

Suddenly, there was an explosion from the other side of the bay. Jessie picked up the binoculars that had been lying next to her and looked toward the eastern exit from the harbor. "Looks like the *Darwin* got the other gunboat." She could see the fire on board the enemy ship as it started to settle into the water. She handed the binoculars to Sanders so he could see.

As he focused the binoculars, Sanders said matter-of-factly, "I guess we now know who wins when a gunboat takes on a submarine." He handed the binoculars to Beth.

All went quiet for a minute as the attackers assessed their situation and the fact that the submarine was now surely coming their direction. Then somebody inside the doorway of the gunboat's bridge waved a T-shirt as a white flag. What was left of the gunboat crew lowered their rifles to the deck.

Captain Mitchell called out from the ark's bridge, "Stand down, Mr. Hunter."

The deckhands slowly stood and looked above and behind to the roof of the bridge. Hunter got up from where he had been lying in a prone position. With his rifle, he motioned to the surrendering crew on the gunboat to raise their arms. Of course, they complied immediately.

"And who wins when a gunboat takes on one tough Indian with a high-powered rifle?" Reese said.

"Damn, Chief," Rodriguez said again, the admiration noticeable in his voice.

Beth lifted the binoculars to look out at the other ships. As the destroyer and the yacht turned to sail the other direction, she muttered, "Son of a bitch. It's the *White Diamond*."

CHAPTER 61

South Dakota

Billy was still bouncing in the launch near the stern of the ark after the firing stopped when he heard Captain Mitchell on the ark loudspeaker. "Mr. Hill, get Doc Harrison from Ararat immediately. We have men down." Billy fired up the launch again and took off for the shore.

Not surprisingly, Doc Harrison was waiting on the pier along with Oliver when Billy arrived. They climbed aboard, and the launch sped back to the ark. As they approached, Billy could see Sanders and Rodriguez pointing their rifles at the prisoners on the gunboat. Billy was also relieved to see Beth and Jessie waiting on the quarterdeck. Billy tied up, while the doctor and Oliver climbed up the ladder and then hurried forward with Beth.

Jessie greeted Billy with a one-armed hug. "Hannigan and others have been hit. I don't know how bad, but—"

Billy interrupted. "I'm sorry to hear it, but your arm—"

"I am okay," she cut him off. "It just grazed me." She paused and looked in his eyes. "I'm glad you made it."

When Billy and Jessie got to the bridge, they learned that victory had come with a serious cost. The hit from the gunboat killed Hannigan, who had been on the port bridge wing. The explosion also sent some shrapnel into the bridge that caught Brooks, who had been stationed on the lee helm near the port side, in the back. He was lying on his side, with Doc Harrison working on him. Seeing the concern in Billy's face, Brooks put his thumb up to indicate he would be okay. Miller had suffered a minor wound in the leg and was sitting on the chart table, where Reichardt was applying a bandage.

They were all stunned to lose Hannigan. Captain Mitchell was always so stoic that it was hard to read his emotions, but they all knew he was shaken. Nevertheless, he was concentrating on what needed to be done and began to issue orders. The ark would go back to Ararat with the wounded. The others would drop the anchor on the gunboat, and then Billy, Jessie, and Hunter would use the launch to take the prisoners to Adamstown, where there was a jail.

The trip to Adamstown was very quiet. Jessie and Hunter stood in back, holding their guns on the prisoners, who sat, stunned, on the floor. The seas were calm, almost glasslike, and the late-morning sun warmed the interior of the little boat. As the adrenaline of the morning started to wear off and the hangover started to come on, Billy felt a strong urge to cut the engines and take a nap. Then he thought about the *White Diamond* and the fact that his uncle had obviously led these invaders to the ark. His anger gave him the energy to stay awake and alert all the way to Adamstown.

Captain Decker was waiting on the pier there with a contingent of sailors as well as some of the Adamstown residents. Archie McLeish showed up just as the launch arrived, carrying a jug of water and some cups.

"Morning," Decker called matter-of-factly as the launch pulled up. He looked at the prisoners as Hunter and Jessie shepherded them off the boat. "Well done. Did you have casualties?"

Hunter answered, "Hannigan's dead. Two wounded." He looked back at Decker. "You?"

The captain answered, "No casualties. It was over quickly. They obviously didn't know we had a submarine." He then looked from Billy to Jessie and back to Hunter with a little smile. "Someday I'd like to know how you Yanks took out a gunboat when the ark has no cannons."

Hunter nodded slightly, took a drink of water, and then answered without emotion, "Someday."

Captain Decker turned to his crew. "Let's get these men to the jail." Reggie McLeish and some other *Darwin* sailors marched the prisoners toward town.

When the residents were out of hearing range, Decker looked back at Hunter, Billy, and Jessie. "Unfortunately, they now do know that we have a sub."

Billy thought of the cruiser and the yacht and asked, "Can you track them?"

Decker shook his head. "They moved out of radar range." He paused before continuing, "My guess is they came looking for food and supplies but didn't want to destroy it by shelling us."

They all involuntarily glanced to the east, where the other ships had gone. Billy thought of his uncle and said quietly, "They're likely to be back."

"Likely," was all Decker said. He then added, "We'll talk more later. Good work today."

The ride back to Ararat started out quietly. The sea in the harbor was still calm, and the launch just zipped along over the waves. Billy stood behind the wheel with Jessie and Hunter on either side, all staring out the front. Then, partly because she sensed Billy was having a hard time staying awake, Jessie started a conversation.

"How's the hangover, Billy?"

"I could use a nap…make that a siesta."

"Of course," she responded and then teased, "Why would today be any different?"

"How's the arm?" Billy asked.

"It hurts…but not bad," she answered.

Billy responded, "I need to get you back to Doc Harrison, get you some stitches."

She asked, "So that was your uncle's yacht?"

Billy couldn't hide the disgust in his answer. "The bastard. Can't trust anybody."

Hunter scoffed audibly.

Jessie looked at Hunter, who had been very quiet until then, and wondered if it was because he was deep in thought about having just killed half a dozen men. "How about you, John Hunter?"

He gave no indications of any feelings of guilt. "Food would be good," he said simply.

"Then I would surely fall asleep," Billy said.

Jessie continued to look at Hunter. "Do you mind me asking, Where did you learn to shoot like that?" Billy, as usual, admired the straightforward way Jessie went about things. She always did ask direct questions, but she was also obviously offering Hunter a chance to talk if he wanted. Hunter didn't say anything for long enough that Billy thought Jessie would give up, but she continued to wait for an answer.

"South Dakota," Hunter finally said.

Billy glanced at him and made a guess. "Wounded Knee?"

He nodded. Jessie looked from Billy to Hunter and then back to Billy again.

Hunter still didn't say anything, so Billy tried. "Wounded Knee was the site of a massacre of Indians back in 1890. A few years ago, a company proposed a pipeline across the reservation land there. Some in the tribe accepted it, some didn't. The protest went on for months. I'm pretty sure—"

Hunter cut him off. "Three years ago." He paused and stared straight ahead at the water. "We lost."

Jessie persisted. "Did it get violent?"

Hunter looked at her. "Yes. That was where I learned to shoot."

Billy didn't know what to say, but he also knew Jessie wasn't sure what that meant, and neither did he, so he offered a comment. "If I remember right, nobody got killed, although some were wounded."

"Yes," Hunter answered matter-of-factly, "I learned to shoot well."

Billy found himself somewhat relieved about the intentions behind Hunter's marksmanship.

Jessie tried to allow him a positive spin. "At least you may have slowed the project down."

"Yes," Hunter answered and then looked at her, "and we might have stopped them, but the council sold us out."

"Your council?" she asked.

"Yes, the tribal council. They accepted the offer from the company." He paused. "And then the council chair turned me in. Damn chiefs."

Jessie was stunned. "Your own chief?"

Hunter looked at Jessie and then, while giving Billy an odd little smile, answered, "He was a slave of nature and the son of hell."

Billy thought for a moment before responding, "*Richard the third.*"

Hunter nodded, satisfied that Billy knew at least that much Shakespeare.

They were all silent for a minute. The only noise came from the boat bouncing on the water. Billy could see Ararat coming in view and throttled back a bit. He wanted to hear the end of this story.

Billy asked, "You went to prison?"

"I was sentenced to five years in Leavenworth. I got out after two."

"Paroled?"

Hunter looked full at Billy before answering. He stared long enough that Billy started to feel uncomfortable.

Hunter finally said, "Your father testified on my behalf." Jessie looked at Billy as his jaw dropped open. Hunter continued to stare at him.

"My father?" Billy asked, even though he guessed the rest of the story even before Hunter responded.

"Yes, it was his company that built the pipeline."

Some of the wheels spinning in Billy's brain clicked into sync. Now he understood more about Oliver's conversion from a giant in the fossil fuel industry. And he knew why a full-blooded Sioux Indian worked for him. He also knew that Hunter's personal Richard III, who he had mentioned on the evening before arriving on Pitcairn, was one of his own chiefs. And finally, he knew why Hunter bristled sometimes when Rodriguez and others called him Chief. Billy vowed silently to never do it again.

Billy looked at the sea in front of the launch, with Ararat coming closer, and then back at Jessie, who just nodded. They both looked back at Hunter.

Hunter stared at them calmly and said simply, "Time to get some food."

CHAPTER 62

Shark Woman

The Battle of the Bay exhausted the residents of Ararat, many of whom were already sleep-deprived from the New Year's Eve party, but they knew they needed to prepare in case the other invaders returned. So after some rest on New Year's Day and a brief burial service for Hannigan's remains, they all, other than the wounded Brooks and Miller, went back to work.

Billy made several runs with the launch to get things moving. One trip took Second Mate Willis along with the engineers and the deckhands to the gunboat, where they could start figuring out how they could use their spoils of war. A quick inspection of the boat revealed a few things, including a Russian-English dictionary. The deckhands began to formulate a plan in case the Russian prisoners did not cooperate in showing how to operate the ship's features, notably the cannon. Billy then took the trustees to Adamstown to meet with Governor Turner and Captain Decker to discuss the next steps. While there, he picked up Reggie McLeish and Lyle, both armed with pistols, as well as the four prisoners, all in handcuffs, to bring back to the gunboat.

On the way back, Reggie said the prisoners had been grateful for food but otherwise uncommunicative. Unfortunately, nobody in Adamstown or on the *Darwin* spoke Russian. But by using a world map and having the prisoners point, the Aussies had figured out that they were former Navy sailors from the port of Vladivostok. Billy told Reggie not to worry as the deckhands had an idea as to how to "encourage" their cooperation.

When the launch arrived at the gunboat, Reese pulled Reggie and Lyle aside. Taking Lyle's pistol, Billy led the Russians up to the forecastle, where the deckhands were cleaning up from the previous day's battle. Billy stopped the prisoners in front of the deckhands at the spot where several of their colleagues had been killed. The deckhands glared at the prisoners. Hunter, Beth, Sanders, and Rodriguez had all been busy cleaning, and they looked filthy, sweaty, and angry. Jessie, unable to do as much work because of her wound, leaned against the cannon, as if supervising, wearing a black tank top and a black wrap on her left bicep, and dark sunglasses enhanced her ominous appearance. Billy also noticed she wore the black shark teeth necklace he had given her for Christmas. He knew why and smiled to himself.

Rodriguez dropped his mop in a bucket of dirty water, said something about "finishing the job," and moved toward the Russians. Sanders was right behind him. Two of the Russians flinched, obviously understanding the intent.

Jessie, from her spot on the cannon, said calmly, "Wait." The others stopped moving and looked at her. She walked over to Billy, took his pistol from him, and held it on the Russians. Then she said to Billy, "Take off their cuffs."

Billy did as he was told. He and the deckhands all knew Jessie was not in charge, but the Russians did not. And chances were good that at least some of them were traditional enough to not expect to see a young woman giving orders. Indeed, from the battle, they surely expected the tall Indian to be the boss. To have him answering to her only added to their confusion. After the handcuffs were removed, Jessie handed Billy the gun and faced the prisoners again.

She gestured behind her at the cannon and said, in Russian, "Work."

The Russians looked stunned. They obviously were surprised that anyone spoke their language, let alone a young Hispanic woman that they had wounded. But she must have gotten the language correct, as the Russians looked at the cannon in a way that suggested they knew what she wanted.

But none of them moved or spoke. Jessie continued to stare at the captives, demanding an answer. She spoke, again in Russian. "Understand?"

Two of the Russians, a tall one and a heavy one, slipped up, belying future efforts to pretend incomprehension by nodding subconsciously, almost imperceptibly.

Jessie smiled slightly, knowingly. She repeated the command for "Work" and pointed at the cannon. This time, the tall Russian smirked as he raised his hands, palms up, as if to say he didn't know how. He stared back at her, defiant in his feigned ignorance.

Jessie took a step toward the tall Russian, pushed the sunglasses up on her head, and stared in his eyes. After a good thirty seconds, she finally said, "Last chance, Ivan." She said it in English, but even if he didn't understand, the meaning was clear.

He continued to stare back at her.

Then, still staring at Ivan, Jessie said calmly, "Flush him."

Hunter, Beth, Sanders, and Rodriguez each grabbed an arm or a leg. Before Ivan could object or any of his colleagues could even move, the deckhands lifted the tall Russian, walked over to the railing, and pitched him over the side. They could all hear the splash as the Russian hit the water. The four deckhands then walked back to where they had been as if nothing had happened.

Recalling a line Hunter had used during their swim call, Jessie said simply, "Sharks gotta eat."

Hunter nodded approvingly. Rodriguez added, "Tiburon alimonte."

Knowing the prisoners might not know the word *sharks*, Jessie held up her necklace so they could all see the shark's teeth and said *food* in Russian.

The remaining three Russians looked significantly different than they had even a minute before as they fidgeted and glanced at one another. Fear showed in their eyes as they looked to Billy at first, as if he would help them even though he was holding a pistol, then at the other deckhands, and finally, reluctantly, back at Jessie. As they did so, they all heard a long, loud scream from down below, where Ivan had been dropped.

Embracing her role, Jessie looked at the remaining Russians, nodded as if to confirm the meaning of the scream, smiled, and repeated *food* in Russian. They looked terrified. She turned her back to them and, as she did so, glanced at Billy and winked.

Billy almost felt sorry for the Russian sailors. They had probably seen very few, if any, women for weeks, and now they were facing an angry, attractive Latina who they had harmed but now seemed able to speak Russian as she had them thrown to sharks without hesitation or remorse. Even Billy thought she was impressively scary in the role.

Jessie, her back to the prisoners, looked at her wrist, where she had scribbled some notes. She then turned to look back at the three prisoners still in line and this time said, again in Russian, "Next."

All three involuntarily tried to back up, but with the deckhands looming behind them, they had nowhere to go.

Jessie looked from one to another and then, finally, at the third, the heavy man, who surely weighed nearly three hundred pounds. Standing behind the big Russian, Rodriguez shook his head slightly at Jessie, quietly saying the words *por favor*, asking her to pick someone else, someone lighter.

Jessie couldn't resist. She smiled at Rodriguez and then pointed at the big man. Rodriguez sighed audibly but then helped his colleagues grab the appointed victim. The heavy Russian started squirming as he called out, "Nyet, Nyet." The big man managed to free an arm and pointed at the guy next to him, then said, "Vlad. Vlad."

The implication, obviously, was that Vlad knew how to operate the cannon. Jessie motioned for the deckhands to let the big man go and turned to Vlad. His resolve disappeared in an instant. He held his hands up and said whatever the Russian word is for *surrender*.

Jessie finally stepped aside and motioned for Vlad to go to the cannon. Beth and Sanders pushed him along.

Jessie looked at the heavy Russian, who had been given the brief reprieve. She said again, in Russian, "Next."

The big man pointed below, as if to the engine room, and said something in Russian, presumably *engines* or *boilers* to let her know he did know how to work those. She nodded and stepped aside to let Hunter lead the man down below to the engine room.

As Hunter passed, he said quietly to Jessie, "Good work, shark woman."

The remaining prisoner cringed slightly as Jessie turned to him, but then quickly pointed toward the bridge. Again, Jessie nodded and motioned for Rodriguez to take the prisoner up to the bridge, where he might be of assistance.

As Rodriguez grabbed the prisoner, he, too, couldn't resist complimenting his colleague. He looked from Jessie to Billy and then back to Jessie before saying, "Santa mierda, senorita! Like a queen of the sharks." He shook his head slightly and then said to Billy, "Better be careful, Shakespeare."

Jessie, her work finished, looked at Billy. He looked back at her and simply said, "Wow!" He knew the word and the tone were the same he had used when they were under the waterfall. And that was appropriate as he wanted to make love to her right then and there.

Jessie smiled proudly. She enjoyed the way he was looking at her. She teased him, "You heard him, Shakespeare. You'd better be careful."

"I guess so," Billy said. "'Queen of the Sharks' sounds like a gangster movie." She smiled back, relishing the title. Billy added, "But as you know, I'm not too good at being careful." He reached for her and, in doing so, bumped her wounded arm.

Jessie flinched a little. "Tell me about it," she said quietly.

"Sorry," Billy answered. "How is it?"

Jessie nodded. "It's okay." She smiled. "Better than it was an hour ago."

"Revenge is sweet, eh?" Billy asked.

They were interrupted by a loud explosion. The deckhands had mastered the cannon, firing a shell that fell harmlessly into the bay.

Seconds later, Reese, Reggie, and Lyle brought the tall Russian up from where they had fished him out of the bay below, wet but otherwise unhurt, and certainly not eaten by sharks.

Billy looked at Lyle as he said, "I thought I heard an Australian baritone in that scream."

CHAPTER 63

Town Meeting

In the evening of January 2, the residents gathered in the center of Ararat to discuss possible plans. They sat or stood in a semicircle facing the west, where Oliver, Maria, and Captain Mitchell rested on wooden chairs. Behind the trustees, the sun was dropping down on the mountains, moving in and out from behind puffy white clouds.

Billy and Jessie sat in folding chairs next to Owen and Sarah, while Annie sat in the sand. The Brooks family approached, James leaning on Janice, with Jonah trailing behind. With a nod of approval from their mothers, Annie and Jonah ran toward the beach, Roscoe scampering behind. Billy and Jessie graciously got up.

Janice Brooks smiled. "Very kind, but we're okay with standing."

"No, we insist," Billy answered. James and Janice said thanks as they settled into the chairs. "How is the back, JB?"

"It'll be all right in a week or so. How's the arm, Jessie?"

Jessie answered, "Same."

Brooks winked as he asked, "Or should I call you Shark Woman?"

Jessie shook her head. "*Jessie* is fine, thank you."

Janice added, "You'd better watch your step, Billy."

Billy shook his head. "People keep telling me that."

"Where's Jamal?" Sarah asked.

Janice looked toward the other side of the crowd. "He's over there with Naomi...of course."

Billy scanned the rest of the crowd. Miller, his face barely visible under his cowboy hat, hobbled in on a cane and sat down with the help of his fellow deckhands. Beth glanced over toward Billy and waved slightly.

Oliver quieted the crowd and began speaking. "Thank you for coming. As the elected council, we bring this meeting to order. Thank you. As you all know, we were reminded three days ago that we are not alone in the world. Further, we anticipate that two of those ships will be back. The three of us met earlier today with Governor Turner and Captain Decker and would like to put a motion on the floor… or, I suppose, the beach."

A few people chuckled as Oliver went on. "Speaking for the council, our motion is to stay, and fight, if necessary. But this is a democracy. We will vote before making any final decisions. We discussed two other options. The second option is to invite the crews of the yacht and the cruiser onto the island to join us. The third option is to load up the ark again and leave."

Several in the crowd groaned audibly. Susan Harris asked, "Can you say more? What does the second option mean, Oliver? That was your brother's yacht, right?"

Oliver hesitated slightly before answering. "Yes. And I want to publicly apologize for having let him know that we were going to Pitcairn. At that time, I had no idea—"

Susan stopped him kindly. "At that time, none of us worried about letting him know. But I would like your opinion on his intentions now."

Oliver paused. Even though Susan let him off easy on his apology, he seemed uncomfortable just thinking about his brother and what had happened. He took a moment and then responded, "One thing that William and I learned from our time on the yacht is that my brother and many of the people on board are interested only in their own aggrandizement. I can only assume that they have little interest in our group or the species."

The crowd shifted uncomfortably, nobody sure how to react.

Billy, trying to break the silence after his father's confession, noticed Reese, standing with Reichardt, in the back of the crowd. "What do you think, Mike? You know Henry Hill."

Many turned to look at Reese. He took a moment and then answered, "No question in my mind that he's a pig. No offense intended, Mr. Hill."

Oliver shook his head and said quietly, "None taken."

Reese finished, "Bringing him and his family and the crew on that cruiser on this island would be like putting rapists in a nunnery."

Miller and Rodriguez snorted their approval of the analogy, but nobody spoke again for a moment. Then Griffiths pushed the obvious issue. "But if they do want in on this island, we are heavily outnumbered. Maybe we should try to talk. At least learn their intentions."

Miller responded, "We learned their intentions last time."

Griffiths pushed back. "Easy for you to say, Cowboy. You don't have kids."

Captain Mitchell offered the idea a minimal lifeline. "We are not advocating this approach, but we should discuss it further."

Jessie picked up on it. "Si. Even if we wanted to give them a chance, do we have enough food for them on the island? Or fresh water?"

Oliver continued the thought. "Owen, can you speak on the water?"

Owen nodded before speaking. "Fresh water should not be a problem. We have plenty of salt water, and the desal system is working well. But I don't know about food…"

Maria answered. "We discussed the food supply. More people would not be good. We are doing well now, but with many more, it would be difficult."

Dr. Steinberg raised her hand and added, "At some point, we would have to worry about carrying capacity. With more people, we might exceed it."

Rodriguez asked, "Carrying what?"

Steinberg was happy to explain. "*Carrying capacity* refers to the ability of an ecosystem to support a certain number of species, whether human or animal. Between Adamstown, the submarine, and us, this island has never had so many human inhabitants. My sense is that we are not currently doing severe ecological damage. Our footprint is lessened by the fact that we use desalination and solar energy, but allowing two other crews to live and eat here would change that."

Nobody spoke for a moment as they digested the thought. The clouds continued to build up in the western sky to the point that the sun's rays only occasionally peeked through.

Hunter finally said, "I say, give them nothing."

Rodriguez laughed out loud and said, "How about giving 'em some more lead, Chief?" A few laughed, but Hunter didn't seem flattered.

After a brief pause, Oliver pushed the larger question. "All right, then. We should also consider the third possibility. We could reload the ark and leave the island. We would then look for another place to settle."

Again, nobody spoke for a few seconds. They all heard a distant rumble of thunder.

Billy said, "I like it here."

Several turned to stare at him, including Beth, who said loudly, "Who are you kidding, Billy? You love it here!" Many laughed while Billy and Jessie both blushed a little.

Maria rescued them. "Si, Guillermo. We all like it here. As do the people in Adamstown. And we would have to leave them."

Mitchell added, "And the *Darwin* sailors. If we leave, they would be without our help if the other ships return."

Oliver responded, "I agree, but I do want us all to keep in mind that we don't know if there are others in addition to the cruiser and the yacht. They could come back with even more ships and people. We could be vastly outnumbered." Nobody said anything for a good thirty seconds. The only sounds were the waves crashing on the shore and another faint rumble of thunder. The palm trees on the west side of the clearing started swaying in the breezes coming down from the mountains.

When nobody else spoke, Oliver gestured toward the building where the repository was housed. "I have spoken with Dr. Steinberg and Mi-Sung about the possibility of moving the lab again, and I would like them to tell you what they told me."

Dr. Steinberg spoke. "We could move it. The ark was adequate. But I will also say that our establishment here is ideal for the species." She glanced at Mi-Sung sitting next to her.

Mi-Sung nodded. "That is correct. The temperatures and other conditions vary more at sea. Here we can keep them much more stable."

Dr. Steinberg continued the thought. "If I may add, we should also be concerned with the prospect of nuclear winter. Scientists have long predicted a nuclear war would lead to several climate disruptions. We don't know exactly how and where these might be the most severe, but in many places the average temperature could drop to just above freezing for a decade or more. We have been fortunate here, at least so far."

Again, people were quiet as they thought about this prospect. Billy immediately thought of the Cormac McCarthy book *The Road* and the grim desolation it portrayed.

Oliver continued the discussion. "Thank you. Those are serious concerns for option number 3. But also for number 2. If things are as bad elsewhere as we think, there may be more people coming our way in the future. And I don't know what other people would do with our repository, but I fear it would not be good. I know my brother had little interest in our project when we talked about it other than possibly exploiting it somehow."

Again, the crowd was silent for just a few moments. Then Sanders spoke as he gestured toward the species shelter. "If it's good for them, it's good for me. I say we stay."

Miller started making the "Mooooooose" sound. Beth and Rodriguez laughed, and even Sanders smiled, if a bit sheepishly. Others sitting nearby were just puzzled.

There was a pause while people talked quietly to one another or just thought to themselves. Another rumble of thunder sounded in the clouds over the mountains.

Doc Harrison called out, "I call the question."

Billy said, "Second."

Oliver nodded and then spoke. “The motion is to stay and fight if need be. All in favor?” Dozens of hands went up in the air.

He continued. “All opposed?” No hands were visible.

Oliver finished, “The motion passes.” Whatever was said after that was drowned in a round of applause.

CHAPTER 64

Preparations

The residents of Ararat had resolved to stay and fight if necessary, so they all pitched in on preparations. Those preparations took several forms.

Willis and the deckhands continued to prepare the gunboat, and especially its cannon, for usage. Captain Mitchell, Grimaldi, Susan Harris, and some of the Adamstown residents worked with the Aussies to improve radar capability on the ships as well as communication lines beyond the range-limited walkie-talkies. The construction crews reinforced the shelter for the species and built two strong shelters for storage of food and water in the event of a shelling. Hunter and Brooks conducted small-arms training for adults with the AR-15s and the few other rifles and pistols they had. Oliver and Doc Harrison set up a system for mustering in the event of an attack.

Lastly, they commenced a rotation of watches so that someone would be on lookout at all times on a station on the top of the hill just behind Ararat, where a person could see the entire harbor and miles in nearly every direction to spot any incoming ships. They would staff it all hours, including during the night, when lookouts could see running lights of any approaching vessels. This situation was different from standing watch on the ark in two ways. First, people could stand watches together, to keep each other awake. Second, since any adult could handle binoculars and the walkie-talkie, all could participate.

The trustees posted a signup sheet at the office and were gratified to see it fill up quickly, including the dreaded graveyard shift from twelve to four, and the sunrise from four to eight. Some families and groups were helpful enough to do the watches together to take two shifts, such as the sunset and the graveyard shift if they wanted to make it a long evening. Indeed, Beth and her colleagues took the first sunset and graveyard shifts and used them for a long poker game on the hill, taking turns to keep an eye on the oceans for any lights. The Brooks family took a sunset shift, Jonah all excited about the prospect, only to fall asleep as soon as it got dark. Owen and his family did the same and had similar results with Annie. The Smith-Garveys stood a graveyard shift. Susan Harris and her daughter, Naomi, did a graveyard shift, and nobody was surprised when Jamal Brooks joined them. The Sirpathia family did a sunrise shift, and similarly, nobody was surprised when Reggie McLeish joined them.

Billy and Jessie saw the chance to use the shifts as an opportunity to spend a night on the hill together. The housing had not been finished, as other matters took priority, so single men like Billy still slept in one large barracks, while single women like Jessie slept in another. The two of them had managed to get away for a night on the beach and another at the waterfall, but they also saw the lookout option as a way to help while getting a night to themselves. So they signed up for the sunset, graveyard, and sunrise shifts on the first night all were available. In the meantime, each of them also volunteered for a daytime shift. Thus, two days after the town meeting, Billy made the climb up the hill to take the midday shift.

CHAPTER 65

Dogs

As Billy made his way up the hill to stand watch, he heard explosions behind him. He looked back at the area west of Ararat to see his brother and James Brooks moving toward the sight of the last explosion with a sign. Billy couldn't read it, but he could see the line of similar signs where other explosions had occurred. He hoped their plan helped, if they needed it.

When he got up to the top of the hill at noon to relieve Sanders, Roscoe came bounding up to greet him, his bushy tail wagging furiously. Billy rubbed his ears as he said, "Hey, buddy, you helping the Moose stand watch?"

"Helping me stay awake, more like," came the response from a few yards away.

Having finished greeting Billy, the dog hurried back over to Sanders and sat down next to him. Billy wasn't surprised to see Roscoe there. Sanders loved to take the dog for walks, and Owen's family was happy to let him do so. Obviously, the dog loved it too.

The lookout station was minimal. A couple of folding chairs sat in the dirt next to a primitive firepit. A small saw and an ax for cutting firewood hung from a tree. A pit toilet twenty yards away was barely visible through some bushes. Sanders was sitting, leaning against a palm tree, where he could face out toward the bay.

"Quiet, eh?" Billy asked.

Sanders reached out his hand. "Like a tomb."

Billy clasped his hand and helped pull Sanders up. He was thankful that the big man did not let Billy do all the work.

"Sounds like I might want Roscoe to stay another shift," Billy answered. Roscoe, too, stood up and looked full of energy, ready to move. Billy didn't think his chances of keeping the dog's company were good.

"Some cool birds up there," Sanders said as he held out the binoculars. "Check out that tree." He gestured high up a tall palm tree on the edge of the little clearing. A pair of beautiful red and green birds sat calmly on a branch near the top.

"Nice!" Billy exclaimed. "Very pretty."

"Lorikeets," Sanders said.

That brought to Billy's mind what Sanders had said at the meeting two nights before. "Say, I wanted to tell you thanks for emphasizing at the meeting why we're here."

"Hey, man," he answered in his deep voice. "We were all thinking it. I just said it."

"Maybe," Billy answered. "Still good to be reminded."

The birds suddenly took off, perhaps on their way down toward the beach for an afternoon feed. Billy and Sanders watched them fly away.

Billy continued, "How come you like animals so much?"

Sanders grinned, a gold tooth showing when he smiled. "You writing a book, Shakespeare?" Billy spread his palms out as if to say maybe.

"That's okay. No secrets here." Sanders thought for a minute. "I had a dog when I was a kid. A mutt about the same size as Roscoe here." Roscoe cocked his ears at the mention of his name.

"We didn't exactly live in the best part of town, and I wasn't always this big. So I was glad for his company." Sanders looked at Billy, who just nodded.

"My dad was never around. And my mom just couldn't stay off the stuff, so they finally checked her into rehab. My older brother and I lived with the dog for a while until he went up the river. Ten years for armed robbery. And me to the juvie facility. And that was when they took that dog away. They said juvenile facilities didn't allow dogs." He furrowed his brow and finished. "Shit, they allowed everything else."

Billy had no idea what to say, so as usual, he fell back on a cultural reference, an old movie line, "Not exactly Ozzie and Harriett, I guess?"

Sanders looked puzzled. "Ozzie and who?"

"Sorry, stupid reference," Billy answered and then sought a positive response. "Anyway, seems like I read somewhere that dogs in those situations can end up in good homes."

Sanders shook his head slowly, a skeptical smile on his lips. "You a nice guy, Billy. But you ain't much of a liar."

"Maybe not," Billy responded quickly, "but you never know."

"Right," he said slowly. "And I never did know. That dog was the best friend I had." He looked down at Roscoe. "I guess I still see that dog in other critters, like this one."

Roscoe looked from one to the other, obviously aware that the two humans were talking about him. His tail wagged a little.

"Dogs are amazing animals," Billy said.

"Better than people," Sanders answered and then continued. "If you're nice to a dog, he don't know if you're Black, Brown, White, or Green. And he don't care. He just knows you're nice."

Roscoe barked once quickly and then did that little circle thing dogs do when they want to get moving.

"Looks like somebody is ready to head down the hill," Billy said.

"Speaking of animal lovers, how's the shark woman?" Sanders asked with a grin.

Billy laughed. "Loving her reputation, I think."

"Better watch yourself," Sanders added.

Billy started to say something about how many people kept telling him that, but Roscoe barked to say it was time to go. Billy said, with exaggerated resignation, "Guess I'll be all alone up here."

"Hey, don't feel like he's picking me over you," Sanders answered. "The dog just knows there's food down there."

Billy looked back at Sanders and grinned. "You know something, Moose, you ain't much of a liar yourself."

Sanders laughed out loud and then started striding down the trail. Roscoe glanced at Billy once and then, realizing he wasn't coming, followed the big man at a trot. Billy settled in against the palm tree and lifted the binoculars to his eyes.

CHAPTER 66

Night Watch

A few days after his midday shift, Billy made his way up the hill again, this time with Jessie. They left Ararat right after dinner, figuring they could relieve the watch up there early and get more time to themselves on the hill. They found Reese and Reichardt deep into a chess game, sitting on the two folding chairs and bending over a little board. Both looked up as Billy and Jessie arrived.

"Hey, it's Shakespeare and Shark Woman," Reese said. He then added, "No offense, Jessie. That was good work."

"None taken," she responded. "In fact, I told my sharks to be on the lookout for more Russians."

Reichardt made the big shark jaws motion with her arms, and they all laughed. Billy looked out over the ocean seemingly calm and empty. "Speaking of Russians, seen anything out there?"

Reese shook his head. "Just water." Reichardt moved a piece on the board, and when Reese looked back down, he frowned. "Damn," he said. "Checkmated again."

Reichardt stuck out her fist for Reese to bump. As he did, he said, "Well, I guess that's how you learn, eh?"

Reichardt made a gesture by pointing at her wrist and then at Billy and Jessie. Reese interpreted, "Linda says you're early." Indeed, the sun was low in the western sky but still at least an hour from going down.

Billy answered, "Yeah, we figured if we got up here early, you could get down and get some warm dinner."

"Much appreciated," Reese said. He and Reichardt stood and dumped the chess pieces as well as the board into a knapsack. Reese offered the knapsack to Billy, who just shook his head. Reese then unhooked the walkie-talkie from his belt and handed it to Jessie. "Hunter's got the duty tonight." Either Hunter or Captain Mitchell was on duty call each night in case someone from the lookout spotted ships.

Jessie said, "Gracias, Miguel. Good night to you both." She started to move the chairs over next to the firepit.

Reese and Reichardt picked up their water bottles and started to walk down the trail to Ararat. Reese looked back at Billy and winked while he said, "Don't forget to keep an eye on the ocean, Billy."

Billy nodded. "We're good." Then he added, innocently, "We'll take turns sleeping."

"Right," Reese said sarcastically and then, with a glance at Jessie, added with a smile, "Better watch yourself, buddy." He turned, and they went down the trail toward Ararat.

Billy and Jessie used the ax and saw to build up the supply of firewood while they still had enough daylight. The only clouds on the horizon were not rain clouds, so they were confident the night would be dry, but a clear night also meant that it would be cool. Billy got the fire started just as the sun started to settle on the mountains to the west, and a full moon popped out over the eastern horizon. A slight breeze came down off the mountains, cooling the air and feeding oxygen to the fire.

They sat down in the folding chairs and relaxed for a few minutes before Billy broke the silence. "Beautiful evening. Cool for summer."

Jessie responded, "Si. I am still getting used to it being summer in the southern hemisphere, not winter."

"Right," Billy answered and then added, "I guess we can't call it the winter of our discontent." Jessie just stared at him but did not respond, so he continued. "That's from—"

"Let me guess." She interrupted. "More Shakespeare." He just nodded, so she continued, "Tell it to Hunter."

"I might. It's from his favorite play," Billy answered.

Jessie looked at him. "Are you feeling discontented, Billy?"

Billy smiled a little. "What do you think?" She hid a smile but didn't say anything, so he went on. "Funny how so many people are telling me to stay out of trouble with you, Shark Woman."

Then she did smile, that little smile he had seen the first day when they were chasing leaves and the one that had made him feel good so many times since. "You have good friends, Shakespeare. And they give good advice."

"Hey," Billy answered, feigning defensiveness, "it's never my intention to look for trouble."

Jessie continued to stare at him. "Oh. And what are you looking for, Billy Hill?"

He stared back. "I'm looking at her."

She smiled appreciatively.

Then he added, "And you? What are you looking for, Jessie Rivera?"

Jessie stood and lifted the binoculars where they had been hanging around her neck. She scanned the darkening skies in all directions while Billy waited for an answer. "I am looking for ships, but I do not see any." She set the binoculars on her chair.

She moved over and stood right in front of Billy. "So...," she said suggestively.

Billy looked up at her, his blood starting to pump faster. "So?"

"So," she said as she started to unbutton her shirt. "So much for your intentions. You may not have looked for trouble, but you have it."

Billy shifted in his chair and leaned back to make room for her. "Hmmm. Someone said the road to hell is paved with good intentions."

"Who said that, Shakespeare again?" Jessie responded as she sat down on his lap, facing him and demanded, "Mr. Shakespeare?"

Billy felt her strength, her warmth. "I can't remember right now," was the only answer he could muster.

Her smiled widened. "You can't remember who said something? You must be in trouble," she said, feeling him stirring beneath her. He was speechless, and she liked it.

"And are you saying this is the road to hell?" she asked, pushing the hair back from her face so she could look in his eyes.

"Whatever road it is, I'm on it," Billy managed. He looked at the scar on her arm from the bullet wound and leaned in to kiss it. Then he moved up her arm into her neck and eventually sank his face into her breasts.

Jessie caressed the back of his head. "You don't know much right now, do you, Billy?"

Billy lifted his face and looked up into her dark eyes. "All I know right now is that I can't get enough of you."

She smiled triumphantly, "Good." She reached down to unfasten his shorts as he shifted his weight to give her room.

Suddenly, the old folding chair collapsed and they were in the dirt next to the fire. They were both speechless for just a moment, and then they started laughing so hard they could hardly catch their breath. They looked at each other, still laughing, and then scrambled to pull off their clothes. She moved on top of him, and they made love while lying in the dirt, the firelight flickering off their naked bodies.

Afterward, they lay there, on their backs, looking up at the stars multiplying in the night sky, as if to defy the light from the moon. Billy reached over without getting up, took a piece of the broken chair, and threw it onto the fire. She giggled.

"Guess we'll hear about that chair," Billy said.

"Si," Jessie agreed. "They can take it out of our paychecks."

Billy chuckled and looked at Jessie. "Well, that was fun."

She looked back at him. "You know, Guillermo, someday I will want an answer to my question. What are you looking for?"

Billy answered, "I know. Someday." He paused. "But not tonight." He thought for a moment and then went on. "We should get some sleep so we can be up in time to see the sunrise. Reggie McLeish did the morning shift yesterday and said the sunrise was spectacular."

Jessie smiled. "Reggie would have said anything was spectacular if he was watching with Naveena." They knew the two of them had been on watch together.

Billy thought of how Reggie had looked when he came running up from the Sarpathia home the morning the gunboats arrived in the harbor, like he really wanted to tell someone how happy he was but couldn't at that time.

"True enough," Billy answered. "Still."

"Okay." Jessie sat up. "I will take the first shift. You get some sleep. I will lay out a blanket for you."

Billy didn't argue. They had slept together enough times that they both knew he would get up in the middle of the night to urinate anyway, as he always did. He could take over then. If she went to sleep first, they knew she might well sleep through the night and he wouldn't have the heart to wake her up. And she wanted them both to get some sleep.

Jessie pulled on her clothes, took a blanket from her pack, and spread it near the fire. Billy pulled a blanket out of his pack, wadded up his clothes to make a pillow, and lay down, pulling the second blanket over him. While he lay there, watching, Jessie put another log on the fire and moved the intact chair closer to the pit. He fell asleep instantly.

As expected, Billy woke up in the middle of the night. He felt like he had been asleep for at least several hours. Without moving from under the blanket, he opened his eyes. Jessie was sitting in the chair, huddled in her jacket, poking at the fire with a long stick. The firelight lit her dark face. Behind her, the sky was full of stars. He smiled, enjoying all parts of the view.

Jessie, her sixth sense kicking in, realized Billy was awake and staring at her. She looked over at him. "Hi," she said quietly.

"Hi," Billy said. "See any lights?"

"Just stars," she answered.

"Ready for me to take over?"

She nodded. "Whenever you are."

He pulled his clothes on and then got up and stretched. "I'll be right back," he said and hustled over into the trees to urinate. By the time that he got back, she had already put another log on the fire for him, used her clothes to make her own pillow, and crawled under the blanket. Neither spoke as she fell asleep.

Billy picked up the night vision binoculars where Jessie had left them and scanned the surrounding oceans. Seeing nothing, he sat down on the folding chair and stared into the fire. Some famous quote about staring into fires started to come to his mind, but then he stopped. She was right. He was struggling to come up with cultural references. He really was in trouble. But it was the best kind of trouble. He had not felt this way about someone in a long time. Ever, he realized. He silently promised that he would tell her that. Soon.

As the night continued, the moon traveled overhead and then started to slip down toward the ocean to the west. The darker sky allowed even more stars to appear, so many that Billy couldn't make out any of the constellations. He didn't feel as sleepy as he expected, but rather incredibly alive. And his brain started to work again. He knew it because he finally did come up with a cultural reference that was appropriate for the moment. "Starry night," he muttered to himself as he remembered the van Gogh painting of the same name. He never did know much about art, but he had seen enough to know why some paintings were famous. He thought of the Rembrandt *Self-Portrait* that mesmerized him once for minutes. And he recalled how good he felt when he saw Rembrandt's *Night Watch* one time while bumming around Europe. Even then, he knew he was looking at a masterpiece, a remarkable statement about humanity. Then he caught himself. That painting and all the others were all gone, lost in a moment of insanity that had been building for decades, centuries. Along with everything else. He felt anger swelling up inside until he forced himself to think about what he and his colleagues had done. They had saved what they could. And that made him proud.

Billy lifted the binoculars again and scanned the ocean. Still nothing. But wait. There, in the eastern sky, he could finally see some light below the horizon, as if someone were opening a chest with a candle in it and the light was starting to seep out. Sunrise was coming. He wasn't sure whether to wake Jessie or let her sleep, but when he glanced at her, she had taken care of the decision. She was watching him from her spot under the blanket, the light from the dying fire revealing a gentle smile on her face. Billy smiled back. She stood, the blanket still wrapped around her shoulders, moved over to him, and took the binoculars so she, too, could look.

Dawn arrived with more lights in the eastern sky, a mix of pink, orange, and blue rays peeking out over the horizon on the far side of the world. A breeze continued to blow down from the mountain off to the west, so the hilltop was cool. But that was only one of the reasons they had wrapped themselves in the blanket. They were enjoying being so close while watching the morning come. And they knew that down in the settlement below the hill, their friends and families were sleeping, and the precious sanctuary that they had built was well protected. So much had happened to them and the world over the last five months, but they were still here and still very much alive. The new day promised new possibilities for a new world.

"Billy," Jessie said softly.

Billy looked where she was looking, off to the north, and then he saw it too. There was light out there, and it was not natural.

He asked quietly, "How many?"

She focused the binoculars and then answered, "Two ships."

Billy unclipped the walkie-talkie from his belt and punched the button. "Hunter," he called and then released the button.

The voice on the other end came back quickly, impressively, given that he had surely just been awakened. "Yeah."

Billy said simply, "They're coming."

Yes, it was a new day with new possibilities, but the new world was like the old one in at least one unfortunate way. They still had to fight for what they held so dear, or it was destined to disappear for eternity.

CHAPTER 67

Invasion

Billy and Jessie hurriedly dressed and cleaned up the site. They were ready to start down the trail when Jessie stopped them.

Billy," she said, looking north through the binoculars. "Something is separating from the larger ship." She handed them back, and Billy looked.

"Hunter." Billy pushed the button on the walkie-talkie and called. When Hunter answered, Billy could hear noises in the background, including the siren from the ark blaring out the warning signal. "They're sending a helicopter."

Hunter's voice came back immediately. "How big?"

Billy held out the walkie-talkie so Hunter could hear Jessie answer, "Forty feet long."

"Damn," came Hunter's voice. "Troop carrier."

Jessie followed up. "Looks like they're headed for the Plateau."

After just a slight pause, Hunter said, "I need to get up there."

They needed a plan. Billy knelt to use a stick to draw in the dirt so he and Jessie could visualize. While he drew, Jessie relayed the map verbally to Hunter. The lookout spot where they were standing was on a hill about a mile southwest of Ararat. What they called the Plateau was a flat area farther up in the mountains, about three miles northwest of Ararat, nearer to the north coast. Billy and Jessie knew it well as they would sometimes run to the Plateau and back, but Hunter didn't know the trails.

Jessie told Hunter, "Start hiking up the trail toward the lookout. One of us will meet you and take you up to the Plateau." She looked at Billy, who nodded in affirmation. "The other will take the walkie-talkie, go up, and find a vantage point from where we can see the helicopter unload."

Hunter called back, "On my way."

Billy and Jessie both dropped their packs. They needed to travel fast and figured they could come back later and get them. Billy reached for the walkie-talkie, but Jessie held it away. "No way," she said.

"It's got to be me," Billy insisted.

"Why?"

"You're faster than I am. You can run down, collect Hunter, and get up to where I'll be going faster than I would."

Jessie frowned. She knew he was right, and there wasn't time to argue. "Okay, but—"

"I know." Billy interrupted her. "Stay out of trouble."

She leaned in to give him a kiss. "There are different kinds of trouble, Billy."

He smiled and took off running, back through the clearing and northwest toward the Plateau. Jessie started running back toward Ararat to get Hunter.

After ten minutes of hard running through the jungle, along an old animal trail he and Jessie had found weeks before, Billy approached the Plateau. He did so at the same time as the helicopter flying in from the cruiser, the sound at first like a ceiling fan that is slightly out of alignment, and then louder, a steady chop-chop of blades keeping aloft a heavy load. Billy worked his way about fifty yards off the trail, where he found a little spot in some trees two hundred yards short of the clearing on top of the Plateau. The trees provided good cover but also a clear line of sight. He watched the pilot maneuver the helicopter and then land where it could disgorge its contents. The troops who emerged were heavily armed, at least thirty of them. But it wasn't just troops. They also had machine guns and mortars.

The helicopter's blades were making enough noise on the Plateau to drown out his voice, so he used the walkie-talked to call Jessie and Hunter. "I've got a spot. I'll meet you on the trail and bring you here." He couldn't hear their response over the noise of the blades. Then he moved back down to the trail to collect his colleagues. He didn't bother to be quiet as he moved through the brush, knowing the helicopter was still masking any noise he was making. After just two minutes, he spotted Jessie leading Hunter up the slope. They were moving fast, Hunter with a long narrow case slung over his shoulder

"Jessie," Billy called out as they approached. She looked up at him just as the chopper finished its unloading and took off again, flying back toward the cruiser. They were both breathing heavily, their shirts wet from sweat. "There's a good spot just up here," he whispered. He turned off the trail into the jungle and led them back to his vantage point. When they arrived, they were all breathing hard but trying to be as quiet as possible as they looked up at the clearing.

The invaders were shuffling around, checking gear, but not yet moving southeast, apparently waiting for another load of troops. Even from two hundred yards away, the sounds of their voices carried through the otherwise-quiet tropical forest. Billy's heart was beating so loudly he wondered if that sound could carry. Jessie looked at him and nodded as if to say she knew how he felt. Hunter inhaled deeply several times to calm his breathing. The sounds of the jungle slowly returned, some birds in the surrounding trees chattering to one another about the intruders suddenly in their area. Hunter uncased his rifle and inserted a bullet.

They only had to wait another few minutes before the sound of the returning helicopter became audible again. As the helicopter came into view, Billy and Jessie both watched Hunter as he rested his rifle on a tree limb for stability and looked through the scope.

The helicopter approached, the sound of its blades filling the air. Hunter waited until it was almost directly overhead and then squeezed the trigger. The sound was like an explosion. The birds that had been resting nearby flew up out of the trees. The shot was true. It shattered the tail rotor like a brick hitting a weather vane.

Immediately the helicopter began to spin as the pilot fought to keep control. He failed. The chopper went down hard a hundred yards from where they watched and blew up in a fiery explosion.

Billy watched the crash and then looked at his colleagues. The flames from the explosion cast an odd red glow on their faces. Neither Jessie nor Hunter changed expression.

"That was one hell of a shot," Billy said quietly.

Hunter barely acknowledged the compliment, simply nodding one time. Then he said, simply, "We have to move."

"Right," Jessie said and then added, "You go first, John. You'll need more time. And they need you in town."

Hunter looked at the two of them and said, "They have to come out where we planned for us to have a chance." They all knew that there were several possible routes from the Plateau down to Ararat, but the residents were prepared to fight the intruders only in one area.

Billy and Jessie glanced at each other and then looked at Hunter. Jessie said quickly, "We'll make sure they follow us."

Billy suddenly remembered an event in American history that had occurred years before the Custer battle at Little Bighorn. Sioux Indians under Crazy Horse tricked an overly aggressive US Cavalry officer, leading him into an ambush that resulted in the annihilation of the soldiers. "Just like Crazy Horse," Billy said.

Rather than being insulted, Hunter seemed to appreciate the comment and smiled slightly as he looked back at Billy. "Yes," he said, "just like Crazy Horse." He slid his rifle back into its case and slung it over his shoulder. He looked each of the other two in the eyes one more time and then, without a word, started hustling back down the trail toward Ararat.

Billy and Jessie were suddenly alone again in the little patch of jungle. They looked at each other and each exhaled deeply.

"I guess we should wait a couple of minutes before we get their attention," Billy said.

"Just a couple," Jessie answered.

Billy looked at her. "It's been quite a morning."

She looked back. "It was quite a night."

He smiled. "Quite a trip."

She said, "I love you, Billy."

She had beaten him to it. "I love you too, Jess."

Jessie started to turn away and then looked back at Billy with that little teasing smile as she asked, "So are we keeping score this time?"

Billy's smile widened as he remembered a run through a eucalyptus forest on a morning that seemed like such a long time ago. "You bet your life we are." And they both knew that was true.

She smiled back. "Let's go."

Billy answered, "Why not?" Even then, with all that was going on, Billy's brain clicked to one of his favorite cultural references, the ending of the movie *The Wild Bunch*. He was proud that they had just repeated the dialogue, but he also knew that had not ended well for the main characters. And there was no time to think about that now.

They started moving through the trees, making enough noise to attract the attention of the invaders. Some of the Russians spotted them and yelled. Then the invaders picked up their weapons and started chasing the runners through the jungle down the trail toward Ararat.

CHAPTER 68

The Battle of Ararat

The people on Pitcairn scrambled to prepare for the invasion. Captain Mitchell got on the walkie-talkie with Captain Decker and Governor Turner so they could mobilize their people. The Ararat residents went to their muster stations. On her way to the pier, Beth ran past Janice Brooks and Susan Harris gathering families at the school. Still running, she yelled "Good luck" to James Brooks, Sanders, and Rodriguez at the arms locker, where they were starting to distribute weapons. When she arrived at the pier, she met Officer Willis, Carter, Reese, and Miller. They hustled down the pier and climbed onto the gunboat. Within minutes, they had it functional. Carter started the engines in case they needed to move. Miller and Reese readied the cannon. Beth and Willis went to the bridge wing, where Willis picked up her clipboard and Beth settled behind the viewfinder, looking back at Ararat.

Beth glanced at Willis. "How's the arm?" Willis was still dealing with the broken wrist she had suffered in the fall weeks before.

"I'm good," Willis answered. She didn't say anything else. Beth appreciated that. From her time fighting forest fires, Beth knew that people dealt with anxiety in different ways. She, for one, was quiet, if for no other reason than to concentrate on the task at hand. She was pleased to learn that the officer was similar. Willis seemed calm, focused on what she had to do. The young woman's fall during the initial voyage had not fostered confidence in her abilities among the deckhands, but their respect had grown as Willis toughed it out and did her job.

Beth heard Decker on the communications system as he said, "We're going after the cruiser." She looked over toward Adamstown to see the sub getting underway. Then she swiveled the viewfinder to watch the town's preparations. The little army of armed residents had lined behind the short rise between the town and the jungle, where they would be less exposed to rifle fire but would still have sightlines toward the trees. Sanders and Brooks, holding AR-15s, were walking behind the others on the firing line, still giving instructions. Rodriguez, Owen, Reichardt, and Luke held the other assault rifles. Griffiths, Jordan Smith-Garvey, Irene Doyle, and Grimaldi all held other older rifles, awkwardly, holding the pieces as if they were strange, dangerous objects. The three trustees held pistols, but none of them looked too confident with their weapons. Doc Harrison, Sarah, Dr. Steinberg, and Mi-Sung crouched behind the firing line with medical kits, ready to help if someone was wounded.

Beth and Willis watched the helicopter fly back toward the Plateau on its second run, only to suddenly go down in a fiery explosion. That helped the odds, but there were still thirty or so troops in the jungle, having been delivered in the first load. The arkonauts were still outgunned. Beth scanned the jungle for Hunter, Billy, and Jessie. They were in there somewhere but would emerge, hopefully where planned, and give the residents a fighting chance. She could read the signs they had posted just days before in the clearing between the town and the jungle, the one on the southern end saying simply "1," and the northernmost one "16." They had spaced them every twenty yards, so they had covered a lot of ground, hopefully enough.

Beth looked away from the viewfinder and back at Willis, who was checking the charts on her clipboard. When Willis looked up, Beth tried to sound reassuring. "It's a good plan."

Willis smiled slightly. "Good. It's the only chance we have."

The walkie-talkie on Willis's belt crackled to life. "Mitchell to Willis. Are you set?"

Beth spotted the captain holding the walkie-talkie as he stood next to Oliver.

Willis answered, "We're ready, Captain. We'll let you know when we see something."

"Roger," Mitchell said. As he held the button down, Willis and Beth could hear Rodriguez behind him shouting at the others on the line.

"None of you gringos shoot until I say so."

Beth chuckled, and Willis shook her head slightly. They were silent again. The entire area seemed to have gone completely quiet. Even the waves seem to have calmed. Willis nudged Beth and pointed toward the bay to the south.

Beth swirled the viewfinder and focused on the little pilot boat coming from Adamstown. McLeish was at the wheel. Two women and three men stood in the hold behind him, looking ahead. They were holding rifles.

Beth said quietly, "Six." It wasn't many, but they might have been the only Adamstown residents who owned arms.

Willis called in. "Reinforcements from Adamstown. Six with weapons."

Mitchell called back, "We'll be glad to have them." Beth watched McLeish pull up to the end of the pier nearest the town, where they unloaded and hurried to join the Ararat army. Brooks distributed them on the firing line.

Then the walkie-talkie came back to life. Hunter's voice came over, from a distance but clear. It sounded like he was running.

"They're coming. Thirty troops with guns." He paused to catch his breath. "Watch for Billy and Jessie."

Then Beth spotted Hunter loping through the trees and into the clearing between the jungle and the firing line. He was carrying his long rifle in one hand. Fortunately, he was so recognizable that none of the nervous residents took a shot at him. He cleared the line and ran to where Oliver and Mitchell were standing.

Beth kept her eyes focused on the line of trees that constituted the border of the jungle. With the benefit of the powerful viewfinder, she noticed birds fly off some of the trees and guessed that was Billy and Jessie stirring them. She focused on the nearest marker and said to Willis, "Looks like marker 4."

Willis spoke into the walkie-talkie. "They should come out at marker 4."

"Copy," Mitchell responded and called to the others on the beach, "Marker 4." Some of the residents on the line, prodded by Brooks and Sanders, moved closer to the spot directly across from marker 4.

Willis finished looking at the notes on her clipboard and yelled down to Miller. "Miller, dial up two-five-five. Lock and load."

"Two-five-five," Miller called back. Due west was 270 degrees, so the Russians were just south of that. The residents had sighted in the markers two days before with live rounds and written down their headings. And from the practice rounds, they knew the exact distance to the tree line. The plan was for the residents to keep the invaders in that tree line with small-arms fire long enough for the gunboat cannon to join the battle.

Beth kept staring through the viewfinder. The morning was warming quickly, and she started to perspire, although she knew it wasn't just because of the temperatures. Finally, she spotted Jessie and Billy coming through the last line of trees in the jungle, right at marker 4.

"Here they come," she said to Willis. They were running hard, Jessie just a few yards in front of Billy.

Shots sounded from inside the line of trees, and dirt splattered just behind the runners. The two of them started weaving as they ran, and then Billy took a hit and went down.

"Damn!" Beth exclaimed.

The people along the firing line in Ararat began shooting at the line of trees, trying to give the runners some cover. Jessie ran back to help Billy as he got up quickly, holding a bleeding arm.

Then, Beth noticed someone in the firing line stand up. To her horror, she realized it was Oliver.

"Get down!" Beth yelled out loud. "Get down!"

Oliver, still standing, aimed his pistol at the trees as he fired. As ineffective as that was, he drew the fire coming from the tree line away from Billy and Jessie and toward him.

Bullets worked their way up the little rise and then into Oliver. He tumbled over backward.

Beth said out loud, "No!"

Some of the residents, stunned, stopped firing. Fortunately, Brooks, Sanders, and Rodriguez kept blasting away at the tree line while Sarah and Doc Harrison crawled over to Oliver to try to help. In the meantime, Billy and Jessie, unaware of why the fire had been diverted, were moving again, limping to the rise and then tumbling over it before collapsing on the ground.

"Beth," Willis, having seen what happened, said calmly. "Are you okay?"

Beth looked away from the viewfinder and at Willis, as if she had spoken in a foreign language.

"Beth," Willis said again, more firmly this time.

Beth stared at her and then, forcing herself to focus, resumed looking through the viewfinder. She told herself that Oliver could be okay and deliberately looked away from him.

Willis looked down at Miller and Reese on the cannon. Carter had come up to join them to help with loading shells and removing the casings.

The first of the invaders came into view. They were moving quickly, especially given that they were carrying some heavy firepower. As they spilled out of the woods, Beth could see assault rifles, machine guns, and even a couple of small mortars. As the fire from the residents increased again, some of the invaders dropped down to kneeling or prone position to continue shooting. The exchange of fire, even from the gunboat's position half a mile away, was loud and intense. Another of the residents, who had been too exposed, took a round in the head and fell backward onto the beach. Some of the Ararat residents were firing wildly at the trees, but others, particularly Brooks and Sanders, were effective. Hunter was taking aim with his long rifle and firing shot after shot. Several attackers were down.

After nearly a minute of the exchange of gunfire, with their men taking some hits, the Russians finally started to back up into the trees. They were obviously well trained. They covered one another as they dropped back and took their wounded with them. The ones carrying the mortars began assembling them.

By falling back, they had moved into the exact range for the gunboat cannon. But they had also shifted location slightly. "A little to the north," Beth said to Willis.

Willis called out, "Make that two-five-seven, Cowboy. And fire one."

"Two-five-seven," Miller repeated while his colleagues dialed it in and the cannon shifted slightly. He pulled the trigger. The gunboat bucked a little from the discharge and then settled down again. Beth watched the shell's trajectory as it flew over the people in the town and landed with a loud explosion on top of the Russians in the tree line.

"Hit," Beth said loudly. The area went suddenly quiet, on the bay and on the beach. Surely, the Russians were stunned, but even the residents who had known what was coming were quiet, waiting to see what happened next.

Beth peered through the scope and tried to see through the smoke where the shell had landed. One of the mortars and half a dozen bodies lay in pieces. But then, after just a few seconds, there was movement. Some of the Russians who had moved just north of their dead comrades began to stir again and moved to get farther away from the explosion site by going deeper into the trees. Two of them began to set up the remaining mortar.

"Shift north," Beth said to Willis. "And add twenty yards."

She called it out to Miller. "Two-five-nine. Add twenty and fire two."

"Two-five-nine, add twenty," Miller repeated to Carter and Reese. While the gunboat crew adjusted the cannon, the Russians fired off a mortar round that landed just in front of the Ararat firing line.

Miller pulled the trigger and the gunboat bucked again. Beth watched the shell slam into the new position. This one did not have the same shock effect as the first, but it did have a similar physical impact.

As the smoke cleared, Beth, looking through the viewfinder, could see nearly a dozen mangled bodies. The jungle and the beach were completely quiet. They all waited again as smoke rose from the tree line. The smell of gunpowder was heavy in the air.

After about a minute, someone in the trees waved a white T-shirt crudely attached to a long stick. The battle of Ararat was over almost as quickly as it had begun.

Willis called down to the gun crew, "Secure the gun, boys. Good job." Miller and Reese and Carter, unaware of their losses on the beach, exchanged high fives.

Beth pulled back from the viewfinder and looked at Willis. There were tears in her eyes. Willis reached out to embrace her.

CHAPTER 69

A Costly Victory

Smoke hung heavy around Ararat, and the smell of gunpowder was pervasive. Many of the defenders were reluctant to get up from their firing positions, still clutching their weapons as if they might need them again. Residents who had sheltered in town during the battle emerged tentatively and approached the battle site slowly.

Hunter, Brooks, Reichardt, and Sanders, all carrying their weapons at the ready, walked cautiously to the tree line to collect the prisoners. Two large craters, littered with broken trees and mangled bodies, showed where the gunboat shells had hit. It was a brutal contrast to what had been there before, a line of palm trees that swayed in the ocean breezes. Now the air was filled with the sickening aroma of burnt flesh. Five of the invaders had survived, although one was in bad shape. They looked dirty and exhausted, not nearly as intimidating as they had been just an hour before. Hunter and his colleagues rounded them up, making them carry their injured comrade, and herded them down to Ararat.

Meanwhile, the residents were taking stock of their losses. Several were wounded; four were dead or dying. Irene Doyle had not moved from her position on the firing line, having been shot in the head and killed instantly. Archie McLeish's friend Ronald Kitchener lay flat on his back, where he had fallen when several rounds hit him in the face and chest. McLeish sat next to him, in shock, shaking his head sadly back and forth. Just down the line from them, Eric

Griffiths lay on his back, also with a chest wound. Doc Harrison and Mi-Sung bent over him, but there was little they could do.

"Here?" Griffiths mumbled, his words barely comprehensible through the blood coming out of his mouth. "Here?" he asked again, as if unable to believe he would die on a remote island. Then he closed his eyes for the last time. The man who had always asked Oliver questions had died asking one more.

Oliver could not hear questions anymore. He lay motionless, his head cradled in Sarah's lap. Owen, Billy, and Jessie all hurried over from their end of the firing line to where Oliver lay. Owen sat down next to Sarah and put his arm around her. Billy stood, holding a handkerchief on his bleeding arm, looked down at the body, stunned. Then he dropped to his knees in the sand. Jessie stood behind him, her fingers caressing his shoulders.

Billy looked at Sarah. "How did he…?" He couldn't finish.

Sarah looked up, tears in her eyes. "He stood up to take the fire away from you," she answered without any accusatory tone. "He was trying…" Her voice caught.

Billy's mouth dropped open, but he had no words. He felt a sickening feeling in his stomach. A memory in his brain clicked, and he thought back to the conversation he had had with his father on the lifeboat, about sacrifice.

Just then, Beth came running up from the pier. She stopped and looked down at her father's body while she caught her breath. She asked, "Did he say anything?"

Billy shook his head for several seconds before answering, "Not in words." Beth stared at her brother, not knowing exactly what he meant.

Others joined the group. The other deckhands, having left Reichardt guarding the prisoners, walked up slowly. They were all still carrying their rifles. None of them said a word. Then Sanders went to Beth and hugged her. Doc Harrison, Dr. Steinberg, and Maria also came over and looked quietly at their fallen leader. Captain Mitchell, limping from a fall, followed.

Doc Harrison started tending the wounded as best as he could. He applied a bandage to a bleeding wound on Rodriguez's arm. Then he began wrapping Billy's arm. Just then, they heard an explosion out past the harbor, so loud many people jerked to attention.

"What the hell?" asked Rodriguez.

"The sub," Captain Mitchell said simply. The others suddenly remembered that while their battle might have been finished, the cruiser was still out there. Mitchell got on his walkie-talkie and called out to Captain Decker.

"Mitchell to Decker. Copy?"

For several agonizing seconds, they heard nothing but static on the other end of the line. Then, very faintly, they heard Decker's Australian accent. "Cruiser is down. What is your status?"

Mitchell, the relief evident on his face, called back, "Invaders stopped."

CHAPTER 70

Postmortem

The residents of Pitcairn tried to recuperate on the day after the invasion and comprehend all that had happened. After the submarine sank the cruiser, Henry Hill had surrendered the yacht and followed the *Darwin* back to Pitcairn. That, of course, necessitated a decision on what to do with the prisoners, both Russian and American. Mitchell and Decker talked to the prisoners. One of the Russians was able and willing to speak English, even without prompting from the shark woman. In addition, while Henry and his family were angry and sullen, others on the yacht were quite willing to tell of their experiences. More specifically, Syszmanski was happy to "sing," to use the prison slang, more than just Polish drinking songs. It turned out that he could in fact speak some English. In addition, Perreau, the helmsman, was also eager to complain about decisions made by the Hill family and for which he took no responsibility. Thus, Mitchell and Decker learned a few things.

Most importantly, conditions in the rest of the world were as bad as feared. After splitting from the ark, the *Diamond* had sailed all along the American coastline, looking for a place to land. In most spots, the Hills and their crew couldn't even get near to shore because radiation levels were so high. In other places, the few people they saw were damaged, desperate, and dangerous. Many survivors had serious wounds, and nearly all appeared to be emaciated. At one spot, several desperate people had tried to swim to the yacht, prompting the boat to mercilessly sail away. The yacht then sailed back to the

South Pacific, specifically the Marquesa Islands, where they found the Russian vessels. The Russian ships, like the *Darwin*, had avoided nuclear fallout by having been on maneuvers near Antarctica. They had then sailed from island to island, looking for a safe place to make port. When Henry Hill told them about the ark and Pitcairn, the Hills and the Russians formed an unholy alliance.

During the day after the two captains learned these things, the residents discussed various options for the prisoners. Hunter and some others advocated the simplest resolution. As Hunter said, "They hang pirates, don't they?" Others preferred something only slightly more humane, banishing them to nearby Henderson Island, a rocky place where some survivors of the whaling ship *Essex* had survived for a short time centuries before. A few others, feeling more charitable, suggested trying to assimilate them into the island society, but the island had only a small jail and nobody trusted Henry Hill and his family. Captain Decker finally offered a solution, but it entailed a loss to the island.

Decker and the *Darwin* crew decided to sail for Australia. They had only faint hope that conditions there would be conducive to staying, but they wanted to check their homeland. Decker said they would be willing to escort the yacht and the prisoners to Australia and then either turn them over to any authorities, if they were still active, or disable the yacht and let the prisoners fend for themselves on Australian soil. As Decker said, "Putting convicts on our continent has some precedent." The downside, of course, was that the Pitcairn residents would be sorry to see Decker and his crew depart.

CHAPTER 71

Memorial Service

Five days after the battle, the residents gathered to honor their dead at a service on the hill behind Ararat, where crosses already stood for Myerson, Green, and Hannigan. The morning was unusually cool, with heavy clouds and a breeze coming down off the mountains, so people wore jackets or sweatshirts. Many Adamstown residents and *Darwin* sailors also wanted to attend, so Billy and Archie McLeish made several runs each in their launches. By the time the service started, over two hundred people had gathered.

Ron Kitchener's widow, the surviving Griffiths family, and the Hill siblings asked Sarah to lead the service. She did so as a non-denominational minister and as the newest trustee of Ararat. The day before, having realized they needed to replace Oliver, the two remaining trustees, Maria and Captain Mitchell, passed out blank pieces of paper as a simple ballot. An overwhelming majority wrote in Sarah's name, and she graciously accepted.

To help with the service, Sarah asked any willing musicians to serve as a band for the opening and closing numbers. All the musicians from the New Year's Eve party accepted. They started with the traditional hymn "Will the Circle Be Unbroken" for any who wanted to sing. Then the band members went down and sat with the other residents.

Sarah began by recognizing those who had been killed. She admitted she did not know Irene Doyle, Eric Griffiths, or Ron Kitchener well, but they all were decent people whose lives had ended too soon. Knowing the families were grieving, she said that was quite natural, citing the book of Jeremiah in the Bible as saying that the purpose of funerals is to mourn so that "our eyes may run down with tears." She added that she wanted to make some more personal comments about Oliver at the end of the service. She then asked for a moment of silence for those who had passed.

Second, Sarah said she wanted to make some comments for anyone who felt any guilt about the battle or all the deaths that had occurred. Most of the people in the battle, including the sailors on the *Darwin*, had never killed someone before, and now they all had blood on their hands. But again, Sarah referred to the Bible, specifically the book of Matthew, to quote Jesus, who said, "You shall hear of wars and rumors of wars, but be not troubled for all these things must come to pass." The residents had truly not had any choice but to fight.

Third, Sarah reminded everyone that their losses would be in vain if they did not finish the job that the arkonauts had started. She looked down the hill at the town below and the building housing the species. "We did not seek to be in this position, but here we are. And if it feels like the weight of the world is on our shoulders, that is because it is. So be it. Ron Kitchener, Irene Doyle, Eric Griffiths, and Oliver Hill have met the call and paid the ultimate price." She paused to collect herself. Her family sat in the front row, trying to keep their emotions in check. Beth closed her eyes and looked down. Owen held his daughter close as Annie buried her face in his chest. Billy felt Jessie's hand close tightly on his.

Then Sarah said, "I want to let any of you say something about those we have lost before I finish with a few thoughts of my own." She paused and looked around. Nobody said anything for a minute. They could hear the waves quietly coming ashore and feel the breeze coming off the mountain. Billy looked at Jessie. She could tell he was thinking about saying something and gestured for him to go ahead. Sarah, too, seemed to sense that her brother-in-law wanted to speak and smiled at him. Billy stood and cleared his throat.

"Thank you, Sarah, for the truth in your words." Billy paused for a moment and then continued. "I do want to say something about my father. I didn't prepare anything, so it won't surprise those of you who know me that I will use a quote for my comments." He glanced at Jessie, who smiled in return. "You know, it's funny that some people here call me Shakespeare when in fact my knowledge of his work is about like my knowledge of the Bible. I don't really know Shakespeare or the Bible as much as I act sometimes."

Owen interrupted quietly. "There's some truth in those words."

Miller and Rodriguez snorted in approval. Others shook their heads to suppress laughter.

Billy didn't mind the levity. Instead, he smiled as he said, "Thank you, brother. Brothers."

Rodriguez grinned at being included as he said, "Da Nada, Hermano."

Billy inhaled and resumed. "But I do know one passage in the Bible that I think is appropriate. It's from Proverbs, chapter 16, verse 16." He glanced at Sarah. "If you know it, sister, please say it with me." Sarah nodded and did indeed join Billy as he quoted the passage. "How much better is it to get wisdom than gold? And to get understanding rather than silver?" Billy and Sarah smiled at each other as they finished.

He then continued. "I've always liked that proverb. Indeed, it's the only one I know. And I used to think that proverb said something about what I was doing with my life, because I sure wasn't collecting gold and silver." Billy's family laughed quietly. "But Oliver was. He was wealthy and getting wealthier."

Billy glanced at Hunter before continuing. "And then he learned. He sought wisdom and understanding and gave up on gold and silver. And that led him here. And led us here." Billy looked around before finishing. "And we're all wealthier because of it. Not only did he learn, but he also kept teaching. Even in death he taught me about sacrifice and love. I will miss him."

Billy sat down. Jessie reached over and patted him on the back. Owen and Beth both turned around to look at him and nodded.

Sarah said, "Thank you, Billy. I, too, want to say a few personal words about Oliver, and they are not dissimilar from yours. He was not just my father-in-law but was also a friend. And as you said, he was the person who brought us all here." She paused to catch her breath. "Oliver was not a perfect man. And he would be the first to tell you that. But who among us is perfect? If he or she was, then he or she would be God, and as many of you like to remind me, you don't even believe in God at all, let alone his or her perfection." Some chuckled.

Sarah resumed. "I will tell you another story about imperfection that leads into our closing hymn. And it's one some of you may know. John Newton was a slave trader. That's as imperfect as a person can be. In the eighteenth century, he was transporting a shipload of slaves from Africa to North America when his ship ran into an immense storm. At some point during that storm, he realized that he was doing a terrible thing. He turned the ship around, sailed back to Africa, and released his human cargo. And he wrote the hymn we will sing to finish this service."

Sarah continued as the musicians returned to their instruments. "Oliver was obviously never a slave trader. But similarly to how traders viewed their slaves, for much of his life, Oliver thought of other living things as something to be used, abused, and extinguished. And then, as Billy said, he learned. And he changed. And he made a difference." Her voice started to crack, but she fought through it and said proudly, "And it was amazing." She paused before finishing. "Please join in singing 'Amazing Grace.'"

As the band started playing, people stood and sang along. Billy looked up from his guitar at Sarah just as she glanced at him, and they both managed to smile. Then he looked out at Jessie and Beth and Owen. They all had tears in their eyes, but they were all singing.

CHAPTER 72

Another Rubicon

After the service and some communion between the attendees, Billy and Archie McLeish ferried the visitors back to Adamstown and the *Darwin*. On his final run with Captain Decker and some of the *Darwin* sailors, Owen and Beth rode along. The three siblings thought they should at least say something, even if condemnatory, to their uncle Henry and his family before their departure on the *White Diamond*. The morning clouds had dissipated somewhat, so the temperatures were warm and the ride across the bay was relaxing, so much so that a couple of the sailors fell asleep.

As soon as the boat docked, the sailors said their thanks and disembarked. Captain Decker lingered with Billy, Beth, and Owen on the pier. They could see Henry, Helen, and Richard Hill standing on the deck of the *White Diamond*, a guard on the pier ensuring that no one came on or off the yacht. Henry looked at the Hill siblings, who stared back, but none of them moved toward the yacht.

Owen started to say, "You know, I've been thinking—"

Beth cut him off. "Yeah, me too."

Billy smiled at his brother and sister. "Don't look at me. I've seen enough of those assholes."

Beth grinned slightly as she looked back. "Screw 'em."

Owen gave a rare smile as well. "Hell, they aren't worth our time. Let's go."

As they turned their backs on their relatives, the Hill siblings looked at Captain Decker to wish him well.

Decker spoke quietly. "I, we, have appreciated working with all of you." He hesitated before resuming. "I've been meaning to get a minute with William alone, but I hope he won't mind if his brother and sister hear this as well."

All three siblings looked puzzled. Billy silently appreciated how Decker used his formal name the same way that his father had.

Decker went on. "Reggie McLeish has opted to stay on Pitcairn. His enlistment officially ended last week, so he has every right to do so. Further, he has no family back in Australia, whereas he does have an uncle here. And…" Decker smiled. "I believe he is smitten by a young woman in your town."

Beth said quietly, "Naveena."

Decker nodded and continued. "Assuming you will have him, Reggie is a good man and will be a good addition to the Pitcairn population." Then he looked directly at Billy. "He was also a good helmsman. As you are, William. I've watched you steer this launch, and Captain Mitchell had the highest praise for your work with the ark."

Billy suddenly knew what was coming even before Decker continued. "I'd like you to consider taking his place in our crew. I realize it's a bit unusual, but these are unusual times. And we could use another helmsman."

Billy was at a loss for words. Beth and Owen turned from Decker to stare at their brother. They knew Billy's history better than anybody and easily imagined what he was thinking. New opportunities. New places. New adventures. In the silence, Billy could hear the Australian flag over the *Darwin* flapping in the breeze. The flag reminded him of all the great things he had heard and how he had always wanted to see the land down under.

"I'm stunned, Captain Decker," Billy finally said, trying to formulate a sensible answer out of the thoughts that were bouncing around in his head. "I appreciate you asking. I need to think and talk to my family…and my friend Jessie…well, I don't know…"

Decker waited and then responded, "I understand. It's the life of a seafaring man. Leaving loved ones is always the worst part." He thought for a moment and smiled slightly at a realization. Then he continued, "Let me suggest the following: We are in fact down two crew members. As you recall, Seaman Fitch passed away shortly after we arrived here. My understanding is that Jessie is a good sailor. Why don't you ask her if she would join us as well?"

Now Billy had even more to think about. His previous answer might have assumed things that even Jessie and he didn't yet understand. But he was intrigued. And he thought she would be as well. He also admired Decker's directness. And it felt good to be wanted.

"Thank you, Captain," Billy stammered. "Let me talk to her. And I, we, will think about it."

"Of course, mate," Decker answered. "I didn't expect you to sign up on the spot. Take some time, talk to your loved ones, think about it." He hesitated and then added, "But we sail in two days." Decker smiled at all three. "For now, I will wish you all well." He reached out to shake each of their hands before turning and walking back to his ship.

Billy, Beth, and Owen climbed quietly into the launch for the ride back to Ararat. As Billy fired the engine and stood behind the wheel, Beth and Owen took places on either side of him. It was a perfect opportunity for Billy to talk to them, as Decker had suggested, but Billy wasn't sure he wanted to, as he had a pretty good idea of what they would say. Neither of his siblings seemed ready to talk about it either, so they started the trip back to Ararat in silence.

Then, halfway back, Beth looked at Billy and said, "You're going to do it, aren't you?"

"Of course he is," Owen said quietly, just a hint of disgust in his voice.

Billy started, "Look, I just heard this, and I need to…" He paused. "Well, I need to talk to Jessie—"

Beth cut him off. "Let me say something. And I think Owen agrees. It's good of Decker to recognize your abilities. Good for you, Billy." The compliment sounded like something she felt she had to say before getting to the point. "But this isn't just about you and Jessie."

"I know that." Billy reacted, even as he wondered just what he contributed to the Ararat community. "But my abilities as a helmsman, for whatever they're worth, are most useful when we're at sea. And let's face it, the ark isn't going anywhere.

"Oh," Owen responded. "Just who is driving this launch right now?"

Billy responded, "Come on, others can learn how to drive this thing."

Beth added, "This is about more than just steering this launch. And you know it."

Billy thought for a moment while the launch continued to bounce across the waves. He decided to say what was on his mind, and it had been on his mind since the battle. "Look, I did what Dad asked me to do. And then he sacrificed—"

"No." Owen cut him off. "You do not get to use Dad's death as a reason for you leaving. If you're going to go, do it for yourself, not for any sense of guilt." Owen asked, "You think Dad would have saved you just so you could go running off to somewhere else?"

Billy shook his head. "I don't know, maybe not, but—"

Owen nearly shouted. "You still don't get it, Bill! The answer is yes. He would have. That's the whole point."

Billy found his temper rising. "You know, I don't really think this is your decision—"

Beth interrupted with their old line. "What, are you scared, Billy?"

This time she was not kidding but rather asking him if he was ready to commit to something. Billy was silent. Indeed, as Ararat came into view, all three were quiet. They pulled up at the pier and tied up the launch. Beth and Owen started to walk away and then stopped.

Beth looked back at Billy. "Look, Billy, you got to do what you want to do. We're just telling you that we don't want you to leave."

Billy nodded. "Thanks." He knew his brother and sister well enough to not expect a gentler message. He added, "I just need to talk to Jessie. But I would appreciate you not spreading this around."

Beth and Owen both stared at him as Owen said sarcastically, "Yeah, right."

Billy didn't know what that meant, so he just watched them go. Then he hustled to find Jessie. Being a Sunday, she wasn't working but rather taking it easy, sitting under a palm tree down by the beach. As Billy approached, she must have been able to tell that it was something serious, as she rose to meet him.

Billy told her what Decker had said and the invitation for both of them to join the submarine crew. Her reaction was, as he expected, impressively calm and direct.

"That's quite a compliment, Billy. You should be proud." She paused and then asked, "What do you want to do?"

"I don't know." He honestly didn't. "But the decision will be a lot easier if you'll think about going with me."

Jessie was silent for a long minute as she looked around and thought. The waves on the shore and the palm fronds waving in the tropical breeze filled the silence.

She finally said, "I will not make it any easier on you, then, except that I will be clear on my position so you won't be uncertain about that." She looked directly into his eyes. "I love you, Billy, and I want to be with you. But I'm not leaving my sister and these people and what we're doing here."

Billy felt a mixture of emotions, joy at her love, but also sadness in her decision. He tried to tell her so, awkwardly. "I'm happy with the first part of that, not so much the second."

Her eyes were kind but steady. "It's that horizon thing again, isn't it? Always another horizon." When he didn't answer, she went on. "Only you can decide what you really want to do."

Billy nodded briefly and said, "Well, I would guess that the *Darwin* won't find much in Australia, other than desolation, radiation, and maybe nuclear winter. They'll probably be back in a month or two."

She smiled slightly. "When we left San Francisco, we thought we would only be out five or six days. If we have learned anything, we have learned that we cannot make predictions."

Billy didn't have a response as he knew she was right. He was silent, staring at the waves as if they would provide some answer. Then he asked, "What do you think I should do?"

Jessie thought about it for a minute and then tried to give what help she could. "This is the kind of thing you've done all your life, Billy. It's who you have always been. So I won't blame you if you go, and I won't ask you to be something you aren't. But what you should ask yourself is if it's who you always want to be." She paused to let that sink in. Gulls flew overhead and landed on the beach near them.

She finished. "I think you should go somewhere now and decide. And I will love you whatever the decision. But I will tell you this, Billy: As you know, I try to protect my emotions, so if you decide to go, please do not come back to give me a goodbye hug or kiss. That is too hard. I would prefer you just go." Then she forced a smile. "Also, my sister won't be happy either, so unlike Treasure Island, I do not think there will be a sack lunch for you this time."

Billy was so fond of her in that moment that he knew any words would be inadequate. So respecting her wishes to not hug her and feeling a lump in his throat, he turned and started walking south along the beach, away from Ararat, to do exactly what she suggested. As he walked, Billy thought. And as was his habit, he started thinking of cultural references that supported different options.

On one hand was the option of going. Billy had spent a lifetime—make that a few lifetimes—never passing on opportunities. And he did not regret it. Indeed, he was aware that he probably bored too many people with too many stories too many times. But the thing was, he always had one, to the point where sometimes people would say something like, "Wow, you did that too?" He liked having all those adventures. And he took some pride in it. He had always loved his freedom and found it incredibly liberating, as had many others. He thought of William Least-Heat Moon's comment that if someone couldn't make things go right, they could always go. He remembered Whitman's line in "Song of the Open Road," wherein he rejoices, "I inhale great draughts of space; The east and the west are mine; and the north and the south are mine." He recalled a famous character from American movies. In *It's a Wonderful Life*, George Bailey asked Uncle Charley, "Do you know what are the three prettiest sounds in the world?" and then answered his own question with "Anchor chains, plane motors, and train wheels." And then Billy thought of himself sitting in an open boxcar, legs hanging over the side as he inhaled the fresh air and the night stars, not sure where the train was going but thrilled that it was going.

On the other hand, Billy knew that freedom has a cost and that there were many other cultural references to that effect. Going back to the *Wonderful Life* movie, George's ultimate resolution to his itch for travel by staying home resonated with Americans for generations. Billy's favorite scene in one of his favorite movies involved the Steve McQueen character in *The Magnificent Seven* who, when pressed by a younger gunfighter to express any regrets about his seemingly exciting, free lifestyle, asked and then answered his own questions: "Home? None. Wife? None. Kids? None. Prospects? Zero." Even one of the most famous wanderers knew this feeling. In his autobiography, Woody Guthrie wrote of one trip by concluding that he just wanted to turn around and go "back up our roads. Back where we come from. Just back." Billy's mind turned to music. In his song "Cautious Man" about a guy who had settled down only to wake one night feeling restless, Springsteen sang, "He got dressed in the moonlight and down to the highway he strode; when he got there, he didn't find nothing but road." The guy turned around and went back home to his wife. Or as Kris Kristofferson said succinctly, "Freedom's just another word for nothing left to lose."

With so many thoughts bouncing around in his mind, Billy felt like he was standing at another Rubicon River and whatever he decided would change his life. Then he smiled to himself and shook his head slightly. Even that was a cultural reference. He could go back and forth with countering cultural references forever and that wouldn't help him with this decision. He kept walking.

CHAPTER 73

The Reckoning

Billy stopped on the beach to watch a large sea tortoise waddle out of the trees and amble down the sand toward the water. The turtle entered the surf and began swimming, much more graceful than he had been on land, seeming to savor his watery excursion. Billy sat down in the sand. He had been so deep in thought that he had walked a mile south of Ararat.

As Billy kept thinking, he realized something. He could never learn as much from cultural references as he could from people who knew him well. And when those people taught you something, even if you didn't recognize it at that time, it could be incredibly powerful. He thought of his friend Joe Washington and their final conversation back in New Orleans. And the words came back as clearly as if they had been said the day before. If you find something worth keeping, you dig in and hold on for as long as you can. He thought about Oliver, who had taught him that some decisions are not just about you. Oliver had changed his own life when he learned that. And he had died for it, making a sacrifice for something other than himself. Finally, he thought of Jessie, who had just said something important in her own, direct, modest, but compelling way. People can change. He could. And by staying, he would not be giving up his freedom but rather embracing the most important freedom of all, the freedom to change.

As he put those lessons together, Billy felt like it was something he should have figured out a long time before. Yes, even wanderers like him could change and make a home, and you could make it for more than yourself. And he finally grasped the fact that so many of the people he cared about back in Ararat were already living those lessons. They understood that humans were at risk of losing everything, so they had gotten together, collected the species, brought them here, dug in, and were holding on as well as they could. Like his father, they had changed their own lives to do something larger than themselves. Billy knew that he was fortunate to be in their company. And after all those years of searching, he realized that, whether due to fate or luck or work or something else, he had now found what felt to him like the center of the universe.

And then Billy heard it, a strange sound that he had never expected to hear on the island. It came from down the beach back toward Ararat. He looked toward that direction with a puzzled expression on his face, wondering if he had really heard it or just imagined it. Then it sounded again, and when he was sure what it was, he smiled broadly.

Billy stood, just as the tortoise finished its brief swim and headed back into shore, surely going home to his family. At least Billy hoped so. Either way, Billy would. He started walking back up the beach toward Ararat and laughed out loud when he heard the strange sound once again.

As he approached the settlement, Billy could see Jessie waiting, right where he had left her. But she was not alone. Beth and Owen had obviously ignored Billy's request to keep his pending decision quiet, and a crowd of people had gathered on the beach. Jessie was standing with Maria, Hunter, and Captain Mitchell. James, Janice, and Jamal Brooks sat nearby with Susan and Naomi Harris. Beth, Sanders, Miller, and Reichardt were in a group down by the waterline, talking while Rodriguez dribbled a soccer ball. Sarah was with Annie, Roscoe, and Jonah as they played in the surf. And Owen and Reese were working on a strange-looking machine that consisted of several vertical pipes standing on a small wooden platform, with a short rope attached. Owen, the engineer, was doing something to the pipes as Reese, the machinist, adjusted their positions.

Reese glanced up and saw Billy approaching. He nudged Owen, who looked up as well. Then Owen, with that funny little grin on his face that he showed so rarely, tugged on the rope, and the sound came again, this time much louder. It was a train whistle.

Billy shook his head back and forth as if in disbelief. As the rest of the group on the beach saw him coming, they all stopped what they had been doing or saying. Annie and Roscoe ran in his direction. The dog reached Billy first and got a quick back scratch for a reward. Roscoe was barking and running around in little circles as Billy bent down to pick Annie up. He carried her as he continued up the beach. When he got within twenty yards of the group, he set Annie down so she could run back toward her mom. Everybody else looked at Billy. Waiting.

It wasn't just the train whistle that got to him. Billy realized that they were all there because they wanted to know what he was going to do. And they had come down to the beach to hear his decision. He was more than surprised or flattered; he was humbled. And at that moment, he knew he was there to stay. Any second thoughts he might have had about his decision vanished into the tropical breeze. He looked at Jessie, and as she looked back, the grin on his face widened. His expression gave away his decision, and Jessie, too, began to smile. Billy walked straight to her, and they embraced in a hug that felt like it would last forever.

EPILOGUE

February 2027

You must live in the present, launch yourself on every wave, find your eternity in each moment. Fools stand on their island of opportunities and look toward another land. There is no other land; there is no other life but this.

—Henry David Thoreau

The storm hid no secrets. Instead, the dark clouds over the mountains announced their pending arrival with rolls of thunder and brief flashes of lightning.

"Looks like this one might need a name, Billy," Brooks called with a smile.

Billy grinned, thinking back to their discussion of naming storms in New Orleans. "Yeah, I almost forgot how to do that. That's a long time ago."

"A lifetime," Brooks answered. He stood on the little hill leading away from the beach, with Janice, Jonah, Sarah, Owen, Annie, and Roscoe, all looking at Billy and Jessie, who were still down by the water.

Jessie sat on the sand, staring out at the darkening ocean and the strengthening waves.

Billy stood ankle-deep in the water, his back to the ocean as he looked west toward his family and friends and the ominous bank of thunder clouds. Their little settlement stood in the foreground with the tree-covered mountains in the distance. In between was the stretch of jungle that had been shelled in the recent battle and the cemetery on a little knoll to the south showing simple crosses for those lost in that fight as well as in the months before. Now the markers stood, silent reminders that those people were gone forever. They would never know another day. They would never see another sunset. They would never have another chance to stand in the surf, feeling the unending power of the ocean. Billy was saddened by the loss of family, friends, and comrades, but their deaths made him feel even more alive. Their deaths were a stark reminder to savor that feeling and not take anything for granted.

The last few days had been busy enough that Billy was enjoying just taking it easy. He had given Decker his decision the day before. And the captain moved quickly to fill his crew, signing on the disgruntled Perreau as a helmsman and Syszmanski as a crew member. Reese and Billy found that amusing, wondering how Polish drinking songs would go over in a submerged Australian submarine. Then, earlier this day, the *Darwin* and the *White Diamond* had departed. Billy and several other Ararat residents had taken the launch down to Adamstown to bid Decker and his crew farewell. They also saw the *White Diamond* leave. And despite the adage that blood is thicker than water, saying goodbye to the Aussies was much harder for Billy, Beth, and Owen than seeing their own relatives disappear out of sight. After coming back to Ararat, Billy and many of the other residents went down to the beach to enjoy the afternoon. But by this time in the early evening, nearly everyone else, seeing the storm coming, had left.

Annie yelled, “Let’s go home, Jessie and Uncle Billy!” She and Roscoe scampered down the rise toward the beach to collect Billy and Jessie but then turned back just in time to dodge the next oncoming wave as it rolled onto the sand, the dog barking at the surf as if it were some watery mailman that had to be shooed away from his home.

Billy called back, “Thanks, but it’s okay. You guys go ahead.” Annie and Roscoe gave up and hurried back up the slope. Jessie waved to let the others know she was staying as well. Brooks, a grin still on his face, shook his head slightly and turned with Owen to head up toward town. Janice, Jonah, and Sarah waited for Annie and Roscoe to catch up and then, with a couple of waves, also walked away.

Billy looked at Jessie and said, "I am home." She smiled.

Billy was in no hurry to move away. It was one of those evenings on the island that he wished would go on forever. And although he knew the moment wouldn't last, he wanted to keep it for as long as he could. So he stayed right where he was as his feet sank deeper into the wet sand with each receding wave. He glanced over at Jessie again sitting where the biggest waves reached her feet and buried them gradually in the sand. Behind her Billy could see the ark bobbing ever so slightly in the incessant waves, the name *Noah* visible just above the waterline.

He thought back to when he had first seen that ship and, even before then, to that night in a New Orleans hospital with Brooks and Washington. How long ago had that been? How different had he been? And how different had the world been? Had it been just six months? Brooks was right—it felt like a lifetime. But not eternity. Not yet.

Thunder rumbled again in the approaching clouds. "Go ahead if you want, Jess," Billy called and added, "But thanks for staying a while."

Jessie continued to stare out at the ocean but, after a few seconds, answered, "No, I'm good." Then she looked back at Billy and asked with that little tease in her voice, "What are you doing? Stand there too long and you will get stuck."

Billy thought about something he had heard once before and answered, "Just digging in and holding on." Jessie smiled knowingly and looked back out at the sea.

A loud rumble of thunder signaled that the storm had arrived. As the raindrops started to fall and the waves continued to crash on the shore, Billy's toes tightened their grip on the island just as the island tightened its grip on him.

About the Author

William R. Lowry is a professor emeritus of political science at Washington University. Before going into academia, he served honorably in the United States Navy, drove a taxicab, worked for the National Park Service, and managed drugstores. Bill was an undergraduate at Indiana University and received his PhD in political science from Stanford University in 1988. He studied and taught American politics and environmental issues with a focus on public lands. He is the author of five nonfiction books as well as numerous other publications. In 2010, he received a Distinguished Faculty Award from Washington University. Bill retired in 2021. He and his wife, Lynn, have a son, Joey, and live in the St. Louis area. He likes to hike, exercise, write, travel, and enjoy time with family and friends. This is his first fiction book.

Printed in the USA
CPSIA information can be obtained
at www.ICGtesting.com
LVHW080359021123
762784LV00001B/88

9 781662 486302